THE MINTERN REPORT

R.D. COPPENS

The Mintern Report

Copyright © 2022
by R.D. Coppens

Cover image by Nevin Speerbrecker

Edited by Benjamin X. Wretlind

Printed in the United States of America

This is a work of fiction. All the characters, locations, and events portrayed in this novel are either fictitious or are used fictitiously.

No part of this book may be reproduced or transmitted in any form or by any means, electronic or mechanical, including photocopying, recording or by any information storage and retrieval system without permission in writing from the author.

ISBN-13: 979-8843173036

First Edition

https://www.facebook.com/authorrdcoppens
https://www.instagram.com/rickcoppensauthor/

THE MINTERN REPORT

For my wife, Kathy

CHAPTER ONE
Present Day - Saturday, October 30

THE AIR REEKED OF CHEMICALS. AN ACRID STENCH PENETRATED MY nostrils. It smelled like an electrical fire, or burning plastic, or gunpowder. Had I been shot? It sure felt like it. Perhaps I'd been punched in the face—or kicked in the chest. It could've been both, but by who? Or whom?

Who and whom. Those two words had always confused me. I couldn't remember what my high school English teacher taught me. I remembered it had something to do with the difference between a preposition and a verb. My head pounded, and I did what came naturally. I screamed my favorite verb.

"Fuck!"

"You alright, Rick?" A voice next to me slurred.

The air was cloudy. Fine white particles floated around my head and burned my eyes. My skin felt hot. I wiggled my fingers—all ten of them—I counted. Twisting my jaw, I stretched my mouth wide and fought off the ringing in my ears.

"Rick! Are you alright?"

"Scruggs?" my own voice echoed in my head.

"Yeah, buddy. Nice move. That asshole almost killed us."

"The hell happened, Scruggs?" I gazed out the windshield of my burgundy F-150. My eyes were blurry. Having fuzzy vision was the least of my problems. A giant oak tree stared back at me.

An oak tree?

What the hell?

A squirrel's nest had landed on my windshield. It was empty.

"That truck came right at us, Rick," Scruggs said with no inflection. "If you hadn't cut the wheel when you did, we'd be dead."

"You sure we're not dead?"

"If we were dead, we probably wouldn't be together."

"The hell does that mean?"

Dan Scruggs belly laughed, and at that moment, I knew we were going to be all right.

Two airbags hung from the dash panel like the droopy eyes of a nightmarish ghost. Everything from the back seat was now in the front, on the floor, or on the dashboard—everything except Scruggs's vintage guitar. We checked. It was the only thing wide enough and heavy enough not to find its way to the front of the cab. Thankfully, the expensive Fender Telecaster was protected in a heavy-duty case.

I kicked a pile of stuff around my feet and found my favorite pocket knife. It had been AWOL for months. I pulled on the handle, and the driver's door opened. Scruggs gave the passenger door a stiff shoulder. Soon, we were both out of the truck and standing in a thick forest.

Dappled light filtered through the high canopy layer. The heels of my Lucchese boots sunk into the moist loam soil. I clipped my knife into the front pocket of my jeans and shuffled through the wet leaves, twigs, and acorns to the front of the truck. Our eyes met over the crumpled hood. Pointing to the damage, I asked Scruggs if my truck was repairable.

He shook his head.

"But you own a body shop," I said.

He acknowledged the oak tree with a nod. "Sorry. It's going to be an insurance claim."

"Shit. I liked this truck. Did you catch the model of the other one?"

He furrowed his brow, and his eyes squinted. "It was a white Ford Super Duty diesel. The body was lifted, and it had dual chrome exhaust stacks."

"Seriously, Scruggs? We were going at least sixty when that truck crossed the double yellow lines. He came around the curve fast, probably doing seventy. Maybe eighty. You remembered all of that?"

"Before you drove into the woods, I thought it might have been the last thing I ever saw, so, yeah, I remembered it vividly."

"Have you ever seen that truck before?" I asked.

He shook his head. "I'll give Jimmy a call."

"Who's Jimmy?"

"Jimmy Hendricks. I use his company for towing."

"Jimmy Hendricks? Seriously?"

He shrugged and tapped on his phone's screen.

Dan Scruggs had been my best friend since grade school. He was tall and handsome, with kind blue eyes. At forty-two, a year older than me, his shoulder-length hair had turned prematurely white. The top had thinned, but his signature ponytail gave it a fuller appearance. His contrasting goatee was thick and wiry enough to scrape the rust off an old tractor.

Stumbling back to the driver's door, I leaned in and found my phone between the seat and the console. The screen had cracked but still appeared to be working. I wiped more white powder from my face and brushed my hands on my jeans. Red and yellow lights flashed from the dash. A constant beeping echoed in the cabin. I called my wife, Kathy, who asked if we were alright. I said yes, but we needed a ride home.

"Where are you?" she asked.

"South of Lansing. Fifteen minutes from your office. I drove Scruggs to Young's Music Emporium to pick up his guitar. We were heading home when a truck came around the curve fast and crossed the centerline."

"You hit a truck head-on?"

"No. I turned at the last minute and swerved right."

"What did you hit?"

"A squirrel's nest."

"What?"

"Okay, the squirrel lived in an oak tree. I hit the tree, alright?"

Kathy let out an irritated breath and requested I visit the urgent care clinic on my way home. Getting into a debate made no sense because it wasn't really a request. She asked if Dan had called his wife, Jo, yet. I told her he was on the phone with his tow truck buddy and I would make sure he called Jo afterward. I reminded Kathy we had a forty-five-minute ride home, which would provide sufficient time for Dan and Jo to finish their conversation. She understood my humor and chuckled. Jo was a talker.

"Have you called the police yet?" she asked.

"I'm speaking with my favorite cop."

"Okay, listen, I can't pick you up right now. I'm three hours north of your location. We're wrapping up a murder investigation. Let me see who I ca—"

"Can you get one of the Erikson brothers to pick me up?" I pleaded.

Kathy sighed. "Kenny Erikson is with me. Let me see who can—"

"Where's Steve?"

"Listen, Rick, just because Kenny and Steve are your hunting buddies doesn't mean they can drop whatever they're doing to be your personal chauff—"

"What if I was seriously injured?" I interrupted again.

"Christ almighty, let me see what I can do."

"Love you."

"Love you too." The irritation in her voice was apparent. Click.

I gathered my belongings, shoved them in a plastic grocery store bag, and set them on the tailgate. Scruggs placed his Fender guitar case next to my stuff and unbuckled it. His face tightened as the tweed case slowly opened. I peeked around his left arm and saw precisely what he did—the guitar was fine. No damage. His posture relaxed, and he delivered a tight fist pump. The '52 Telecaster, Butterscotch Blonde, was safely snuggled in red velvet.

"Kathy is arranging transportation," I told Scruggs.

He checked his phone and said the tow truck was on the way.

I snickered. "Are you going to let Jimmy Hendricks play your guitar?"

Scruggs shook his head and asked if I had suffered a concussion. I said, possibly. We laughed. What just happened could have been much worse. He walked toward me with his arms extended, and I knew what was coming, so I stretched out my arms and reached up. At six-foot-three,

Scruggs towered over me by at least six inches. I had to stand on my tiptoes to reciprocate his hugs. I wished he would simply bend over or at least meet me halfway.

Whatever. We hugged.

He lifted me high and squeezed. When my feet finally hit the wet carpet of leaves and twigs, I backed away. Something in my peripheral vision caught my attention. It was a log, thick, covered in moss, horizontal — a dead tree. An animated squirrel stood on the scaly bark and chattered in my direction.

It looked pissed.

Gravel crunched beneath the tires of the Michigan State Police Dodge Charger as it pulled onto the shoulder. Red and blue lights flashed. Detective Steve Erikson hopped from the vehicle and greeted us with a gentle handshake. He looked us over for visible injuries. The airbag had left a rash on my chest. Scruggs had minor facial abrasions where his sunglasses used to be.

The tow truck pulled up minutes later, and the driver surveyed the scene. Scruggs introduced us. I asked the lanky driver if he was left-handed. He gave me a blank stare. Obviously, it wasn't the first time he'd heard the joke. Jimmy Hendricks pulled on his long, scraggly ponytail and continued about his business.

Steve summoned us to his vehicle. He turned off the flashing lights, and we pulled away. I craned my neck and glimpsed the right-handed Jimmy Hendricks yanking my truck backward out of the woods. Yellow lights from the tow truck reflected off the wet forest floor. A few passing cars slowed to see what had happened.

The urgent care clinic was less than thirty minutes away.

Thankfully, it was mid-morning on a Saturday, and there weren't many people in the waiting room. After a few pokes and probes, Scruggs and I were back in the car.

Steve Erikson gave me a sideways glance and asked, "What did the doctor say?"

I fastened my seatbelt. "Doc said we needed to grab a beer and relax for the rest of the day."

The car's tires barked on the blacktop road, and we continued south for the village of Dunville. Our hometown.

CHAPTER TWO

Present Day - Saturday, October 30

ESTABLISHED IN 1837, DUNVILLE WAS REGISTERED AS THE OLDEST village in Michigan. An hour's drive from any major city, it was predominantly a farming community and home to four thousand residents—at least, that's what the welcoming signs at the edge of the village advertised. They needed updating.

Our little town was growing, and I hoped it wouldn't turn into one of those congested communities people fled. I'd seen it happen to neighboring towns and villages. Traffic, noise, bright lights, air pollution, asshole neighbors, and high taxes had city folk searching for a simpler life—or their perception of simplicity—a fantasy, like the TV shows they'd binged watched on their big-screen televisions. It was a myth the Hallmark channel sold to the dreamers. In reality, rural life wasn't as easy, romantic, or peaceful as cable television portrayed. It took extra effort to live in the country.

On the twenty acres where Kathy and I lived, there was no city water, no sewer system, no cable television, and often—when storms rolled through, or a pickup truck knocked down a power pole—no electricity. Our house sat on top of a modest hill. A large stand of hardwood trees surrounded two sides. Open fields on other sides provided a faithful breeze, where conversations from neighbors could be heard from a distance of a half-mile or more. Smells traveled even farther. During harvest season, the air in the country smelled like baked bread, like wheat — like grandma's kitchen. When the wind blew in the wrong direction, the wafting aroma from neighboring farms could smell like pig shit.

The Hallmark channel never mentioned that. Big city transplants always complained about the smell of pig shit. The dozens of romantic shows they'd watched had misrepresented their expectations.

I was raised in the country, just a few miles outside the village of Dunville. It was a great community. Locals were friendly, and neighbors looked out for one another. Businesses took pride in their community. Farmers helped other farmers without question and without bitching. The minor inconveniences of country living were just that: minor. And the smell of pig shit every now and again didn't bother me.

ON THE outskirts of the village, Steve Erikson's police cruiser slowed to comply with the lower speed limit. He nodded toward my hardware store, which was quickly approaching on our right, and asked if I wanted to stop. I shook my head and pointed my finger through the windshield. We continued south.

My father, Richard Cooper, opened the hardware store in the mid-fifties. I had kept the family business and my dad's memory alive for the past two decades. It's been my one and only job since my early teenage years.

Minutes later, the Charger entered the historic town square of Dunville. Scruggs groaned and fidgeted in the back seat. I rolled down the window and hung my right arm in the breeze. My head followed my arm and was outside the window enough to catch a face full of fresh country air.

Dunville, Michigan, was a great place to call home. As a

kid, I didn't realize I had it so good. Over the years, I've grown to appreciate my free-range childhood in the gently rolling hills of southern Michigan and the Norman Rockwell-like setting of our village. The four blocks of the town square were paved with rectangular bricks, installed in a herringbone pattern. The historic buildings, now mostly retail, were seasonally decorated to perfection like they were competing for a "best of" award. I smiled and hummed a favorite tune.

Sometimes even now, when I'm feelin' lonely and beat.
I drift back in time, and I find my feet.

The streetlight poles along Main Street were beautifully adorned with fall foliage garlands that varied in yellow, orange, red, purple, and brown shades. Large banners hanging high above the brick-paved street advertised the upcoming "Holiday Festival," which took place in late November. It was our town's most popular event. Live music, food trucks, and a carnival-like atmosphere attracted thousands of visitors from southeastern Michigan and northwest Ohio.

In the middle of the town square was a tall, hundred-year-old statue of a Native American Pottawatomie chief hoisting a broken spear over his head. The fractured lance was a symbol of peace. The founding fathers of Dunville dedicated it to celebrate the heritage of our Native American ancestors—after they'd been displaced.

In the shadows of the bronze statue, wooden steps led to a large octagon pergola. It was a popular gathering place for locals and tourists alike. Beyond that, the majestic Raisin River directed rain run-off and snow-melt southeast to Lake Erie.

It was almost noon when we entered the town square. Tourists had already crowded the streets. Shoppers lined the narrow sidewalks, jaywalked across brick-paved roads, and bounced from store to store. The bakery on my left was doing a brisk business, and next to it, the River Raisin Boutique hawked a variety of Native American souvenirs. They sold t-shirts, moccasins, miniature statues of the famous Pottawatomie Chief, coffee mugs, and arrowheads. Tourists loved the arrowheads. They were probably mass-produced in China.

A sign on the front door of the boutique informed consumers that a small percentage of sales would be donated to a Native American charity. It didn't say *how* small and didn't disclose *which* charity. Probably the casino, I guessed, a half-hour west, in the town of Parma—our high school football rivals.

Across the street, a national candle shop franchise exchanged legal tender for knick-knacks, miniature statues, silk flowers, and, of course—candles. I saw dozens of women through a large window. They laughed and chatted as they wandered the store, probably trying to decide whether their house should smell like Goji Berry Mango or Huckleberry Sugar Blossom.

Dozens of men, who probably wished the store sold a candle that smelled like apple-wood smoked bacon, mingled outside near the pavilion. Their mannerisms appeared exaggerated as they bragged about who had the best fantasy sports team, or at least that's what I guessed they were doing. They'd probably already been in the candle store with their wives and needed a testosterone check.

The steady pounding of conga and bongo drums in my

head reminded me of the front-row seat I'd once had for a Carlos Santana concert. My whole body felt out of sync. Bob Brewster's Social Club was up ahead, on our left. Steve laughed as I pumped my fingers wildly through the windshield. Scruggs's comical attempt to sit up straight in the back seat brought memories of an awkward newborn giraffe I saw a few years ago at the Toledo Zoo. The baby giraffe was more graceful.

FIFTEEN YEARS ago, when my wife Kathy began her career as a CSI investigator with the Michigan State Police, she was assigned a senior partner—a mentor. His name was Robert Brewster. We've been friends ever since.

Robert J. Brewster was known to everyone as "Brewster." He was almost tall—two fingers shy of six feet, with dark brown hair, brown eyes, and a politician's smile. His wife, Dina, was the town dentist. Her Plaque Attack Dental Clinic in the historic town square was sandwiched between a hair salon and the candle franchise.

A few years after mentoring Kathy, Bob Brewster retired early from the Michigan State Police. With a small pension and a healthy inheritance, he pursued his lifelong passion and built the most popular dining and drinking establishment in Dunville. Brewster's Social Club, a restaurant and bar, was on Main Street, one block north of the town square. Across the street from the club was Tinsdale Park, named after a past mayor. Beyond that—a spectacular view of the Raisin River.

The interior of Brewster's Social Club was divided into two sections. Entering the restaurant's front door, the large dining room was straight ahead. It was the perfect place for family gatherings. The lighting and soft music were pleasing and relaxing. Evenly spaced black and white pictures on the wall represented the humble origins of our town.

I rarely went to the restaurant. Instead, once inside the front door, I turned right, where, at the end of a long hallway, an arched stone entrance welcomed me to the bar. It's where I enjoyed my daily lunch visits with friends and locals. A hand-crafted mahogany bar, once the centerpiece of the famous Starlight Lounge nightclub in Detroit, covered the right side of the room. It extended nearly the entire length. My favorite barstool sat next to the server's station at the far end of the bar. Past that, swinging doors led to the kitchen.

A half-dozen antique tables lined the left side of the room. Above the tables, brass frames filled the wall with images of a post-depression Detroit. Antique lighting fixtures dangled from tall tin ceilings. Visitors felt like they had stepped back in time — a simpler time, an exciting time, and more often than not, as the photos on the wall reminded them — a violent time.

A decade ago, during the design process of Brewster's Social Club, the gentrification period in Detroit was at its height. The big city mayor called it a new renaissance period and offered significant tax incentives to investors. Voters approved a revitalization and sustainability bond. Real estate prices in the big city soared. Many historic buildings were sold to wealthy developers and demolished. Expensive condos and high-end retail emporiums soon replaced them.

Collectors purchased antique street lights, building marquees, and other vintage items. The vacant Starlight Lounge nightclub was targeted in the city's commercial resurgence plan. While most structures were simply demolished without respect to their history and culture, a few contractors had the character and integrity to preserve the city's history.

Ten years ago, an advertisement in the Detroit Free Press had announced the time and date for an auction on Park Avenue, where the interior furnishings and fixtures of the Starlight Lounge nightclub were available to the highest bidder. Bob Brewster had bought the handmade furniture and the large mahogany bar for his new restaurant.

CHAPTER THREE

Detroit, Michigan - 1935
'Those were the good old days'

WITHIN ANY MAJOR CITY, THE 80/20 RULE APPLIES. EIGHTY percent of the people are law-abiding. Most businesses are legit. Most cops are honest.

Politicians are an exception to the rule.

The eighty percent—who practiced good morals and ethics, lived within the rules of polite society, and followed the law—rarely met the other twenty percent. It didn't mean they didn't exist. They would always be there—in the shadows of the law, in the pockets of politicians, and one step ahead of the devil.

In 1935, in Detroit, Michigan, the law-abiding majority enjoyed the post-depression economy. Employment was at an all-time high. The population in Detroit grew by double digits. Henry Ford introduced the first V8 engine and raised workers' wages. Laborers from across the country, mainly the South, flooded the motor city.

Professional sports figures and teams mimicked the economic recovery and contributed to its momentum. In 1935, Detroit's Joe Lewis was the world's boxing champion, the Tigers beat the Cubs to win the World Series, the Lions won their first NFL championship, and the Red Wings were on the way to securing their first Stanley Cup victory.

The less law-abiding twenty percenters weren't interested in someone else's winning streak. Their streak ended with the passage of the 21st amendment. The repeal of prohibition signified the end of the gangster era. Detroit's infamous Purple Gang reign, known for kidnapping, murder, and bootlegging, ended violently. Moonshiners, distillers, and mobsters had reached the pinnacle of their illicit careers, creating a void in the unprincipled twenty percent. They drank legal whiskey, reminisced about the good old days, and maneuvered for power. The void needed filling, and plenty of twenty percenters lined up for the challenge.

It was a hell of a time to live in the Motor City

David Gonyea was not in the mobster category. Not yet, anyway. At twenty-five years of age, the tall, barrel-chested artisan owned a prosperous furniture-making business in the homogeneous suburbs of Detroit. He craved more. More diversity. More opportunities. More excitement. He embraced challenges. The synergistic partnership he enjoyed with his new bride, Eve, heightened David's confidence and freed his mind from limitations.

Building on his good luck and being a natural risk-taker, he gambled on Detroit's resurgence, moving his furniture-making business from the suburbs to an antique brick building on Woodward Avenue in the city's heart. David Gonyea was now fresh meat in the big city.

Within months, David's decision to move had been validated. His business was flourishing. *Gonyea Custom Furniture* employees worked overtime to satisfy the demands. Their reputation for building and delivering high-quality furniture became their trademark. As the demand for products rose, so did their prices.

As the summer of 1935 drew to a close, David Gonyea

received a lunch invitation from Sam Durocher, a man he knew of but had never met.

Unlike David, Sam Durocher was not a suburban transplant. He was born a Detroiter. Handsome, charming, and recognizable to most in the city—at least to those who mattered—his gentle public demeanor revealed nothing of his hard-hearted potential. If his piercing blue eyes and unforgettable smile couldn't open doors, his wallet could.

In 1935, Sam Durocher's highly profitable bootlegging career had ended. He needed another enterprise to satisfy his accustomed lifestyle and, of course, his social status. Sam had powerful friends in prominent positions: political friends, beholden friends, who—under duress—helped him secure a two-story brick building on Park Avenue for pennies on the dollar. It was the most sought-after real estate in Detroit.

The elegant building he would refurbish on Park Avenue would soon be the most famous nightclub in the city. He needed to be relevant. Sam would maintain his status in society at all costs. His prominence as one of Detroit's wealthiest entrepreneurs would once again flourish.

The exterior construction for Sam Durocher's new business venture, Starlight Lounge, was nearing completion. The interior, still unfinished, was the reason for their midday meeting. In early August 1935, on an overcast Friday with a light drizzle, the two men met at an empty building on Park Avenue.

Dressed in his best business attire, David Gonyea entered an open doorway and shook the rain from his umbrella. He was greeted by a man of similar height, with unforgettable blue eyes and a recognizable smile. Ten years David's senior, Sam Durocher removed his fedora, shook hands with his guest, exchanged pleasantries, and invited him to be seated at a lone table in the middle of the open space.

A short, robust man with a thin mustache, wearing a starched white shirt and a black vest, greeted them. He held two crystal glasses and a decanter of red wine. The gentleman poured. Sam and David thanked him and toasted a budding relationship.

Attractive female servers entered the area from a back room, placed sterling silver serving plates in front of them, and carefully removed the dome covers.

Sam's blue eyes met David's deep-set brown ones. "I hope you don't mind. I ordered lunch."

David shook his head. "Not at all. It looks wonderful."

"I'm glad you're punctual, David."

"I'm always punctual, Mr. Durocher. My reputation depends on it."

"Please, David, call me Sam."

Sam Durocher didn't enjoy wasting time. Bouncing small talk back and forth during lunch, he told his guest as much. Not that Sam didn't enjoy the idle conversation and becoming acquainted with the young artisan. He wanted David's services for his new business venture, and Sam was a master at building relationships. He excelled at getting what he wanted.

Finished with their meals, the men stood from the table and strolled through the empty first floor, wine glasses in hand. Sam revealed his furniture design ideas to his slightly inebriated guest.

"This very building," Sam said, pointing at their surroundings, "will be the envy of everyone in the city. Our services will appeal to only the highest of clientèle. I will provide exclusive liquor, elegant dining, and the finest quality of interior furnishings."

With a gleam in his eyes, David nodded. The compliment was justified. He *was* the best furniture maker in the city. He knew it, and so did Sam. David also knew of Sam's reputation, which caused some concern. Yet, he remained silent and listened.

"I want the best for my Starlight Lounge," Sam continued. "For the centerpiece, the main bar, I want something grand. And here's the caveat, David. I need to be open by Thanksgiving."

"That's a pretty aggressive timeline. Barely three months away. I'll need a couple weeks to complete the design drawings for your approval."

"You have my approval," Sam said. "Can you get the job done?"

"It won't be cheap."

"That's not what I asked."

David sipped his wine and considered the opportunity. He appreciated the candor, but Sam's piercing stare sent a shiver of anxiety through David's body.

Sam wrapped an arm around David's broad shoulders with a tight hug. "Listen, you can do whatever you need to for the furniture your team builds, but I have special design requests for my custom bar. I want it to be built on-site, under my supervision—no drawings."

David frowned. "That could delay your opening."

Sam would not be dissuaded. After a brief discussion about a significant bonus for completing the project on time, David was on his way back to his furniture shop on

Woodward Avenue. He was excited, moderately nervous, and fully aware he was about to enter a business arrangement with one of Detroit's most recognizable, intimidating, and influential individuals. David told himself that a deal with the devil is better than no deal. His wife reminded him, more than once, that he was too quick to accept some business decisions.

"Now and then," Eve would say, "it might be better to walk away."

This time, he prayed he was making the right decision. The devil be damned; he wanted this job.

THE DEADLINE Sam Durocher demanded was tight. No contracts were signed, no money exchanged hands, and yet, David Gonyea committed to the project.

Or did he?

David reviewed the furniture drawings with his lead designer for two days, calculating the schedule repeatedly, each with the same disappointing outcome. Eve, who also acted as his financial advisor, continued to counsel him to walk away from the deal. "Too many things can go wrong," she told him. "I don't trust that man." Eve was wise enough to foresee the consequences of failure. Defaulting on the expectations of a man like Sam Durocher worried her.

Knowing Sam was not the person he wanted to disappoint and remembering that he had already told him he was punctual—even bragging about his reputation—David still wanted to make it work. He wanted to be associated with the Starlight Lounge. Sam's demands to oversee the construction of the bar stirred his curiosity, but it wasn't a deal-breaker.

Or was it?

The designing, building, and delivery of the small furniture was not the problem. The large mahogany bar that Sam demanded was David's Achilles heel. Without architectural drawings and a complete materials list, the on-site construction of the customized bar would be time-consuming and labor-intensive. David struggled with his commitment.

DAVID KISSED Eve and gave her a tight hug. He left her with a playful pat on the ass on the way out the door.

Today is going to be a good day.

He drove to the Starlight Lounge building on Park Avenue again, recording the mileage and calculating the time. He needed to convince his wife and his team that they could pull it off. First, though, he needed to convince himself.

During previous reconnaissance visits, he hadn't noticed the vacant building next to the Starlight Lounge. Taking it as a sign from God, he smiled and continued driving. His excitement level peaked. If he could lease this adjacent building, it would allow him to set up a temporary wood shop. It would expedite the manufacturing process of the furniture, increase productivity, and solve his delivery predicament. Improved profitability was a bonus.

Driving away from the building, his heart raced. So did his Lincoln Roadster. The wind blew violently on his thick, wiry hair, creating the illusion that a porcupine was attacking his head. Zigzagging through the busy streets of Detroit, he made the seven or eight blocks in record time. Parking his yellow Roadster, he glanced toward the sky. No rain. Besides, this wouldn't take long. He left the top down and hurried to the City Hall building with a renewed vigor. It was only a half-block away. Trotting up the stairs to the main entrance, he tossed a coin into the open case of a street musician.

Karma, he thought.

This could be my lucky day.

The directory in the lobby led him to the city planning department on the second floor. He bounded up the stairs two or three steps at a time. At the top of the broad marble staircase, he turned right. It was just a guess. He was correct.

The thick, frosted glass door looked heavy, although it opened easily. Introducing himself to the tiny woman at the receptionist's desk—whose name tag said "Judith"—he found his tall frame leaning forward, peering at her.

Maybe a Sears, Roebuck catalog would make it easier for you to see over the desk.

"What?"

"Sorry." *Did he really say that out loud?* "I'm looking to lease a building on Park Avenue, ma'am. To whom would I speak?"

"Hold on," she said, checking her directory and scowling at David. "Down the hall. It's the second door on your right."

David thanked her politely, shook his head, and followed her directions. The tiled lobby echoed a word he hadn't heard in a long time. "Yutz."

His neighbor used to call him a yutz, he remembered. It was Yiddish for "asshole." He laughed and continued down the hallway.

She didn't look Jewish.

A short, disappointing conversation with the department manager quashed David's enthusiasm.

"Isn't there another possibility?" David pleaded with the lanky gentleman named Charles. "Is there someone else to whom I should speak?"

Charles, an awkwardly built man with a noticeable hunch, rubbed the large silver cross that hung around his neck so hard as to polish it. "I'm the manager," were his final words. That was it. He played the power move. There was no more to be said after 'the manager' exercised his authority.

So much for karma.

Charles slithered away from his desk, retreating with a kyphotic gait to a door near the rear of the office, never looking back.

Prick.

On his way out of the office, dejected, David picked up a Bible placed purposefully on the prick's desk to gain attention — to prove his faith. It was the Old Testament, the thick one. He tucked it under his right arm and headed for the lobby.

David smiled at the diminutive woman at the reception desk. Judith sneered as he approached, turning her head sideways, away from the yutz. He slammed the thick Bible on her desk, and she snapped to attention, maybe even increasing her height by an inch or so. She may have even jumped. Who can tell?

"That's for you," David barked. "I've just created a miracle. Sit on this! You're now three inches taller!"

He stormed out of the building, down the marble stairs, past the mediocre violinist, crossed the street, and opened the door to his shiny yellow Roadster.

Splattered white bird shit covered the driver's seat.

Fuck!

ONE WEEK after their lunch meeting at the Starlight Lounge building on Park Avenue, David Gonyea and Sam Durocher met again in a private box behind home plate at Navin Field.

The Detroit Tigers played a home game against the Washington Senators. They chatted about weather, sports, politics—they agreed. Wives—both seemed in love. Children—neither had any and eventually, the conversation turned to business.

Sam Durocher sipped his beer. "The last time we met, you said the timeline was good."

"I thought it was, Sam, but I've reviewed the details for the past week. My lead designer, our production team, and my financing adviser have spent countless hours reviewing the logistics of this project. Unfortunately, we're not comfortable with the deadline. I don't want to let you down. Is your schedule flexible?"

"I'm not willing to change my schedule. Nobody in the media will give a shit about a new business opening in February. There's no advantage. I need to be open by Thanksgiving, and I want you and your team to create the vision we discussed. Do you need more money?"

"No, absolutely not." David's hands waved emphatically. "It's not about the money. Your offer is more than fair. It's just the timing and the distance between my shop and your building. My employees would have to spend a lot of time traveling back and forth across the city, measuring, designing, and delivering. We might pull it off if it weren't for the custom mahogany bar. What you've requested will take a lot of time and labor. I even looked into leasing the vacant building next to yours to create a temporary workshop. Unfortunately, it's already been committed to someone else."

Sam furrowed his brow. "To which building are you referring?"

"It's the one to the right of your building, facing it from the street. On the east side."

"If you were to lease this building next to mine, would you be comfortable committing to the Thanksgiving deadline?"

"Yes, but that's not possible. I've already looked into it. I even spoke with the manager of the city planning department. He was a bit of a dick."

"Hunchback?"

David cocked his head. "What?"

"Never mind, his name is Charles."

"How do you know Charles?" David asked.

Sam grinned. "Don't worry about it. When would you need the lease to start, and how long would you need it?"

David told him he would need immediate occupancy, and for cleanup, he would need the temporary location until the end of the year. Sam Durocher said he would take care of the details and handed the young artisan a thick envelope containing a significant cash deposit.

They enjoyed the rest of the game and chatted about business, friends, and family. Accepting the retainer, David had given Sam his commitment.

The Tigers beat the Senators by a score of six to three.

CHAPTER FOUR

Present Day - Saturday, October 30

Dan Scruggs set the hard-shell tweed guitar case on the floor beside his stool. I did the same with the plastic grocery bag as the harassment from the Social Club lunch regulars continued.

"Oh, look, a hobo and a musician." Someone slurred.

Another shouted. "Is that your overnight bag, Rick?"

I let out an insincere chuckle and saluted a few friendly faces with an extended middle finger. Some returned the gesture.

Ward Watkins, the Social Club bar manager, approached us with a grin. "Hey, fellas." He looked at me. "I heard through the grapevine that you saved Scruggs' life this morning."

An amiable guy with a pleasant smile, Ward stood between my five-foot nine-inch frame and Scruggs' towering height. He was a retired car salesman and treated patrons with respect, listened to everyone's issues without judgment, and didn't drink—which didn't hurt.

Scruggs shoved a finger in my face. "Rick killed a squirrel."

I slapped his thick hand. "Not true. I saw him running away."

"Yeah, well, now the poor rodent is homeless."

Ward shook his head.

Scruggs and I laughed, and shared a fist bump.

Brewster entered the bar.

"Hey Brewster!" the lunch crowd shouted.

"How's everyone doing today?" he replied to the crowd, both of his hands waving in the air like he was trying to say hello to them individually, only simultaneously. Somehow it worked. "Don't forget to try the bison burgers this afternoon. They're incredible."

Brewster walked towards us, stopping along the way to shake hands with a few of the regulars. He placed his palms on the bar, leaned forward, and asked about my truck. I told him it couldn't be repaired. "Jimmy Hendricks picked up my truck," I said. "He's taking it back to Scruggs' shop."

Scruggs confirmed with a nod.

Ward snickered at the mention of Jimmy Hendricks.

"I'll call my insurance agent when I get home," I said. "I'll need to stop by the Ford dealership on Monday. We need rides home after lunch."

Brewster took a step back and crossed his arms. "Did you guys recognize the vehicle that ran you off the road?"

I shook my head.

Scruggs said, "I would recognize it if I saw it again. It was unique. That asshole nearly got us killed."

Brewster recommended I ask for Karl Gustafson when I called Dunville Ford. Said he was an ex-cop, reputable, and would take good care of me.

"I'll shoot him a text to expect you," Brewster smiled and turned to the entrance, where Dunville Police officers Carter and Dean walked through the arched opening and ambled in our direction. I hopped from my stool with a mock salute. The cops reached for their weapons in a simulated response. We laughed and shook hands.

Officer Willie Carter patted me on the shoulder. "Sorry about your truck, Rick. Steve showed us the pictures. I'm sure glad you guys weren't seriously injured. That looked like a nasty collision."

"Thanks, Willie. I'd like to find that asshole that ran us off the road and bounce *his* head off an oak tree."

Officer Owen Dean smiled, nodding in agreement.

Scruggs shared the description of the vehicle that had nearly killed us. The two local cops promised to keep a lookout.

Marianne, my favorite waitress, reached across the counter with the cops' take-out lunch orders. I waved off their attempt to pay and asked her to put their lunch on my tab. Carter and Dean thanked me with firm handshakes and headed for the exit.

Ward scanned the bar for thirsty customers and then turned to us. "What can I get you guys?"

"Modelo for me," I said, pointing my thumb towards my chin.

Scruggs said, "I'll have a Corona."

"How can you drink that piss, Scruggs?" I shrugged, stretching my arms wide.

"What? They're both made in Mexico." He pointed his thumb toward the south, although it was pointing east. I knew what he meant.

"Yeah, but they don't piss in the Modelo."

"I'll put a lime in it." Scruggs laughed.

Marianne was back to take our orders. Tucking a loose strand of long, brown hair behind her right ear, she stared at Scruggs and me with concerned eyes. Shaking her head, she crossed her arms and looked at the two of us, saying something about not drinking alcohol after a violent collision. Scruggs tugged on his ponytail and looked away.

"I'm not drinking alcohol," I said. "It's just beer." I smiled and then shouted to Ward. "Don't forget the lime for Scruggs's bottle of piss!"

"You want a lime, Scruggs?" Ward asked with a sideways glance in my direction.

"I guess so," he answered dryly.

Ward pointed at me. "Is he making you put a lime in your beer?"

"Yep."

"Why?"

"Says there's piss in it."

Ward shook his head and, from his expression, probably wondered if there was such a thing as an IQ detector. He sauntered down the bar.

Scruggs and I chatted with Brewster until he excused himself to take an incoming phone call. Ward returned with our beers, set them on the counter, cocked his head, and retreated with a sinister smile.

"Wait!" I hollered. "Hold on! Come back here! You put a lime in my Modelo!"

"Yep."

"Why?"

"If Scruggs gets a lime, you get a lime." He turned and walked away.

I picked the slimy green foreign substance from my ruined beer and tossed it at Ward's head. He must have seen my reflection in the large mirror behind the bar because he turned quickly and swatted the lime slice out of the air like Jackie Chan.

He laughed. "Ha! You missed."

"You ruined my beer!"

"Suck it up, Rick."

Brewster returned from his phone call. "What's with the commotion?"

"Rick threw fruit at my head!" Ward pimped.

Brewster laughed. "All right, bozos, you clowns are my favorite part of the day, but somebody needs to find out where that lime slice went. I don't need more ant problems. The health department frowns on insects crawling around my restaurant."

Scruggs snorted. I apologized to Ward and offered to find the missing lime slice for a fresh beer. I asked Brewster if he had a flashlight. He gave me directions to the maintenance closet and moved his way up the bar to schmooze with the regulars.

The adolescent bantering between Scruggs and me had been going on since we were kids. Harmless bickering. The locals understood. They were used to it. Maybe they weren't used to it, but they tolerated us. Tourists were sometimes caught off-guard. Some probably felt uncomfortable. Oh well, it's what we did.

I hopped from my stool, patted Scruggs on the shoulder, and asked him to order me the bison burger lunch special. Dismounting my stool, I walked around the server station and turned right toward the kitchen area. I pushed on the hinged double swinging doors a little too forcefully and nearly knocked Marianne on her ass. She carried four lunch specials on her arms, sidestepped my advance, and kept her balance. Luckily, I was a big tipper, and she liked me.

"Whoa, sorry, Marianne."

She tipped her head to the side and blew a long strand of hair from her vision. "No worries." She continued toward the hungry patrons.

I entered the kitchen and was amazed at the cleanliness of the large, open room. Dozens of workers were decked out in aprons and white hairnets. There was stainless steel everywhere. Gaining a new appreciation for what happened behind the scenes at the Social Club, I promised myself I would never complain about food prices again. The beverage prices, well, that was a different matter.

I strolled toward the maintenance closet with a bit of a bounce in my step and an unwarranted feeling of importance.

CHAPTER FIVE

Present Day - Saturday, October 30

I FOUND THE MAINTENANCE CLOSET AND HOPED THE DOOR wasn't locked. The handle turned, and the door opened inward. The lights turned on automatically. It was a much larger room than I had expected. Well lit and well ventilated. A recessed fan whirled overhead. There were tall metal shelving units on the left and rear walls. The cleaning supplies, disinfectants, paper products, first aid supplies, and many other boxes and bottles appeared well organized. Product labels and government warning stickers were everywhere.

Danger - Caution - Hazardous chemicals - Keep away from small children - Contents under pressure - May cause cancer, and on and on it went. Bold lettering and bright colors warned the average idiot not to drink the bleach. It's no wonder there were instructions on Pop-Tarts.

A large yellow toolbox was on the right side of the room on the floor. I opened it and removed the flashlight. Above the toolbox, hanging on a metal bar, were janitorial uniforms. I grabbed an empty hangar and noticed a clipboard attached to the wall next to the door. The papers on the clipboard had a series of elongated boxes for check-marks, dates, times, and people responsible for cleaning specific areas of the restaurant. Holding the clipboard and flashlight, I headed back to the bar. I glanced at the workers periodically and pretended to take notes. I hummed a tune that was stuck in my head and sauntered through the kitchen. Nobody made eye contact with me. It was an interesting psychological experiment to observe how people behaved differently when someone with a clipboard was surveilling them. I returned to the bar as Marianne set our lunch specials in front of us.

Scruggs cocked his head. "What's with the clipboard?"

"Just an experiment." I snickered.

"On what?"

"People."

"What people?"

"Other people, Scruggs, not you."

"That's good." He laughed.

After placing the clipboard and flashlight on the floor next to my feet, I grabbed the hand sanitizer from the bar top and took a few healthy squirts. The elusive lime slice would still be there, wherever it was, after lunch, so I ate my bison burger while it was still warm.

"Hey, fellas." Ward stepped up to check on us. "How was everything?"

Scruggs wiped his chin. "Great."

I nodded. "Brewster was right. This bison burger was fantastic."

"Yea, it's been popular today."

"Sorry about the lime thing, Ward."

"No worries, but you throw like a pussy."

"Next time." I laughed.

Ward went about serving other customers.

Interlacing my fingers, I raised my arms over my head, cracked my knuckles, and leaned back to stretch, trying to find motivation. Placing my hands on top of the stool, I pushed myself to my feet and faced my buddy. "Are you taking off, Scruggs?"

"Not yet. I want to watch you humiliate yourself."

I groaned, grabbed the flashlight, and stepped around the server station. Lifting the hinged portion of the bar top, I stepped through and lowered the countertop back into place. Glancing at the areas where the elusive fruit could have landed, I saw nothing. I checked the shelves and openings in the back of the bar again. No luck.

On the front side, where the customers were seated, the mahogany bar met the laminate flooring seamlessly. There were no gaps. On the other side, where Ward Watkins and the bartenders worked, this was not the case. Behind the bar, decorative hand-carved legs kept the bottom off the floor, creating a three-inch gap.

I exhaled a long breath, positioned myself on the floor, and prepared to explore the blackness beneath. I needed to find that lime slice. Scruggs and Ward weren't the only people who enjoyed my discomfort. Brewster sneaked up from behind and stuck the toe of his right shoe up my ass.

"What the hell?"

Lying on my right side and holding the flashlight in my right hand, I slowly scooted along the sticky floor. The beam of light created creepy shadows in the dark, three-inch opening. There were indiscernible objects scattered about. Searching and scratching, I slithered along the floor while the locals heckled me. Finally, I spotted the elusive fruit slice in the tiny three-inch opening. Ward had whacked the lime slice out of the air so hard it had flown under the bar towards the front side where the customers sat. Today's modern bars are barely two feet deep. This mahogany classic was all of three feet in depth, maybe more. "Shit," I muttered. "I can see it, but I'm not sure how I will get it."

"Need a coat hanger?" someone asked.

"I have a coat hanger," I grumbled. I stood up fast and felt a little lightheaded. The hanger didn't provide the reach needed to retrieve the forbidden fruit. I summoned Ward for another beer.

"Make it two beers, Ward," Scruggs chuckled, rubbing his meaty paws together. "This is getting interesting."

I glared at him. "Don't you have a business to run, Scruggs?"

"Right now, this *is* my business." He laughed.

I punched him in the shoulder. "Help me out, buddy. I need ideas."

"Get something longer than a coat hanger."

"Oh, that's brilliant. Aren't you a genius?" Then I had an idea. "Hey, Ward," I said, ignoring Scruggs. "Where's that mop you used to clean up spills?"

"At the other end of the bar," he replied.

"Can you grab it for me?" I implored him. "See if the handle unscrews from the mop head, will you? I only need the wooden handle part."

Scruggs and I took big pulls from our beers. Ward sauntered away.

A few minutes later, he was back with a five-foot-long wooden pole. I took another slug of beer and prepared to lie on the floor again. Shining the flashlight with my left hand and grabbing the wooden stick with my right, I swept at the lime slice a few times. After a few more strategic attempts and my irritation level elevated, I took a heavy swing at it. The pole whacked hard against the front underside of the bar, echoing from the narrow gap. I peered into the opening. The fruit hadn't moved, but I'd knocked something else loose.

Brewster looked down. "What happened?"

"Think I broke something."

"My mop handle?" asked Ward.

"No, Ward. Your mop handle is fine. Hold on—" I rose to my feet. "I'll be right back."

Scruggs picked up the clipboard from the floor by my stool and handed it to me across the mahogany counter. I grabbed it and turned on a heel. Exiting the back of the bar, I returned the hinged countertop to the flat position. Turning right, I entered the kitchen and marched forward.

I opened the door to the maintenance room and replaced the clipboard on the inside wall. Opening the yellow toolbox, I grabbed what I'd come for and headed back to the bar. Less than five minutes had passed when I returned.

Grabbing the duct tape I'd found in the toolbox, I wrapped a piece around the end of the wooden mop handle. There I was again, on the floor, sticky side down. The wooden pole was in my right hand with the duct tape on the end, sticky side out. I carefully pushed it towards the debris, using the flashlight as guidance. Reaching the front side of the bar, I swished it around from side to side for a few seconds and gently retrieved it. At the end of my sticky mop pole was a small piece of mahogany wood, thin, about six inches square. I stared at it for a few seconds, then tossed it up for Brewster to catch. No need to stand. I'd had enough exercise for the day.

Pushing the pole into the abyss again and swishing it in an elliptical pattern, I retrieved it gently, slowly, hand-over-hand, and stared at my discovery. "What the hell?"

Brewster stared down at me. "What's the matter, Rick?"

"It's a coin. A gold coin." My face twisted in confusion.

Brewster furrowed his brow. Ward ambled over and stared. Scruggs's upper torso created a long shadow as he leaned over the bar's edge and stared at me with wide eyes.

"You pulling our legs?" Scruggs asked.

Ward added. "You're joking, right?"

Brewster gently kicked me in the ass. "Did you get the lime?"

I gave him a look, stood from the floor, and flipped him the coin. Scratching the three-day growth on my chin, I watched as the locals leaned forward and peered over the bar, staring at my discovery in disbelief.

Brewster rubbed the coin between his thumb and forefinger. "This is interesting."

I reached for the sanitizer on the counter. "Now what?"

CHAPTER SIX

Detroit, Michigan - 1935
'Brothers in Arms'

THE BUREAU OF INVESTIGATION, FOUNDED IN 1908, WAS growing exponentially. Late the previous year, Congress combined the BOI with the Bureau of Prohibition and renamed it. The newly established agency was called the FBI.

By early 1935, every major city held training centers for new recruits. New agents were given assignments to tackle the growing epidemics of gambling, prostitution, organized crime, white supremacy, kidnappings, bank robberies, and murders. The twelve-week program was the forerunner of today's FBI National Academy.

John Douglas and Dale Mintern served together in the Marines. Both were tall, muscular, and handsome. Except for eye color—Dale with blue, John with brown—they looked like brothers. Both were blessed with square jaws, dimpled chins, and thick, wavy dark hair. They commanded attention. Having met in Marine boot camp, they *were* brothers—Brothers in Arms.

Honorably discharged, John and Dale joined the Detroit Police Department and often joked about seeing more combat as police officers than serving in the military. During their tenure with the Detroit Police, violence and criminal activity complaints were regularly submitted for investigation and follow-up. These reports were mostly ignored. Follow-up wasn't the Detroit Police Department's strong suit.

John and Dale's disappointments multiplied with the lack of leadership in their department. The previous fall, discontented with their profession and dispirited, both had pursued other law enforcement options. There weren't many available. Not without relocating. They felt stagnant and underutilized. The Detroit Police Department had become, in their experience, a corrupt organization that favored the privileged over the disadvantaged, the rich over the impoverished, and, much worse, white over colored.

After a difficult shift on a difficult day in a city that was becoming more and more difficult to work in, they slid up to the curved bar at Baker's Keyboard Lounge on Livernois Street and ordered drinks. John was a beer guy, Dale, bourbon.

Chatting up a gentleman who saddled up to his right, John Douglas asked the distinguished gentleman about his business. The polished man with the salt and pepper hair and tailored suit said he was on his way to New York and turned forward to sip his Scotch.

John admired the perfect knot in his tie.

Reaching for the bowl of nuts on the bar top, the suit coat of the dapper man opened slightly, revealing a holster.

He's right-handed. John made a mental note and elbowed his partner. Dale Mintern and John Douglas communicated without speaking. It wasn't a gift. It came from years of working together and protecting each other. Dale rose from his stool and walked behind John, tapping him on the shoulder as he passed. Smiling at the fashionably dressed man, Dale sat. The cops had flanked the suit.

Dale swirled his bourbon and turned his head slightly left. "Waiting for trouble or looking for it?"

The man in the suit didn't flinch. "Excuse me?"

"Your gun? Is it registered?"

Dapper Dan looked straight ahead. A tight smile pulled on his lips. "You guys are cops, right?"

They nodded.

The man in the middle grinned. "May I reach into my jacket pocket for my 'permit?'"

The cops nodded and slid in closer, ready to pounce if necessary. The gentleman wasn't nervous. Placing his right hand — his shooting hand — palm-down on the bar top, he reached into his jacket pocket with his left hand. He never flinched. Removing his 'permit,' he set it down gently and placed his left hand on the countertop.

John Douglas picked up the badge and stared at him. "Son of a bitch. You're with the FBI?"

"May I remove my hands from the bar?" The man asked.

John nodded. "What's your name?"

"Special Agent James Klein." He said, placing his badge into his jacket.

"I apologize."

"You didn't know. Actually, I'm impressed by how well you two handled the matter."

"We take our safety and the safety of the citizens of this fair city seriously," Dale said.

Special Agent Klein said, "Your leadership must be proud."

They spoke in unison. "They're assholes, sir."

"Listen," the suit chuckled. "I just finished interviewing two candidates here in your city for positions with the FBI. I didn't like either of them. Are you guys interested in applying?"

THEIR APPROVAL letters from the FBI were received in late April 1935. John Douglas and Dale Mintern entered the FBI academy together, and although their previous military training was physically demanding, their new careers would test the limits of the mind. Under the direction of J. Edgar Hoover, the FBI became a formidable force against the less law-abiding. The latest developments in scientific crime investigations were being studied. Ballistics, latent fingerprint research, handwriting, typewriting analysis, and toxicology were just a few of the newest technologies being advanced.

In every city across the country, informants became a valuable asset to the bureau. The politicians and newspapers had declared the depression over, but not everyone could participate in the recovery. Picking up a few extra bucks for snitching on gangsters wasn't difficult; it was dangerous, but not difficult. Information from paid informants flowed into the Detroit FBI branch. Most of them were low-level violations and not worth the resources. Others were quashed with simple threats of prison time.

On November 7, reliable information about an upcoming gambling operation was reported by multiple informants. License plates from across the country were spotted in Detroit. They were recorded, crosschecked, and verified. The newly formed agency considered the information to be credible. Phones were tapped, and suspects were followed. The FBI chose not to inform the Detroit Police of their ongoing investigation. The risk of leaks was unacceptable. Secrecy was warranted.

Six additional agents were assigned to assist Agents

Douglas and Mintern on their first major assignment. Surveillance was conducted around the clock. Cars were tailed, and shady individuals were shadowed as they frequented local restaurants and clubs. Photos of the suspects, their family, friends, and meeting places were tacked to the corkboard on the wall in the local FBI branch on Michigan Avenue.

THE FOLLOWING week, Wednesday morning, November 13, the FBI agents' relentless investigation concluded after five long days and sleepless nights. A high-stakes gambling event was to take place Friday night on the second floor of the soon-to-be-opened Starlight Lounge. Wealthy and nefarious individuals from across the country would be in attendance. They had two days to prepare.

Douglas and Mintern consulted with experienced agents across the country. With their help, a plan of action was approved. The cast of characters on their radar included gangsters from Detroit and Chicago, a defense attorney from Cleveland, a big city mayor from California, a congressional representative from Ohio, and a prominent jeweler from New Jersey. At a minimum, they surmised, a dozen individuals would be in attendance.

Monetized informants were paying dividends. The informants said that the owner of the Starlight Lounge, Sam Durocher, had guaranteed the protection and security for all the attendees. Durocher had hired four extremely large and well-armed ex-convicts to secure the property. The informants learned personal bodyguards would not be allowed inside the lounge during the "alleged" gambling operation, which eased the FBI's concerns, if only slightly.

They hoped the intelligence was accurate.

John Douglas, Dale Mintern, and their colleagues knew what needed to be done: follow their motto.

Train for the best. Train for the worst.

FRIDAY, NOVEMBER 15th, two days after their plans were approved, John Douglas, Dale Mintern, and the six additional FBI agents prepared for their first significant case. They were physically and emotionally ready for the task ahead. The raid was scheduled to be executed precisely at midnight. The Detroit Police precinct commander would be contacted for backup five minutes before the execution, eliminating any possibility of leaks.

Watches were synchronized at 10:00 p.m. Rehearsed positions were assumed. Two agents were assigned to watch the beefy goon who protected the cars with the out-of-state license plates in the parking lot. Two more were assigned to guard the front door of the Starlight Lounge and instructed to apprehend anyone exiting the building as the operation unfolded. The rear entrance of the building, in the alley, was the access point to penetrate.

Douglas, Mintern, and the other two agents would enter from this location with force. From an abandoned warehouse across the alleyway, they kept a keen eye on the rear delivery door of the Starlight Lounge, taking notes and photos and silently communicating with practiced hand signals. Shortly after 11:00 p.m., a striking yellow Lincoln Roadster entered the alley behind the building and parked. Two occupants exited the convertible. They shook hands and shared a few laughs. The driver, David Gonyea, waved goodbye to his passenger and drove away down the alley and out of sight.

The passenger was Sam Durocher, the owner of the establishment. He unlocked the rear delivery door of the Starlight Lounge and entered the building.

As planned, five minutes before midnight, an agent guarding the front door placed a call from a payphone on Park Avenue, across the street from the Starlight Lounge. He contacted the night-shift commander at the Sixteenth Precinct. Providing his name, position, and badge number, he reassured the commander of the consequences of not taking his call seriously.

Minutes later, gunshots echoed from the vicinity of the private parking lot. Sirens could be heard in the distance. The rear delivery door of the Starlight Lounge was breached. Agents rushed in with guns drawn. Adrenaline peaked as the G-men moved in unison to their left, cleared the immediate area, and proceeded quickly up the wide staircase to the second floor.

A large goon emerged from the shadows at the top of the staircase and fired downward in the agents' direction. Bullets ricocheted off the metal staircase railing. The pungent odor of gunpowder filled the air. Chunks of concrete from the interior brick walls exploded inward. Expensive Italian marble tiles shattered, and a massive dust cloud engulfed the first floor.

John Douglas sidestepped the threat and returned fire. He wasn't the only one. The noise was deafening. Muzzle flashes were so close it burned his skin. Screams were barely audible as the gunman was pelted with lead.

The overweight gangster tumbled down the stairs. If the many bullets didn't kill him, which they did, the force of his head bouncing off the tiled steps on his way down would have. His face was no longer recognizable at his final resting place, just short of the ground floor. His fat body twisted in a manner that seemed to have been impossible. Puddles of crimson blood oozed from the man, creating a slick surface on the Italian marble, forming a pool as gravity took its course.

Clearing the staircase, the agents continued to the second floor. Behind a pair of double doors, the commotion grew louder. Forcing entry into the large room, the agents shouted practiced commands to stand down, drop your weapons, don't move, this is the FBI, and so on. The only objection came in the way of a small-caliber derringer. A short, awkward-looking man with a face resembling a turtle carelessly pointed his pocket gun toward the agents. Multiple bullets hit their target. The tiny fellow in the three-piece suit slumped to the hardwood floor, his weapon still fully loaded.

The agents took quick control of the chaos, scanning the room for further resistance. Physically and rather forcefully, the suspects were positioned on the floor, face down on the white tile, which had now taken on a different hue. Some suspects groaned. Others protested. A few shouted for their attorneys. Swift kicks from heavy leather boots silenced the complainers. The confrontation was over.

Minutes later, Detroit Police officers entered the building and announced their presence. Participants from two distinctly different law enforcement agencies met each other. The suspense was palpable. Agent Douglas holstered his weapon and yelled, "Clear." It seemed to settle nerves, and tensions abated.

Handcuffs were placed on the *alleged* criminals. Names

were taken, and evidence seized. Ten people were placed under arrest. Another lay dead, blood pooling around his body, turning his expensive three-piece gray suit a deep burgundy color. A walnut-handled derringer lay on the floor, just a few feet away from his lifeless hand. One of the G-men swept it aside, later to be bagged as evidence.

Tens of thousands of dollars in currency, jewelry, and coins were removed from a handcrafted table in the middle of the large room. Two guns, a couple knives, and brass knuckles were confiscated from the remaining bodyguards — the smart ones who were still breathing. Detroit Police officers walked the suspects down the stairs, corralling them near the rear entrance. They would be transported to the local precinct for fingerprints and mugshots. Two federal agents guarding the front door were let inside by their colleagues. Notes were compared. Nobody had attempted to escape from their direction. Both agents from the parking lot arrived at the rear delivery door. Neither of them had been injured in the gun battle. The beefy goon in the parking lot wasn't as fortunate. He died of lead poisoning.

Dale Mintern placed jackets, hats, assorted papers, and other belongings into a large box, securing it with a tag that included the time and date. John Douglas took photos, inventoried the evidence, and placed the cash, jewelry, and coins into his dark brown customized briefcase. The leather briefcase, a gift from his father, was branded with the official FBI logo and John's badge number, 316.

The FBI team huddled in the corner of the second-floor room and shared a quick prayer. There were no injuries, at least on the good guys' team. Mintern and Douglas reconciled their notes.

Still, something didn't jive.

Surveillance notes taken before the raid revealed a discrepancy. Twelve individuals had entered the building. Only eleven had been accounted for. Ten were arrested, and one was dead. The math didn't work. The team reviewed their notes and crossed off the suspects' names who were arrested. Sam Durocher was missing, possibly still in the building. Perhaps still a threat.

With guns drawn, the two teams split up. Cautiously and systematically, room by room and floor by floor, they set out to clear the rest of the building. Confident that the upper level was clear, Douglas and three agents proceeded cautiously down the staircase to the main lounge. Mintern and the remaining three agents continued down the cement stairs to the basement.

In a private office on the first floor, down a short hallway at one end of the mahogany bar, Douglas opened a door that appeared to be a closet. It wasn't. Stunned, he found a metal spiral staircase that led in two directions: up to the second floor and down to the basement. Assigning two of his agents to proceed down the tight staircase, he and the other agent squeezed up toward the second floor. They met a dead end at the top of the metal staircase. A wall. John Douglas pushed on it, and it hinged open. Exiting the hidden doorway, the two men exchanged glances. They stood shoulder-to-shoulder in a small second-floor office that had already been cleared.

What the hell?

At the other end of the metal staircase, two agents also pushed on a hinged wall in the basement. It opened to a dimly lit room. They announced their presence to avoid startling their colleagues and made eye contact with Dale Mintern, who signaled for them to join him. Mintern pointed to a locked door that led to the adjacent Park Avenue building. They had no authority to breach it. It was clear how Sam Durocher had cleverly escaped.

THE CORONER placed the bodies of the beefy parking lot goon, the overweight bodyguard who'd bounced down the marble staircase, and the small unidentified man with the stained gray suit into body bags and headed for the county morgue. Detroit Police officers drove three fully loaded paddy wagons to the Sixteenth Precinct with ten suspects, each proclaiming their innocence and demanding they speak with their attorney.

Mintern gathered the box of evidence with the suspects' belongings. Douglas put the camera with the surveillance photos in his custom leather briefcase with the cash, jewelry, and coins.

AT AROUND 2:30 a.m., eight federal agents walked three blocks west to their parked vehicles. Seven agents drove to the FBI office on Michigan Avenue to complete their paperwork and file after-action reports. The eighth agent, John Douglas, went in a different direction. He drove his vehicle down a dark alley and parked near the previously breached delivery door of the Starlight Lounge. He would remain on site, protecting the scene from intruders and looters, hoping he might spot the elusive twelfth suspect— Sam Durocher.

The following morning, Saturday, November 16, the first cleaning crew employee arrived. He was early; it was seven-thirty, and a dead man was sitting in a car in the alley. Panicked at his discovery, the employee unlocked the rear door, rushed inside the Starlight Lounge, and dialed the Sixteenth Precinct.

Agent John Douglas was dead. Two .38 Special bullets lodged in his head, just behind his left ear. The custom dark brown leather briefcase, with the branded FBI seal and number 316, was not in the vehicle.

CHAPTER SEVEN

Present Day - Monday, November 1

TEMPERATURES WERE NEARLY FIFTEEN DEGREES ABOVE AVERAGE. It was almost t-shirt weather—almost. Morning rays of sunshine forced their way through the narrow slats of the wall-to-wall patio doors in our master bedroom. Dappled shadows danced across the hickory hardwood flooring. Opening the blinds fully, I found myself in a trance-like state, inspired by the beauty of the scenery outside, and marveled at what could have been a Bob Ross painting. The cloudless and vibrant blue skies created a breathtaking backdrop. Brushstrokes of yellows, oranges, reds, and browns of the deciduous trees enveloped the horizon. And, just like the famous painter might have done himself—a few dark green coniferous trees were randomly placed.

It's your world.

Outside, harvesting combines droned in the distance. Thick dust clouds followed them across the rolling hills, suspended in the air. Hundreds of acres of corn fell, eight to twelve rows at a time. Carried by the breeze, corn stalk debris danced across our yard. Muted gold and red leaves floated softly to the earth from the mature trees around our property. Autumn's encore was playing out right in front of my eyes.

A pleasant bouquet wafted down the hallway. The wonderful aroma of rum, vanilla, cocoa, and almond made the morning even better. Kathy had fired up the coffee pot with a favorite Jamaican blend. I craned my neck to inhale a deep breath and sped up my morning rituals.

My daily attire was blue jeans, a flannel shirt, and a well-worn pair of western boots. Of course, I owned more proper clothing—the kind Kathy forced me to wear when we traveled to the big city for dinners and such, but unlike my wife, most of my shopping happened at Cabelas. I checked myself in the mirror, ran my fingers through my shaggy brown hair, buckled my leather belt, and hustled to the kitchen.

My wife, Special Agent Kathy Cooper, wielded the spatula like a short-order cook, flipping eggs like a ninja. I lightly cleared my throat to broadcast my presence. She turned and blew me a kiss. The dichotomy between her personal and professional existence was something most people never saw. Those who knew her socially recognized her as a kind and nurturing person. Professionally, her calm demeanor could be deceiving. She was as tough as a mixed martial arts fighter. Petite and barely an inch over five feet, her smooth olive complexion had people guessing her age. She certainly didn't look like she was on the north end of forty.

I grabbed the bread from the toaster and applied butter and jelly. Opening the cupboard above the toaster, I pulled a couple of plates from the shelf, set them on the counter, and reached in the top drawer for clean forks. My phone buzzed with a text. I read a message from Karl Gustafson. He would deliver a loaner vehicle to my house in the next thirty minutes. Huh? Brewster's doing, I guessed. I'd forgotten I no longer had a truck and made a mental note to contact my insurance agent.

Kathy added hot water to her teacup and asked if I'd

spoken with Brewster since I found the gold coin on Saturday afternoon. I told her Brewster was meeting with a friend who owned a coin shop in Ann Arbor.

Kathy slid the eggs onto the plates. "This is exciting, isn't it?"

I poured a fresh cup of java. "Yes, I feel like a pirate who found a buried treasure."

"I'm amazed the coin was still there after all these years."

"You're right, babe. The Starlight Lounge was built in the 1930s. I'm surprised nobody found it when Brewster purchased the mahogany bar and moved it to Dunville."

"There must be an interesting story behind the coin and how it ended up hidden in the bar. Who gets to keep the coin?"

"I haven't thought about that. I found the coin, but Brewster owns the joint."

Kathy grabbed two full plates and met me at the kitchen table. "What do you think the coin is worth?"

"Probably more than it was in 1933," I answered. "The back of the coin said it was worth twenty dollars. I'm guessing the price of gold today is much higher than it was back then."

"Maybe you guys should frame it and display it at the bar."

"That's an excellent idea." I mopped up my eggs with toast. "It'll be a great conversation piece."

Kathy told me it was already the talk of the town. The news spread quickly, which shouldn't have surprised me. She'd received many phone calls and texts from locals who fantasized about the coin's origin and speculated how it wound up in Dunville. Small-town people weren't concerned with details. Sure, they wanted them, but gossip—that's what they lived for. When she told me the line to enter the Social Club yesterday stretched around the block, I thought she might be joking. She assured me it was no joke. "Apparently," she went on. "Everyone wanted to visit the bar because that's where the gold coin was found."

I threw my hands in the air. "What the hell? Are you serious?"

"Yep, and from what I've heard...."

Kathy continued speaking, but my mind had already shut down. Scruggs and I had been eating lunch at the Social Club since Brewster opened it ten years ago. Now, what was going to happen? Would my favorite bar be ruined? How long would this nonsense last? Would somebody else sit on my favorite bar stool? It wasn't *really* my stool, but the lunch regulars respected tradition—they all had their favorite seating arrangements. Kathy said I reminded her of the Sheldon Cooper character on *The Big Bang Theory*. It probably wasn't a compliment.

Whatever.

"Are you even listening to me?"

Her cop voice penetrated my compromised attention span. I stood from the table to deliver a tight hug. Kathy smiled, kissed me, and headed down the hallway toward the bedroom.

I cleared the table, rinsed the dishes, and placed them in the dishwasher. A loud horn honked outside. I hollered to let Kathy know I was leaving and ambled to the mudroom. I cut through the garage with my backpack and met the car salesman in the driveway.

Built like a tank. Large head and large square teeth—

with a significant gap between the front two on top — Karl Gustafson met me in the driveway. His handshake was firm. He was my height, only thicker — much thicker. I guessed his age to be in the mid-to-late-fifties. His Popeye forearms and faded Marine tattoos were noticeable. It *was* t-shirt weather for Karl. A spotless F-150 Platinum series truck sat behind him in my driveway. He extended his arm and dangled the keys between us. The loaner truck was white. I didn't like white vehicles. All the farmers had white trucks. He handed me the keys, and I returned the handshake.

Karl slipped in closer and patted me on the shoulder like we were old friends. Told me to stop by the dealership anytime. Said he would either find something that fit my needs on the lot or help me order a new one from the factory. Then he left without unnecessary chit-chat or a driveway sales pitch. No bullshit. I liked him already. Waving a thick hand in the air, he hopped into the vehicle that had followed him and drove away.

I adjusted the seat and steering wheel in my temporary transportation, rolled down the window, and was startled by the deafening sounds of a leaf blower emanating from the side of the house. A blue haze of two-cycle smoke wafted in my direction. *What the hell?* Why did landscapers need to start so early? The damn birds were barely awake. I closed my window, which reduced the sound of the small engine racket to an acceptable level. Bluish smoke lingered in the cab. A tall, thin young man who wore a sponsored baseball cap and t-shirt grinned at me. He lifted his right arm high and waved to me enthusiastically. I feigned a smile and returned an insincere wave. Picking up the phone from the center console, I called Brewster. It went to voicemail.

I called Scruggs. No answer.

There was a voice message from someone named Sarah Owens. She introduced herself as a reporter with the *Dunville Dispatch*.

What did she want?

My mind raced with thoughts of the gold coin and, of course, the town gossip. In a small town like ours, rumor-mongering was a hobby for most people, a profession for others, and to some, it was a call of duty.

MY HARDWARE store was fifteen minutes from our house, and I barely remembered the ride. My mind whirled. I'd never been officially diagnosed with ADHD, or whatever the proper acronym was, but it didn't matter — I had it in spades. I glanced at the glass doors at the front of the store. Paulie Dowd, my store manager, waved at me. He had a big smile on his face. He always did. Meandering towards the front doors, I returned the wave.

"Morning, boss," he said as I reached the vestibule. His typical attire, jeans and a bright aloha shirt, looked clean and neatly pressed.

For years I'd tried to get him to quit calling me boss, and somewhere along the way, I gave up. It was what he did. Paulie Dowd was a highly agreeable human being, and everybody liked him. He was a five-foot ten-inch tall teddy bear, weighing just north of two hundred pounds. His clean, shaved head and barrel chest could be intimidating if you didn't know him or never saw him walk. He waddled like a duck. *Quack, Quack.*

I gave him a pat on the back and a cheerful smile. "You got here early today."

"Yes, boss. I wasn't sure what time you would get here. I wanted to make sure the store was open on time."

"I'm always here before eight o'clock."

"I know, but with all the excitement, I just wanted to be su—"

"What the hell are you talking about, Paulie?" I interrupted. "What excitement?"

"You know, boss. The gold."

"Does everybody in town know about it?"

"Probably."

"Shit."

"What's wrong, boss?"

"Nothing, I guess. I wish we had found the gold coin in my hardware store. I might have customers lined up across the parking lot."

"What?"

"Never mind. Let's get this place ready for business."

Without further conversation, we turned on the lights, opened the gates to the outdoor garden area, and reconciled the cash register. It was the same morning routine, and I enjoyed working with Paulie. He brightened my day with his laissez-faire attitude toward life. This morning, though, he seemed fidgety. I knew something bothered him. He waddled over and refilled my thermal coffee mug. I thanked him, observing with interest as he meandered aimlessly around the room. I considered ignoring his erratic behavior and simply walking away, but curiosity prevailed. Then, when I asked—I regretted my decision.

"What's eating at you, Paulie?"

"You're not going to like this, boss." His head looked like it belonged on a bobblehead doll. He rocked back and forth like a human metronome on tennis shoes. "The band I'm playing with asked me to go on the road with them for two months."

Now I really regretted asking the question.

Paulie Dowd, Scruggs, and I, along with our drummer Rob, had our own rock-n-roll cover band until the previous year before breaking up. We had played music for weddings, private parties, and corporate events for nearly twenty years. After we split up, as most bands did, primarily for stupid reasons, Paulie joined a new group. It didn't affect our friendship or our working relationship, but there was always an underlying awkwardness that we unconsciously ignored. It felt like a divorce, and we never approached the subject.

I spread my arms wide, splashing hot coffee on the sleeve of a favorite flannel shirt. I told him I didn't like the guys in his new band, especially the lead guitar player. I was a pretty good judge of character, and I knew some of the guys he was jamming with were troubled. I couldn't prove it, but I felt they were into some stupid shit. And I told Paulie as much.

"I don't do drugs, boss."

"Why would you assume I was talking about drugs, Paulie? Is Ron doing drugs?"

"You mean Rocco?"

I furrowed my brow. "Who the hell is Rocco?"

"It's Ron, but he goes by Rocco now, and he's a fantastic guitar player, boss."

I reminded Paulie he was going on the road with a group of musicians and anything—and I stressed the word *anything*—the rest of the band got involved with, he would be just as culpable. I didn't want Paulie implicated in any of the other guys' stupid or illegal activities.

His face tensed. "They have a manager now, and the first show is already scheduled."

"What the hell are you talking about? You're too old to be a rock star, don't you think?"

He fell silent. I felt like an asshole. I'm sure I could've handled that better and apologized quickly. "Listen, Paulie, that's not what I meant. It's just tha—"

"It'll be fun, boss."

"I know, I know." I groveled. "When are you leaving?"

"Sometime on Thursday. We have to be in Chicago for a show this Friday night."

"Are you sure you're ready for this?"

He beamed. "I can't wait!"

"All right," I said, trying to lighten the mood and redeem some self-respect. "We've been friends for a long time. I'll support you on this adventure and hold your position for two months. No more."

"Thanks, boss. I'll send you postcards."

The rest of the morning was a blur. Time dragged on, and my mind felt numb. The thought of Paulie leaving and, of course, the crowds at my favorite bar overwhelmed me. I checked my phone and saw a text from Karl Gustafson. I scrolled through the half-dozen images he sent. Of the six F-150 trucks on his lot, four were white, one was silver, and another was black. I asked Karl to search other dealerships for a burgundy truck. He said my last truck was burgundy and wondered if I should try a different color. I said no—I liked burgundy. Within seconds, I received a thumbs-up emoji. Once again—I liked him.

A crushing thought paralyzed my brain. Would Karl

take care of all the paperwork for me? Or would I still need to deal with the unpleasant experience of jumping through the red tape, lines, and grouchy government employees at the Secretary of State's office? Which reminded me to contact my insurance agent. So I did. She was pleasant and told me someone would visit Scruggs Auto and Body, where my truck had been towed, to assess the damage and complete the claim. Staring at the growing pile of paperwork on my desk, my phone vibrated, thankfully diverting my attention.

"What's up, Brewster?"

"I'm on my way to your store with Gary. We'll be there in about thirty minutes. We need to talk."

"Why are you coming here, and who the fuck is Gary?"

"Gary's the guy from Ann Arbor I told you about. He and his wife Joan own the rare coin and jewelry store."

"Oh, is this about the gol—"

"Quiet!" Brewster hissed. "Not over the phone."

"What the hell is wrong with you?"

"This is serious," he said. "We'll be there as quickly as possible."

"You're sounding weird."

"It's about to get weirder."

CHAPTER EIGHT

Detroit, Michigan - 1935
'Don't Blame Me'

WITHIN HOURS OF FINDING THE BODY OF JOHN DOUGLAS IN THE alley behind the Starlight Lounge, agents from the FBI picked David Gonyea up at his house. Escorted to the bureau's offices on Michigan Avenue, he said little during the ride. David looked pale, sweat beading on his brow. Inside the federal building, they guided him to a thick metal door with chicken wire sandwiched between two small square pieces of glass. It opened to a drab green room that was designed to be uncomfortable. A single heavy metal table sat in the middle with four chairs surrounding it, two on either side.

Mintern would employ a new interrogation technique that the bureau had recently developed. Instead of the prior intimidation method, which often led to shouting matches between adversaries, the new tactic built rapport with suspects, keeping them more comfortable. Open-ended questions, empathy, and compassion had proved successful in previous interrogations. This rehearsed, practiced approach often led to a quicker confession or another investigative avenue.

Entering the cinder-block room with a fellow agent, the door closed behind them with a solid clunk. Mintern approached the gray metal table, nodding at his suspect. They sat facing each other. He stared purposefully at David for an extended period, watching him shift in his seat, uneasy, picking at his fingernails. The other agent remained by the door and observed.

Scooting his chair closer to the table, relaxing his shoulders, Dale leaned forward and placed a notepad and pencil on the metal table. The agent at the door glanced toward a one-way mirror, where a few more colleagues observed the interview. Dale leaned back in the uncomfortable metal chair, acting at ease and inhaling a deep breath. He paused, looked David Gonyea directly into his dark brown eyes, and began his technique.

"David, we have evidence that places you at the scene of a murder. Is there anything you'd like to tell us?"

David threw up his hands. "What the hell are you talking about?"

"We would like to get your side of the story, David. An FBI agent was murdered last night. What can you tell us about what happened?"

David's posture stiffened. "I had nothing to do with any murder. This is insane."

Exhaling a breath of confidence, Dale asked David if Sam Durocher had accompanied him to the hockey game last night. David acknowledged he was at the game and said that many people, upstanding people, people of importance, could attest to his and Sam's attendance. Dale continued the questioning, trying to find a crack in his story.

"What time did you leave Olympia Stadium?" Dale pressed him.

"10:30 p.m., I guess."

"After the game, where did you go?"

"I drove straight home and went to bed," David

squirmed. "I'd been with my wife, Eve, all night until you pulled me away from my breakfast this morning."

Dale leaned forward, placing his elbows on the metal table. "Did Sam Durocher ride with you to the hockey game?"

"Yes! Sam and I rode together, all right?"

"You just told me you drove directly home."

David wiped the sweat from his brow. "I did, right after I dropped Sam off."

"Where did you drop Sam off?"

"At his house."

"On the way to your house?"

"Yeah. So?"

"What time did you drop off Mr. Durocher at his house?"

David pushed his chair back from the table and placed his hands on his head. His face was twisted. Dale Mintern could see David's face becoming redder with each question, and he couldn't let him relax. Dale asked about the whereabouts of Sam Durocher and said the FBI had visited his house this morning. He was not at home.

"Did you stop anywhere between the stadium and Mr. Durocher's house?" Dale asked.

"No!" David barked.

"Would you like to think about your answer for a minute? Lying to a federal agent can have serious consequences."

David stood from the chair and nervously requested his attorney. His head twisted, glancing around the room, apparently searching for another means of egress. Dale rose to his feet and waved his hand forward toward the door. The second agent pushed the door, holding it open. Before David reached the threshold, Dale Mintern stepped in front of him, his palms held high, impeding any forward progress.

"I only have one more question for you, David. Was the murder planned, or did it just happen on the spur of the moment?"

David Gonyea brushed past the agent at the door and stomped out of the room. Nobody stopped him. His cursing carried through the barren hallway.

Dale Mintern slipped out the back door of the FBI building on Michigan Avenue and hustled around the corner. He hurried across the street to where he had parked his car. He watched David enter a taxi. It sped away, heading west. Dale followed.

EVE HAD been waiting for her husband in the living room. She hugged David tightly and looked up into his brown eyes. "Is everything all right?"

Running his fingers through her long blond hair and staring into her beautiful blue eyes, he lied, assuring her it was simply a business matter. "Nothing to be concerned about," he told her. "Everything will be fine."

They interlocked fingers. Eve planted a kiss on her husband's cheek. Knowing there would be no answers to her questions this morning, she offered a second breakfast since the first had been interrupted. David declined the breakfast, returned the kiss, and said he needed to visit a colleague. He wouldn't be gone long; he lied again and reminded Eve they would attend the grand opening of the Starlight Lounge that night. "A night on the town is what we need," he said, fabricating his best smile.

David left Eve with a tight hug and a kiss on the lips. He

continued down the porch steps and shuffled across the sidewalk, where he fired up the yellow Lincoln Roadster and sped away—paranoid.

The FBI interrogation worried David. Except he hadn't done anything, had he? Weaving his way through the busy streets of downtown Detroit, he pulled near the spot where the federal agent was killed the night before and parked. A heavy pulse pounded in his ears. A shiver raced up his spine. A quick pull from the stainless-steel flask he kept in the glove compartment helped. One more couldn't hurt.

A few large trucks were in the alley behind the Starlight Lounge. He surmised they were deliveries for tonight's grand opening and asked a few workers if they'd seen Sam Durocher. They had not. Hustling inside, he checked the office. It was empty. David marched down the cement stairs to the basement of the Starlight Lounge and turned left. Approaching the door on the far wall, he pulled a unique key from his inside jacket pocket. The door squeaked as he pushed it open. David exited the Starlight Lounge and entered the basement of the adjacent building. Letting the door close securely behind him, he reached for the light switch and called out for Sam. There was no response.

His heart pounded as he climbed up the cement staircase to the first floor of the adjacent building. The drills, lathes, and other woodworking tools had already been removed and returned to his Woodward Avenue shop. The room was empty and eerily quiet. Adjusting his eyes, David squinted through the dusty shadows and spotted Sam sitting at a desk near the far wall, gazing out a grungy window. He walked towards the desk.

"I watched you pull in," Sam said, startling David.

With a slight quiver, David asked, "What the hell did you do, Sam?"

Sam's head dropped. "What had to be done?"

"I just left a meeting with federal agents. They picked me up at my house. They're asking me about the murder."

Sam lifted his head, turning his body slightly left. "I was up early this morning and heard their cars approaching my house. I thou—"

David interrupted. "Why didn't they bring you in for questioning, Sam? They asked me where you were."

Sam pushed himself to his feet. "I woke Lilley up when I heard the cars approaching our house. Told her not to speak with anybody and slipped out the back door. I hid in the wooded area behind my house until they left."

David stepped back, palms raised. "Have you spoken to your wife since that happened?"

"I called her from a phone down the street. I told her I needed to be alone for a bit."

"Does she know you're here?"

"Of course not. Lilley is a sweet woman. I don't want my wife involved in any of this shit." Sam returned to the chair and gazed out the window.

"Well, they're looking for you, Sam. You understand that, right?"

"What did you tell them?"

"What did you do?" David barked.

Sam slapped his palms on his thighs. "I watched them from this window. I sat right here, at this desk. I heard what they were saying. They had evidence from the raid, including a leather bag full of money and valuables and a camera with photos of us—which would prove that I was here on the night the FBI agent was murdered. I can't have that, David. Nope. Can't have that. And, what about my friends? The people I invited to my place? My guests? I can't let them go to prison because I messed up. The bodyguards I hired failed, and I need to do whatever is necessary to free them."

"What are you going to do now?"

Sam shrugged. "I need to make sure everyone gets out of jail, or I might end up as fish bait. Since they have no evidence, everyone should be released quickly. Remember, these are powerful people, David, with deep connections."

David scowled. "Where is the evidence?"

Sam grinned. "What evidence?"

"The photos of me and you, meeting in the alley the night the FBI agent was murdered. *That's* what evidence. I did nothing. I had no part in whatever happened, yet you have a camera with photos of us meeting the same night the cop was shot in the alley. If those photos end up in the hands of the police, it won't look good for me—or you. Just give me the camera, and we'll never speak again. I'll take care of it. We'll never talk to each other again, ever."

Sam glanced down, pausing with a long exhale. Near the left side of the desk, a dark brown leather briefcase sat in the dappled shadows on the floor.

David followed Sam's eyes. "Is the camera in there?"

"Everything is in there."

"I want the camera."

Sam stood from his chair quickly. David's body stiffened. Sam told David he didn't trust him. "There's no way I'm giving you the camera," he said and told David Gonyea to leave the premises immediately, threatening him with unthinkable alternatives.

David's eyes rounded. "You can't do this to me!"

"Watch me, asshole." Sam moved forward. David stepped back. "Get the hell out of here and make damn sure nobody sees you leave, understood?"

Sam's face took on a deeper shade of red. David noticed the veins in Sam's forehead growing larger and hoped a stroke was imminent. "I told them I dropped you off at your house after the hockey game, Sam. You better stick to that story because I'm not going to prison for what *you* did."

"Get out of my face! I have a big night tonight. For Christ's sake, it's my grand opening, and don't worry, I'll give those assholes at the FBI a call. Yes, I'll meet with them. And as long as our stories match, and there is no evidence, there's not a goddamn thing they can do to us."

David contemplated overpowering him and grabbing the leather bag. On the desk within Sam's reach, a revolver overruled the impulse. He reversed his advance and hustled down the basement stairs, through the secret basement door, and up the stairs to the first floor of the Starlight Lounge.

Returning to his car in the alley, David Gonyea glanced in every direction, looking for a tail. He drove away, west, towards St. Albion Street.

CHAPTER NINE

Present Day - Monday, November 1

TWO-CYCLE EXHAUST MAY HAVE LONG-LASTING EFFECTS. I MADE a mental note to Google it later for confirmation. I felt foggy. Perhaps a drink would clear my stupor. I reached into the bottom drawer of my desk and stared at the bottle. The seal was still intact. My cell phone vibrated in my shirt pocket, startling me and nearly causing me to drop the expensive Irish blend. Carefully sliding the liquid commodity into the bottom drawer, I answered my phone.

"Hey, Kath."

"Just checking in. Did you speak with Paulie?"

"Yeah, he quit," I blurted.

"He quit?"

"Yep. For two months."

"Are you drinking already?"

How the hell does she know these things?

"Paulie is taking a two-month leave of absence, and Brewster is on his way here with some guy named Gary," I whined.

"Who's Gary?"

"The guy Brewster met with this morning about the gold coin. Apparently, he and his wife own a coin shop, a jewelry place, or something like that in Ann Arbor."

"Gary and Joan King?" she asked.

"What?"

"Gary and Joan King. You've met them many times at social events."

"When?"

"It doesn't matter. What's the scoop on the coin?"

"That's the weird part." I scratched the stubble on my chin and searched my memory bank for someone named Gary or Joan King. Then I made a mental note to Google the side effects of concussions and how long they lasted.

"Brewster and Gary are on their way to meet with me. Brewster sounded stressed." I said.

"When are they supposed to meet you?"

"They should be here in about thirty minutes. Why?"

"Mind if I join you?"

"That would be great. I could use some tangible sanity."

"Okay, then. I'll be there in about twenty minutes. I'll bring you a sandwich."

"How about a drink?"

"Sure. Pepsi Zero good?"

Click.

I tossed my phone onto the desk, leaned back in my chair, and stared at a small dark stain on the ceiling. It seemed to grow larger. I made a mental note to research roofers. *Wait?* What was the other mental note I just erased? Or were there two? Hmmm. I made a mental note to Google the side effects of concussions and how long they lasted.

After a much-needed break, albeit short, I felt somewhat human — almost approachable. With my attitude recovered, I checked my cell phone for text messages and weather updates. Then, I answered a call from a prospective vendor. I liked his pitch and scheduled to meet with him next week. Someone else called about my car warranty — assholes.

Paulie opened my office door and then knocked. "Boss, there's a call for you on line one." He waddled away.

I grabbed the phone from its cradle. "This is Rick."

"Hi, Rick, my name is Sarah Owens. I'm a reporter with the *DunvilleDispa—*"

"What do you want?" I reached for the Advil.

"I have some questions about your discovery at the Social Club. I wondered if you'd mind me stopping by to meet with you?"

"No."

"Great," she said. "What might be a good time to meet?"

"No, I meant no, you can't stop by. I have a business to run and don't have time for this nonsense."

"Can we chat on the phone, then?"

"We are chatting on the phone."

"You're funny. Can you tell me about the gold you found at the Social Club?"

"Where are you getting your information?" I demanded.

"I have a witness that can corroborate what happened on Saturday afternoon."

"Was the witness at the bar?"

"Yes, he was."

"Was this witness drinking?"

"Well," she stammered. "I don't see how that is relevant."

"Really? Not relevant?" I fumed. "You're following up on a story you heard from a drunk? Do you think that's responsible reporting?"

She continued with her interrogation. "Are you denying there was a gold coin found at the Social Club on Saturday?"

"Shouldn't you focus on your award-winning 'best of' series?" I snapped back. "That's what your readers really want, isn't it?"

"Tell you what, Rick. Give me fifteen minutes of your

time this afternoon and let me see what I can do about featuring Cooper's Hardware as one of our 'best of' winners this year."

If I were in a different mood, a better mood, maybe a touch more agreeable, I might have been more receptive to her inquiry. Today wasn't that day, so I continued with my sarcasm.

"You mean I could receive the 'best hardware store' award this year?" I asked excitedly.

"That's right; I think I could make that happen."

"How would that work?" I baited her.

"What do you mean?"

"I mean, would it really matter if I won the 'best of' award or the 'worst of' award?" The sarcasm came quickly today.

"I'm confused," she admitted.

"Coopers Hardware is the *only* hardware store in town. Do your homework!"

"It would be great publicity for your store."

"Listen, I've got customers to take care of. I'm hanging up now."

"I'm going to get to the bottom of this, Rick."

"You're already at the bottom." I slammed the phone into the cradle.

I could have handled that better.

PAULIE SWUNG open my office door while knocking. He waved Kathy forward and closed the door behind him. *Quack, Quack.*

Kathy smiled as she approached my desk and placed the small Yeti cooler on the floor. She was dressed in perfectly fitting yoga pants and a snug-fitting top. Anything Kathy wore looked great. Her CSI Special Agent work attire was professional and sexy at a different level, but I enjoyed her day off clothing the best. She looked relaxed. And natural.

Walking behind the desk, she leaned over and gave me a big kiss on the cheek and a tight hug around the shoulders. I told her she looked hot and meant it. Always a straight shooter, she told me I looked like shit. I shrugged, tapping my fingers on the desk. Kathy held her palms wide and gave me a talk to me look.

I leaned back, letting out a long sigh. "Brewster sounded weird."

She leaned forward with her elbows on my desk and chin planted in her hands. "What kind of weird?"

I shrugged. "I don't know. Just weird."

"Well, that's helpful. Can you be more specific?"

"I've never heard Brewster sound nervous before."

Kathy leaned back, crossed her arms, and studied my face. "Do you think his behavior is connected with the discovery of the gold coin?"

"Probably. Why else would Brewster bring that Gary guy from Ann Arbor to meet me?"

"Maybe it's good news," she said. "Maybe the coin is so valuable they want to discuss our early retirements."

"That's a joke, right?"

"Maybe, maybe not. I'm just trying to help you sort things out."

"And this chick from the newspaper is hounding me," I added.

"Really, Rick. This *chick*?"

"Whatever. The reporter left a voice message on my cell

phone this morning and then called me at the store."

"What did she say?"

"She was rude."

"What did *you* say?"

"I hung up on her."

"Do you think you could have handled that differently?"

Kathy was right, of course. I'd been in a funk, and it certainly wasn't the reporter's fault. It was simply an amalgam of adverse outcomes. First, my truck was totaled, then the gold coin thing at the Social Club happened, and now Paulie was leaving on some wild ass adventure with a bunch of misfits.

Kathy paused and took in a breath. "Regarding Paulie, you can't control what he does. We'll know more about the thing at the Social Club when Brewster and Gary get here. Until then, there's nothing you can do, so eat your sandwich."

I wondered what else might go wrong.

CHAPTER TEN
Present Day - Monday, November 1

My stomach felt settled, and I thanked Kathy for bringing me lunch. My attitude had recovered, or so it felt. We shared small talk about family and chatted about our upcoming Caribbean vacation over the Christmas Holiday. A loud knock on my door ended my therapy session.

"It's unlocked," I said, clearing my throat.

Brewster stood in the doorway, flashing an above-average smile. He wore expensive-looking jeans, an open collar shirt, and a blue blazer. Waving his left arm forward, he motioned Gary to enter, and they ambled into my office.

"Morning, Rick—hey there, Kathy. I didn't expect to see you here. How are you?"

"I'm fine, Bob. Sounds like you've had an interesting morning?"

"That's an understatement." Brewster waved his arms in two directions. "Rick, this is Gary. He and his wife own a rare coin and jewelry store in Ann Arbor."

"Yeah, we've met before, many times." I shook Gary's hand. "How is Joan?"

Kathy rolled her eyes.

I winked back.

"Nice to see you again, Rick." Gary smiled. "Joan is doing great. Thanks for asking."

Gary King looked taller than I remembered—a few inches more than me. I checked his heels. They looked thick.

Gary was solid and built like an athlete. It wasn't his sculptured face or matching brown hair and eyes I remembered — it was his handshake. His hands were large, with crooked knuckles. I remembered someone telling me he was an amateur boxer in his teens.

Brewster pointed to the two chairs at the customer side of my desk. Then he walked to the corner of my office, and grabbed the third chair. Kathy sat down on the far left. Gary was in the middle chair. Brewster sat on the far right and placed his elbows on the desk, resting his chin on his folded hands. "Where do we start?" he asked.

"How about telling me why this meeting is so important?" I snarked.

Brewster smiled, scooted back in his chair, and rested his hands on his lap. His shit-eating grin confused me. "Why don't I let Gary explain?"

Gary's eyes flickered about. He leaned forward and cleared his throat. With an extended inhale, followed by a long, audible exhale, he slapped his meaty paws on my desk and beamed. "The gold coin you guys found is extremely valuable."

"So, we're rich," I said sarcastically.

"Not so quick," Brewster interrupted. "Please, give Gary a few minutes to explain."

Kathy gave me a look. I rolled my eyes and leaned back in my chair, which earned me another look. Damn. Today wasn't my day.

Gary witnessed the 'look exchange,' and with a sympathetic nod, he continued. "I'll be straight with you, Rick. I didn't believe the coin was authentic when I first saw it, and I couldn't confirm anything without further testing and research. Bob called my cell phone yesterday, Sunday morning, and asked if he could drop the coin off at my house. He wanted a quick appraisal. I drove to my store and spent most of the day researching and performing tests to confirm the coin's legitimacy. Last night, I called Bob to share my results. We discussed my findings at length when we met at my store early this morning. At our meeting, he told me who found the coin, where it was found, and how it was found. That's a great story, by the way."

Kathy asked. "So, what do we have?"

Gary beamed. "It's a 1933 double eagle coin."

She rotated the index finger of her right hand. "Which means what?"

Brewster interjected. "For everyone to understand this coin's value, let's give Gary a few minutes to provide background on it and the consequences of ownership."

I grimaced. "What consequences?"

Kathy gave me another look. I wondered what my daily limit was. I let out a soft grunt and settled back in my chair.

Gary went on, "The story of your double eagle coin began in 1904 when President Teddy Roosevelt commissioned one of the premier sculptures in America to design a new twenty-dollar gold piece. His name was Augustus Saint-Gaudens. His design of the twenty-dollar gold piece is considered one of the most extraordinary pieces of art on any American coin. In fact, the name Saint Gaudens has become the nickname for the legendary double eagle liberty coins.

"But *here's* the reason the coin is priceless. In 1933, President Franklin D. Roosevelt issued an executive order to end the depression-era bank crisis. He stopped the coinage of gold and made it illegal to own the metal. The proclamation prohibited the private ownership of gold. It declared that gold coins were no longer legal in the United States. People had to turn in those coins for other forms of currency. Nearly half a million double eagle coins were minted after he signed the executive order. Because the government minted them *after* the executive order, they were no longer considered legal tender. Two intentionally spared coins are on display in a museum in Washington, DC. With only one exception, no 1933 double eagle coins were ever legally released, although some were stolen from the government, possibly by the U.S. Mint cashier. Over the years, several of them were recovered, returned to the government, and melted. However, a few of them found their way into the hands of private collectors via a New Jersey jeweler named Isaac Swift. Let me close with this, and hold on tight. The sole legal 1933 double eagle coin, originally purchased by King Farouk of Egypt in 1944, is currently in private hands. Last year, that gold coin was auctioned to an unknown buyer. It sold for 18.8 million dollars."

My body stiffened. "Holy shit!"

"Yep," Gary agreed.

"I wonder how much jail time that poor Isaac Swift guy got?" I asked.

Gary shook his head and chuckled. "Ironically, Isaac Swift, the jeweler who admitted to selling some coins, said he could not recall how he got them. The Justice Department tried prosecuting him, but the statute of limitations passed."

Kathy leaned in. "If this jeweler didn't get prosecuted because of the statute of limitations, wouldn't we be exempt?"

He shook his head. "The law states that 'since the coins were never issued,' they remain the property of the United States government. These coins cannot, even today, be legally owned by the public."

"But it's perfectly legal to own *other* gold coins today, right?"

Gary affirmed with a solid nod. "Correct. Since 1974, in fact, but not the coin you found. They're still illegal to own. Any double eagle coins recovered by the feds before 1974 were required to be melted. That's really unfortunate. A few coins recovered after that date were spared from the melting pot and returned to the government."

Kathy leaned back and tucked a thick strand of hair behind her ear. "So, what's the upside and downside to owning this coin?"

"The upside is that we have one of the world's rarest coins in our possession. The downside is that it's illegal to be in our possession."

Bob had already heard Gary's story that morning, so he sat silently, listening and observing our reactions. I asked Gary what our next step was and if the coin was in a secure location. He guaranteed its safety and said it was in an impenetrable safe at his store in Ann Arbor.

I was curious. "Does Joan know about the coin, Gary?"

"Hell, no." Gary chortled. "Shit, she'd probably melt it down for jewelry."

I laughed. "I don't remember you being this funny, Gary."

Kathy rolled her eyes.

I gave her another wink with a slight grin.

Brewster leaned in. "All right, now you see why I wanted

to meet with everyone in private this morning. Sorry about being short with you earlier, Rick. I didn't want to have this conversation over the phone." He turned to Kathy. "What are your thoughts?"

She leaned back and set her folded hands in her lap. "Good question. As I see things, Bob, we have two options. Our smartest is to contact the feds, let them know what we found, and turn over the coin. Or," she paused. "We could pursue our own investigation and find out the real story behind this mysterious coin." Her head swiveled around the room, making eye contact with us.

"So, we're keeping the coin?" I asked.

"No! Absolutely not! We could get ourselves in big trouble. I'm not willing to downsize my lifestyle to a ten-by-ten cell for the next twenty years."

Nervous chuckles filled the room. I didn't know if keeping the coin, even for an investigation, was the smartest thing to do, but what the hell? It could be interesting. Then again, I wasn't known for making the best decisions, so I raised my hand. "I believe it would be exciting to pursue an investigation. I really want to know the story of how this treasure ended up in a bar in Dunville. That's *my* vote. But if we decide to do this, we have a huge obstacle to overcome."

"What's on your mind?" Brewster asked.

"The press, man, the gossip. Everyone knows we found the coin. How do we investigate it while *we're* being investigated for not revealing that we even found it?"

Brewster grinned. "Ah, my friend, everyone knows we found *a* coin. Not *the* coin." Then he continued, "Gary, do you have any gold coins at your business we can borrow?"

Gary's head cocked. "What are you thinking?"

"I need something valuable enough to satisfy the town gossip but not expensive enough to invite the IRS to stick their noses up my ass."

Kathy nodded. "Brilliant. How much were you thinking, Bob?"

He shrugged. "I don't know. Hopefully, less than five grand. You're the investigator, Kathy. What's our next step?"

"Gary, how quickly can we get a replacement coin?" Kathy asked.

"I'll find something in my inventory after Brewster drives me back to Ann Arbor."

Kathy turned to me. "Rick, you need to call that newspaper reporter and apologize to her. Get together with her as soon as possible."

"Really?"

"Yes. Really. Bob, what time does the Social Club close?"

"The restaurant closes at ten, but the bar doesn't close until 1:00 a.m. My staff will be there until at least two, cleaning up."

"Let's plan on meeting at your club around 3:00 a.m. I want to find out if there were any clues left behind. There could be additional evidence under the bar. I'll grab a couple of colleagues to assist with our investigation."

Brewster objected. "I'm not sure that's the best idea, Kathy. The more outsiders we bring into this thing, the higher the chance of being exposed."

Heads nodded, the office emptied, and I realized what must be done. I had to do my part in our crazy scheme and call the newspaper chick.

"Make amends," Kathy told me. "Get her to buy into our plan."

I sucked at apologizing.

CHAPTER ELEVEN

Present Day - Monday, November 1

I PULLED THE VIBRATING PHONE FROM MY SHIRT POCKET. BREWSTER had sent a few images of the gold coin Gary King had loaned him. I expanded the photos with my index finger and thumb for greater detail. A Native American wearing a large headpiece was proudly displayed on the front of the coin. On the back was an eagle—or an angry chicken, I couldn't be sure. Either way, I had already put off calling the newspaper reporter for over an hour, so I scrolled through my recent phone calls and found her number. When Sarah Owens answered, I sucked in a deep breath and swallowed my pride.

"What can I do for you, Rick?"

"I was thinking about that 'best of' award we spoke about."

"Really?"

"Yep."

"You were a little short with me earlier."

"I hadn't had lunch yet."

"Is that an apology?"

"I was hungry."

"Okay, listen," she chuckled. "Your hardware store has a good reputation, but I'll still need to interview you. I have some questions that need answers."

I thought the 'best hardware of the year award' would be pretty cool, and I also knew I was in an excellent position to receive it. After all, Sarah had questions about the gold coin, and I had answers—so, there's that. I told her I would be at the store until 6 p.m. She said she was on her way.

I ended my phone conversation with the reporter and called Kathy, letting her know everything was in place. She asked about the coin, and I gave her a description. Told her it was a little north of Brewster's budget but should work just fine for what we needed. She thanked me for sucking it up and taking one for the team.

I called Brewster. We discussed our strategy with the reporter. In the end, he suggested bringing the reporter to his Social Club.

"We can show her the coin, satisfy her curiosity, and invite her to stay for lunch," he said. "Call me when you're on the way."

I liked the plan. Besides, I was hungry.

Paulie opened my office door without knocking. "Hey, boss."

"What's up, Paulie?"

"There's some chick here from the *Dunville Dispatch*. Said she has a meeting with you?"

Jeeze, that was quick.

"Really, Paulie, some *chick*?" I said with a shoulder scrunch.

"Sorry, boss. She's really good-looking."

"Hold her off for five minutes. Tell her I'm on the phone with a customer."

Quack, Quack.

I spent a few minutes developing my strategy for dealing with the reporter. Truth is, I had no idea how our meeting would go. I had no plan. Zip. Zero. Nada. Suck it up and see what happens is not exactly a winning strategy, but I had no experience with reporters. They made me nervous. A slip of the tongue or an offensive comment might get me unwanted ink in tomorrow's newspaper. I had every right to be worried. Unfiltered rhetoric left my mouth as often as carbon dioxide.

The door swung open. Paulie waved his right hand towards the petite brunette. "Hey, boss, this is Sarah Owens." He had a big smile on his face. His chest puffed out a bit.

I exhaled a deep breath and stood, waving her forward. "Come in. Please, take a seat."

Sarah twirled a strand of hair between her thumb and index finger. She smiled and sat across my desk. "It's a pleasure to meet you, Rick. I've heard good things about your business."

"Thanks, I guess."

She had a cute laugh. "I appreciate you meeting with me."

"I had a choice?"

"That's funny. Where should we start?"

"It's your show."

"Well, we're here to talk about a couple of things. Should we start with the 'best of' nomination or begin with your interesting find at the Social Club on Saturday?"

"It's *not* a nomination," I clarified. "It's an award."

"Sounds good, Rick, but I can't guarantee the award. I can only interview you as a nominee."

"Then I can't guarantee any answers to your questions."

She told me a bit about the business of newspaper reporting. Said she enjoyed writing and cared deeply for our community and finished by bragging about how good she was at her job.

"With a little humility, you'd be perfect." I smiled.

Sarah and I weren't 'hitting it off,' per se, but our conversation took on a more relaxed feel.

"Funny again," she said. "Your hardware store is the perfect candidate for this year's 'best of' award, so let's clear the slate and get that out of the way."

"So, I'm in?"

"Yes."

"Can I get that in writing?"

"You have my word." Her right hand was raised high as though a judge had just sworn her in for testimony.

"Fine." I settled back in my chair. "What other questions do you have for me?"

She pulled out her phone, and I believe I saw her push the record button. "Let's talk about your discovery at the Social Club. What can you tell me about what you found?"

For the next fifteen minutes, Sarah asked a lot of questions. They were good questions, short and to the point, and easy to answer. I was completely candid, with one obvious exception. It was a good interview, and she did her best to make me feel comfortable, which made me uncomfortable. I hoped I hadn't said anything inappropriate or stupid.

She pounded the keypad on her iPhone and then looked up and asked the closing question. "May I see the coin you guys found?"

"Bob Brewster has it. It's at his club."

"Can we go there? I'd like to see it."

I had to agree with Paulie. She *was* cute. She reminded me of my wife, Kathy. Sarah had long brown hair, brown eyes, a petite, athletic figure, and an agreeable sense of humor. She continued pounding her iPhone with her thumbs. I turned up the speaker volume on my phone and dialed Brewster. After a few rings, I recognized Ward's voice. Based on the background noise, the bar must have been crowded. I told Ward the Dunville newspaper reporter was with me, and she wanted to meet with Brewster. He asked if the meeting was about the 'best of' award for the Social Club. I told him maybe, just to keep the conversation short.

"Hold on," he said. "This is exciting."

I glanced at Sarah. Her head still buried in her phone, machine gun thumbs pounded the screen.

When Brewster answered, I told him we would be at the club in about fifteen minutes. Sarah looked up from her electronic tether. I provided an enthusiastic thumb up. She smiled.

SARAH INSISTED on riding together and jumped into the passenger seat of my loaner F-150. Fifteen minutes later, we entered the restaurant, continued through the vestibule, turned right, avoided the main restaurant, and continued through the stone archway and into the bar.

"Hey, Rick," Ward greeted us with a loopy grin. His hair was perfect. I guessed he had primped for the reporter. I introduced them, and they shook hands.

Brewster walked from behind the bar with an extended reach. He exchanged pleasantries with Sarah and then turned to Ward.

"We'll be in my office. Can you hold all calls and visitors while we chat?"

Ward nodded. "Will do. The fire marshal might still be back there."

"What?" Brewster's head cocked.

"Said he was a state inspector. Flashed his badge and told me he needed a few minutes to look everything over. Said it was routine, and not to worry."

"When was this?"

"Fifteen minutes ago?"

"That's weird." Brewster scanned the bar.

I introduced Sarah to Marianne and a few locals. When the bantering ended, I hurried her along. Brewster's office was on the right side of the hallway, across from the maintenance closet. He held the door open, invited us inside, and pulled a chair away from the desk for Sarah.

"Please, be seated," he smiled. "Would you like something to drink?" She declined. I followed her lead. "It's a pleasure to meet you. I enjoy your articles in the *Dispatch*."

"Thanks, Mr. Brewster. I appreciate that. You have a beautiful place here. I had lunch here yesterday. It was really crowded."

Brewster smiled. "I understand you were interested in our discovery on Saturday?"

She nodded. Sarah asked the same questions she had asked me, in the same order as far as I could remember. While they chatted, I left text messages for Kathy and Scruggs, letting them know where I was and who was with me. I shoved my phone into the breast pocket of my flannel shirt and heard Sarah ask Brewster if she could see the coin.

He walked to a door near the corner of his office, a few short steps behind his desk. The door hinged outward. When he opened the door, it reminded me of a large galley-style walk-in closet. Shelves on the left side of the room were full of boxes, which I guessed were office supplies. A hangar bar with a few pairs of pants, shirts, and jackets was on the right. Brewster's golf bag sat in the far corner. In the middle of the galley, hanging on the back wall, was a beautiful black and white artist's rendering of the Social Club. Brewster grabbed the left side of the frame and tugged it lightly. It hinged open, revealing a safe. He punched in a series of numbers, and with his left hand, he grabbed a small pouch.

Returning to the desk, he offered the cotton pouch to Sarah. She slid her chair closer to the desk. Gently pulling the drawstrings, the pouch opened, and the coin fell into her small, manicured hand. We watched as she examined it and balanced it in her hands as if on a scale.

"May I take a few photos?" she asked.

Brewster nodded.

"May I also take a few pictures of you and Rick with the coin?"

When she had finished, ten minutes later, Brewster placed the coin into the pouch and returned it to the safe. He offered us lunch. Sarah declined, and I followed her lead — again, reluctantly. We waved to Ward and Marianne on the way out of the kitchen. The locals studied the reporter as we passed the row of stools at the mahogany bar.

I fired up the white F-150 and drove back to my hardware store. Sarah spent most of the fifteen-minute ride pumping her fingers on her phone. She thanked me in the parking lot for the meeting and strolled to her late-model Jeep Grand Cherokee. I made one more call. Karl Gustafson said he was available to meet.

I headed for the Dunville Ford dealership.

CHAPTER TWELVE

Detroit, Michigan - 1935
'Prove It'

SAM DUROCHER KILLED THE ENGINE OF HIS FORD DELUXE Touring Sedan in the parking lot of a church on Griswold Street. He ignored the "no parking" signs that were prominently posted. Societal rules didn't apply to people like him. People like him made the rules. It was a beautiful Saturday afternoon, and the sidewalks of downtown Detroit were congested. The "little people" were shopping. A four-story retail building on the corner of Michigan and Griswold overflowed with consumers. Bright, colorful awnings extended over the sidewalks, keeping the sun out of the patrons' eyes and pigeon shit off their cheap hats.

Detroit Police officers monitored the chaotic intersections, blowing their whistles, shouting, and waving their arms randomly, or so it appeared. It was textbook-managed chaos. The traffic cops supervised the havoc between automobiles, streetcars, horse-drawn carts, and pedestrians. In 1935, three-quarters of auto accident fatalities were pedestrians.

Sam Durocher pulled down on the brim of his fedora to shade his eyes and cover his face. He was a celebrity to some, to others, a scoundrel. Some men recognized Sam and gave him a respectful nod. A few women smiled flirtatiously as he passed. He held his head low as he walked, always cognizant of his surroundings. His eyes darted back and forth as he reached his destination on Michigan Avenue. The nondescript building contrasted with the beauty of the surrounding architecture. Built at the turn of the century, the famous Detroit architect didn't intend his three-story Beaux arts-style industrial building to look intimidating. It was not designed that way. The transformation was intentional. Upper-level windows on the front of the building were tinted dark. Previously, the second and third floors offered office space for accountants, lawyers, and other entrepreneurs. A failed clothing retailer left the first floor unoccupied. The large glass windows that once invited consumers to view the handmade, expensive dry goods had been replaced with brick. The door was wood and windowless. A brass McCloskey Building sign on the front of the building, honoring a past mayor, had been replaced with a smaller one. It didn't need to be large. There were only three letters: FBI. In 1935, renovations like this were being expedited in major cities across the country.

Entering the FBI building, Sam sauntered deliberately across the marble floor. The room was sparsely appointed. An almost well-dressed woman with dark, frizzy hair, deep-set eyes, and thick glasses pointed to the two chairs against the far wall. Her appearance confused him. *What the hell?* He thought. *She might be a spy.*

The reception desk where Sally sat—that was the name on the desk plaque—was plain. Her desk was clean. No clutter. Behind Sally, hanging high on the wall, an intimidating photo of J. Edgar Hoover overlooked the lobby and appeared to be staring over Sally's broad shoulders. Sam imagined the FBI director's eyes following him as he paced the floor. He studied Sally's face. She seemed not to notice or care. Sally picked up the black headset and spoke into it, slowly, methodically, with an annoyingly high-pitched voice. Minutes later, descending the staircase to the main floor, an agent turned left, nodded at the cartoonish-looking receptionist, and extended his right hand to his guest. "Thank you for stopping by, Mr. Durocher."

Sam returned a reluctant handshake. "I understand you wanted to speak with me."

"Indeed. Please, follow me." He waved Sam forward, down the wide hallway towards a drab green room.

"I hope this won't take too long, Agent…?"

"Mintern. Agent Mintern. Please, call me Dale."

"Like I said, *Agent Mintern*," he snarked, their blue eyes meeting, "I have a hectic day ahead."

Dale nodded. "Tonight is the grand opening of your Starlight Lounge, correct?"

They reached the dark green metal door at the end of the hallway. Another agent opened the door and remained in the hallway. Sam Durocher entered first, followed by Dale Mintern. Dale waved him forward, pointing to the lone table in the room. The heavy door closed behind them.

"That's correct, Agent Mintern," Sam acknowledged while leaning back in the metal chair. "Tonight is my grand opening, and I have much to do yet, so please, let's make this quick."

Dale slid his chair forward, interlaced his fingers, placed his arms on the metal table, and began. "Please, call me Dale. This meeting is informal. I just have a few questions that need answers."

Sam nodded, remaining silent.

"Your new club is beautiful," Dale said.

Sam's eyes narrowed. "Excuse me?"

Dale gambled. "I was there last night. It's quite elegant."

Sam didn't bite. "So I've heard. I wish I were there, you know, to greet you."

"We may have just missed each other." Dale leaned back.

"I don't know where you're going with this sarcasm. From a conversation I had this morning with a business associate, I was told you needed to confirm my attendance at the hockey game last night."

"I've already confirmed your attendance at the game, Sam. I'd like to confirm your attendance on the second floor of the Starlight Lounge last night."

"You're grasping at straws, Agent. I can't be in two places. I enjoyed the hockey game, went home, and crawled into bed."

"I was at your house early this morning. I spoke with your wife, Lilley. You weren't home."

Sam said he was out of the house early for his morning walk. "Exercise, Dale. It keeps me in shape. You should try it. It's wonderful for relieving stress. The early walks around the neighborhood are relaxing. I use the time to plan my day. I'm sorry I missed you this morning. Had I been home, I would have invited you inside for coffee."

Dale took a different approach. "The secret staircase was clever. I'll give you credit, Sam," he winked.

"It's not secret—it's hidden. Hell, *you* found it, so it *can't* be secret. It was designed so my staff wouldn't interfere with my high-profile guests. The staircase is simply a means of getting from floor to floor without distracting my guests."

"Have you used this staircase? I mean, personally, have *you* been in there? It's a tight squeeze."

"I must have." Sam's lips pulled into a tight grin. "My fingerprints are probably all over the place—in that *secret* staircase."

Dale knew he wasn't going to break him. Not today, anyway. Sam Durocher's past arrest record and lack of convictions proved he was comfortable under pressure, confident under suspicion, and even arrogant when questioned by law enforcement. Dale told Sam he was a suspect in the murder, and of course, Sam had already made that assumption. However, Dale made that point several times during the short interview, hoping it would rattle his nerves, but he wasn't sure sociopaths were ever nervous. Sam seemed restless a few times but nervous—nope, just fidgety. Sam Durocher was a different breed of criminal. Dale and his team would have to work hard to find the evidence needed to lock him away for what he did. He needed to make the charges stick, sending Sam to prison for a long time.

Synthetic smiles and insincere handshakes ended their brief meeting. Dale swung the door of the interrogation room open, waving Sam forward. He escorted his suspect down the narrow, tiled hallway and watched him exit the front door.

Sam strutted like a peacock along the narrow sidewalk that paralleled Michigan Avenue. He never looked back.

Never look back.

CHAPTER THIRTEEN

Present Day - Tuesday, November 2

SHORTLY AFTER 2:30 A.M., I IDLED DOWN MY LONG, WINDING driveway. Gravel crunched beneath the tires. A lone deer and a couple rabbits scattered when the truck's headlights interrupted their nocturnal activities. Light drizzle lowered the already chilly early morning air. Kathy sat in the passenger seat. She turned the heated seats on and adjusted the vents to direct warm air at her feet. Turning left onto the blacktop road, I gave the gas pedal a heavy foot. The tires slipped on the wet surface. The V8 engine on my loaner vehicle had more power than I expected.

Traffic was non-existent in the early morning, and Dunville town square felt as peaceful as it appeared. The colorful "Holiday Festival" banner hanging over the brick-paved street swung in the light breeze. A few blocks later, we pulled behind the Social Club.

Brewster waved at us from under a small canopy covering the rear door. I flashed my lights to alert him of our arrival and slid into the parking space next to his white Lincoln Navigator. Kathy threw a small nylon bag over her shoulder and strolled toward Brewster. He held the door open, and she disappeared inside. I walked behind the truck, lowered the tailgate, grabbed the two hardshell cases and a soft-sided tool bag, then hustled to the shelter of the small arched canopy, shaking the light mist off my Gortex jacket. Brewster patted me on the shoulder, ushered me inside, and the door closed behind us. Walking through the kitchen, I hummed a favorite Traveling Wilburys song that was stuck in my head.

"Rick!" Kathy shouted.

My body stiffened. "Sorry. Was I humming again?"

"No, you were singing."

"Really? Who did I sound like?"

She shook her head. "Hell, I don't know. Bob Dylan, I guess."

I scratched my cheek. "The young Bob Dylan, or the old Bob Dylan?"

"What the hell is wrong with you? Get your head in the game."

Brewster laughed. I kept singing the rest of the tune while I placed my tool bag on the counter and the two hardshell cases on the floor behind the bar. Kathy ignored the snickers that echoed through the empty room. She placed the nylon shoulder bag next to my tool bag on the countertop. Brewster grabbed our jackets, shook any remaining raindrops, and tossed them on a table nearby. We spent the next few minutes reviewing the details of what happened on Saturday. Kathy's eyes scanned the area. She took notes as she listened to our story.

Brewster placed his hands on the bar top and leaned forward. "So, what's our first step?"

Kathy ran her eyes up and down the mahogany bar. "Is there any access to that space under the bar where the coin was found?"

"That's the weird part," Brewster said. "Early Sunday morning, before I drove to Ann Arbor to meet with Gary King, I stopped by the club to investigate further. I took the drink glasses from the shelves and removed anything and everything from behind the bar that wasn't nailed down. I pulled and tugged on every piece of wood along the entire bar and found nothing unusual. No removable panels. No access."

Kathy's expression twisted as she reached across the counter for her gear. "Why would someone design a secret compartment in this bar without having access?"

The metal buckles of the hardshell cases snapped open, echoing through the room. Kathy opened the lid and revealed the content — a metal detector. Then she got down on her knees, on the customer side of the bar, with the wand in her right hand. Beginning at the far left side of the bar, near my favorite stool, she shuffled slowly to her right. Moving the device in a small, slow, elliptical pattern, she closed in on the area where the coin was discovered. The machine made a short, quiet beep. It soon became a long, annoying sound as she continued moving right. Marking the suspicious area with a piece of yellow tape, she continued shimmying along the bar. Fifteen minutes later, the task was complete.

Brewster stepped closer. "So, what do you think?"

Kathy rose to her feet. "There's something in there."

"Can you tell what it is?"

"Nope, it's just something metallic. This bar is handmade. No nails or screws were used in the construction. Whatever it is, it's definitely not an original part of the bar."

I watched her open the second hardshell case, the larger one, and remove another device. I lifted the hinged countertop for her, and she slipped behind the bar and knelt down. The endoscope from the large case was guided into the three-inch opening under the bar. A sizable wireless video monitor—which resembled an iPad—was positioned near the base of the cabinet. The LED light from the camera provided clear images on the large screen. Brewster and I stared at the monitor anxiously as she navigated the three-foot wand into the darkness.

Kathy focused on a small opening near the front section of the bar while we stared at the image on the monitor. "That square opening appears to be the same size and shape as that piece of wood you found, Rick. Wait a minute," Kathy said. "Hold on." She stood up quickly and looked up and down at the bar, deep in thought.

She asked me for a tape measure. I grabbed it from my tool bag, sliding it across the polished surface of the bar. Her eyes darted as she bent down, stood up, then bent down again. Her forehead scrunched with confusion. Kathy slid the measuring tape into the three-inch opening below the bar and recorded her findings. She then measured the area above the three-inch space where the drinking glasses would typically be and compared her notes.

"That's it!" She said, rising to her feet with a satisfied smile.

"What are you talking about?" I asked.

"It's a false panel. The underside of the bar is thirty-eight inches deep. The shelf above is only thirty-two inches deep. That's a six-inch difference. You'd never know by looking at it. It's so clever, it's brilliant!"

Brewster shrugged. "What good is a false compartment if you can't access it? Why wouldn't they have designed the access panel above the bar's base? It's useless where it's at."

"I don't have all the answers, Bob, but one thing is for sure. There is something in that hidden compartment that someone wanted to be kept secret."

I held my arms wide, surveying the bar. "What now?"

Kathy shrugged. "Well, now that we know the secret compartment wasn't an accident, we need to find out what's inside."

Back on her knees, she wasted no time guiding the camera into the three-inch opening below the bar and then up into the secret compartment. We stared at the screen as a yellowed piece of a newspaper came into focus. The wand had barely reached. The image on the monitor provided a crystal-clear look at past history: a portion of the *Detroit Free Press* sports section, dated Saturday, November 16, 1935. An article about the Detroit Tigers was partially legible. The crumpled condition of the paper made most everything else indiscernible.

Brewster recommended she use the claw grips at the end of the camera wand, but Kathy disagreed, not wanting to damage any evidence.

"So, what do we do?" Brewster asked.

Letting them know what I wanted to do, they nodded and stepped aside. Owning a hardware store qualified me as a professional handyman. I pulled the cordless drill from the tool bag and grabbed a drill bit. After drilling four corner holes, the portable jigsaw went into action. I carefully cut an opening into the bottom of the bar, large enough for Kathy to stick her arm into it.

Lying on her belly, she carefully slid her right hand into the cut-out and slowly reached for the opening in the underside of the bar. Neither of our large hands would have fit. Her body contorted as she wiggled herself into what appeared to be an uncomfortable position. A few moans, a few groans, her upper torso twisted unnaturally. It seemed her Yoga classes were paying dividends.

"There's something wrapped in this newspaper," she said.

I bent down and peered over her shoulder. "Is it another gold coin?"

Kathy clutched the yellowed antique newspaper and finessed it out of the six-inch opening. "It's much larger than a coin. It's heavy."

Rising to her feet, she opened the newspaper above the countertop and stared at the discovery. Her eyes rounded.

So did ours.

"Holy shit, guys. It's a gun!" She pointed it in a safe direction and set it aside. Gently unraveling the crumpled paper, another object fell. It landed softly on the bar top. It was a small pouch secured with a drawstring. When she opened it, our eyes focused on the spill. A dozen brilliant round diamonds scattered across the polished mahogany surface. Brewster picked up one diamond and held it high. The lighting above the bar glistened off the facets of the gem.

I handed Kathy a couple Ziplock baggies from the nylon tote. She placed the yellowed newspaper into one baggy, zipped it tight, and put it aside. The diamonds were set in another bag. The cylinder of the revolver was opened and examined.

"Two bullets are missing," she said.

"How many bullets are there?" I asked.

"It's a six-shot Colt revolver. There are two spent cartridges and four live rounds."

The .38 Special revolver was placed into a third Ziplock bag.

"Well, this was interesting." She removed her nitrile gloves, tossed them on the counter, stared at the three clear bags, then at Brewster and me.

I scratched at the stubble on my chin. "This is like something you'd read in fiction novels."

"Well, this isn't fiction," she confirmed.

Brewster pointed to the baggies. "Will you be able to get fingerprints from these things?"

Kathy shrugged. "It's doubtful. Prints on metal objects only last for a few years. I'll check the newspaper for fingerprints. After eighty years, though, I wouldn't get my hopes up. Thirty years is usually the limit to lift fingerprints from paper, and that's pushing it. As for the diamonds, I have zero forensic experience in that field."

"What about ballistics?" Brewster said.

"Ah, thinking like a cop again?"

He chuckled. "You know it."

"Finding this gun certainly broadens our investigation. I'll get Steve and Kenny Erikson to help with some research." She returned her equipment to the hardshell cases, secured the latches, and placed three Ziplock baggies into her nylon backpack.

"What about me?" I huffed. "I'm a cop too, you know."

"A reserve cop," Kathy chuckled, knocking my bravado down a notch—maybe two. I feigned hurt feelings, holding my fist over my heart.

"You're a volunteer," Brewster added with exaggerated laughter. "You get to work the traffic detail at the Holiday Festival."

"I've helped Owen Dean and Willie Carter on a few cases," I reminded them.

They both consoled me and admitted they were having fun with my ego. Honestly, I didn't mind the ribbing. It made me feel like I played a part, albeit a small one, in the law enforcement brotherhood.

It had been a long day, and it was possible the adrenaline dump from our discovery was taking its toll. Kathy said she needed more time to process her thoughts. She asked Brewster to get her as much information as he could on the history of the mahogany bar and who built it.

Brewster tapped his fingers on the polished surface of the bar and smiled. "I can't tell you who built it, but I can tell you where it came from. I purchased the bar and all the furnishings you see here from a club in Detroit that was demolished over ten years ago."

"Do you have receipts for everything?"

"I have the receipts for the furniture and many photos of the Starlight Lounge before it was demolished. I just need to find them. It's been a while."

"What about the diamonds, Kath?" I asked.

"I'll give Gary King a call about those. He should be able to get me an appraisal." Kathy clapped her hands together. "Let's pack things up and get out of here before we attract any suspicion. Keep the lid tight on this. Nobody can know we were here tonight or what we found."

Kathy threw the nylon tote bag over her shoulder. I placed my tools back into the soft bag and slid it off the counter. Then, I picked up two hardshell cases from the floor and followed Brewster to the back door. He set the alarm, and we exited the building. I gave Kathy a sideways glance and finished singing the Traveling Wilbury's song.

Brewster chuckled, and although Kathy shook her head,

I believed I detected a thin smile.

In the shadows at the far end of the parking lot, I spotted a dark SUV and couldn't remember if it was there when we arrived.

Huh.

CHAPTER FOURTEEN

Present Day - Tuesday, November 2

With only a few short hours of not-very-sound sleep, I found it difficult to leave the comforts of the soft cotton sheets. Kathy groaned and rolled to her side of the bed, obviously awake enough to call "dibs" on the shower. Before I could challenge her to a race, she bounced out of bed and scampered to the bathroom.

I sauntered down the hallway toward the kitchen and added an extra scoop of my favorite blend. Filling the water reservoir to the brim, I dropped the overflowing filter into the upper cavity and pressed "brew." Pulling the toaster from the lower cabinet, I set it on the counter and slid in a couple of bagels. Waiting for them to brown, I wandered to the living room and turned on the television for today's weather forecast. The young man with too much shit in his hair told his adoring fans that the overnight drizzle and clouds were moving east.

"We should expect a beautiful day today with temperatures in the mid-sixties," he said and then rambled about the perfect weather for a better-than-expected voter turnout.

It was Election Day, and Ben Winston, a close friend, held a substantial lead over his competitor. Ben had already served two terms as Dunville's mayor without controversy, which was not typical of a politician. I worried that such a significant lead might cause complacency with his supporters. His challenger was a recent transplant from a larger city. He was young and also used too much goop in his hair. I guessed it made him appear taller.

Whatever.

Steve Dumas was the challenger's name. His campaign slogan was 'growth and change.' Growth was already a problem in our expanding town. Change? Hell, nobody really wanted change. Country people welcomed measured growth. The vast majority of residents enjoyed the slower pace. The herd mentality of dumping too many big-city people into the country might benefit the tax base, but it was a negative asset to our rural culture. I couldn't prove it, but I believed it was Steve Dumas who recently authored the anonymous *Dunville Dispatch* editorial complaining about the smell of pig shit in his neighborhood.

I headed for the toaster and, on the way, grabbed a stick of butter from the refrigerator. Pulling a knife from the top drawer, the toaster dinged, and two bagels popped up with perfect timing. I poured myself a large cup of caffeine, buttered my bagel, and took a huge bite.

"The shower is all yours." Kathy's voice carried from the hallway. "I'm going to get dressed."

"Okay," I shouted. "There's a bagel on the table for you."

Grabbing a napkin, I shoveled another bite into my mouth. On my way to the bathroom, I passed the television. The Channel 6 News anchor told her adoring fans to stay tuned for a breaking story. "One you won't want to miss," she beamed. "A gold treasure was discovered at one of our local restaurants. We'll be right back."

I hollered for Kathy to join me. I didn't mean to startle her, but apparently, I did. She rushed into the living room, throwing her blouse over her head. It was actually pretty sexy. I pointed to the flat screen above the mantle and turned up the volume. A commercial for an automobile injury accident law firm concluded. The seasoned anchorwoman smiled into the camera with teeth as bright as the sun.

"Welcome back to Action 6 News Hour. We're going directly to our on-the-scene reporter, Jessica Logan. She's breaking a story about a gold coin discovery at one of Dunville's most popular restaurants this past Saturday. Jessica, what can you tell us?"

"That's right, Monica. We're still piecing together the details. Right now, we can tell our viewers that over a dozen witnesses have confirmed a rare gold coin was found during a lunchtime scuffle at the Social Club restaurant on Main Street. According to the witnesses, a bartender and at least one patron were involved in an altercation so violent that it caused significant damage to the bar. The rare gold coin found inside the damaged bar is extremely valuable."

"This is an incredible story, Jessica. Do we know what started the brawl? Was anyone injured?"

"I've spoken with the chief of police, Monica. He's as confused as we are. My sources are telling me it was alcohol-related. Our Action 6 News team is also following up on credible reports that it may have been a hate crime."

"Well, that's certainly concerning. Please be safe out there and keep us updated as this story unfolds. Stay tuned to Action 6 News tonight at five o'clock. We'll be speaking with Reverend Jesse Johnson about the latest epidemic of alcohol abuse and hate crimes. Back to you, Bill."

I tossed the remote onto the couch. "What the hell is wrong with these people?"

"Sex, money, and murder. That's what their viewers want. They gobble it up," Kathy said.

"Nothing in that story is true." I protested.

"Well, they got the *gold coin* part correct."

I nodded. That was the *only* part of the story the news team got right. There was *no* fight at the Social Club, and the bar *wasn't* damaged. I wondered if Sarah Owens, the newspaper reporter, spread the story. Kathy headed to the kitchen. I strolled down the hallway to the bathroom. After a hot shower and a clean wardrobe, I called Brewster. He didn't answer, but his text came through quickly.

I'm on the phone with the chief of police. I'll call you back.

I searched my caller ID, found the number I was looking for, and called the reporter.

"Is this Rick?"

"Yes! This is Rick."

"Whoa, whoa, whoa. Settle down. I just saw the Channel 6 News report on TV."

I growled at my phone. "I thought you were writing a legitimate story about finding the gold. You told me you were good at your job. What did you do? Sell your story to the highest bidd—"

"Hold on a minute," Sarah replied sharply. "I haven't told a single person about the gold. I didn't even tell anyone about our meeting at the Social Club."

I inhaled a deep breath. My face reddened. Kathy reached out for my phone before I could say something I might regret, which happened much too frequently. Slapping my phone into her hand, I left the room and headed out the door for fresh air. I heard her introduce herself to the newspaper reporter. The door slammed behind me.

FIVE MINUTES later, maybe ten — it could have been longer — I returned to the kitchen and topped off my insulated coffee mug. Kathy was seated at the kitchen table, sipping from another National Park souvenir cup. On the table in front of her were Sarah Owen's conversation notes.

I gave her a peck on her cheek. "I was a little short with the reporter."

"You think? Sarah wasn't responsible for sharing the information with Channel 6 News."

"How do you know?"

"Apparently, there was a guy at the Social Club on Saturday when you found the gold coin. Sarah said he reached out to her and wanted to sell his story. The *Dispatch* has a strict policy against paying for information, so she refused his offer."

"Who was the guy at the bar?"

"Stuart Applegate. Do you know him?"

"I don't recognize the name."

"She believed Stuart's story credible, so Sarah visited the Social Club, chatted up a few of the regulars, and got the details of what happened. She found out *you* were the one who actually discovered the coin. That's why she reached out to you directly. She wanted to confirm the details for her front-page story tomorrow."

Kathy told me Sarah didn't want to publish her story with the hearsay from someone who claimed to be at the bar when the coin was found. I wished Sarah would have shared that information with me yesterday when we met with Brewster. It might have saved me from embarrassing myself. Probably not. But who knows.

I apologized for the earlier outburst and topped off my coffee. "Should I fire up another pot?"

Kathy shook her head.

"Okay. I've got to get going, babe. Paulie is leaving in two days, and I still don't have the employees' work schedules figured out."

She handed me my phone and said Bob tried to call me when she was on the phone with Sarah. I made a mental note to call Brewster on my way to the hardware store and reminded Kathy about Paulie's going away party tomorrow.

"He's not quitting, Rick. He's taking a sabbatical. It's simply a few months off for a musical adventure."

"He says that now. After a couple months on the road, I'm not sure he'll be returning to a normal routine."

"I hope you're wrong. This adventure is not his best decision. I really don't like the misfits he's traveling with— Wait! Hey! Paulie and the Misfits!" Kathy said.

"What?"

"That should be the name of their band—Paulie and the Misfits."

"The hell is wrong with you?"

"I thought that was good."

"All right, it was pretty clever."

"I'm glad you liked it," Kathy smiled.

I wrapped my arms around her waist and kissed her on the lips. "Are you going to check out that stuff we found this morning?"

"Stuff? You mean the evidence?"

I shrugged.

"Yes. I've got some work to do today on the gun and the newspaper. I'll call Gary King about the diamonds on my way into the office. Hopefully, he can meet with me soon."

"Tell Gary I said hello."

Kathy rolled her eyes.

CHAPTER FIFTEEN

Present Day - Tuesday, November 2

I TURNED LEFT ONTO THE BLACKTOP COUNTY ROAD AT THE END OF my driveway and gave an insincere wave to an early morning jogger. His face was twisted with pain. The suffering was self-inflicted, and I held no sympathy for him. I hadn't set up the automatic voice calling feature on my loaner vehicle, so I thumbed through my contacts and pressed the recall button. Brewster's wife, Dina, answered and said Bob was busy.

"Give him a few minutes," she said and asked how Kathy and I were doing.

Dina and I chatted about life, health, family, vacations, and whatever else the Energizer bunny dentist had on her mind. She kept the conversation interesting while Brewster finished his morning routine. At least, that's what I assumed he was doing. Dina's energy level seemed high; I guessed she'd already been to the gym. Brewster told me his wife was a fitness freak. Said she worked out six days a week. The petite blond-haired, blue-eyed dentist also craved competition. Earlier this year, Dina earned a respectable finish at an Iron Man competition in Phoenix. I wondered how she found time to treat patients at her Plaque Attack Dental Clinic.

I had already reached the town square when I heard Brewster's voice.

"Sorry about that," he said. I heard Dina say goodbye in the background.

"Did you watch the Channel 6 News report this morning?" I asked.

"I did. I also received a call from Police Chief Adams. Told me the reporters hounded him for a comment."

"What did Chief Adams tell them?"

"Told them he had no comment. Said he would look into the story. That's why he called me. Asked me what really happened and wanted more detail. I provided him with the truthful version of events, and he seemed satisfied—maybe even a little pissed."

Brewster told me nobody from the Channel 6 News team contacted him. Shit, he owned the club where the gold was found, and not one reporter reached out to him for a comment?

"So they aired a bullshit story without contacting the restaurant owner where the gold coin was discovered?"

"Appears so, Rick. Don't worry. This will blow over in a few days. They'll be on to some other exaggerated story by the weekend."

I tapped my breaks and blasted my horn at a lanky kid who had stopped to check his phone in the middle of the road. He jumped, gave me a side glance, and shuffled away slowly.

"I called that reporter this morning and might have the answer to how those talking heads got wind of the story."

Brewster said, "What was that background noise?"

"Animal in the road."

"Huh. What did the reporter say?"

"She received a phone call from a guy on Saturday afternoon. Apparently, he was at the bar when I found the gold coin. He was looking to sell his story to her. His name was Stuart Applegate. Do you know him?"

"I do. You'd recognize Stuart, too. He's a lunch regular like you and Scruggs. A machinist, I believe. Works at a small tool and die shop at the edge of town, further up the road from your hardware store."

"Farther." I corrected him.

"What?"

"It's farther. Not further."

Brewster's annoyance level peaked. "The hell are you talking about?"

"Farther is the correct word you should have used. Farther is the word for travel, for distance. Further is used for, hmmm, let's say, furthering your education, which maybe you should consider."

"You're an asshole." Brewster chuckled.

I spread my arms wide. "Just saying."

Brewster said he would talk with Stuart if he showed up at the club for lunch. I changed the subject to confirm Paulie's going away party tomorrow night. He said the event was good-to-go but told me it would be in the main restaurant, not the bar. I heard him suck air through his teeth as he reminded me there had been so much publicity about the bar; it was jam-packed — day and night.

"That's just wrong!"

"I understand. Think positively, Rick. The larger restaurant will provide much more room for everyone who will show up to wish Paulie good luck on his adventures."

"Son of a bitch, Brewster. This is getting out of control."

"Let's go to Little Italy's for lunch. It'll be my treat, and you love their food. We can stare at that waitress's big tits. What was her name?"

"Bambi?"

"That's it. We can eat Italian food and stare at Bambi's tits."

"You're twisted in the head, Bob. This story better blow over quickly. I'll call Scruggs and have him meet us at Little Italy's at noon. I'll let him know you're buying his lunch, too."

PAULIE WAS already inside as I rolled into the hardware store parking lot. The interior lights were on, and I saw him through the large glass windows. I parked my truck, threw a backpack over my shoulder, and continued to the front entrance. A reflection on the large windows caught my attention. I saw a vehicle sitting at the far end of the parking lot. There was movement inside.

Just past the check-out registers, inside the store, was an area of glass with a large window decal. It advertised a national brand of paint. The perforated color graphic made it nearly impossible to see into the store. Looking out of the store was easy—like a one-way mirror. I watched two individuals sitting in the vehicle and wondered what they were doing. Drugs? I wouldn't think a drug deal would go down in my parking lot at 8:30 in the morning. What would I know? I didn't do drugs. Were they casing my store to rob us? That would be stupid. What moron would rob a store at the start of the day?

Shaking off the paranoia, I strolled to the employee break room. I needed caffeine. After a few cups of coffee and a longer-than-normal morning huddle, I sent my team on their way to take care of customers.

Paulie paced back-n-forth, dulling the polished linoleum flooring.

"Is everything okay, Paulie?"

"I don't know where he put the report, boss."

I shot him a quizzical glare. "What are you talking about?"

"The fire marshal was here, boss. I can't find where he left his inspection report. Maybe he'll mail it to you."

I lifted my hands, palms out, and faced him. "Stop moving and talk to me, Paulie. You're making me dizzy. What the hell are you talking about?"

His face tensed. "He knocked on the front door a half hour ago and flashed a badge. I let him in, and he walked around the store with a clipboard."

"Did he ask questions?"

"He wondered if you were around. Told him you'd be arriving around eight-thirty."

"How long was he here?"

"Don't know, boss. I was in the break room making coffee, and the next thing I know, you pull up. I never saw him leave."

I wondered if it was the same inspector that had visited Brewster's Social Club. My intuition told me it was. I didn't believe in coincidences. The morning hours passed quickly as I bounced back and forth between my office and the sales floor. The exit polls for the election were being reported every thirty minutes over the store speakers.

It was late morning when Kathy called. "The National Integrated Ballistic Information Network confirmed the gun we discovered inside the Mahogany bar is connected to the murder of an FBI agent over eighty years ago, in 1935."

The mobster era of the 1930s had always fascinated me. "Are you talking about the gun we found at Brewster's place?"

"Yes. And listen up. Here's what I know from today's research," Kathy continued. "The Starlight Lounge in Detroit, the original location of Bob Brewster's mahogany bar, was owned by Sam Durocher. Appears Sam had deep criminal connections. Before opening his nightclub, he had been arrested a few times for bootlegging and other illegal activities but was never convicted. The night before the official grand opening of his Starlight Lounge, the FBI raided his building and busted a high-stakes illegal gambling operation on the second floor. After the raid, an FBI agent was found dead—murdered. The very next day, everyone who had been arrested in the illegal gambling raid was released from jail. All charges were dropped. Are you with me so far?"

My imagination whirled, and I wanted to hear more, so I instinctively said yes, and Kathy continued.

"Okay, so nobody was ever arrested for the murder of federal agent John Douglas, that was his name, and the murder weapon was never found—until now—because it's in *my* possession. I've researched and found information from newspaper articles about the 1935 raid, but it's all third-person reporting. Agent Douglas had a partner. His name was Dale Mintern. He surely would have filed a report with the bureau. I'd like to get my hands on his report and thought I should reach out to your friend in Georgia."

"You want to contact Ron Grimwade?" I asked.

Kathy told me she needed to turn the gun, the murder weapon, over to the FBI and wanted to use my childhood friend, Ron Grimwade, as her contact. She called him *my* friend, but Kathy knew him well. She was also friends with Ron and his wife, Laura. We had spent many trips to the

Grimwade's mountain house in North Carolina for motorcycle riding. The South had great winding, twisting roads. She probably asked for my permission out of respect for the longstanding relationship between Ron and me and because she knew Ron wasn't a glory hog. That was important. He would do his best to process the gun internally without leaking it to the national media.

"Are you going to tell him about everything we found?" I asked.

"Probably not. The gold coin and diamonds don't fall under the FBI's purview, so there's no need to share this information with Ron, although it wouldn't matter if I did. I'll turn those items over to someone in the Treasury Department after I've had a little time to investigate it personally. Right now, my official caseload is slow, so I have some free time to pursue this mystery. I'm intrigued, actually."

"Are Steve and Kenny aware of what you just shared with me?"

"They are. I called them first. They're scrambling to reconcile my ballistics report with their preliminary research."

"Should I call Brewster?"

"No. I've already reached out to Bob and left him a voice message. I'll explain the details to him when he returns my call."

"Okay, Kath. I'll text Ron and let him know you'll be calling. I'm processing invoices at the store today and am up to my elbows in paperwork."

"Did you get your schedules worked out with your team?"

"I did," I sighed. "Fortunately, everyone was excited

about the additional overtime while Paulie was away. I didn't tell my team yet, but I will give all of them a healthy Christmas bonus. They've earned it. I'll also promote Jim Anderson as the temporary store manager."

"It's the right thing to do," she said.

Click.

I walked to my office, sat at my desk, and stared at the mountain of paperwork. I tackled half the pile before calling Scruggs to tell him we would meet at the Italian restaurant for lunch today. Hearing the news that Brewster was paying cheered him up a bit. He was never happy about breaking up our Social Club lunch routine.

With less than a half-hour before leaving for Little Italy's, I was making good progress on the stack of invoices on my desk. Paulie entered and then knocked on the door.

"Hey, boss."

"Sup, Paulie?"

"There's a guy out here asking for something we don't carry."

I threw my hands up. "So, how can I help?"

"He wants to know if you can special order it for him."

I sighed. "Special order *what*, Paulie?"

"He'd like to purchase a metal detector."

"What?"

"Yep. Maybe he's searching for Indian arrowheads along the Raisin River, boss."

"Tell him to get it from Amazon."

"I thought we were all about customer service, boss?"

I gave him a hard stare and shooed him from my office. Then, I hustled to the parking lot, fired up the plain white F-150, and headed for Little Italy's.

CHAPTER SIXTEEN

Detroit, Michigan - 1935
'Never Apologize'

SAM DUROCHER FELT CONFIDENT AFTER MEETING WITH AGENT Mintern, maybe even cocky. Too cocky? Maybe. His hands trembled as he stood outside the three-story Beaux arts-style FBI headquarters on Michigan Avenue. Removing his fedora, he pulled a handkerchief from his vest pocket and wiped his brow. Self-doubt confused him. Sam was usually a clear thinker. Today felt different. Had he just pissed off the FBI? Probably. Which was worse, he wondered — a pissed-off federal agency with endless authority, or politicians and gangsters, who didn't give two shits about authority — or consequences? A conundrum for sure.

One block from the church parking lot on Griswold Street, where he had parked his car, Sam stopped in front of a popular department store. Hoards of shoppers and sightseers seemed to grow more significant by the minute. Early Christmas shopping, he presumed. Sam returned a nod from a gentleman who looked like he wanted to be a gangster. The guy was clueless. He tipped his hat to the young woman that flirted with him. He kept walking. Not today, lady. Today he had a mess to clean up.

Sam found a payphone secured to the brick facade of the nationally recognized department store. He removed a business card from his jacket pocket and deposited five cents. A sexy voice on the other end of the line asked him to 'hold please.' His call had been transferred. Sam Durocher and Anthony Bocelli, the prominent attorney from Chicago, shared a heated conversation. Most of the heat came from the lawyer. Sam was informed that the ten people arrested at his place of business had been released.

"Since the FBI agent was dead," the Chicago lawyer told him. "And there was no evidence." He chuckled. "The judge dismissed the case. Everyone has been released from jail."

Sam exhaled a relieved sigh. "That's great news, right?"

Anthony Bocelli shot back. "They're not happy, Sam."

"I understand, Tony. Just know that I'll make things right."

"Restitution for the tangible items is one thing, Sam. They expect this to happen quickly, but how can you make reparations for Isaac Swift? He's dead. Killed by FBI agents in your building, under your protection. What about his wife and two young children in New Jersey? You've got a lot of explaining to do, my friend."

Sam pleaded, "Listen, Tony, do me a favor. Please, this is very important. Contact everyone and have them meet me at St. Joseph's church in one hour. I'll make sure they are fairly compensated for their troubles. Before my grand opening tonight, I need to make things right."

"How is that gonna work, Sam? A federal agent was murdered. All the evidence, the money, the jewelry is missing."

"Not over the phone, Tony. Just have the guys meet me at the church. I may not have the missing evidence, but I can make things square."

Anthony sighed. "I'll make the calls. Don't fuck this up, my friend."

―

SAM'S ANXIETY distracted his situational awareness. Reaching for another nickel, he waved off a burly young man who insisted on using the payphone. Dismissing him nonchalantly didn't sit well with the big man's ego. A meaty paw grabbed Sam's right shoulder. Sam stepped backward quickly and released a powerful elbow. It stunned the beast, knocking him off balance, but not off guard. The brawny lad grinned, shook his large head, and wiped the blood from his nose with his forearm. With a loud growl and a bloody smile, he lunged forward. Sam sidestepped the counterattack and focused on the weakest part of his opponent's body. Goliath fell hard against the brick wall, barely missing the payphone he wanted to use. The gathering crowd of spectators cringed. Some covered their eyes. Others placed their hands over their ears. The sound of bones breaking could be disturbing to hear. A large man wailing and squirming on the ground was not a pleasant sight. He didn't know it yet, but his shattered knee was the least of his problems. Two beat cops patrolling the area recognized Sam Durocher. They stepped in quickly.

Crack!

More spectators covered their ears as the baton came down hard on the back of the brawny lad's head. The large dumb ass was dragged away, and the crowd handily dispersed.

Sam waved off the attention, dropped another nickel into the slot, and dialed a number he had committed to memory.

FATHER PATRICK Malloy agreed to host the meeting. "St. Joseph Church could benefit from such a generous donation. My parishioners thank you. I'll see you and your friends in an hour. God bless you, my son."

Having set the stage for his upcoming meeting, Sam returned to the soon-to-be-opened Starlight Lounge. He parked his Deluxe Touring Sedan in the alley behind the building. Entering the rear door, he watched as his team prepared for tonight's grand opening.

It was going to be an exceptional event.

Ignoring the hard-working, *simple* people, Sam proceeded down the basement stairs to the adjacent building through the adjoining door. Once there, he grabbed a dark brown leather briefcase from under his desk and retraced his footsteps.

Back inside the basement of the Starlight Lounge, Sam pulled three items out of the leather briefcase and set the bag on the floor. A recent edition of the *Detroit Free Press* lay on a nearby bench. Sam grabbed a newspaper section and used it to wrap the .38 Special revolver. He reached up to the low ceiling, pushed on a hidden panel, and slid it off to one side. Extending his hands through the opening, Sam placed the pistol inside the secret compartment he had designed in his custom mahogany bar and added a cotton pouch and a coin. The items would be safe until he could return them to the family of the poor bastard who made the fatal decision to pull his peashooter on trained FBI agents. Isaac Swift's family deserved that much, at least.

Placing the cover on the secret compartment of his mahogany bar, he slid the ceiling panel back into place and headed upstairs quickly. His friends would meet him soon. Father Malloy was at St. Joseph's church, handling the details Sam had requested — or paid for. Semantics. Matters needed to be resolved quickly, or his dreams of a prosperous future would be over. To hell with his dreams. His life was in jeopardy.

INSIDE THE vestibule of St. Joseph Catholic church, Father Malloy bowed his head and accepted the envelope. Pressing his hands together, the veteran priest mumbled a short prayer, signaled the sign of the cross, thanked Sam, and retreated to his private quarters.

Sam waited anxiously for his friends. He closed his eyes and recited a prayer of his own. A prayer he had learned from his mother. He'd never prayed before, not really, at least not earnestly. This time, Sam prayed and told God he meant it. He felt edgy as he paced the hardwood floor in the formal dining room. Sam hated waiting. He wasn't comfortable with idle time, but this was important, so — he waited. There was no alternative.

At the top of the hour, the door swung inward. Minutes apart, the guests staggered in. All ten of them. As instructed by Sam, Father Malloy had set twelve chairs around the large dining room table. Ten chairs for the visitors, one for Sam, and one for the missing person, Isaac Swift. In reverence for the recently departed jeweler from New Jersey, Sam had strategically leaned an empty chair against the table. He placed a crystal vase of white tulips — typically used to show worthiness, to seek forgiveness — in front of the vacant chair. It was a well-thought-out introduction to his pseudo apology. Greeting his guests individually, he shook a few hands and kissed a few cheeks.

Sam deliberately made eye contact with each person at the table. He motioned for his friends to be seated. After a brief semi-rehearsed speech, he asked for a minute of silence for their dear friend, the beloved Isaac Swift. Then, like a seasoned politician, he said, "Forgive me." Sam paused, bowed, took a noticeable breath, and began. "On the table is a leather bag. Please, take what is yours."

Dramatically, he emptied the contents on the table, slowly dragging the leather bag away, almost religiously, making damn sure not to smile. Once again, he bowed his head in submission. Cash, watches, jewelry, rings, and other personal items were among the large pile in the middle of the handcrafted Oak table. Gracefully and respectably, each participant reached across the table, shuffled through the large pile of valuables, and retrieved their belongings.

It was a surreal moment.

Reaching inside his tailored jacket, Sam addressed the table, "Also, gentlemen," he said reflectively. "I have ten envelopes in my hand. Please accept them as a gift from my security team."

Never apologize. Never admit defeat. Never show weakness.

"The men I hired to protect you will never work for me again. In fact, they may not work for anyone in the future."

Laughter and head nods filled the room. A few wine glasses clinked. Sam smiled. He was back in control, where he was comfortable.

Anthony 'Big Tuna' Batterelli, the Chicago gangster, sipped his expensive wine and was the first to speak. "What about Isaac Swift?" he said. "He might have been a bit of a weasel, but he deserves respect. I don't see any of *his* belongings on the table."

Sam nodded. "That's correct, Mr. Batterelli. I have Mr. Swift's possessions in a safe place. I will return them to his family and make sure they never have to worry about anything in the future. They will be taken care of. You have my word."

In a condescending tone, the mayor of San Clemente, California, spoke next. "How safe are Isaac Swift's possessions, Mr. Durocher? If the FBI searches your property, will they discover anything that might incriminate *us*?"

Sam ambled a few steps to his right and faced the disagreeable Mayor. He placed his hands together, as if in prayer, and addressed the politician. "That's an honest question, Mr. Mayor, and I appreciate your candor. I have separated Mr. Isaac Swift's possessions intentionally. They are in the safest place possible, where the FBI, or any other law enforcement agency, would *never* find them. In fact, Mr. Mayor, if I were to meet an early demise, no one would ever see these items again." Sam shared a tight smile and said, "Only a fool might stumble upon them."

His comment about death was intentional. Sam might escape the executioner if they wanted Isaac Swift's family to receive his inheritance.

The politicians and gangsters laughed out loud.

CHAPTER SEVENTEEN

Present Day - Tuesday, November 2

LITTLE ITALY'S PARKING LOT WAS NEARLY EMPTY. I WAS WELL ahead of the lunch crowd, which was good. Their daily specials targeted the senior citizen population, and there were plenty of pensioners and social security recipients in the area. Soon, the parking lot would overflow with handicapped license plates, rubber-tipped walkers, and emotional support animals. The unforgettable bouquet of medical ointments and perfume was something you wished *was* forgettable. Mind you, I had nothing against the seasoned citizen population. Heck, I hoped to be one someday. My concern centered on the restaurant's marketing strategy to attract seniors. The lunch specials were discounted by half from noon to three, which I supported. What I disagreed with was their buy-one-get-one-free offers on the house wines. Red or white, it didn't matter. Buy-one-get-one.

The bi-weekly police blotter in the *Dunville Dispatch* was filled with stories of post-lunch parking lot altercations at Little Italy's. Detailed accounts of fender benders, slip-n-fall injuries, and the occasional octogenarian assault charge read like a cheap gossip tabloid magazine at the grocery check-out.

I parked my truck far away from the entrance and the handicapped parking area. Those blue lines on the blacktop were prized spaces, and I didn't want to return a damaged loaner vehicle to Karl Gustafson. After crossing the parking lot, I opened the front door of the brightly illuminated vestibule and entered the restaurant through the second door. Once inside, I wondered if they'd lost power. I rubbed my eyes and blinked a few times to adjust my vision.

A young college-age beauty caught my attention and greeted me at the check-in desk. The name tag she wore resembled an Italian flag. My eyes worked overtime, adjusting to the darkness.

"Hi, Trina," I smiled.

She returned a much better smile. "Welcome. Table for one?"

"No, I'm a bit early. There will be two more joining me. Is Bambi working today?"

"Sorry, no. It's her day off."

"Damn."

"What?"

"Never mind. Can I get something in the back, please?" I turned and pointed to my favorite table.

Trina confirmed the table was available, wrote something on a laminated sheet, and put a colored erasable marker aside. Grabbing three menus, she guided me to the table.

"Randy will take care of you today," she said. "Can I get you anything to drink while you wait for your guests?"

I ordered a glass of house red wine. She pirouetted, and with her feet pointed slightly outward, slipped away gracefully, like a ballerina. Moments later, Randy introduced himself. He placed three glasses of water and one glass of red wine on the table. I thanked him and asked him to bring two more glasses of wine when my friends arrived. He nodded, but his hair didn't move. His head was buzzed on the sides. His thick blond hair stood up straight. It looked like he'd been scared, or maybe he'd stuck his fingers into an electrical outlet. Perhaps he was going to school to be a television personality. Maybe he just wanted to be taller—whatever. There seemed to be a lot of that going around.

"Thanks, Randy."

"My pleasure."

I always enjoyed eating at Little Italy's. It reminded me of the mobster movies I liked to watch. The ambiance and décor were genuine Italian. It felt like I could have been in Florence, Venice, or Naples. Hundreds of wine bottles lined the wall behind the bar. Light fixtures were handcrafted with wrought iron, a gaudy design, with dim bulbs. Linen table coverings were red and white, checkered. Italian flags hung proudly above each table. Black and white photos of fat, smiling Italian faces hung on the walls. Most were hairy. A large movie poster of *The Godfather* was proudly displayed in an ostentatious gold frame. Signed photos of Sinatra, Pacino, Stallone, Travolta, Pesci, DeVito, and other Italian heroes were haphazardly placed wherever a space on the wall permitted.

The locals had voted Little Italy's "Italian Restaurant of the year" via the *Dunville Dispatch's* annual survey. They had "best of" contests for everything—every year. It was a brilliant means of selling newspapers.

The guys walked in, and I waved my hand high. Brewster carried a large manila envelope and met me with a handshake. Scruggs gave me a hug, and we took our seats.

Randy was a few short steps behind and placed two more glasses of red wine on the table. "I'll give you gentlemen a few minutes to check out the menus. The daily specials are on the back page." He sauntered away.

Scruggs furrowed his brow. "What's wrong with his head?"

We chuckled.

"What's in the envelope, Brewster?" I asked.

He tapped the package and smiled. "I found the information on the furniture I bought from the Starlight Lounge in Detroit. I have the itemized bill of sale. A bunch of photos as well."

"Cool. Find anything interesting?"

He shook his head. "I haven't had a spare minute to review the information. I thought we could make this a working lunch. Each of us could review the photos, pass them around, and see if there's any information that might be helpful. After lunch, I want you to take the envelope home to Kathy. I'd like her to get eyes on this as well."

"Speaking of Kathy, she called me this morning, and you won't believe what she discovered." I leaned in, looking left, then right, like there might be a secret agent listening in on our conversation. "The ballistics report from the revolver we found in your bar matched the murder of an FBI agent in Detroit in 1935."

"No shit." Brewster's eyes widened. "Was she able to lift any fingerprints from the weapon?"

"No. Here's the deal, though. Kathy is turning her ballistics report and the gun over to my FBI friend."

"What about the diamonds and the coin?"

"Oh, she still wants to pursue our investigation into those items. Kathy loves a good mystery."

Brewster raised his glass for a toast. "Gentlemen, we

should do our part and see if there is anything we can uncover that might help her move this case forward."

BREWSTER OPENED the large manila envelope and placed the thick stack of papers on the table. Keeping the invoices in front of him, he handed the photos to Scruggs and me. The decade-old pictures from the auction day were crystal clear. The other images, much older, were a mixed stack. They were smaller, square, with faded colors and white edges. Most reminded me of the pictures my parents used to keep in a cardboard box in a closet.

Randy was back to take our food order, and we hadn't even researched the menu. Lasagna was their specialty, so we ordered it. I requested extra bread for the table.

"Excellent choice, gentlemen. I'll get your orders placed right away." He bounced to the kitchen.

"He's weird." Scruggs laughed.

Brewster scanned the dining room. "Where's Bambi?"

"She's off today," I said.

"Maybe we shouldn't eat here on Tuesdays anymore." Brewster chuckled and picked up a stack of papers. "These are the detailed invoices for the furniture I purchased. There's not a lot of information here. It only states that the items were owned by the Starlight Lounge."

Scruggs held up one of the older black and white photos high. "This must have been a really cool place to visit."

I held up another. "Check out your mahogany bar in *that* place. How did you remove the mahogany bar, Brewster?"

"That's a great story, and my timing couldn't have been better." He weaved a tale. "The city of Detroit held an auction three months before the Starlight Lounge was scheduled to be demolished. I was the high bidder and purchased everything—tables, chairs, office furniture, and the mahogany bar—at a great price."

I tipped an imaginary hat. "Whatever you paid was worth it."

"It was indeed. Ironically, my restaurant was still under construction when I purchased everything, so I negotiated a deal with the city to leave the furniture on-site for a few months. Then, I hired a company to wrap it all in protective blankets. They also built a heavy-duty wooden crate around the mahogany bar. When the construction team arrived to demolish the Starlight Lounge, I paid the crane operator and his guys to load the bar and furniture onto a flatbed trailer."

I pointed at one photo. "How did you get that huge crated bar into your restaurant without dismantling it?"

His eyes lit up. "That's a great question and another great story. I knew the mahogany bar would be a challenge. Most of my building interior, especially the flooring, needed to be completed before installing the bar. Our architect was brilliant. He designed special roof trusses. They were installed directly above where the bar is currently located. When the time came to install the bar, the construction crew removed a portion of the roof and lowered the bar in place with a crane. Once in place, they removed it from the crate, and the contractor replaced the roof boards and metal roofing."

Scruggs grabbed the photo. "That's an awesome story. I never knew tha—"

Just then, a commotion demanded our attention. We rose in unison from our red and white checkered table and hustled toward the loud voices resonating from an adjacent dining area. I could feel the tension before we rounded the corner. The look on Brewster's face told me the tingling on the back of my neck was warranted. Ten feet in front of us stood our server, Randy, squared off with a large man built like a bulldozer, whose thick beard, deep-set eyes, and overalls were the same color of charcoal. I guessed the heavy boots to be in the size fourteen range.

The biker—I assumed he owned a motorcycle—turned his Harley Davidson baseball cap backward, pulled on his long black ponytail, and stretched his arms in front of him. After cracking his knuckles slowly, like a forgettable scene in a foreign martial arts film, he topped off his pre-fight ritual with a crooked grin and a deep guttural belch.

A little over-the-top, I thought.

There they stood, toe-to-toe. The giant towered over our svelte server. Randy's feet were spread wide and staggered. He didn't appear worried. The loud noises that had caught our attention moments earlier turned eerily quiet. It felt like we had just entered the eye of the storm.

I gave Scruggs a side-glance. "Big son of a bitch."

He nodded.

Brewster had only taken a single step forward when the action began. The large man punched Randy in the chest. The shit-eating grin never left the biker's face. I sensed something was about to happen, and when it did, it reminded me of a mixed martial arts pay-per-view event. If I were a betting man, I would have lost money.

Our server crouched low and rushed the giant. He lunged up and slammed both palms into his chin with open hands held together closely, rocking a colossal head backward. I winced at the sound. Randy twisted his thin frame around the beast's body, never leaving more than an inch of space between them, and slipped behind his assailant. With the heel of a fashionable shoe, he kicked the black overalls just above the bend in the right knee. The heavyweight fell.

Brewster stood a single step in front of Scruggs and me. His feet could have been stuck in cement, his expression frozen in disbelief. Other patrons formed a semi-circle around the combatants with their mouths agape.

Randy wasn't done. He wrapped his right arm around the thick neck, locked his left forearm into a trained position, and stepped back. His opponent's frame bent awkwardly, and he fell back. Randy pulled the big man tight and appeared to have whispered something in his ear as he administered a textbook chokehold.

Brewster advanced and tapped him on the shoulder. Randy released his death grip on the biker and shuffled backward. I watched the ex-cop do what he had probably done a hundred times throughout his career. He checked the thick wrists for a pulse, rolled the sleeping giant onto his side, and inspected his airway. Blood pooled on the floor, and his barreled chest was motionless.

The big guy was out cold.

I pulled the phone from my breast pocket and dialed Dunville PD. "Send the paramedics, too," I suggested.

Then I heard more noise. Hands clapped from the customers who had witnessed the incident. Scruggs turned to the closest spectator and asked what happened. I listened as the guy laughed. "The big guy called him a faggot."

When Officer Willie Carter arrived, the defeated bully sat on the floor. We had leaned him against a wall. His eyes were glossy. It didn't look like the hulk could move his arms. They lay limp at his side. An ice pack, covered with a bar towel, was held in place by an employee. Blood dripped from the towel, which used to be white.

Paramedics arrived minutes later. It took six of us to get him on the gurney. He was strapped down and wheeled into the ambulance. Officer Carter said he would escort them to the hospital and asked his partner Owen Dean, who had just arrived, to take statements.

I saw Officer Dean speaking with our server in a far corner. Randy rubbed his chest. He hadn't broken a sweat, and I couldn't know, but I doubt his blood pressure had elevated. He looked calm, totally composed.

Scruggs saddled up beside me and pointed at Randy. "His hair is perfect."

We provided our statements to officer Dean, which undoubtedly matched the accounts of the other witnesses. I took one more glance at Randy, and our eyes met. I gave him an approving nod and detected a slight smile. He turned to face a large framed photograph on the wall and checked his hair in the reflection. Satisfied, he headed to the kitchen.

We sauntered to our table, where a different server met us with lasagna and bread. We nodded in unison at the suggestion for another glass of wine, then finished our meals without discussing the Starlight Lounge, photos, or invoices. Murmurs resonated throughout the dining area. The legend of Randy's courage and ninja-like skill set had grown exponentially with each passing minute and each new whisper. As new guests arrived, they appeared to be briefed on what had transpired. Heads turned, and curious patrons searched for the Kung-Fu server.

"Sorry about that disruption, gentleman. Your lunch is on the house today."

What the hell?

Kung-Fu Randy refilled our wine glasses. It had been less than thirty minutes since his bout, and he hardly seemed frazzled. Of course, the fight only lasted one round.

"Nonsense," Brewster laughed. "You should charge your customers double for the entertainment."

Randy pulled his lips back into a tight grin. "The manager insists."

I saw Brewster tuck a couple of what I assumed were large denomination bills into the palm of his right hand. He stood from the table, reached out, and offered a handshake. Randy accepted the gesture with a slight head bow.

"Just curious, Randy—where did you learn to defend yourself?"

He kept eye contact with Brewster as he placed the bills into the front pocket of his skinny jeans. He paused for a moment and shrugged his shoulders. "My father owned a Jiu-Jitsu academy in Ann Arbor. I learned how to defend myself before I could ride a bicycle.""

"Lunch was on the house." With each table Randy visited after leaving ours, he must have presented the same news from the manager. Each response was the same—a handshake and a smile. I wondered why he hadn't taken the rest of the day off. Pride, I surmised.

Brewster placed the photos and invoices back into the manila envelope and handed it to me. "Have Kathy look at this. Maybe she'll see something that might be important."

I picked up the large envelope and grabbed my vibrating phone from the breast pocket of my flannel shirt.

"Hey, Kath."

"Are you at the Social Club with Dan?"

"Nope, we're at Little Italy's. They have entertainment here on Tuesdays." I had her on speakerphone, and the guys tossed their heads back with laughter.

"Really?"

"I'll explain later. What's up?"

"We need to meet. Kenny and Steve have gathered some information, and I've invited them to our house for dinner tonight. Check with Bob and Dan. See if they can join us."

"Sounds good. What time?"

"Seven o'clock. On my way home, I'm running to Ann Arbor to meet with Gary King."

"Ann Arbor isn't on your way home," I reminded her.

"I know, but Gary's available to meet with me, so I'm heading there. I'll be home by seven. By the way, check your email. I just forwarded you the report Ron Grimwade sent me. I don't have time to study it before our meeting tonight. Can you review it and share what you find with the rest of us?"

"Of course."

Click.

I glanced at my screen and saw Kathy's email. Brewster confirmed he would attend the meeting and bring dinner from his restaurant. Scruggs said he'd have to check with Jo before making any commitment. I chuckled and slid the manila envelope back to Brewster since I'd see him later tonight.

I RETURNED to the hardware store and pulled into a busy parking lot. Paulie was near the fenced-in gate on the right side of the building, loading a pickup truck with bags of fall fertilizer and such. I whistled at him as I exited my vehicle and walked towards the front door. "When you get a minute, can you stop by my office?" I said.

"Sure thing, boss. I'll be there shortly."

I walked to the office, sat down, and looked at the pile of papers on my desk. I didn't feel very responsible today. I probably shouldn't have drunk wine for lunch.

I sent a text to Kathy. *Brewster is bringing dinner tonight from the club.*

Paulie knocked on my office door and then entered. "You wanted to see me, boss?"

I stood from my chair and closed the gap. "I've prepared a little going away party for you tomorrow night."

"I'm not quitting, boss. Just taking a little time off." His face was twisted.

"Whether you're leaving or coming back is not the point. We'll miss you while you're away, and I wanted to plan something special for you before you left. We're excited for you and want to send you off with a positive vibe."

"Thanks, boss. I'm touched."

"You may well be." I smiled.

Quack, Quack.

CHAPTER EIGHTEEN
Present Day - Tuesday, November 2

BREWSTER WAS THE FIRST TO ARRIVE, JUST BEFORE 7:00 P.M. THE Erikson brothers came minutes later. A Social Club employee had placed the buffet warming pans on our center island. The tiny flame below kept the food warm. The air smelled of Italian, heavy on the garlic. After a few minutes of mingling, chatting, and grabbing beverages, the plates were filled.

Kathy met me near the lasagna and kissed me on the cheek. "Is Dan coming?"

"No," I smirked. "Jo had something planned for him."

"But it's Tuesday night?"

I shrugged, and Brewster chuckled as he reached for the garlic toast.

Kathy asked if I had reviewed the report she emailed me. I confirmed that I'd studied it in detail. Then I winked and teased her with a 'wait and see' look. She shook her head lightly, but a smile pulled on her lips. When I asked her if she'd sent the weapon we had found to Ron Grimwade, she nodded and told me a federal currier would pick it up in the morning and deliver it to Georgia.

I passed Kenny and Steve in the hallway and gave them a nod. Although the Erikson brothers were two years apart, Steve being the oldest, they acted like twins. Both had the Swedish look—blue eyes and blonde hair. Kenny was a few inches taller and clean-shaven. Steve sported a tight beard.

They set their shoulder bags on the floor by their chairs and headed for the kitchen. Brewster was on my heel and sat next to me, on my right. He nodded and grabbed his fork, never saying a word. He looked as hungry as I felt. After a quick meal, I cleared the table and delivered four cold beers and a glass of white wine.

Kathy sipped a northern California blend and glanced around the table. "Where should we begin?"

Brewster stood from the table and turned to Kathy on his way to the vestibule. "The ballistic match was a huge surprise. I can't believe the gun we found inside my bar is linked to a murder."

Kathy nodded. "Now we need to find out how the gold coin and diamonds ended up in your bar, who owned them, and how this is tied to a murdered federal agent. With the information we'll be sharing this evening, we may be able to better grasp what really happened."

I turned to Kathy. "How did your meeting go with Gary King?"

She leaned forward. "I got there as the store was closing. Gary inspected the diamonds briefly and appeared to be impressed. He put them in his safe and said he would call me tomorrow."

Brewster had returned with the manila envelope he'd retrieved from the console in the entryway. He unfastened the metal clasp and sat. "I have the invoices from the auction and many photos to review. They might not help much because they only provide information on what I purchased and the amount I paid."

Kathy leaned back in her chair, addressing Brewster and me. "Did you guys uncover anything interesting during your lunch meeting today?"

"Not really," Brewster snickered. "Most of our time was spent reminiscing about the good old days and the mahogany bar I purchased from Detroit. Also," he paused for a chuckle, "we got sidetracked with an altercation in the restaurant."

I choked back laughter. Steve and Kenny leaned forward with curiosity. Kathy gave me a stern gaze and probably assumed I was involved in the altercation. Past experiences allowed permission for such assumptions. Brewster held up his hands, palms forward, and shared what had happened during our lunch gathering. I added color commentary.

Kathy shook her head, took a sip of wine, put on her cop face, and made eye contact with the group, providing directions for our exercise. "Let's look at the photos," she said. "And don't rush anything." Then, nodding to Brewster, she continued speaking as he passed the photos around the table. "Take your time with each photo. Look beyond the obvious. I'm searching for anything that doesn't make sense. If something looks out of place, it might be important. Don't take anything for granted. Look beyond the focal point of the lens. Focus on the periphery."

Kathy's strategy was simple. If anyone had suspicions or questions about a photo, it would be placed in the middle of the table. Those that passed through everyone's hands without questions went into a large cardboard box she had placed on the floor.

At the end of the first hour, one photo needed further review. Kathy held it high. "This photo caught my attention both times around the table," she said. "It's from the auction period when Brewster purchased the furniture and mahogany bar. As you can see, the bar had already been removed from the Starlight Lounge, and the main floor was empty. Rick, can you grab me the magnifying glass?"

I walked to the console in the hallway near the front door and retrieved the Sherlock Holmes device from a small drawer. When I returned and handed it to her, she leaned forward and pulled the photo to the table's edge. Holding the lens steady in her right hand, she examined the image. Her breathing was light and measured. She let out a slow exhale and passed the photo to Kenny—along with the magnifying glass.

Kenny squinted through the lens. "What am I looking for?"

"Do you remember the photos and video footage I gave you this morning?"

"Yes." He shifted in his seat. "I brought the photos with me."

"Do you recall the specific location in the mahogany bar where the secret compartment was located?"

"It was about one-third of the way down the bar, from the left side. Would you like me to grab those photos?" He reached for his shoulder bag.

Kathy tugged on his sleeve. "No, no, that's not important. Focus on *this* photo. Let me know if anything catches your eye?"

"Hmmm." His head shook. "Nothing jumps out at me, Kathy. Sorry."

"No worries. It's a process. Please pass the photo."

Steve scrutinized the photo and tilted his head. "I'm confused. What do you see that I'm not seeing?"

"It might be nothing. That's why we're doing this exercise."

"Damn. I don't see anything unusual." He analyzed it for another minute and passed the photo clockwise to me. I sat at the end of the table.

"Can you give me a clue, Kath?"

"I don't even know if I'm right, Rick. Examine the photo. Let me know if anything strikes you as interesting, maybe even out of place. Focus your eyes below where the secret compartment of the bar was located. Focus on the floor."

I studied the photo. The room was quiet as a Catholic church service. Removing the magnifying glass from my eye, I tilted my head back, then forward again, and focused through the lens. "Huh. When was this photo taken?"

Kathy beamed. "After the demo crew removed the bar with their crane."

"Is that what I *think* it is, Kath?"

Her brown eyes sparkled. "You see it, don't you?"

"Do you think it's possible?"

Kathy held up her wineglass and winked. "Seems likely, doesn't it?"

Hushing the whispers from the table, she took a sip of her Sauvignon Blanc and set the glass on the table. "Bob, can you confirm the Starlight Lounge had a basement?"

"Yes, there was a basement. I walked through the building when the demo crew prepared the crane to remove the large crate. The second floor was pretty trashed and wasn't safe to visit. There was a basement, though. I remember walking down the cement stairs and being startled by a big fat rat."

"I'll be damned. You nailed it, Kathy!" I said. "You're a genius!"

She bowed her head, raised a wine glass, and winked. "Ta-da."

Brewster wrestled the photo from my hand. "Let me see that. What the hell are you two talking about?"

Steve and Kenny rose from their chairs and walked behind Brewster, peeking over his shoulder. Nobody said anything for a long moment.

Kathy leaned over the table, pointing at the photo. "Bob, look at the tiled floor underneath where the bar was located."

His eyes narrowed. "What am I looking for?"

She pumped her index finger over the image. "Look at the grout lines between the tiles, where the secret compartment of the bar was located. Do you see anything that looks out of place?"

He furrowed his brow. "Do you think *that's* how he did it?"

"That's what I'm thinking, Bob. There is no grout around that one tile. It's the only one that looks like that. What other reason could there be? The missing grout isn't an accident. Someone must have accessed the compartment in the bottom of his mahogany bar from the basement by moving that tile to access the secret hiding place."

Kenny picked up his shoulder bag from the floor. "I have some information on the furniture builder." We watched as he pulled a thick stack from his bag, neatly arranged and held together with large paper clips, and began."David Gonyea was his name. He was only nineteen years old when his father died in 1929. After his father passed away, he took over his furniture shop. He changed the company name to *Gonyea Custom Furniture* and, in 1935, moved from the downriver suburbs of River Rouge to a much larger building in downtown Detroit. That's where Brewster's furniture and mahogany bar were built. My initial investigation found

David Gonyea extremely successful and well regarded. His company's furniture included signature brass tags with their company logo. That's how their furniture can be identified. I found records of one of their china cabinets being auctioned in 2007 for over twenty thousand dollars."

Brewster's eyes rounded. "I don't remember seeing the brass plates on *my* furniture."

"Look underneath your tables and chairs tomorrow. I'll bet you find them. Also, I learned the furniture company flourished through the mid-sixties and closed its doors right around the time of the 1967 Detroit riots."

"Much of downtown Detroit was permanently ruined in the late sixties," Brewster said.

Kathy nodded. "Yep, it's unfortunate. The city has never been the same. What else have you got?"

"When David and his wife, Eve, were in their late forties, they had two sons. Both are still alive. One still lives in River Rouge. The other is in Florida. After David died in 1974, his wife, Eve, moved to Poland, but we've been unsuccessful in locating her whereabouts."

"Have you reached out to David's sons?" Kathy asked.

"I called this afternoon and haven't heard back from them."

"Maybe they have some information from their father that would help us solve the mystery of the gold coin and the murdered FBI agent. What else have you got?"

"This is interesting. We still have some additional research to do, but here's what I have so far…."

Kenny picked up a single photo from the tidy stack in front of him and held it high. He introduced us to the owner of the Starlight Lounge—Sam Durocher. He was standing on the brick-paved streets of Park Avenue—in front of his nightclub. It must have been taken after 1935.

"He's a handsome guy," Kathy said. "With a bit of a shady look about him."

Kenny nodded in agreement and held up another picture. "This photo shows David Gonyea on the bank of the Detroit River with John Vitale, Angelo Zerilli, and William Tocco. These three guys were prominent East Side gang members and rivals of the famous Purple Gang. They were ruthless, feared, and some of the most dangerous gangsters in the country."

Photographs of David and his friends were passed around the table for the next fifteen minutes. I couldn't speak for everyone, but I enjoyed the nostalgic trip through those early Detroit days. Sticky notes, with names on the back of each photo, enlightened us to a few acquaintances David Gonyea associated with. They included gangsters, politicians, prominent businessmen, and gorgeous women.

He seemed like an interesting character.

In front of me, lying on the table, neat, folded, and marked with different colored highlighters, were the internal FBI reports from my Georgia buddy. The information I was about to share would raise a few eyebrows. And so I began.

"After Kathy called me about the ballistics match this morning, we reached out to my friend Ron Grimwade. Some of you may remember him. Growing up, he and I lived a few houses apart, but he left Dunville when we were teenagers. His family moved south to Georgia. He's currently an FBI agent based out of Atlanta. Kathy is turning over the gun—the murder weapon we found inside Brewster's bar to Ron. He'll process the weapon and tie up the loose ends of the murdered federal agent."

I tapped on the papers in front of me and continued. "Ron sent me this detailed after-action report from the dead FBI Agent's partner, Dale Mintern. We spent a great deal of time on the phone reviewing this report. Ron was curious about what we were looking into and said he trusted my judgment. Not sure trusting my judgment was his best decision, but what are friends for, right? Here's what he sent me." I waved the papers high. "Let's begin with the murdered FBI agent in Detroit. His name was John Douglas. After an honorable discharge from the Marines, he joined the Detroit Police Department at twenty-two. He continued with them until he was accepted into the FBI academy in April 1935. Sadly, he was a federal agent for barely seven months. His EOW, which stands for end of watch, was November 16, 1935."

"We're all cops, Rick. We know what EOW stands for," Kathy said.

I offered a reverent nod. We bowed our heads in respect for a fallen brother. After a moment of silence, I continued. "Anyway, I took Ron's information and reconciled it with the information Kathy had uncovered. Here's what I've learned. Are you ready?"

Knowing it was a rhetorical question, everyone leaned forward with anticipation.

"Let's start with Agent John Douglas's assassination, and that's precisely what it was — an assassination. Two gunshots to the head from the revolver we found in the secret compartment of Brewster's bar. The night before his body was found, Douglas and his partner Dale Mintern and six additional FBI agents had raided a high-stakes gambling operation on the second floor of the Starlight Lounge.

According to Mintern's typewritten after-action report, ten suspects were arrested in that raid. There should have been *eleven* arrests, but one of the dumb asses drew his weapon and was killed by FBI agents." I paused for dramatic effect, then leaned forward and spilled the news. "I know where the gold coin came from." I leaned back in my chair, smiling like a Cheshire cat.

"Enough with the drama," Kathy said. "Spit it out."

I leaned forward with a tight grin, elbows on the table, and my face felt flush with anticipation. "The dumb ass who pulled a gun and was subsequently shot by FBI agents in the raid was none other than Isaac Swift, the jeweler from New Jersey."

Brewster spent a quick minute catching Steve and Kenny up on our meeting with Gary King and provided them with a synopsis of how Isaac Swift fit into the story. "If there was ever any doubt about the legitimacy of the coin we found," Brewster added, "the information Rick just shared establishes irrefutable provenance."

Kathy's eyes narrowed. "That's great information, Rick. What else is in Ron's report?"

I exhaled a long breath and continued. "Within hours after Agent Douglas was found dead, a prominent Chicago attorney had the suspects released from jail. All charges were dropped because of a *lack of evidence.*" I used my best finger air quotes. "According to the report, the murdered FBI agent had the evidence from the raid in a brown leather briefcase in his car. When his body was found, the briefcase was missing."

Kathy asked, "What evidence did he have in the leather briefcase?"

I flipped the page and slid my finger to where I had highlighted a few paragraphs. "According to the report, agent John Douglas had collected a camera, a large amount of cash, jewelry, and a gold coin."

Brewster tapped his beer bottle with his index finger. "That's suspicious for sure. No evidence, no crime, right?"

"You got it, buddy. The Chicago attorney told the district judge that the group of eleven had gathered in Detroit for a *prayer meeting*."

"I can smell bullshit a mile away. Was any of the evidence ever recovered?"

"There's no record of anything being recovered. That shouldn't be surprising. Shit, who would turn it in? It was 1935, for Christ's sake. Times were tough."

"Did agent Mintern have a suspect list for who might have killed his partner?" Kathy asked.

I nodded. "He focused on two main suspects. According to his notes, he interviewed David Gonyea, the furniture maker; however, he noted David didn't fit the profile of a murderer. His conclusion was that Sam Durocher, the owner of the Starlight Lounge, killed the agent and then removed the evidence from his car to protect his high-profile friends who had been arrested. But here's where it gets interesting." I paused for suspense. "Two days after John Douglas was murdered in the alley, Sam Durocher was executed inside his Starlight Lounge. He was found slumped over the mahogany bar."

Kathy said, "So if Sam Durocher *did* kill agent John Douglas in the alley, who executed *him* two days later? Does Ron believe Agent Mintern might have sought revenge for his partner's murder and killed the lounge owner?"

"The plot thickens, Kathy. Not long after Sam Durocher was found dead, slumped over the bar, agent Mintern was shot multiple times outside a diner in Ohio. He was returning from an interview when he was ambushed by gunfire from a vehicle in the parking lot."

"He survived?" Steve asked.

"Yes. Mintern spent some time in the hospital and survived the shooting, but his career didn't survive the aftermath of his investigations. He resigned from the bureau within weeks of being released from the hospital. Ron told me that his personnel file was vague in details. Ron assumed that he had pissed off some very prominent politicians and businessmen. He questioned the timing of Mintern's resignation and believed he was forced to resign from the bureau."

"So, the powerful people he pissed off got him fired?" Kathy asked.

"That's Ron's theory. Said he probably received an ultimatum from the bureau — resign with dignity or be fired. The FBI was relatively new, so there wasn't much precedent in handling such matters. Ron also told me that Mintern received a two-year severance package, which raised even more suspicions. That would have been rare in the 1930s."

"Who was arrested in the gambling raid?" Kathy asked. "Who did agent Mintern piss off enough to cause his career to come to an abrupt end?"

I shuffled through the pages, searching for more colored highlights. "The arrest records showed that Congressman John Kelly from Ohio was one of the ten arrested. By the way, Mintern was on his way home from a meeting with the Ohio Congressman when he was ambushed and shot, which sounded suspicious to me, but hey, I'm naturally conspiratorial." I looked around the table to ensure everyone was still engaged, then read the rest of the names. Influential figures included a big-city mayor, a high-profile attorney from Cleveland, and a few well-known mobsters.

"Was the owner of the Starlight Lounge arrested in the raid?" Kathy asked.

"Great question. Sam Durocher was *not* arrested in the raid." I flipped ahead a few pages. "And here's another twist. According to the Mintern report, he was monitoring the rear entrance of the Starlight Lounge before the raid and references an 11:00 p.m. time frame where he and his team witnessed David Gonyea parking a bright yellow convertible in the alley behind the Starlight Lounge. Sam Durocher was his passenger. The two gentlemen exited the vehicle and had a brief conversation. Gonyea then returned to the car and drove west, leaving the alley. According to the Mintern report, Durocher then entered the building."

Brewster said, "If Sam Durocher was in the building, why wasn't he identified on the arrest report?"

"Another great question. Check this out. After the ten suspects were arrested and hauled off to the Sixteenth Precinct by the Detroit Police, the federal agents found a secret staircase in a first-floor office closet. This hidden spiral staircase connected all three floors of the building. They also discovered a door in the basement of the Starlight Lounge that led to an adjacent building. Mintern's written assumption was that Sam Durocher escaped through the hidden staircase and sneaked out of the building through the secret basement door."

Brewster furrowed his brow. "Nobody saw Sam Durocher exit the building from any other location?"

"The report said the front door was guarded by two agents. The only other exit point was the rear delivery door and the fire escape, which was directly above the rear door in the alley."

Steve said, "If David Gonyea was seen in that alley, could he be the one who murdered the FBI agent? The report said he drove away, but what if he returned and killed Agent Douglas?"

Kathy shook her head. "I don't buy it. My money is on Durocher as the killer, and here's why," she said, tapping her index finger on the table. "While it's possible David Gonyea *could* have murdered the agent, I don't see why he *would*. He pulled into an alley, got out of the car to chat with Durocher, and left the scene. Nope, it's not him. I believe it was Sam Durocher. He had the strongest motive, and, since he was seen entering the building but never seen leaving, add to those facts that he wasn't arrested in the raid—nope, he did it. He had motive and opportunity."

We spent a few more minutes at the table discussing the information and exchanging ideas and theories. When the bantering ended, Kathy read from her spiral notebook and summarized the events leading up to the raid at the Starlight Lounge and the subsequent murder of the FBI agent, John Douglas. She looked around the table and ended her summation, sounding like she was a prosecuting attorney presenting a closing statement. "Would you agree with me that Sam Durocher is our number one suspect for the murder of an FBI agent?"

Everyone nodded.

We gathered our belongings and helped tidy up the dining room. Kathy stuffed two large Ziplock baggies full of leftovers for the Erikson brothers, and everyone headed to the front door. Kenny jumped into the passenger seat of Steve's red 1969 Mustang. Steve fired up the beast and pulled out of the driveway, tires barking on the blacktop road as he accelerated. Following the Erikson brothers down the driveway, Brewster stuck his left arm out of the driver's side window of his Lincoln Navigator and waved goodbye. Turning right, he pressed the accelerator hard as well. For a large luxury vehicle, it was fast.

Kathy turned off the porch lights. She and I held hands and stared at the beautiful autumn sky. The night was black as ink, and the stars appeared to fall from the heavens. Brewster's taillights disappeared over a rolling hill into the eastern horizon. Then we spotted a dark SUV pull out of a side street near a patch of woods across the road from our house.

"What the hell?" Kathy stared at the silhouette. "Where did that car come from? Why aren't the headlights on?"

"What's even odder? *That* SUV looks like the one I saw yesterday morning in my parking lot when I opened the hardware store."

"Should we follow it?"

"We'll never catch it. I'll give Brewster a call on his cell."

CHAPTER NINETEEN

Detroit, Michigan - 1935
'The Grand Opening'

WITH GREAT FANFARE, THE GRAND OPENING OF THE STARLIGHT Lounge took place as scheduled. Officials from the FBI requested the lounge be closed until they could complete their investigation. Their pleas were unsuccessful. In typical Detroit-style politics, a late-night ruling by a district judge, a friend of the mayor, denied the request. Despite objections from the FBI and a last-minute appeal to a higher court, the grand opening continued. The ruling pleased Sam Durocher but created a different level of stress. Had he won the legal battle or been tricked into a comfortable lull? Today, he wouldn't dwell anymore on the subject. Today was *his* day.

Sam Durocher was delighted. The alleged gambling bust at his place late last night by the FBI was just that — a bust. Without the evidence, his friends and colleagues had been released from jail. Sam thought they had all been compensated more than fair. Except for the politicians, everyone who attended the alleged gambling event — the *prayer meeting* — stayed in Detroit for the grand opening. The politicians had enough 'ink' to last a while. Some were up for re-election.

Hearsay and scuttlebutt of the previous night's raid at the Starlight Lounge by the FBI built the anticipation and expectations of the grand opening to unprecedented levels. On the bustling, crowded streets of the Motor City, people talked. From the average schmuck in the corner barbershop to the high society gentlemen drinking 'legal' whiskey at the *Detroit Athletic Club*, it was the gossip du jour. Rumors on the street ran rampant about who was arrested in the raid. The 'little people' wanted a reason to smile, applaud, and rejoice. They whispered and gossiped, secretly hoping their favorite politician was involved in the raid and behind bars. While the working men and women—the laborers—were not-so-silently rooting for the collapse of the upper class, the upper class attended the grand opening. It was an invitation-only event, and the little people were not invited.

Detroit boasted many beautiful buildings, but this latest addition, the Starlight Lounge, was a cut above the neighboring structures. From the street view, the outside of the building was precisely the grand statement Sam Durocher had envisioned. Massive hand-carved wood doors, compliments of the *Gonyea Custom Furniture Company*, included solid brass hardware and centered the inviting entrance. The colorful marquee, donated by a city council member up for re-election, was prominently displayed above a sizable red canopy and gracefully illuminated the dark brick pavers on Park Avenue.

Inside the lounge, the glossy sheen of the Italian marble flooring glistened in the soft glow of the elegant light fixtures that dangled gracefully from the tall, tin-covered ceilings. The shadowing was perfect. A large Persian rug at the bottom of the staircase covered the broken tiles and blood-stained grout from the previous night's activities. A few strategically placed plants covered the bullet holes on the interior brick wall. The large mahogany bar, beautifully designed and handcrafted, was prominently displayed on the far wall—the centerpiece of attention, welcoming guests as they entered. The custom tables and chairs were hand-rubbed and polished to a lustrous glow.

Men of wealth and stature sported tailored suits and tuxedos. Prominent women of culture and importance competed for the most elegant evening gowns and formal dresses. Business cards were exchanged, handshakes were plentiful, and the drinks flowed freely. Everyone attending the event described it as incredible, well organized, and elegant. Attention to detail was the consensus. The following day, the *Detroit Free Press* ran a front-page story about the event above the fold.

It appeared as though Sam had succeeded. Nothing could stop him now.

CHAPTER TWENTY

Present Day - Wednesday, November 3

I FOUND A RARE STREET PARKING SPACE IN THE TOWN SQUARE, across from the Native American statue and community pergola. Squeezing my truck into the tight opening, I strolled the narrow sidewalk to the Dunville Bakery. I waved to a few familiar faces along the way and held the door open for an elderly lady whose attempt to corral three small children failed miserably. Grandkids, I guessed. She seemed so sweet.

Most weekday mornings, I stopped at the bakery to pick up treats for my employees. Weaving around the unruly toddlers, I made my way inside.

"Morning, Charlene." I gave her my best smile.

I knew little about Charlene, except that she owned the bakery. I guessed her to be in her late twenties. She lived in town, but I never saw her outside the bakery, and we never crossed paths. Her soft, curly, shoulder-length hair, warm brown eyes, and cheerful smile could snap anyone from a foul mood. It certainly worked for me.

"Morning, Rick. Nice to see you. By the way, your blue eyes jump out in that photo."

I returned a perplexed stare.

"Today's newspaper." She grinned. "You and Mr. Brewster look rather handsome."

Charlene must have recognized my confused expression. She turned on her heel, darted behind the counter, returned with today's edition of the *Dunville Dispatch,* and held the front page high for everyone in the bakery to see. A few people clapped. Some appeared annoyed. Most had their heads buried in electronic devices—clueless.

The large color photo of Brewster and me was prominently displayed—above the fold. We were smiling. I was holding a gold coin. The Indian head on the front of the coin was crystal clear. Below the fold, a much smaller article confirmed Ben Winston had been re-elected.

I knew I'd catch hell from him about upstaging his election victory.

The bakery was crowded, and, local celebrity or not, I had to wait for my order like everyone else. I made room for the steady stream of customers entering the front door and walked outside. A blue and white metal box was a few steps away. I slipped three quarters into the oxidized slot. They didn't seem to register. I gave the rusty contraption a swift kick while an elderly woman with a walker scowled at me. With an apologetic nod, I removed my newspaper, tucked it under my arm, and walked back inside.

"Here you go, *Mr. Cooper*." Charlene bowed from the waist. "Don't forget about us *little* people." She flicked her limp hands high while the rest of her body feigned submission.

I reached for the colorful box. "You're funny, Charlene. See you soon."

Reversing my footsteps along the narrow sidewalk, I strolled to my truck. A few cars were waiting for my premium parking space. I waved to the lucky person who pulled in behind me and headed south to my hardware store. The crisp air from an open window filled my lungs. Within the first mile, a dozen donuts became eleven. I periodically glanced at the large photo of Brewster and me, which sat on the passenger seat.

Yep, it was a pretty good photo.

The feel-good experience at the bakery turned from sweet to sour when I pulled into my parking lot. The Channel 6 News team was camped outside the front entrance. I stared at the bold red lettering on a large white van. An antenna extended high above the roof. A half-dozen people milled around, straightening cables, yelling, pointing fingers, and staring at their cell phones.

Jessica Logan, the on-the-scene reporter, smiled into the camera. Her signature purple hair looked like it had been sprayed with lacquer. Even when she shook her head, it didn't move. A female make-up artist patted the reporter's face with a powdery substance. Whatever didn't stick to her skin was carried away by the morning breeze. On television, she was beautiful — easy on the eyes, as they say. Staring at her through the windshield, I thought she looked thinner than on TV — even better looking.

Screw this. I didn't have the time or the patience to deal with a media ambush. Executing a flawless U-turn, I picked up my phone and called Scruggs.

"Good morning, Mr. Cooper."

"Hey, Scruggs, glad you answered. I thought I'd stop by your place this morning and check out that race car you're working on."

"Sure! That's cool. Come on over. Wait. What's going on?"

"What?"

"You're up to something."

"Can't a friend just stop by and see his buddy?" I chuckled.

"What's really going on?"

"Did you see this morning's newspaper?"

"Yeah, Ben was re-elected."

"The other story, asshole."

Scruggs laughed. "You and Brewster actually look good on the front page."

"Well, the Channel 6 News van is in my parking lot."

"That's funny. Is that good-looking reporter with purple hair there?"

"Fuck you. Do you mind if I stop by for a coffee? I have donuts."

"Of course," he laughed hysterically. "Are you taking the day off?"

"Nope, and it's not *that* funny. I'll give Paulie a call on the way to your place. He can handle the store until that reporter leaves. I'll head back afterward."

"Sounds good. I'm just waiting for the fire marshal to finish. I'll put on a fresh pot of coffee."

"What?"

"The fire marshal is here. Said I was overdue for my inspection. Flashed a shiny badge and told me it was routine."

"What's he doing?"

"I don't know. Walking around the offices, checking for hazards, I guess. I've been in the shop all morning."

I told Scruggs I had a surprise inspection at my hardware store yesterday and asked him if he could sneak a few photos of the fire inspector. He wondered why I hadn't met him, and I told him that Paulie had let him into my store before I arrived.

"He's walking out of the office area now, Rick. I'll duck behind this car and take a few shots. Gotta go."

Click.

I called Paulie and asked if the news crew was still in the hardware parking lot and was happy to hear they were packing up their gear and moving on. I asked him if he had spoken with the reporter.

"Yeah," he confirmed. "That good-looking chick with the purple hair asked about you. I said you weren't coming in today."

"Really, Paulie. *Chick*?"

"You call her that all the time, boss."

"Whatever. Thanks for covering for me. By the way, what did that fire marshal look like?"

"What do you mean?"

"The guy who visited the hardware store yesterday. What did he look like?"

"Kind of badass looking, I guess. He was taller than me by a few inches, with broad shoulders and blue eyes. He reminded me of the guy who starred in that NCIS television series."

"Which NCIS show?"

"The good one, boss. Not those stupid spin-offs from LA or New Orleans. They have terrible actors and shitty plots."

"Are you talking about Mark Harmon?"

"Yeah, he looked just like him, with black hair."

"Thanks, Paulie. See you soon."

WHEN BREWSTER answered his phone, I told him the Channel 6 News team had ambushed me at my place of business and warned him they could be at his place next. It gave him at least an hour to prepare for their arrival since his restaurant didn't open until 10 a.m. He asked how I handled the interview. I told him I didn't. When he pressed for clarification, I told him I avoided the news crew, took a quick about-face and peeled out of the parking lot.

He chuckled. "Where are you now?"

"I'm heading to have coffee with Scruggs."

"Tell him I said hello."

"I sure will. And hey, did anything come of the SUV that followed you from our house last night?"

"No, I never saw it. The vehicle must have turned off the road before I reached the main drag."

"That's weird."

"After you called me, I called Steve and Kenny to see if they were in the area. I was going to have them tail the vehicle. They weren't available."

"Yesterday morning, I saw a similar SUV in my parking lot as I pulled in to open the store."

"Any chance you saw the license plates?"

"I did not. It was backed into a parking space facing the store. There was no license plate on the front of the vehicle."

"Only nineteen states don't require a front license plate, and the only one that borders Michigan is Indiana. The rest aren't even close. Did you catch the color of the rear plate?"

"Nope. Never saw it. There were two guys in the front seats. I watched them from inside the store for a few minutes and headed to get coffee and a donut. They were gone when I returned."

"Okay, now that we're all aware of this mystery SUV, let's keep a vigilant eye on our surroundings."

"Should I be worried?"

"No, being worried is never good," Brewster advised. "You should be aware. Always be aware."

"Shit's getting weird in this town."

"Are you and Scruggs coming by for lunch today?"

"I'll check with him and get back to you. I'm pulling into his place now."

"Keep me posted."

Click.

MY VISIT with Scruggs was enjoyable. It had been far too long since I'd visited his place of business. I was usually only there to drop a vehicle off or pick one up. He showed me the fancy car he was working on and explained what he was doing to make the car perform better. I feigned interest and smiled a lot. We read the front-page article Sarah Owens had written about the gold find at the Social Club. Both of us agreed she did an excellent job of reporting the facts. I was pleased with her professionalism. Scruggs complimented me on the front-page photo. I asked if he wanted an autograph. He said something stupid. I laughed. Pulling out his phone, he showed me the images of the fire marshal and forwarded them to me.

I set the newspaper on the workbench. "Did the inspector leave you any report, Scruggs?"

He stuffed another donut in his mouth. "Nope," He mumbled, wiping his chin with his sleeve. "Seemed to be in a hurry. Told me everything was in good order, not to worry."

"Any chance you saw what kind of vehicle he was driving?"

He shook his head.

I placed my coffee mug in the sink and walked to the front door with Scruggs. He hugged me goodbye. I had caffeine jitters. Although my blood sugar would soon drop to a normal level, the education I'd received about engines was already forgotten. I sent Paulie a text, pulled out of Scruggs' parking lot, and turned left onto the blacktop. Then I pressed the recall button to return a missed phone call.

"Sorry I missed your call, Kath. I was visiting with Scruggs."

"How's Dan doing?"

"He's doing great. He really enjoys working on cars."

"What prompted your visit this morning?"

"Channel 6 News van was in my parking lot."

"Did they ask you questions about Sarah's article?"

"I never spoke with them. I scooted out of the parking lot before they saw me."

"Coward."

"What?"

"Never mind. I'm on the way to pick up Steve. We're headed to see David Gonyea's son. He lives in River Rouge. Just wanted to let you know."

"Can I go with you?" I begged.

"Aren't you working today?"

"Yeah, but it's Paulie's last day. He can handle everything. I'm not sure when I'll be able to get another day off for a while."

"Sounds good. We can use the ride to chat. Where are you?"

"Just left Scruggs' place. Where should we meet?"

"Meet us in Chelsea. At the truck stop, on the north side of I-94."

"Thanks. I'll be there in twenty minutes. I have extra donuts."

I hung up with Kathy and called Paulie, letting him know I may not be in until late that afternoon. Then I sent messages to Scruggs and Brewster to let them know I would not be having lunch with them today. I cranked up the radio, heading north, singing along with Van Morrison.

CHAPTER TWENTY ONE
Present Day - Wednesday, November 3

For decades, Michigan State Police vehicles were black, with gold shields and striping. In 1954, the color was changed to the bright shade of blue Michiganders are accustomed to today. Not everybody was sold on the new paint color, and some troopers thought the color was gaudy. The brightly hued cruisers were soon dubbed 'Blue Goose,' to parody a well-known commercial bus line from that period.

Kathy's 'Blue Goose' Ford Explorer waited for me in the rear parking lot of the gas station. Steve jumped from the passenger side, offering me the front seat. Waving him off, I climbed into the back.

"Hey, Rick. It's good to see you again," he said over his shoulder.

I gave him a wave. "So, what's going on?"

"Fill him in, Steve," Kathy said, reaching for her Yeti water jug in the console.

"There is definitely something weird afoot," Steve said and turned in his seat to face me. "After many attempts to speak with David Gonyea's sons, I finally spoke with both of them this morning. The one who lives in Florida—his name is Doug—hung up on me three times before I finally had a short conversation with him, and I mean *short*. Told me he never got along with his father. Said he hasn't spoken with his brother Danny, who we'll meet today, in over thirty years. Also told me to never call him again and hung up the phone. I tried calling him a few more times without success."

"Do you think there's anything suspicious about his behavior, or is he simply a dick?"

"Either way, he's a dick."

"Sounds that way. So, where are we heading?"

"This is where it gets interesting." Steve continued. "After my conversation with the dick in Florida, I contacted the other son, Danny. He lives in River Rouge. He was extremely polite. I gave him my State Police identification information, why I was calling, what information I was interested in, and guess how he responded to me?"

I shrugged.

"He said I was welcome to stop by with questions, but I had better have my identification credentials. Told me an FBI agent visited his house yesterday afternoon with similar questions. Said the man at his front door, who claimed to be a federal agent, couldn't provide a valid ID."

"What did he do?"

"We didn't get that far into our conversation. I guess we're going to find out. I'm just glad Danny agreed to meet with me." Steve turned back to face the windshield.

Continuing on I-94 eastbound for another thirty minutes, we exited onto the southbound Southfield Freeway and chatted about our expectations for the upcoming meeting. Kathy would control the interview. Steve and I would ask questions when and if it was appropriate. Continuing south for a few more miles, we turned on Fort Street, another mile to Kingwood Street, and another left. We pulled into a newer subdivision with young trees and manicured lawns. The driveway was on our right. A stealthy figure, prominent in stature, appeared from the side of the garage and strolled past us nonchalantly. Kathy turned off the engine and exited the vehicle.

"Mr. Gonyea?" she asked.

"That's me." He continued down the driveway and walked around the back of Kathy's Explorer, keeping a vigilant eye.

Kathy's brow furrowed. "Is everything all right?"

"Yes, ma'am," he said with a slight nod. "I was just checking your license plate. Wanted to see if this vehicle was registered with the State of Michigan, that's all."

"It is indeed." She approached him with her right hand extended. "My name is Kathy Cooper. I'm an investigator with the Michigan State Police, and yes, this vehicle has been paid for with your taxes."

"Ha! You'd be pulling up on bicycles if you relied on my taxes." He snorted.

Kathy chuckled. "I hope you pay as little tax as legally possible."

"You should probably get your rear door repaired."

"Excuse me?"

Danny Gonyea pointed at her tailgate. "That's a huge dent. You should take pride in your vehicle."

Kathy closed the gap and acknowledged the blemish. "It's a recent accident. I'll make the repairs a priority."

"May I see your badge?"

Removing the badge from her belt, she held it high for him to inspect. Then she pointed in our direction. "This is Detective Steve Erickson, and this is Rick."

Danny's eyes squinted. "Are you a cop, Rick?"

"Reserve cop. Kathy is my wife."

"Why are you here?"

Steve stepped forward, his right hand extended. "Rick is the person who found the gold coin we spoke about, Danny. He's the reason we started this investigation."

Danny shrugged and strolled to the front door. We followed him up the two cement steps. "Take off your shoes," he said, waving us inside.

The house was clean and appeared well organized. We placed our shoes on a plain black mat in the tiled vestibule. Above a leather couch, an American flag hung on the living room wall to our right. On the left, two Lazy Boy recliners flanked a white brick fireplace. Military photos lined the mantle above the fireplace. Above them hung a large black and white print of a Huey helicopter landing in some faraway jungle long ago. Ronald Reagan stared at us from the far wall, and beyond our 40th President was the kitchen. Danny pointed to our seating choices and continued to the kitchen. Steve and I sat in the recliners. Kathy remained on her feet, walking between us toward the white fireplace with the thick wood mantle.

Returning from the kitchen carrying an oak chair, Danny placed it between the couch and the recliners facing the vestibule. He didn't sit. He stood and faced the fireplace.

Kathy turned from the mantle and met Danny's deep-set brown eyes. "You look just like your father."

"So I've been told."

"He was a good-looking man."

Danny cocked his head. "Is that part of your training?"

"Excuse me?"

"The compliments," he said.

Kathy waved her palms. "No. What I said was sincere."

"Then, I thank you."

"Marines?" she asked.

"Yes, ma'am."

"Vietnam?"

"Yes, ma'am."

"We appreciate your service."

"It was a different time." He waved his left hand towards the couch and took a seat on the oak chair. Kathy sat on the small couch and met Danny's gaze.

She leaned back and crossed her legs. "Was my colleague, Steve, clear why we wanted to meet with you, Danny?"

He looked to his right towards Steve, then back to Kathy. "I understand that something valuable was found in a piece of furniture that my father's company built."

"A rare coin was discovered in a mahogany bar." She gestured to me. "Rick was the person who found it."

"I'm not sure what this has to do with me, but I'm willing to entertain your questions."

"I appreciate that," Kathy said with a thankful nod. "Before I get to those questions, I'd like to know more about the visitor you had yesterday."

"*Visitors.*"

She uncrossed her legs and leaned forward. "What?"

"*Plural.*"

"I thought Detective Erikson told me you had *one* visitor?"

"I told the detective," he nodded at Steve, "that a man knocked on my door and introduced himself as FBI agent John Smith. Your partner never asked if there was anyone with him."

Kathy's lips pulled into a tight grin. "Okay, then. I'll ask the question. Were any other persons with the man who approached you?"

"Yes, ma'am. There were two younger men in the vehicle."

"What do you mean...younger?"

Danny pointed to the front door. "The guy on my porch claiming to be a federal agent was in his sixties. The two guys in the black Chevy Tahoe were in their mid-thirties."

"Did you recognize any of these men?"

"I did not. The two men in the car were ex-military or law enforcement."

Kathy crossed her arms. "How do you know that?"

"I just know."

"So, the two younger men never exited the vehicle?"

"That's correct."

"Did the gentleman on your porch show any official identification?"

"I asked him for identification, but it wouldn't matter if he showed it to me."

She leaned forward, palms on her thighs. "What do you mean?"

"FBI Special Agents have a mandatory retirement age of fifty-seven, ma'am. He was well over the forced retirement age."

"Did he threaten you at all? Were you ever afraid of him?"

Danny grinned. "The only thing I'm afraid of is me."

"Wait," I interrupted. "Danny, you said the two younger men were in a black SUV?"

"No, sir. I said they were in a black Chevy Tahoe."

I leaned toward Kathy and whispered that it could have

been the same vehicle we saw last night across the road from our house. She acknowledged with a nod and continued with her conversation.

"So, Danny, the alleged FBI agent and the two younger men simply left your house causing no trouble?"

"That's correct, ma'am."

"We spoke to your brother Doug earlier this morning. He didn't seem to be very approachable."

"He's a dick."

Steve and I chuckled. Kathy did not and said, "He may very well be, Danny. He was extremely reluctant to speak with us. Can you think of any reason he might not want to answer our questions?"

"It's just the way he's wired. He's been different since we were kids. Doug and my father never got along. I haven't spoken to my brother in decades. He never seemed to get along with *anybody* and was constantly in trouble."

"I'm sorry to hear that."

"It's not your problem, ma'am."

"Let's talk about the reason we asked to speak with you. I understand you have your father's business records. Is that correct?"

Danny threw a thumb over his left shoulder. "Yes, ma'am. I have a few boxes of his stuff in the garage. I haven't looked through it since he passed. Didn't give it much thought back then, either."

"How did your father die?"

"Massive heart attack."

"Is your mother still alive? Eve, right?"

"That's correct, ma'am. And no, unfortunately, after dad passed, mom went into a deep depression. After losing my father, she packed her belongings and moved to Poland. Her sister, Irene, lived there. Mom lived abroad for less than a year before she died. Natural causes, they said. It happened quickly. My biggest regret is not finding the time to visit with her, you know, in Poland."

We nodded. Danny stood and summoned us to the garage door at the far end of the kitchen. "You won't need your shoes," he bragged. "The garage is spotless."

We passed Ronald Reagan, entered the kitchen, and continued past an elegant, handcrafted oak table. When I asked, Danny said the table was a wedding gift from his father. "It lasted forty years longer than my marriage," he laughed.

We entered the garage and stepped down twice. The floor was spotless, clean, and professionally sealed with a glossy beige epoxy coating. I had garage envy. There were two vehicles inside. An F-150 truck, similar to my loaner, white, sat nearest the entry door. A spectacular, yellow, antique rag-top convertible was on the far side.

"Wow, Danny!" I pumped my finger. "What is that? It's beautiful."

"That, my friend, was my father's favorite car. It's a 1934 Lincoln K-series Roadster. Believe it or not, it has less than five thousand miles. Dad only drove it for a couple of years before storing it at his shop. He gave it to me a few years before he passed." Then he pointed to three old Stroh's beer cases on the floor along the back wall. "Here are the business records you're looking for."

Kathy cocked her head. "You keep them in beer boxes?"

"What difference does it make where I keep them, ma'am? You should be happy I still have them. I've already told you I'm nostalgic. It's the only reason I haven't thrown them out."

"I apologize for the insensitive comment, and yes, I'm glad you are nostalgic, Danny. They may have some value to our case."

"They have no value to me anymore. You can take those with you. I don't want them back. That's the deal."

Kathy's eyes rounded. "Are you sure you don't want them back? Even for nostalgic reasons?"

"No, ma'am. After you complete your research, please have them disposed of. My father left me a sizable inheritance, that beautiful yellow Roadster, and his revolver. I have enough nostalgia to last me for the rest of my life. These papers won't be missed."

I exchanged glances with Kathy and Steve.

"Your father left you a revolver?" Kathy asked.

"Yes, ma'am."

"May I see it?"

He shrugged. "It's in the attic. I haven't even thought about it for decades. It's not registered, you know. I have never fired it. It's one of those sentimental things."

"I understand. As we explained earlier, there were two murders within forty-eight hours in 1935. The gun may be involved, and it may not be. If it is, it could help us solve one, if not both, murders."

He gazed toward the yellow convertible. "Do you think my father actually killed someone?"

Kathy shrugged. "We won't know until I run a few tests. Do you believe your father could use the gun on another person?"

"He was a gentleman, ma'am, with a temper. That didn't

sound good, did it?" Danny's eyes were downcast. His shoulders relaxed as he let out a long exhale. "My father had some interesting friends. You might not believe me if I told you about the people I've met at our family dinner table. It was an exciting childhood, for sure. Let me say this. I know my father better than anybody, and if he used a gun on another person, they deserved it."

He stood between the F-150 and the Roadster and pulled on the white nylon string attached to the attic ladder. It opened with a loud squeak. He stepped up, reached for the light switch above the ceiling, and disappeared. Minutes later, we watched him descend the ladder, holding a dark brown leather bag in his hands. Jumping from the bottom step, he turned and strolled towards us.

"The gun is in the bag," he said, handing it to Kathy.

"Whose bag is this?" she asked. "Do you know where your father got it?"

"No idea."

Branded on the front of the leather bag were the official FBI seal and the number 316. Kathy unbuckled the weathered straps and gazed inside. Reaching into her jacket pocket, she pulled out a pair of nitrile gloves. Kathy reached into the bag and pulled out a shiny stainless-steel revolver. With the gun pointed in a safe direction, she scrutinized it.

"You've never fired this gun, Danny?"

"No, ma'am."

"There's a spent cartridge in the cylinder."

Steve peeked over her shoulder. "What kind of gun is it?"

"It's a six-shot revolver. Hold on." She punched the information into her phone. "It's a Smith and Wesson.357

revolver, Model 19. According to the serial number, it's an early model, first released in 1935."

Danny's face tensed. "So, what does this mean?"

Kathy placed the weapon in the leather bag and turned to Danny. "I'll take the gun with me and perform a fingerprint and ballistics background check."

"What if I don't like the results of your findings?"

"I follow the evidence, Danny. I don't have an agenda."

"*C'est comme ça,*" he replied.

"What does that mean?"

"It's French, ma'am. It means, '*It is what it is.*'"

CHAPTER TWENTY TWO

Present Day - Wednesday, November 3

KATHY THANKED DANNY GONYEA FOR HIS TIME AND HELD OUT her business card. "Call me anytime. If there's something you think might be important, I'd like to know about it."

"Sounds good, ma'am. Let me know how the investigation turns out. Keep the papers. Bring Dad's gun back."

Kathy assured him she would return it. We exchanged a few more pleasantries and said our goodbyes. We drove slowly past the newer homes with manicured lawns and headed for the freeway. Antique beer boxes and a dark brown leather briefcase were in the back of the Explorer.

Kathy glanced in the rearview mirror. "Are you heading back to the store, Rick?"

"Yes. I'm going to spend a few more hours with Paulie. We'll close the store and see you at tonight's going-away party."

They dropped me off at my truck on their way to the MSP offices in Lansing. I headed south and cranked up the radio. The Tom Petty channel played one of my favorite tunes. I banged on the steering wheel and sang along.

BACK AT my hardware store, the rest of the afternoon breezed by like grade school memories. After the last customer signed their credit card receipt and the doors were locked, I climbed into my truck, fired it up, and shouted out the driver's window, "Are you following me, Paulie?"

He beamed. "You betcha, boss. I'll be riding your bumper."

In typical Brewster fashion, two street-side parking spaces were reserved with orange construction cones near the front entrance of the Social Club. I pulled into the first open space and heard Paulie's brakes squeak as he slid behind me. I jumped out and walked toward him as he exited his vehicle.

We hugged.

"Thanks, boss. This is awesome, man."

"No problem, buddy. Let's go share a few adult beverages with your friends. I'm looking forward to your postcards."

I followed him into the vestibule, and we continued straight—to the main restaurant. A few dozen people gathered around the reserved tables. They waved and clapped as we entered. Against the far wall were three long tables. The middle table held the main course—chicken, glazed salmon, BBQ ribs, mashed potatoes, two styles of rice, and a colorful blend of mixed vegetables. Chilling on a bed of ice, to the left were a couple of salad options, shrimp, and fruit. I saw Dina and Jo taking inventory at the dessert table on the right.

Paulie mingled, laughed, and chatted with friends. I grabbed a large plate of food and spotted Kathy sitting with Brewster and Scruggs. I shuffled in their direction and took a seat next to Brewster, across from Kathy.

She leaned forward. Her voice lowered. "I have a couple of things to share with you guys." We leaned in. "The gun we picked up from Danny's house did not match any ballistics in the national database. That's disappointing news. But, since we're in party mode tonight, I won't let *that* news bring me down. So, here's the good news, and I mean—great news. I received a call from Gary King this afternoon." She paused with a smile.

Brewster tipped his beer towards Kathy. "Well, what did he have to say?"

Kathy's face glowed. "After Gary finished rambling about the cut, clarity, color, shape, and size of the diamonds, he gave me a rough appraisal." Kathy raised her wineglass. "Gentlemen, we have a dozen two carat round brilliant cut diamonds. They are worth between twenty-five and thirty-five thousand dollars each in the current retail market. Gary was quite impressed and said they could be worth maybe even half a million dollars."

Our conversation was interrupted as Ward, Marianne, and another worker approached the table, each carrying a guitar and a stand. They set them down in an open space between the dining room tables, motioning to Scruggs and me. Paulie could smell the neck oil of a guitar from a mile away. He hustled in our direction.

The three of us slid our chairs into a circle, facing each other. Together for the first time in a long time, we performed an extended acoustic set. The crowd loved it. We hadn't played together in over a year. Tonight, something clicked. The sounds from the instruments reverberated throughout the restaurant. Our vocals harmonized better than I expected. Several patrons walked over to listen, and soon, it was no longer a private party. We finished our set with a resonating power chord and placed the instruments in their stands.

Paulie was surrounded by his fans, and he soaked up the adoration.

Scruggs walked away to join his wife, Jo. She introduced him to her new friends. I was on my way to the bar when Kathy flanked me. She grabbed me by the elbow and pulled me aside.

"We need to talk," she whispered in my ear. "Sarah is in the hospital. She's unconscious and in pretty bad shape."

"Who's Sarah?"

Kathy barked softly, "Sarah Owens, the reporter *chick* from the newspaper?"

"Fucking serious?"

"Watch your language," she scolded me and then turned her head to ensure no one else was within earshot.

I stepped closer. "Sorry, babe. What the hell happened?"

Kathy had received a call from a colleague. Sarah's neighbor called the police. Said he heard yelling and screaming coming from her house and became concerned. After he hung up the phone with the police, he checked on her. The front door was open. He walked in and found her lying on the living room floor. Thankfully, he's a nurse and kept the bleeding under control until the ambulance arrived.

"Will she be alright?" I asked.

"I don't know. I'm heading to the hospital now. Steve and Kenny have been notified, and they're on the way to interview her neighbor."

"I'll go with you."

She waved me off. "You stay here. Enjoy your time with Paulie. There's nothing you can do at the hospital."

I glanced back at the table. "Does Brewster know?"

She followed my eyes. "Nope. You can fill Bob and Dan

in after I leave. Let's try keeping the chatter to a minimum."

I walked back to the crowd and whispered to the guys. We slipped away and followed Brewster to his office.

I THREW my hands in the air. "That's all I know, man."

Brewster growled. "Is she married? Does she have a boyfriend? What the hell happened?"

"I told you. That's all I know. Kathy is headed to the hospital. Said she'd call me when there's more information. Steve and Kenny are on their way to interview her neighbor."

Brewster wasn't satisfied and pulled out his cell phone. We heard Kenny's voice through the speaker.

"What's up, Brewster?"

"I just found out about the reporter being attacked. What's going on?"

"I don't know yet," Kenny said. "I'm just pulling up to the scene. Dunville Police are on sight. Looks like officers Carter and Dean are both here. Let me have a chat with them."

Brewster paced the floor. "Will you call me as soon as you know something?"

"Of course. As soon as I have any information, I'll call you."

We rejoined the celebration in the dining area, where a growing crowd applauded. Paulie continued entertaining with classic songs and storytelling. A Gibson guitar rested on his right knee. He sounded great, and I knew his upcoming tour would be a huge success.

Around midnight, the party thinned. Our guest of honor was not a drinker. It wasn't what he did. Tonight was the exception. He waddled sideways from the dessert table with something chocolate in his hands. I slid a chair out for him, and he fell into it. A dark brown substance was stuck between his two front teeth.

"This was a great night, Rick," he slurred, stretching out the word "great."

I patted him on the back. "I'm glad you enjoyed it, buddy. I'll miss you."

"How did our guitars end up here?" he mumbled, spitting a few chunks of a brownie on the white table covering. His blue and white aloha shirt was speckled with an uncomplimentary color.

"You can thank Scruggs for that," I smiled. "He brought the guitars with him today during his lunch break."

"How did he get *my* guitar?"

"You never lock your doors, dumb ass. We all know that."

"Oh. Okay. That's cool. I should get going. What time is it? Where are my keys?"

Scruggs was already at my side. We each grabbed an elbow and picked Paulie up from the chair, guiding him to the front door. There were still enough people in the restaurant to create loud applause as he stumbled towards the vestibule. Paulie attempted a graceful bow, which sparked laughter from the small crowd.

We struggled to get Paulie belted into my passenger seat. Scruggs hopped into the Equinox and followed me. We dropped Paulie at his house, made sure he was comfortable, and headed back to the Social Club. It was nearly 1:00 a.m., and the crowd had thinned. I checked my phone. No calls or texts from Kathy. I looked across the bar at Brewster. "Any news yet?"

He shook his head. "Maybe we should drive over there."

"Nope, it'll be a shit show," I advised. "We should stay put and wait. How about grabbing me a cold beer?"

"I'll have a Corona with a lime slice." Scruggs laughed.

I furrowed my brow. "That's how all of this shit started!"

The three of us laughed, taking our minds off the news about Sarah, if only briefly.

My phone rang. I answered a call from Kathy.

"Hey, babe," I said. "Talk to me. I've got you on speakerphone. I'm at the bar with Brewster and Scruggs."

Kathy said there wasn't much to share. No good news. No bad news. It was a waiting game. She told us that Sarah had swelling on her brain—minor. She had been placed in an induced coma for precautionary reasons.

"The next twenty-four hours are critical," Kathy continued. "For now, she's in good hands."

"That's terrible. Have you heard anythi—"

"Hold on," Kathy interrupted me. "Steve is calling me. I'll bring him into our conversation?"

Seconds later, Kathy was back. "Steve, I'm on the phone with Rick. He's with Bob and Dan at the club. You are now joining our conversation. What news do you have for us?"

"They're still canvassing the neighborhood. We're hoping one of Sarah's neighbors had a video doorbell camera. Maybe we could get lucky for a change. Shit's getting weird around here."

I drained my beer. "What do you mean?"

"This is off the record, right? So, I spoke with Peter Green. He's the neighbor who called the police. According to the paramedics I spoke with, Peter was a nurse and probably saved Sarah's life. Said he heard loud noises coming from her house at seven o'clock. Mr. Green was sure of the time because his favorite news program had ended. He pulled the curtains on the window facing her house and watched for a few minutes. According to what he told the deputies, he went to the kitchen to wash the dishes. Afterward, heading to the bathroom to brush his teeth, he said the noise grew louder. Swears he heard a female voice screaming. Rushing to the front door, he stepped onto the porch and saw two men dressed in dark clothing hurrying across her front yard."

Kathy asked if Peter Green could identify the men. Steve said no, not really—it was already dark, but Mr. Green confirmed the SUV had a Michigan license plate—the one with the image of the Mackinac Bridge on it. And, he said, the assailants drove the same model car as he drove. A Chevy Tahoe.

"What color?" Kathy asked.

"It was black. Mr. Green's is white."

Steve said. "How the hell does a reporter fit into this story?"

I let out a noticeable grunt. "Ever since we found that coin at Brewster's place, weird shit has been happening. Yesterday morning, a black SUV was in my hardware store parking lot. Last night, when everyone was leaving the meeting at our house, we saw a dark SUV pulling out of the side street. And, at our meeting this morning in River Rouge, Danny Gonyea told us that the *supposed* FBI agent who knocked on his door was driving a black Chevy Tahoe."

"How is the reporter involved?" Scruggs asked.

"She released a detailed interview with Brewster and me in today's newspaper," I snarled. "It's too much of a coincidence. The same day her article gets published, she gets beaten up by two guys in dark clothing? The gold coin *has* to be the connection."

"What I don't understand," Brewster countered, "is why anybody would go through this much trouble. Seriously? Hurting people over a coin that's worth, what—five grand? That's what Sarah said in her story today. Five grand. That's nothing!"

"Well, there has to be another angle," I said. "What about that guy who was at the Social Club on Saturday? Stuart Applegate. The guy who most likely sold his bullshit story to the Channel 6 News team. What about him?"

"I don't know, Rick," Brewster sounded skeptical. "Let's run through the timeline again."

"Not tonight, man. I'm wiped out. My head feels like someone played tetherball with it. Kathy, are you on your way home?"

"I'll be leaving shortly. I'm waiting to speak with the doctor."

I slid my empty bottle forward. "Okay. I'm heading home."

"Don't wait up for me," she said. "Guys, let's sleep on this tonight and regroup tomorrow. I'll call everyone in the morning to set up a convenient time to chat."

Steve and Kathy signed off, and the call ended.

It was nearly two o'clock in the morning, and I needed sleep. I heard Brewster say good night to his cleaning crew. He trailed us out the back door. Scruggs and I strolled to our vehicles and headed home.

Brewster's headlights followed us out of the parking lot.

CHAPTER TWENTY THREE

Detroit, Michigan - 1935
'One Last Drink'

BY ANY MEASURE, LAST NIGHT'S GRAND OPENING WAS A COMPLETE success. The latest addition to Detroit's growing list of nightclubs instantly became *the place to be*. Sam Durocher had finally been rewarded for all his hard work. Those fortunate enough to gain access inside the club were instantly elevated to a higher social status. Those lucky enough to infiltrate the outside perimeter of cops and security thugs spent the evening collecting photos and autographs of famous people they'd only seen or read about in gossip magazines. Movie stars, sports heroes, and other distinguished celebrities paused outside the Starlight Lounge, smiled, and waved their hands high. Cameras flashed. Adoring fans shrieked with excitement. The little people loved it.

Today, Sam had a headache. He had only recently climbed into bed when his wife, Lilley, woke him for a phone call at two in the afternoon.

"Whoever it is, tell them I'll call back," He mumbled into his pillow.

Lilley apologized for the interruption and whispered, "I'm sorry, honey. He won't take no for an answer. He calls me every fifteen minutes. Maybe it's important?"

Sam crawled out of bed, threw on a robe, and made his way to the living room. He picked up the phone from the end table and fell back into his favorite chair, rubbing his eyes.

"Who is this?" he barked.

"I think I'm being followed."

"Gonyea?"

"Yes, it's me, Sam. We need to meet. I need to know what's going on. I feel like I'm on the outside, looking in."

"Well, you're *not* an insider, David, so get over it. Why the hell are you bothering my wife and me? Jesus Christ, I'm trying to rest."

"The FBI won't stop their investigation because you need rest, Sam. Especially the agent that interviewed me, the dead agent's partner. This is personal for him. He worries me. I think I'm being tailed."

Sam stood from his chair and kicked the matching ottoman. "I'm not talking to you anymore over the phone. If you must meet me, I'll be at my club when it closes tonight."

"Can we meet earlier, Sam? I mean, we could do lunch or dinner."

"That's your option—*your only option*. Meet me after the lounge closes, or shut up and leave me alone." He slammed the phone down.

Lilley turned her head and shuffled towards the study.

Sam stormed to the bedroom.

DAVID ROLLED over and faced his beautiful wife. His deep-set brown eyes stared affectionately into her blue eyes, which didn't seem as bright at the moment. He listened to her pleas not to leave the house, but he had already decided.

"It'll be fine," David told her. "I just need to clear up a couple of things. I need to speak with someone about an important business matter."

Eve didn't look pleased. "Nothing good can come from

a meeting at this time of the night."

David promised the meeting wouldn't take long and he would be home as quickly as possible. "I'll be snuggled up in bed with you soon," he said. "Everything is going to be fine."

David watched Eve pull back the quilted bedspread and swing her long legs over the side. "I can't sleep. I'll go with you," she said.

David hopped from the bed and pulled her close. He planted his hands on her cheeks and gently kissed her lips. "This is something I need to do, Eve," he sighed. "Alone."

He watched Eve remove her robe from the hook on the back of the bedroom door. She wrapped it tightly around her body and glanced back at him with a sad smile. David's eyes felt moist as she gracefully exited the second-floor master bedroom.

She deserved answers.

David stepped into a clean pair of pants, tied his shoes, and buttoned a freshly starched shirt. He slid a shoebox from the shelf inside the walk-in closet. Replacing the box, he tucked a shiny revolver into his waistband. A blue blazer covered the bulge on his right hip. Within minutes, he was on the road.

He parked his vehicle on Park Avenue and walked three blocks east. A half-block later, he turned left on St. Aubin Street, where he walked for another block and then turned right, down a dark alley, heading for the rear entrance of the Starlight Lounge

SAM DUROCHER opened the door to the annoying knocks and wondered why David was so late. Sam stepped into the dark alley, glancing past David in both directions. "Where's your car?" he asked.

"I walked."

"From your house?"

"Of course not. I told you: I think I'm being followed. I didn't want my car seen anywhere near your business, so I walked for a few blocks."

"That explains why you're late. I'm just about wrapped up here, so you better get to your point quickly. You're getting on my fucking nerves."

Sam waved his hand forward, and David entered the building. Sam took another couple of looks around the alley, concerned that David might not be as paranoid as he thought. They walked in silence to the main room, stopping near the bar.

"I want the camera," David said, pointing at the dark brown leather bag sitting on the mahogany bar top. A large cotton money bag with the First National Bank of Detroit logo sat beside it.

Sam turned, stepping closer to David, blocking his view of the leather briefcase. "Is that what this is about?" he laughed. "I thought you might try to rob me. There's a lot of cash in that bank deposit bag."

David stepped back. "You can keep your fucking money, Sam. I want the camera that's in the other bag."

Sam stepped closer. "What the hell are you worried about, Gonyea? Haven't you figured it out yet? If you go down, I go down, and guess what? I'm not going down, not now — not ever!"

David shook his head. "I had nothing to do with your gambling friends. I certainly had nothing to do with the murder of an FBI agent. The camera is what I want. There are photos of you and me meeting in the alley on the night of the murder. I don't want the cops thinking I had any part in that."

"I don't trust you, David," Sam said. "That's why you'll never get the camera. It's the only leverage I have to keep you from running to the cops and ratting on me."

Sam turned away and meandered behind the bar. He pulled an expensive Bourbon from the top shelf and observed David's movements in the large mirror. "Would you like a drink?"

David shuffled his feet and fidgeted with his hands. His eyes were fixated on the mahogany countertop and the brown leather briefcase. He noticed Sam's reflection staring back at him in the mirror and staggered a few steps backward. David's hands were shaking. His blood boiled. He ran his fingers through his coarse black hair.

Sam spun around slowly, smiled, and placed his hands on the bar. "Your time is up, Gonyea. You can drive home, walk home, or fly home—I don't care. Get out of my lounge and never bring this subject up again. Do you understand?"

"But, I really nee—"

"And lose my phone number!" Sam screamed. "Never call me at home again!"

David Gonyea was startled. His heart raced.

Sam grinned at David's uncomfortable state. *My karma is good right now.* Earlier, he had handled the federal agency brilliantly. He smiled, knowing the gangsters and politicians were satisfied. This troublesome piece of shit, David Gonyea, was the weak link in his alibi, and now, he had put him in his place.

It was a good day.

With his belly pressed against the mahogany bar, Sam

glanced right towards the leather briefcase, which was within his reach. In his peripheral vision, he caught the angry look on David's face and laughed. "Dumb fuck", he mumbled, loud enough to be heard.

Grinning, Sam turned away from David, placed a gray Fedora on his head, lit a cigarette, and reached for his glass of Bourbon. One last drink, he thought.

One last drink.

CHAPTER TWENTY FOUR

Present Day - Thursday, November 4

KATHY REACHED FOR TWO COFFEE MUGS AND SET THEM ON the counter. I fumbled through an upper cabinet, ignoring the vitamins, and grabbed the bottle of Advil.

I turned to give her a tight hug. "What time did you get home last night?"

"A little after three. You were sound asleep."

"I tried to wait up," I lied.

"No worries. It was a long night for everyone."

"How is Sarah?"

"No change. She took a hell of a beating. I'm told she must have fought back pretty hard. There were scratches on her arms and blood under her fingernails."

"What the hell is wrong with people?" I asked rhetorically, then popped two oval gel capsules in my mouth and swallowed them without water. I nearly choked.

The scent of Caribbean blend coffee filled my nostrils before the brownish-black liquid filled the carafe, so I dawdled to the living room with an empty cup and turned on the television. After a short, useless weather report, the Channel 6 News anchorwoman introduced Jessica Logan, the on-the-scene reporter. Bright lights illuminated her serious facial expression as she stood on the well-manicured lawn of a modern mid-century bungalow. In the background, yellow police tape stretched across a small cement porch. Damage to the front door was noticeable. The camera panned the neighborhood as the reporter shared the story of a brutal attack on Sarah Owens. Jessica Logan concluded it was random — an unfortunate wrong place, wrong time, crime of opportunity. An act of violence against women. She hadn't considered the discovery of a gold coin in the Social Club bar last Saturday, and the subsequent front-page report that Sarah Owens had filed in yesterday's *Dispatch* newspaper was connected to her beating.

The reporter's lack of reasoning disappointed me in some respect and pleased me on another level. For the time being, the discovery of the gold coin would be placed on the media's back-burner. There were two attackers on the loose, and that would take precedence. It's the way the news cycle worked.

The video on the television screen switched to a recorded interview with Sarah's neighbor, Peter Green. He provided a detailed description of Sarah's two assailants and their vehicle.

"Two men, six feet tall, dressed in black and driving a black Chevy Tahoe," Jessica Logan repeated to her audience. "These men should be considered armed and dangerous. If you see them, do not approach them. Call 911 immediately."

I punched a button on the remote, and the screen went dark. Back in the kitchen, Kathy met me near the center island with a full carafe in hand. I held out my thermal mug like a Halloween trick-or-treater. I blew the steam from the top of my cup and watched Kathy shuffle to the blender, where she added milk, protein powder, and fresh fruit. I grabbed the newspaper from the kitchen island, sat at the table, and spoke over the noise from the blender.

"Have you spoken with Ron yet?" I asked.

The blender whirled. "I'm playing phone tag with him," she said. "He's supposed to call me this morning. By the way, I'm going to the hospital today. I need to check on Sarah's condition."

"Let me know how she's doing," I yelled, not realizing the blender had stopped.

Kathy laughed, shuffled in my direction for a quick kiss, and headed for the shower. I spent a few minutes catching up on the news from the *Dunville Dispatch* and checked my phone for an accurate weather forecast. My phone vibrated.

"What's up, FBI guy?"

"Hey, tool man." Ron laughed.

"How's the weather in Atlanta, brother?" I asked.

"It's hot and sticky, man. Hot and sticky. I tried calling Kathy. It went right to voicemail."

"Yeah, she's in the shower."

"Then why are you answering your phone?" Ron laughed, never allowing space for a smartass rebuttal. "Let Kathy know I received the courier delivery this morning. I'll process the revolver through proper channels and do my best to keep the hype down, but I can't guarantee it won't go public."

"I appreciate that. By the way," I paused because I didn't exactly know what I would say next, but I had to say something, so I blurted, "The saga continues."

"Now what?" The frustration in Ron's voice was evident.

I let him know about yesterday's meeting with Danny Gonyea. Reminded him of the raid at the Starlight Lounge, the murder of a federal agent, and the subsequent murder of the lounge owner. He reminded me he already knew everything I had just said. "What the hell are you trying to say? Spit it out, for God's sake."

So I did. I spit it out. "When we met with Danny Gonyea, he told us his father had left him a gun. A revolver. Kathy examined it. Said there was a spent cartridge in the cylinder. She took it to her office and ran a ballistics and fingerprint test. There were no matches in the national database."

"That's the second gun you've found."

I wasn't sure if that was a question or a statement, but it caught me off guard. Ron was right. What were the odds? I've never found a winning lottery ticket lying on the sidewalk. I've never been fortunate enough to greet Ed McMahon knocking on my front door with a Clearing House Sweepstake check in his hands. Maybe I've seen a four-leaf clover, but I can't remember when or where. Yet, I have found or helped to find two antique revolvers in the past week.

Two murder weapons?

Maybe.

What the hell?

"Yeah, I know. Weird, right?" I cleared my throat.

Ron didn't think it was weird. He thought *I* was weird, but that wasn't new. He'd always known that. I knew what Kathy wanted to ask Ron, and since I was acting as a proxy CSI agent, I asked if he could get us the bullet that killed Sam Durocher in Detroit in 1935.

Ron spoke in a lower tone, with a slower tempo. "Do you believe the gun you got from this Gonyea fellow is involved in the murder of a Mr. Sam Durocher?"

"You're taking notes, aren't you?"

"Answer the question."

"All I know is Kathy has her suspicions, and that's good enough for me," I said.

"Ok, so here's the deal," he replied quickly. "I'm looking at the copy of the report I provided for your wife. The Mintern report. Have Kathy call me and request the physical evidence for the murder of the lounge owner, Sam Durocher, and I'll get it approved. I expect a follow-up report from her, either confirming or denying the gun in question was involved in the murder. Understood?"

"I'll have her call you. Thanks, FBI guy."

"Whatever, tool man. Stay safe."

I ended the call, placed my phone on the counter, and topped off my coffee mug. I checked my watch. There was still time before I needed to leave for work. Thankfully, the Advil had kicked in.

"What?" I heard Kathy yell from the hallway.

I hustled in her direction. "Is everything all right, Kath?"

She raised her left arm and extended her "hold on a minute" index finger. The phone was tight to her ear. I couldn't hear anything she said, and she wasn't saying much, just listening intently. I sipped my coffee and studied her facial expressions. Her face didn't show horror, only concern. Nobody had died; I was pretty sure of that. She thanked the person and ended the call.

"Brewster's restaurant has been robbed."

CHAPTER TWENTY FIVE

Present Day - Thursday, November 4

KATHY SLID HER PHONE INTO THE POCKET OF HER ROBE AND leaned in for a hug. She told me it was Kenny who had called.

"Brewster's restaurant has been robbed," she repeated. "Two of his cleaning crew employees were taken to the hospital."

"When did this happen?" I asked. "His place doesn't even open until ten."

"Kenny only briefed me. As soon as I get dressed, I'll head over there."

"I'm going with you."

She backed away from my hug and headed for the kitchen. "What about the store?"

"Shit, hold on."

I sent Paulie a text. Asked him when he and the band were heading for Chicago. Said he was packing his gear. The guys would pick him up around noon, and he didn't mind managing the store until I arrived. I asked him to provide Jim Anderson last-minute advice, and of course, he said, "No problem, boss."

Kathy headed to the bedroom to get dressed. I took a two-minute shower, threw on clean jeans, and slipped on a pair of boots and another favorite flannel shirt. I press checked my Glock and placed it into the leather holster for an appendix carry.

Minutes later, she pressed the accelerator hard, and we were on site in record time. There were a few police cars parked near the club's rear entrance. Brewster's Navigator was parked next to Kenny's SUV. I followed Kathy to the back door of the building, where Brewster paced the cement patio.

She shook his hand and asked what had happened. He waved us forward. We followed him inside, not stopping or speaking until we reached his office. Glass and a broken frame on the floor in the corner of his office caught my attention.

Brewster sat in his plush, high-back leather chair. Kathy sat across from him and pulled out her spiral notebook. I saddled up next to her. Kenny was on our heels, pulled another chair from the corner of the office.

"At around six-thirty this morning," Brewster said, "a jogger was on Main Street and took a shortcut through my parking lot. When he noticed the back door of the Social Club was ajar, he called inside. With no response, he became concerned and called the police.

"Kenny, you know more details than I do. Can you finish this for me?" Brewster exhaled a long, slow breath, hung his head, and stared at the floor.

Kenny nodded. "No worries, man. Here's what I know. Officer Owen Dean pulled into the parking lot and notified command of his position. Entering the open door, he found one male and one female tied and gagged. After requesting backup and an ambulance, he checked on the injured victims. They had been smacked around and hogtied to one of the carved legs behind the bar. When backup arrived, the officers cleared the building. Dean kept vigil over the two wounded individuals until paramedics arrived. Let's see here. Logan and Eva, that's their names. They had been cleaning the club for the past ten years. There was no one else inside the building. Found something strange, though. You won't believe it. Check *this* out."

In the corner of Brewster's office, behind his desk, was a small room, modest, like a walk-in closet. Near the threshold, on the floor, was a large black and white rendering of the Social Club. Kenny stood from his chair, took a few short steps to his left, and pointed. The glass had been smashed, the frame destroyed.

Kathy surveyed the damage. "What happened here?"

"See that large hole in the wall?" Kenny pumped his finger.

"How could we miss it?" Kathy said. "Why is part of the wall missing?"

"There used to be a safe inside that wall. That damaged photo covered it."

Kathy tossed up her hands. "Instead of breaking into the safe, they simply cut out a piece of the wall?"

"Yep," Kenny nodded. "They took that piece of the wall with them. Somebody *really* wanted that safe. Two guys gained access to the building, assaulted the cleaning crew employees, and cut the safe out of the wall. They left a reciprocating saw behind. We'll run it for fingerprints, but I doubt we'll find any."

"Why are these walls so thick?" Kathy asked.

"It was an architectural design for sound abatement. The walls in this office are three times as thick as a typical wall. Even the ceiling has two layers of drywall.

"The guys with the Sawzall must have been pissed," I

said.

"I imagine they didn't expect the walls to be so thick," Kenny gave a nervous chuckle. "Anyway, Brewster gave us permission to access the video camera footage from the club. We've already contacted his security company and are waiting for the files to be transmitted." He scratched his chin. "Wonder how they knew about the safe behind the photo?"

Kathy sighed. "My guess is they knew about the safe from Sarah. She must have been interrogated by her attackers and told them about the safe."

"Sarah knew the safe was there," I confirmed. "She and I watched Brewster open it during our interview for her newspaper article."

Kathy peeked outside the room and whispered, "Did Bob tell you what was inside the safe, Kenny?"

"Said there was a substantial amount of cash, a few watches, some jewelry, and the gold coin in the wall safe."

Kathy said she wanted to take the lead on the investigation. Kenny nodded and said he'd already spoken with the Dunville Police. "Chief Adams was fine taking a back seat to the State Police as long as he was kept abreast of our progress," Kenny confirmed.

When asked where they took the two injured employees, Kenny said they had been transported to Tecumseh Hospital as a precaution, but the paramedics said their injuries were minor. "At least their physical injuries." He winced.

"Thanks," Kathy said. "I'll head to the hospital and get their statements. Do you want to ride with me?"

He nodded, stood, and waved his hand forward.

"I'm going to hang with Brewster for a while, guys," I said.

Kathy nodded. "That's fine. He probably needs some

quiet time. Don't overstay your welcome."

We left the small room and stopped at Brewster's desk. He was on the phone with Dina. I heard him tell her everything was fine, but it wasn't.

"Love you, too," he said, staring at his phone.

Kathy asked him a few more questions, taking notes. Ten minutes later, the Ford Explorer squealed from the parking lot with two pissed-off cops.

I SHUFFLED closer to Brewster and gave him a concerned stare, asking an obvious question. He lied and said he was fine. I knew better.

"I've been thinking," I said. "When we spoke last night, at Paulie's party after we found out about the attack on Sarah—wait a minute." I paused, turned toward the hallway, and pointed. "Let's step outside for some fresh air." I held out my palm.

We walked in silence through the break room and exited the rear door. Outside, on the cement patio, Brewster paused. He looked exhausted. His skin was ashen, eyes vacant, and his gait slow. His head fell back, resting on his neck, his mouth agape as he spent a quick minute staring at an overcast sky.

"Good call, Rick," he exhaled loudly. "I needed to get out of there. Fresh air feels good."

His equilibrium seemed uncertain. I stepped closer in case he needed help and guided him to the bench while cradling his right arm. He took a seat at the lacquered picnic table.

"That's not why I wanted us to leave your office," I said. Brewster's forehead furrowed with confusion. "I've tried to put the pieces of this puzzle together, and I've tossed and turned for nights trying to figure it out. Actually, I've been wracking my brain since Tuesday. Call it conspiratorial," I waved my arms wide. "Call it paranoia, but there is a common denominator I find very suspicious. Do you think Ward is awake yet?"

He gave me a quizzical stare. "I spoke with Ward this morning. He's already aware of what happened."

"I know, but I need to speak with him. What's his number?"

Brewster shared Ward's information. I added it to my contact list and called.

"Ward, this is Rick Cooper. I'm at the club with Brewster."

"This is terrible," Ward said.

"It is, but I have a question. I just sent you a couple photos. Pull them up on your phone and let me know if you've seen this guy before."

"What's this about?"

I was short with him. "Please, Ward. Humor me."

Waiting for the images to be magically transported, I glanced at Brewster. He listened to our speaker-phone conversation and sat up a little straighter. Curiosity filled his eyes.

"I'm looking at the photos," Ward said. "It's the fire marshal. What's this have to do with anything?"

I pounded my fist on the table. "I thought it might be. Thanks, Ward. I'll fill you in later."

I broke off the call and texted the photo to Paulie.

Is this a photo of the fire marshal you told me about?

Within a minute, he confirmed my suspicion with a

"thumbs up" emoji.

I slid the phone across the picnic table. "This guy has something to do with this, Brewster."

He stared at the photo and asked who it was. I sarcastically told him it sure wasn't a fire marshal.

"There are a few more images," I said. "Flip the screen to your left. Scruggs took these photos of the inspector who visited his shop yesterday. I just confirmed this is the same guy who was at my hardware store on Tuesday morning. Ward identified him as the mysterious inspector who visited your club."

He looked up from the phone. His eyes narrow. "Is that why you invited me outside?"

"Yup," I said, thumping my chest with a balled fist. "This time, I'm thinking like a cop." Then, ignoring his chuckle, I asked, "Do you think this fake fire marshal could have planted cameras or listening devices in our places of business?"

"There's only one way to find out." He slid my phone back to me, picked his phone up from the table, put it on speaker, and pressed a few buttons.

Steve Erikson answered softly. "I heard the news, Brewster. Kenny called me this morning. Anything I can do?"

"You know it, brother. I'll be sending you a few photos. I need you to run them through facial recognition."

"Not a problem. We're also reviewing the security camera video files that your security company emailed us."

Brewster stood up and paced the patio. His energy rebounded like he had just slammed a Red Bull.

"Perfect. I have another request. I need a few electronic surveillance sweeps. Can you bring an RF detector?"

"What the hell?"

CHAPTER TWENTY SIX

Detroit, Michigan - 1935
'What Did I Do?'

DAVID GONYEA DID NOT DRIVE DIRECTLY HOME FROM HIS parking space, blocks away from the Starlight Lounge. Instead, he raced his Lincoln Roadster to a large brick building that displayed his family name. Street lights illuminated the bright yellow convertible on Woodward Avenue, and for once, David wished the streets were crowded with other vehicles. At three o'clock in the morning, he imagined the lights getting brighter with every street lamp he passed. Passing the large sign that advertised his business, *Gonyea Custom Furniture*, he turned east to Montcalm Street and into the dark alley behind the building. Turning off the ignition, he promised himself that soon, very soon, he would park his eye-catching convertible in the garage and replace it with something less memorable. Black, he thought. Everyone has a black car.

David no longer wanted to stand out.

His head was on a swivel and not for the typical precautions that should have concerned him in Detroit's early morning hours. Street thugs and bums were the least of his problems. The door closed with a heavy clunk when he entered the building. The sound echoed through the expansive wood shop.

Racing to the front of the building, he peered out the large display window that faced Woodward Avenue. He looked in every direction, more than once. Every noise, every movement, every shadow startled him. His panicked disposition magnified his paranoia. Confident that no one had followed him, he turned away and hustled to his office.

Son of a bitch. What did I do?

Setting the dark brown leather briefcase on his desk, he removed six rolls of film. One by one, he pulled on the film and stripped them from their cartridges. Removing a pair of scissors from his top desk drawer, he cut the 35-millimeter strips into smaller pieces, knowing it was an unnecessary step. The overhead lights would have rendered the undeveloped film useless.

Why take any chances?

Placing the small pieces of film into a metal wastebasket at the side of his desk, he added a few crumpled up pieces of newspaper and tossed them in. He lit a match. The fire raged. Then he placed the film canisters on the floor, crushed them under the heel of his size eleven shoes, and added them to the fire. Almost instantly, they melted into an unrecognizable state.

A slight panic set in as thick clouds of black smoke filled his office. Hurrying to the wood shop, cussing to himself along the way, he returned with a heavy copper fire extinguisher. Pumping the handle, David sprayed the metal basket with a liquid jet to douse the flames. Ashes from the burnt film clippings flew into the air and gently floated to the ground, like the aftermath of a volcanic eruption. The foul odor of the burning plastic permeated the entire building.

Son of a bitch.

Cleaning up the mess to the best of his abilities, he wondered what else might go wrong. The cleaning company would not be back until the following Friday. Hopefully, he thought, five days from now, the odors from the fire won't be recognizable.

Pacing the hardwood floors in his office, David wiped the sweat from his brow and the tears from his eyes. He removed the camera from the leather briefcase and placed it on his desk. His hands trembled. His mind whirled. If Sam had just given him the damn camera, none of this would have happened. Sam would still be alive. David would not have turned the camera over to the police. He wasn't planning to turn Sam in, either. It didn't need to end like this, but now it was too late, and the evidence needed to disappear.

Opening the briefcase wider, the pungent smell of gunpowder burnt his nostrils. The soft glow of his desk lamp reflected off the shiny revolver that lay at the bottom of the bag. He removed the pistol and polished the heavy object with his cotton shirt, eliminating fingerprints. He returned it to the leather bag, buckled the straps, hung his head, and wiped the moisture from his eyes.

Shuffling to the corner of his office, he turned a large, silver tumbler left, right, then left again, stopping at the specific numbers only he and Eve knew. He twisted the chrome handle. The heavy steel rods clunked, and the large safe opened. David placed the dark brown leather briefcase deep in the darkness, shut the door, turned the handle left, spun the tumbler, and promised to never look at the shiny revolver again.

Yellow light from the street lamps cast eerie shadows through the front display window. David peered out for one last look at Woodward Avenue. A taxi drove by, then a patrol car.

Scurrying away from the large window, he made his way past his office towards the rear door through the large workshop. The burning smell of plastic permeated the building.

Tossing the camera on the passenger seat, he fired up the Roadster and headed south through the alley, then east on Columbia. At nearly four o'clock in the morning, the streets were mostly deserted.

Avoiding the main drags, weaving his way through dimly lit side roads, he stopped briefly in an alley behind a famous department store on Michigan Avenue. David pulled alongside the large dumpster, heaved the camera high in the air, watching it land inside, and headed for home.

CHAPTER TWENTY SEVEN
Present Day - Thursday, November 4

KATHY ANSWERED ON THE FIRST RING AND SAID SHE AND KENNY Erikson were at their offices in Lansing. When I asked, she told me Sarah was awake, groggy, and expected to make a full recovery.

"That's great news," I said with honest enthusiasm. "I'm still at the Social Club."

Brewster couldn't hear my phone conversation but smiled when I gave him a thumbs-up and whispered Sarah's name.

"I thought you were going to give him some space?" Kathy questioned.

"Things have changed," I said. "And there's more you should know. Brewster just sent some photos to you and Kenny. Steve already has them and will process the images through facial recognition. We're pretty certain the guy in the photo is one of the people from the mysterious black SUV."

"Really? How do you know?"

"Because I'm a talented reserve Police officer."

She chuckled. I thought I heard Kenny choke on whatever he was drinking.

"You can fill me in later," she said. "I'll check out the photos. Gotta go."

Click.

Brewster and I walked back inside the Social Club. The investigators were gathering evidence. He pulled each of them aside and whispered in their ears. I assumed he was telling them to keep the chatter to a minimum and only to speak freely outside. Their heads bobbed.

I let Brewster know I needed to be on my way. It was Paulie's last day, and he'd been kind enough to cover for me this morning. I couldn't keep him waiting.

"Tell Paulie good luck for me," he said, adding, "You're a good cop, buddy." We shook hands, and he gave me a pseudo guy hug. His compliment made me smile.

I told Brewster I'd be back for lunch, headed south, and called Scruggs, letting him know what was happening or what I thought was happening. Our conversation was short. He understood what I was saying and agreed not to have conversations inside his shop. I sent Paulie a text, letting him know I was on my way and watched for suspicious vehicles along the ride—especially any black Chevy Tahoe. I wasn't paranoid anymore; I was alert. Always be alert. That's what I'd been told.

The hardware parking lot was not crowded, and the traffic inside the store was sparse. I summoned the half-dozen employees to the break-room for a quick meeting. They gave Paulie hugs and wished him well. I thanked Jim Anderson for taking the reins while Paulie was away. Jim was excited. So was Paulie.

I gave Paulie a firm hug. "Be careful out there, brother. Have a blast on stage with those misfits, and don't get involved in anything besides music. Got it?"

Paulie shoved a fist pump in my direction, which I reciprocated. He threw his jacket over his shoulder and left the building.

Quack, Quack.

―

TODAY'S WEATHER was, again, unseasonably warm. The Channel 6 weather team smiled at me from the computer screen on my desk. The long-term Michigan weather forecast included colder temperatures and snow showers. "Possibly heavy snow," the weatherman warned.

Significant snowfalls weren't unusual for this time of year in Michigan. Still, many people redirected their brains to a hoarding mentality when any forecast included the words "winter weather advisory." Some prepared for the seasonal change like it was the first time it had ever happened.

My employees converted the seasonal inventory. Pallets of rock salt replaced fertilizer and mulch. Lawnmowers, garden tools, and patio furniture were placed outside near the front of the fenced-in area, where large, colorful signs and helium-filled balloons advertised reduced prices. In their place, snowblowers and various models of snow shovels lined the cement patio outside, near the entrance.

Mid-morning, my cell phone vibrated. It was Kathy. I headed for the rear delivery door, walked outside, and answered.

"Can everybody hear me?" She said.

"Yes" was heard multiple times.

"I had hoped we could meet in person this morning to review our notes. Obviously, that's not going to happen. Kenny and I are heading to St. Joe's to check on Sarah. Let's take a few minutes and see if we can't understand what's happening."

Steve interjected, "Just so you know, we were unsuccessful at gathering additional evidence on Sarah's attack through our neighborhood canvassing. A few driveway videos captured the black Chevy Tahoe leaving her house. Nothing else helped to identify the assailants or the license plate information."

"That's too bad," Kathy said. "What about that photo Bob sent you? Do you have any information on our alleged fire marshal?"

I heard Steve shuffle his notes. "I had a colleague enter the photo in the database. If we get a hit, we should have his information shortly. In the meantime, I've been reviewing last night's video surveillance at the Social Club, and here's what we've got." More paper shuffling. "The parking lot camera caught a dark blue Chevy Colorado pulling behind the building. It came into view immediately after Brewster drove away. It approached from the opposite end of the parking lot. Two masked men, dressed in dark clothing, knocked on the rear door of the club. When it opened, they aggressively assaulted the two employees and secured them to the heavy legs of the bar. The assailants kicked down Brewster's office door, cut out a section of the wall, carried it to the rear of the building, and tossed it into the dark blue pickup. We can assume they were professionals. Their total time on-site was less than fifteen minutes. I ran the license plate on the truck. It was registered to Hazel Kruk, a Dunville resident. She's an employee at a local accounting firm and reported her truck missing this morning. We've got a BOLO out on the vehicle."

Brewster asked, "How are Logan and Eva?"

"They're going to be fine, Bob," Kathy said. "Logan has a pretty good shiner. Eva had a few scratches on her face, but nothing serious or long-lasting, except maybe the trauma.

Logan said he heard knocking on the back door within seconds of you leaving. Assuming you had forgotten something, he opened it. Obviously, he now regrets it."

"He should know better."

"Listen, Bob," Kathy said. "He's been through enough. Don't make it any worse. I can guarantee it'll never happen again. He's learned a life lesson. Both said two men wearing dark clothing and ski masks forced their way into the building. Eva said Logan put up a fight and got punched pretty hard. When Eva tried to help, they subdued her quickly. The assailants zip-tied their hands to the bar, bound their legs, and placed gags over their mouths. They took their cell phones, smashed them with their boots, and tossed them into the bar sink. Both victims said the attackers knew exactly what they were doing. Neither of them could see what was happening in your office. They only heard voices echoing from the kitchen. We already know the loud noises they told us about were from the reciprocating saw that was left behind."

"When are they being released? I'll pick them up from the hospital and drive them home."

"Don't worry about that, Bob. Their discharge forms have already been processed. I have one of my detectives picking them up."

"Hey, Brewster," said Steve. "My team will continue to review the video files from your club. Maybe they'll find something I didn't see. Either way, I'll be heading your way in a few minutes and should be at your place within the hour. I'm bringing Bill Evans, our TSCM expert, with me—"

My ADD kicked into high gear as I stared at my phone. I had myself wrapped up in something I had never expected or experienced before. Listening devices may have been planted in Brewster's club? *What the hell?* Would they also find them in my hardware store or Scruggs's auto shop? What about our homes? I subconsciously patted my Glock and rejoined the conversation as Steve spoke.

"—Bill Evans is the head of our Technical Surveillance Countermeasures task force. He is an expert in counter-surveillance and will perform electronic sweeps. Everyone needs to understand that this is not like the movies. There are five primary categories of bugging devices. Depending on what they used—if they used anything—Bill might detect them in minutes, or it could take hours."

"Listen, guys," Kathy said. "If they planted listening devices, we don't know *who* they targeted or even *when* they began their surveillance. After we visit Sarah at the hospital, we'll visit Gary and Joan King at their store in Ann Arbor."

Brewster asked if Gary and Joan King were in danger. Kathy said she wasn't taking any chances and would have around-the-clock protection details assigned to their home and business.

"Undercover teams are on their way," Kathy said. "I want to speak with Gary and Joan personally. They need to know what's happening."

"Do you think they tapped our cell phones?" I asked.

Kathy asked if anyone had misplaced their phones or been without them in the past week. Negative was the reply from the team.

"Bill has already checked my phone," Steve confirmed. "I'll have him check everyone else's when we arrive. I don't believe our phones have been compromised."

After a few goodbyes, the conversation ended. Before

leaving the parking lot, I glanced around, suspicious of every vehicle. I left Jim Anderson in charge, and with one last glance in the rearview mirror, I was on my way to meet the lunch crowd.

CHAPTER TWENTY EIGHT

Present Day - Thursday, November 4

When I arrived, Steve's Charger was parked near the Social Club's rear entrance. A blue Ford Explorer had parked next to it, and although it looked like Kathy's, there was no damage to the rear door. I slipped into an empty parking space. It was almost noon, and I expected Scruggs to arrive any minute. This wouldn't be our typical lunch get-together.

Brewster, Steve, and a gentleman I had never seen before sat at the picnic table. They were in deep conversation. I ambled across a small grassy area, stepped onto the large cement pad, and approached with a subdued smile. Steve slid off the bench seat and made the introduction.

"Rick, meet Bill Evans."

My parents had taught me to never judge a book by the cover. They were great teachers. I was not a great student. I immediately pegged Bill Evans as a geek. The lenses of his glasses were thicker than the frames. Shorter than me by a few inches, his thinning black hair had been combed forward to misrepresent where the hairline began. Stylish blue slacks were tapered at the ankles, where they met a pair of brown and blue bargain-basement sneakers. Two pens were clipped into the breast pocket of his plaid, slim-fitted shirt.

Bill Evans stood and held out his hand. I accepted the wet noodle greeting with a firm tug, feeling uncomfortable with the wince I had caused. Brewster must have read my facial expression. He rolled his eyes, rose to his feet, and sauntered toward us.

"Bill," Brewster said, giving me a sideways glance. "I'd like the entire building swept, but let's start with my office." He opened the rear door and swept his right hand forward like he was rolling a bowling ball. Bill entered the building. Brewster pointed down the hallway. "It's just through the break room. First door on your left. I'll be right here if you need me."

The geek grabbed his black nylon backpack, thanked Brewster, and headed inside. We lost sight of him as the door closed.

Steve glanced at his phone, raised a hold-on-a-minute finger, and stepped away to answer a call. He paced the parking lot like an expectant father. Minutes later, he hustled back to the picnic table, his face animated. Excitement filled his voice.

"Brewster! Rick!" he shouted.

We hustled toward him. He pulled the phone from his ear. "His name is Tyler Jackson!"

Brewster's brow furrowed. "Who are you talking about?"

"We got a hit on the photo," Steve said directly. "I have Sergeant Ian Ford on the line with me. I'm going to put him on speakerphone." He pressed a button. "Ian, are you there?"

"Yes, I'm here. Hey, guys."

Brewster barked. "Who is this piece of shit, Sergeant?"

"His name is Tyler Jackson, sir. Caucasian, thirty-three years old. A Michigan resident with a current address in Hubbard Lake. I just received this information, so bear with me. Let's see. The report says he served nearly two terms in the military. He spent most of his time overseas in Afghanistan. He was an Army Ranger—Special Forces."

Brewster paced the patio. "What does that mean, Sergeant—*nearly* two terms?"

"He received an OTH discharge, sir. He didn't complete his second term."

"What did he do to warrant the other than honorable discharge?"

"Not sure, sir. He was released in 2012. His military records have been redacted."

"Son of a bitch." Brewster kicked at an imaginary object on the ground. "Besides knowing his current home location, do you have any other history on him?"

"Not much, sir. No current employment information on file. He's been off the grid for quite a while. Before 2016, he worked at a few construction and landscaping companies. Even those jobs were sporadic, and he's been AWOL from public records for at least five years. No arrest record and no W2 forms. He is *seriously* off the grid."

Brewster pounded a fist on the picnic table. "Thanks, Ian. Can you please forward everything you have to my cell?"

Sergeant Ford paused. "I can send it to Detective Erikson's cell phone, sir."

"Understood. Thank you for the information. If anything else comes up, please let me know. I mean—let Detective Erikson know."

"Yes, sir. Will do," he said, and then his voice added concern. "Sir, exercise extreme caution if this guy is involved in whatever you guys are investigating."

"I understand, Ian. Thanks again for your hard work."

Click.

Brewster said, "Give Kathy a call. Fill her in."

Steve dialed her number, pressed the speaker button, and placed his phone on the picnic table.

"Hello, Steve," she answered.

"Where are you, Kathy?"

"Kenny and I are just leaving Gary's store in Ann Arbor. We're heading home. Why?"

"I'm at the club with Brewster and Rick. You're on speaker. Sergeant Ford just contacted me. We have a positive ID on our suspect. His name is Tyler Jackson. Army Ranger. His current address is listed as Hubbard Lake."

"That's great news. Forward the file to me?"

"As soon as I receive it, you'll have it."

Kathy said, "Has Bill Evans arrived at your place, Bob?"

"Yeah. He's inside doing whatever it is he does. How did your meeting go with Sarah Owens?"

"Sarah is still groggy, but that's expected with the beating she endured. During our conversation, she confirmed the two men who forced entry into her house were asking questions about *your* place of business. Unfortunately, they knew where your safe was because she saw you open it during her meeting with you and Rick."

"So I've heard. Is Sarah going to be ok?"

"Yes, I believe so. I spoke with the attending physician before I left the hospital. He told me Sarah was recovering quickly and said she was a tough young lady."

"Did her assailants tell her what they were after?"

"No. From our interview, Sarah thought it was simply a robbery. Knowing that your restaurant is busy, she assumed the two thugs were after a quick cash payday."

"How are Gary and Joan King?"

"A little concerned. Maybe *more* than a little concerned. They both know what's happening. Until we sort this out, I'll have two teams assigned to them, one for their personal protection and another to monitor the store—"

"Gotta go," Bob interrupted. "Bill Evans just walked out the back door. He's waving me over."

Click.

Movement in my peripheral vision caught Scruggs as he walked in our direction from the parking lot. I stood and waved my hands high. He waved back, picked up his pace, and arrived simultaneously with the geek.

Bill Evans stood face-to-face with Brewster, smiled, and said, "Hold out your palm."

CHAPTER TWENTY NINE

Present Day - Thursday, November 4

B REWSTER, STEVE, SCRUGGS, BILL EVANS, AND I STOOD SO CLOSE together it felt like a team huddle—the ones I remembered from my high school wrestling days. Scruggs hadn't been fully briefed on the latest developments, and I watched his head follow the conversation like he was at a tennis match. His mouth hung open wide enough to stuff an apple in it.

"What?" Brewster's eyes narrowed.

Bill Evans grinned broadly and repeated, "Reach out your hand. Show me your palm."

Brewster extended his right arm. Bill Evans placed two small silver objects into his open palm. They looked like watch batteries.

Brewster stared at the miniature objects. "Is this what I think it is?"

"Yep. Place them in here, please." Bill closed the lid on the black box.

"Is that all of them?" Brewster asked.

"Yes, sir. Found one underneath your desk, and the other behind the bar, by that large mirror. They're inexpensive RF devices that can be purchased at thousands of spy stores, even Amazon."

"Are you certain there aren't anymore?"

"Well, there are other types of devices on the market, but if they used these cheap models to listen in on your conversations, I doubt they would have invested in anything more complicated. Nope, I believe this is it."

Steve slapped Bill on the back. "You're awesome."

"Thanks, man. Where are we going next?"

The counter-surveillance geek set his backpack on the picnic table and removed a notebook. With a pen from his breast pocket, he jotted down the addresses for my hardware store and Scruggs' auto shop. Said he would stop by my place first. I sent a text to Jim Anderson, letting him know to expect a visit from Bill, and recommended Scruggs reach out to someone at his shop. He nodded and stepped aside to make the call.

I answered a call from Kathy. She had already contacted a family friend, Judge Stevens, who had reviewed the information we had uncovered on Tyler Jackson. She expected a probable cause warrant to be issued within hours and told me the State Police in Alpena were already conducting preliminary intel on the suspect's house in Hubbard Lake. I pulled Brewster and Steve Erikson aside and shared the news with them.

When the rear door of the Social Club opened again, I couldn't hide my excitement. My smile broadened, and my mouth salivated. I didn't know what the lunch specials were today, and I didn't care. I was hungry. Marianne and another employee carried two large food trays. On their heels, Ward Watkins balanced a large tray of beverages.

Brewster said to Bill, "Don't leave. Have lunch with us." He slid over on the bench to make room. Bill seemed a bit of a loaner but looked comfortable around us, making me feel good.

Everyone leaned forward and filled their plates. Scruggs

sat down next to me. He'd only taken a few bites of his food before he leaned close and whispered in my ear. My brows lifted, and I pumped my fists. I wanted to jump from the bench and dance on the table. He hushed my enthusiasm and told me Jimmy Hendricks said the intel was solid, and we should eat quickly and leave—so we did just that. There were curious stares from the group as we tossed our napkins on the table and excused ourselves. I followed Scruggs to his shiny silver F-150 at a quickened pace and hopped into the passenger seat. Adrenaline pumped through my body.

TEN MILES northwest of town, Scruggs slowed his speed and pulled onto the gravel shoulder, sliding in behind the parked tow truck. The right-handed Jimmy Hendricks met us between vehicles. We shook hands, and he gave us the scoop. High on the hill was a popular hangout for tourists, bikers, and wannabe bikers. It was appropriately named Hilltop Bar and Grill.

Jimmy pointed. "He's still in there. A big guy with a crazy-looking face."

Scruggs and I knew the place well. Along with Paulie and our drummer, Rob, we had been their house band many years ago. We had great times and met many good people there. The person we would meet today was *not* one of those good people.

A thick stand of hardwood trees lined the road and obstructed the view of the summit. From our vantage point on the shoulder of the road, the bar wasn't visible. Fifty yards ahead, a winding dirt road turned right, traveled up the hill, turned right again, and then left, ending at a large dirt parking lot.

Jimmy asked if we had a plan. I shrugged and suggested we wait until the asshole came out of the bar. We'd ambush the piece of shit and give him a proper beat down.

He shook his shaggy blond head. "I'm not getting involved in a beat down. That's not my thing."

Scruggs slapped a fist into an open palm. His ponytail whipped around his head. A guttural sound escaped his throat.

I sized up the lanky tow truck driver. "Fucking-A Jimmy, you've got to be close to six-foot-tall."

"Dude, I weigh one-forty-five. Do I look like a fighter to you?"

I gave him a second look. "Let's play it by ear," I said. "We'll drive up there and check it out."

"What if he recognizes us?" Scruggs said.

"Are you stupid? We were doing sixty, and he was going even faster when he blew by us and ran us off the road. He doesn't know what we look like."

Scruggs shrugged his shoulders and fired up his truck. I hopped into the 'shotgun' seat. Jimmy opened the rear passenger door and pulled himself in, setting a large nylon bag next to him.

The F-150 pulled onto the road, weaving around the parked tow truck, and continued another fifty yards past a thick row of trees. Up ahead was the sign for the Hilltop Barn-Grill. It looked like someone had hand-painted it on a sheet of plywood. We turned right at the sign and proceeded up a winding path to the parking area.

Near the top of the hill, Scruggs punched me in the shoulder and pointed through the windshield. "Son of a bitch," he grunted. "That's the truck!"

There it sat—a white Ford super-duty diesel pickup truck, just as Scruggs described last Saturday, high off the ground on massive tires. Thick chrome stacks extended above the cab. It was backed up against the building, occupying two parking spaces. My heart raced.

Scruggs backed into an open spot near the entrance. We strolled inside, our heads on a swivel. Jimmy pointed to an available table next to a blaring jukebox, where Waylon Jennings belted out a song about a good-hearted woman. Scruggs and I sat with our backs against the wall and faced the open dining area. Jimmy took a seat across from me. He jerked his thumb over his right shoulder, leaned forward, and whispered, "Black cowboy hat with the red flannel shirt."

He must have read my facial expression because he added, "Still want to give him a beat down?"

I shook my head and glanced at Scruggs. "Jesus Christ, he must be over three-hundred pounds."

A scantily dressed waitress slapped three menus on the table and leaned forward, purposefully flashing her cleavage. It was distracting. A colorful butterfly tattoo covered her left breast. I wondered what it might look like in thirty years. Shaking off the disturbing thought, I told her we weren't hungry, only thirsty, and ordered three draft beers. Scruggs handed her back the menus. She frowned and turned on her heels, heading for the bar.

"We could call the cops," Scruggs suggested.

I shook my head and sized up the giant cowboy again. He was sitting with two other enormous rednecks. Together, the three of them had to weigh a half-ton.

"I've already spoken to officer Dean," I told Scruggs. "He

said there was nothing the police could do. There were no witnesses to our accident, and it would be the cowboy's word against ours." I tossed my hand in the air, signaling the end of our discussion.

I turned away from Scruggs and glanced out the dirty window facing the parking lot. The white Super Duty diesel was not visible. I guessed it sat five or six spaces away, closer to the corner of the building. With a couple of quarters in hand, I shuffled to the jukebox to get a better view of the window. I slid the coins into the slot while looking left — studying the scene outside.

I had an idea.

I punched a few buttons on the music machine and wondered what songs I had selected. Then I patted Jimmy on the back as I walked around our table, told him I'd be right back, headed outside, and meandered to the diesel truck. My eyes scanned the walls and roof of the building for cameras. I didn't see any. The driver's door of the white diesel truck was locked. I peeked into the window and saw the keys lying on the console. The lunch crowd had waned. The parking lot was half empty. There were two open spaces across from the cowboy's truck, and beyond that, a steep hill led to the thick row of mature hardwoods.

I hustled back inside.

Scruggs and Jimmy held frosted mugs to their lips. I took a seat, quenched my thirst, and saw the butterfly-breasted waitress deliver another pitcher of beer to the cowboy's table. It was time to act.

I leaned forward. "Can you break into his truck?"

Jimmy Hendricks flashed a smile. "It's what I do."

Scruggs' eyes rounded. "What's your plan, Rick?"

"An eye for an eye. Follow me."

We slammed our beers. I tossed a twenty on the table, and we hustled to the vestibule. As I pushed on the heavy wood door, the crowd behind me moaned loudly as a Michael Jackson song blared through the speakers. My eyes watered, and I couldn't stop laughing.

Perfect!

Scruggs opened his truck and lifted the rear bench. He tightened his ponytail, donned work gloves, and tossed me a pair. Good thinking. Jimmy grabbed a small black device that looked like a blood pressure cuff. He slipped on his gloves and shushed our giggling. We followed him to the target vehicle. Within thirty seconds, the air wedge had widened the gap in the door frame enough to slide in a metal rod. Seconds later, the door opened.

Scruggs pushed Jimmy aside, leaned in, grabbed the key from the console, and slipped it into the ignition. He turned the key enough to power the truck without starting it. With his left hand on the brake pedal, he reached for the console with his right hand and pulled back on the lever, putting the transmission into neutral. My heart rate elevated. I watched Jimmy shuffling his feet in perfect timing with his shifting head.

"Fuck, fuck, fuck, let's go!" Jimmy looked like he needed to use the restroom.

We met at the rear bumper and gave the truck a heavy shove. The gravel parking lot was on a slight decline that matched the surrounding topography. The vehicle moved forward—slowly.

Scruggs had already started his escape down the winding gravel path when I glanced left. The white diesel truck had covered the thirty yards to the edge of the dusty parking lot. Then, it appeared to stop, hung up on a convex section of grass that lined the edge of the gravel.

My heart sank.

"Look!" Scruggs said, pumping his finger wildly. I leaned forward to see past his colossal frame and saw why he was so excited. The two front tires of the Super Duty diesel had crested the small mound and moved forward. Downhill. It picked up speed. Then more speed. Then....

I craned my neck, trying to see what was happening. The thick row of trees blocked my vision as we approached the hand-painted sign by the main road. I couldn't see what was happening—but I heard it. Damn right, I heard it.

Crunch!

A sudden feeling of guilt coursed through my body. I shrugged it off as an adrenaline dump. Scruggs punched the gas pedal and turned left onto the blacktopped road. He sped to where the tow truck was parked and stopped abruptly. Jimmy let out a holler, grabbed his large nylon bag, and jumped from the back seat.

"Are you out of here?" Scruggs shouted out his window.

Jimmy tossed the bag into his tow truck and turned to us with a satisfied grin. "Nope. I have a gut feeling someone close by will need my help shortly."

I removed my work gloves, tossed them over my shoulder into the back seat, and shared a high-five with my buddy.

Revenge is sweet, but karma is sweeter.

CHAPTER THIRTY

Detroit, Michigan - 1935
'The Grand Finale'

LIEUTENANT GREENBAUM OF THE DETROIT POLICE DEPARTMENT'S Sixteenth Precinct picked up the black handset from his desk. The caller was frantic, screaming about a dead man and blood. The Lieutenant tried calming the person on the other end of the line. *Speak slowly. Breathe. Who are you? What's the address?*—and so on. First introduced three years earlier in the New Jersey Police Department, two-way radios had been recently installed in all the Detroit Police patrol cars. The Lieutenant used the new technology to radio a patrol car. Two officers were assigned to follow up.

Officers Malley and Nunez arrived minutes later at an address on Park Avenue. It was early in their shift and their day was about to get interesting. Standing in a light drizzle, they pounded on the front doors of the Starlight Lounge. There was no answer. Returning to their patrol car, they drove west to St. Aubin Street, turned right, then right again, traveling east down the alley behind a long row of two-story brick buildings. At the rear entrance of the Starlight Lounge, a tall young man dressed in blue overalls stood in the shadows. He paced back and forth under an overhang that protected him from the raindrops. A cigarette dangled from his lips. A half dozen butts lay in a puddle at his feet.

Malley and Nunez exited their patrol car and scanned the alley for anything suspicious. The nervous lad pulled a crumpled pack of smokes from his overalls. He waved the cops toward the open rear door of the Starlight Lounge and lit another cigarette. He did not follow the patrolmen inside.

Cautiously entering the building, the cops strolled through the empty club. When they reached the main lounge, it was apparent why they were there. The body of an adult male was slumped over the mahogany bar. Long legs dangled from his waist. Ankles bent awkwardly near the floor. It appeared as though he was still standing. The dead man's left arm hung limply at his side. His right hand lay across the bar countertop, clutching a drinking glass. The dark-colored liquid had spilled, pooling around an outstretched hand. A bloody gray Fedora lay next to a lifeless head. A cigarette butt lay next to the expensive hat, leaving a burn mark on the polished surface. Piercing blue eyes, wide open, stared expressionlessly across the room.

Malley cringed at the massive amount of blood pooling around the man's head. A large puddle of the sticky crimson substance spread across the bar surface, threatening to mix with whatever spilled from his drinking glass. Checking for a pulse, he found none. He didn't expect to.

Nunez walked to the front side of the bar and grimaced. "Shit," he told his partner, staring into the dead man's far-away eyes. "I knew him."

Malley stepped closer. "Isn't that the owner of this club?"

Nunez nodded. He had known the man. Two nights ago, the same prominent Detroiter, Sam Durocher, paid Victor Nunez a large sum of cash to stand guard outside the same building. That was the grand opening.

This was the grand finale.

Malley pointed to a cloth bag that sat on the mahogany

countertop. The dark blue ink on the cream-colored bag caught his attention: *First National Bank of Detroit*. Although it sat precariously close to a mixed puddle of booze and blood, the cotton bag was dry. Nunez followed his partner's eyes and strolled to the bar. He opened the bag and looked inside. A thin smile pulled on his lips. He nodded to his partner. "I'll throw the bag in the trunk. We'll talk about this later."

Malley nodded, and headed for the back of the bar, where a black phone sat on the counter below a large mirror. He picked up the handset, stuck his index finger into the base, and turned the dial. Lieutenant Greenbaum took his statement and told Malley he would send the precinct commander to the scene. Then Greenbaum contacted the coroner.

The precinct commander interviewed the two cops, questioning their integrity on the crime scene. "Have you touched anything?" he asked. "Has the body been disturbed? Have you moved, touched, or removed any of the evidence?"

Officer Malley shook his head. "Everything is exactly as we found it, sir."

Procedures were followed. Photos were taken. Nunez was keenly aware of recent events, activities, and publicity surrounding the Starlight Lounge and questioned whether they should contact the FBI. The commander advised him to stick with the investigation and leave the details to his supervisors.

On a dreary Monday morning, two days after the grand opening, the Starlight Lounge was quiet and empty, except for one body. Sam Durocher was dead from a single bullet to the back of his head.

The cops watched as the lifeless body was covered, placed on a stretcher, and wheeled through the rear door to a waiting van.

Officers Malley and Nunez returned to their vehicle and left the scene.

CHAPTER THIRTY ONE

Present Day - Friday, November 5

NATURE'S WAKE-UP CALL WAS ALWAYS EARLIER THAN I LIKED. Morning rays of brilliance peeked through the blinds in the bedroom and shone in my eyes. The rising sun competed with my internal alarm clock. I rolled away from the bright light and reached for a hug from my wife, but found the bed empty. Tossing my feet over the side, I slid them into well-worn slippers and made my way to the kitchen. I heard Kathy finish a phone call as I rounded the corner from the hallway.

She sat on a tall stool, hunched over, left elbow resting on the island, a teacup in her right hand. Approaching from behind, I let out a soft cough to avoid startling her. I kissed her on the cheek and rubbed her shoulders.

"Are you all right, Kath?"

"I've been better." She set her cup on the counter and stood for a proper hug.

I squeezed her tight. "What's going on?"

She shrugged. "I couldn't sleep last night."

"I know. You tossed and turned."

"Coffee's ready." She pointed to the counter, sat down, and stared at her phone.

"Thanks." I shuffled to the counter, filled my insulated cup, and took a seat on the other side of the island. "Talk to me."

She released her words with a slow, soft exhale. "Earlier

this morning, I spoke with Captain Marx. He's the commander of the Alpena State Police Post. When his team executed the search warrant yesterday at Tyler Jackson's house in Hubbard Lake, they were met with gunfire. Don't worry," she raised her palms. "No officers were injured, which is great news, but they pronounced the suspect dead at the scene."

I clapped my hands together, startling Kathy. "Good! Tyler Jackson is dead!"

She leaned back on her stool and raised her palms again, giving me the I'm-not-done look. "It's much more complicated than that," she said and continued with the details of the encounter in northern Michigan. "The gunman who opened fire on the police and was killed was *not* Tyler Jackson. His name was Lowell Thomas. The report Captain Marx emailed me this morning," she pointed at her phone, "contained information from the medical examiner. Apparently, Lowell Thomas was stoned out of his mind. They discovered large amounts of methamphetamine in his system during the autopsy. I'm still waiting for the full report. Also, I just got off the phone with Steve Erikson. Less than a half-hour ago, Steve and a team from my department executed a search warrant on Lowell Thomas's residence in Brightmoor, a Detroit suburb. He rented a small ranch house in a very tough neighborhood. I'm told they dusted for fingerprints and gathered physical evidence. They found a payroll stub, dated a few weeks ago, from a construction company in Redford Township. We're trying to get a hold of the owner to find out how Lowell Thomas is involved with Tyler Jackson."

I didn't respond right away. It looked like Kathy had more to say, and I was right.

"There was another body on the property, Rick." She pulled in a deep breath, followed by a long exhale. Our eyes met. "His name was Stuart Applegate. He was a Dunville resident. Lived in the Commons subdivision east of town and worked as a machinist at Burch Tool and Die, right up the road from your hardware store."

I scrunched my forehead. "Why does that name sound familiar?"

Kathy pulled up a photo of the deceased resident and slid her phone across the granite counter. "He was fifty-seven years old, widowed, and had no children. His name sounds familiar because he was the guy at the bar when you found the gold coin. He's the one who was trying to sell his story to Sarah Owens."

"Damn," I blurted. "I recognize Stuart's face from our lunch gatherings at the Social Club. He was a nice guy." I slid the phone back to Kathy.

"According to the report, they chained him to a pole in the basement. I'm told he took a serious beating. The preliminary cause of death was a heart attack, but I'm still waiting for a copy of the final autopsy."

"Holy shit, Kath. What the hell have we got ourselves mixed up in?"

"I've been asking myself the same thing. Until now, our investigation into what we found inside Bob's bar has been a side job, a hobby of sorts, a Nancy Drew mystery. Now, somebody named Lowell Thomas is shot and killed in Tyler Jackson's house, up north, in Hubbard Lake. A Dunville resident is tortured in his basement, and for whatever reason, heart attack or not, he's dead. Hell, until this morning, I'd never heard of Lowell Thomas. Where is Tyler Jackson? Why was Thomas on Jackson's property? How are those two connected? And how the hell was Stuart Applegate involved?"

I shifted on my stool. "So, what are you going to do now?"

"Get as much help as I can. Whether or not he's off the grid, we'll find Tyler Jackson. Somebody knows where he is. I'm hoping the construction company owner where Lowell Thomas worked has information tying these two derelicts together."

I slid a couple of pieces of bread into the toaster and tossed a few eggs into the frying pan. The blender whirled in the background as Kathy mixed a protein shake. She glanced in my direction, I gave an affirmative nod, and she made enough for two. I buttered the toast and slid the eggs — over easy — onto the plates.

After a quiet breakfast, we kissed, hugged, and headed in different directions, each carrying a Yeti cup brimming with a banana and strawberry shake.

As Kathy headed for the garage door, I said, "When you find out where that construction company is in Redford, I'm going with you."

"We'll see," she replied.

"You want me to be a better cop?" I baited her.

She stopped in her tracks, furrowed her brow, and stared at me for a long moment. After one more hug, she grabbed a light jacket and continued to the garage. I followed her, seconds behind, fired up my truck, and headed for the hardware store.

JIM ANDERSON, my interim store manager, waved to me as I entered. Lanky and always smiling, he resembled George

McFly, Marty's dad in the *Back to the Future* movie. Not the wimpy, cowardly McFly. No, he seemed more like the character toward the end of the film when he was confident, charismatic, and in control of his destiny. His smile reminded me to call Paulie. I missed him. No need to bother him now. He was probably still sleeping. Paulie had a big night ahead of him, and I decided to call him after his performance in Chicago tonight. The show ended at eleven, so I'd call him afterward, around midnight. I made a mental note.

"Morning, Jim." I waved back.

He beamed. "Good morning, Mr. Cooper."

I made my way to the office and called Brewster and Scruggs, letting them know about my conversation this morning with Kathy. I briefed them on the events that unfolded yesterday afternoon at Hubbard Lake. As expected, Brewster had already heard the news. He still had a connection inside the department. Scruggs seemed shaken, and after a minute of silence, he told me Stuart Applegate was his customer.

"It was Stuart's race car I've been rebuilding," he said. "I can't believe he's dead."

I provided condolences. Scruggs sniffled and told me he'd see me for lunch.

Click.

CHAPTER THIRTY TWO

Present Day - Friday, November 5

SCRUGGS SPENT A FEW MINUTES SOCIALIZING WITH THE REGULARS, shaking hands with a few friends, and headed in my direction. He tapped me on the shoulder. I hopped off my stool and reached up for a hug. I didn't have a choice. Ward Watkins was busy behind the mahogany bar, eradicating dehydration one customer at a time. Marianne shuffled quickly back and forth from the kitchen to the dining area, reminding me of a time-lapse video. Whenever I looked around, she placed a full plate down or picked up an empty one. It's no wonder she was in such good shape. Brewster made his way down the bar, smiling, waving, and fist-bumping.

"Hey, Brewster," we shouted, mounting our stools.

"Afternoon, gentlemen," said the consummate salesman. "You guys should try the chicken wrap today. It's delicious."

Scruggs rubbed his belly. "Sounds good."

Ward grinned. "Hey, fellas." He placed two bottles on the polished mahogany top.

Scruggs winked as Ward shoved a lime wedge into his Corona.

Brewster laughed out loud, then stepped closer and whispered to me. "Thanks for calling me this morning. Shit has hit the fan, huh? I guess our Hardy Boys mystery investigation is over."

"That's funny, Brewster," I said. "Calling it a Hardy Boys mystery."

"Why is *that* so funny?" he asked.

"This morning, Kathy called it a Nancy Drew mystery."

"I guess we all have different perspectives." He chuckled and moonwalked away from the bar.

Marianne filled the void that Brewster had created. She smiled, took our orders, and confirmed we had made the right decision.

THE LAST bite of my chicken wrap was crunchy. I pulled a small, hard, white thing out of my mouth with my index finger and thumb and studied it. My tongue worked back and forth, searching for where the foreign object belonged. Moving my tongue again to the left side, I found the spot.

I'd chipped my tooth.

I raised my hand and shouted, "Hey Brewster, got a minute?"

Holding his hand high, with the index finger extended, he politely excused himself from a conversation with a chatty customer.

"Thanks for that." Brewster placed his right hand on the bar top and waved back with his left at the gentlemen he'd just ditched.

"Thanks for what?" I questioned.

"Thanks for pulling me away from *that* conversation. You saved my ass. I thought the guy would never stop talking. He's a truck driver from Illinois who's going through a divorce. Has three teenage kids — one son, two daughters — a German shepherd, two cats, and is heading to Saginaw to meet with someone he met on an online dating service."

"Is he meeting a guy or a girl in Saginaw?" I asked.

"What?"

"Could go either way. Not that it matters. You should go back and ask him."

He threw his head back and laughed. "You're an asshole. Did you *really* need to speak with me?"

I pointed to my mouth. "Is Dina working today? I chipped a tooth."

"She doesn't see patients on Fridays, unless it's an emergency. Does it hurt?"

"No. Just a small chip on one of my back teeth. There's no pain. I'll call her office on the way back to the store and schedule something for Monday."

"Call her if there's any pain before Monday. She accepts emergency patients all the time." Then Brewster changed subjects. "How was Stuart Applegate involved with Tyler Jackson, and why was he murdered in northern Michigan?"

"I think you already know the answer," I said. "Stuart was at your restaurant when I found the coin, and somebody believed he had intimate knowledge about it and possibly where they could find it. It's undeniable this person, or persons, knows more about this coin than we imagined. It's also indisputable that they're dangerous and willing to do whatever is necessary to get their hands on it."

I checked my phone. Kathy had left me a message. She was on her way to the Social Club and would be here within minutes. I said my goodbyes and headed for the front door. The Blue Goose Ford Explorer pulled up to the curb.

It was time to practice being a better cop.

THE CINDER block building, painted a bright canary yellow, wasn't significant. Neither was the handmade sign hanging from a rusty chain between two weather-beaten wooden fence posts. It was displayed haphazardly on the scraggly lawn near the sidewalk on Grand River Avenue in Redford. *DMJ Construction*. That was it. I saw nothing else. No phone number. No catchy logo. No welcoming signs. I certainly wasn't expecting to find the Better Business Bureau sticker anywhere on the building. As we pulled into the gravel driveway on the right side of the building, no windows or doors were evident. Kenny must have been nearby because I saw his vehicle in the sideview mirror. He rode our bumper up the dusty driveway.

The massive gravel lot behind the canary yellow building was a stark contrast to the ugliness of the building itself. Dozens of construction vehicles and heavy equipment were parked in an organized manner. They were clean and presentable—a remarkable juxtaposition. A blue two-story building sat about a hundred yards away, at the far left edge of the property.

Kathy knocked on the steel door. I tried peeking into a small window on the right side of the door. Years of dirt, grime, neglect, and a thick metal grate obstructed any visibility.

"Come in," a rough voice shouted from the inside.

Kathy pulled on the heavy door and we entered. The room was scantily appointed. Dark brown wood paneling covered the walls. Soiled ceiling tiles were probably white a few decades ago. The only visible furnishings were an institutional metal desk, three chairs, and a filing cabinet. A large clock hung on the back wall behind the desk. A disturbing photo of a woman hugging a large, fuzzy cat with crazy eyes was haphazardly displayed to our left. The cat looked scared. The woman in the picture, who I guessed was a younger Jean Simmons, expressed a bizarre smile. Smoke from a recently discarded cigarette butt wafted in our direction.

"Please, call me Jean." The woman hacked.

I looked for the cat.

"Thanks, Jean. I'm Special Agent Kathy Cooper. I'm with the State Police. I'm here to ask you a few questions."

A walking cane balanced precariously against a gunmetal gray desk. The gangly woman peered over her thick glasses. With a tight frown, which might have been her natural appearance, she grabbed the cane, stood, and took a few awkward steps forward. "I've been divorced from him for over a year. Whatever that dumb son of a bitch did, I had no part in it."

Kenny grinned.

I suppressed a chuckle.

"We're not here about your ex-husband, Jean," Kathy said. "We'd like to ask you a couple of questions about one of your employees."

"Let me guess." She scratched an itch beneath the thick, tangled bird's nest covering her head. "You're either looking for Loco Thomas or Billy Bartlett?"

Kathy furrowed her brow. "I'm sorry? We *are* here about a man with the last name of Thomas, but our records show his first name as Lowell."

"Same asshole. Lowell Thomas is nicknamed Loco because he's a fucking lunatic. His friend, Billy Bartlett—mostly known as Bully—was his friend. Another piece of shit."

Kathy took a few steps closer to the androgynous figure. "Excuse me, Jean. If these two men were so difficult and unpleasant, why did you hire them?"

"I didn't hire them. I purchased this business over a year ago with my deadbeat ex-husband, and they came with the deal. The agreement stated that these two bums would continue their employment for at least one year. I would have fired them as soon as their one-year commitment was over, but they scare me. Looks like I don't have to worry about that anymore. I haven't seen either of those assholes in weeks."

Kathy gave her the news. "You won't need to worry yourself about Lowell Thomas anymore. He's dead."

"Good," Jean said rather quickly. "What about Thomas's friend, Billy? Is he dead, too?"

Kathy shook her head. "This is the first we've heard of Billy Bartlett. Can you get me the files on both men? Also, I need to know if Thomas or Bartlett were friends with any of your other employees. Was there anyone they hung around with?"

"Not here. No way! Everyone stayed clear of those two losers. They were scary. I've lost a couple of good workers because of them. Nobody who works for me was involved with either of those two thugs. You can interview all my employees, and each one will smile when you tell them Loco will never return. How did he die?"

"Violently," Kenny answered.

"Perfect." Jean grinned.

Kathy stared up into her deep-set brown eyes. "I would like to interview all your employees, Jean. Also, I need information about the previous owner who hired Thomas and Bartlett. Due diligence. I'm sure you understand."

"I understand, but I never met the previous owner. It was all handled by attorneys—expensive attorneys. I'll see what I can find, though."

"Thanks, Jean. Can you have this information prepared for me quickly? My colleagues and I can find a place to have lunch and stop by afterward."

"No problem. Everything is on the computer these days. I'll have it ready shortly."

"Thank you." Kathy handed her a business card.

Jean's hands dwarfed Kathy's.

"If there is anything you can think of or anybody you believe might be involved with them, please let me know. Every little detail is important."

Jean scratched at the perpetual itch. "The only friend those troublemakers seemed to have was this guy who stopped in occasionally, but he was *not* an employee. Whenever he came by, those two assholes would disappear for days. They still insisted on getting paid while they were away. Good riddance, I say!"

Kathy's eyes widened. "Does this other guy have a name?"

"I'm sure he does, but I don't know it. Whenever I saw him on the property, I retreated to my office. He might have been as nuts as the other two. Who knows? I wanted nothing to do with him."

"Can you describe him?" asked Kenny.

"He didn't look like Loco or Bully. They *looked* like trouble, with their long hair and beards. Their friend was cleancut, dare I say, good-looking, with gorgeous blue eyes. He always wore camouflage clothing, like he was ready for war or something. I assumed he was one of those wacko survivalist types you hear about on the news, right after he just blew up a building."

Kathy and Kenny exchange glances. I peeked over

Kenny's shoulder as he pulled out his cell phone and clicked on the icon for his case files. He stopped scrolling when he found the photo that looked like a younger Mark Harmon, the *NCIS* heartthrob. Expanding the picture, he turned the phone towards Jean Simmons.

"Yep, that's him," she said. "Is he dead too?"

"Not yet." Kathy grimaced. "Jean, can you get us the Lowell Thomas and Billy Bartlett files while we wait?"

"I thought you were coming back after lunch?"

"I just lost my appetite."

KATHY WALKED outside, her phone plastered to her ear. I followed but couldn't tell who was on the other end. A few minutes later, she stared at her phone, turned to us, and read an email.

We learned a bit more about Billy Bartlett.

Less than four months ago, Bartlett had been released from one of Michigan's finest correctional institutions. He was thirty-four years of age, Caucasian, six feet tall, brown eyes, gang affiliations, and prior arrests. His long police record included possession, breaking and entering, soliciting prostitution, and one conviction for assault with a deadly weapon. Jean Simmons had painted an accurate profile of him. The last known address was in Inkster, about twenty minutes from the construction site.

Kathy swiped at her phone. "Billy Bartlett might be the linchpin to locating Tyler Jackson."

"Let's go," I said.

Just then, another State Police vehicle pulled behind the construction building. A female officer exited the car and motioned me to the passenger side.

My head bounced back and forth between Kathy and Kenny. "The hell is this?" I asked.

Kathy introduced me to Trooper Vicky Trotter. "She's taking you back to Dunville."

I glared at Kenny. He shrugged and turned away. This wasn't an argument I was going to win. So I didn't start one.

Speeding from the parking lot, stones flying, a mixed cloud of sand, gravel, and limestone in their wake, Kathy and Kenny peeled out of the DMJ Construction parking lot in Redford. They were on their way to the last known address of Billy 'Bully' Bartlett.

I was being escorted back to Dunville.

So much for learning on the job.

CHAPTER THIRTY THREE

Detroit, Michigan - 1935
'Early Retirement'

DETERMINED, UNWAVERING, AND HELL-BENT. THESE AND DOZENS of similar adjectives were written and verbalized to describe the actions and behavior of Agent Dale Mintern over the days and weeks that followed the death of his partner — his friend, John Douglas.

Mintern had traveled by air as far as the continent permitted — from New Jersey to the east and California to the west — and by paved and dirt roads to several Midwestern cities in the middle. The expense accounts he submitted to the bureau for reimbursement were substantial and legendary for the time.

Every person arrested and subsequently released during the gambling raid at the Starlight Lounge on the infamous night of November 15th received a visit from Mintern. He visited most of them more than once. Agent Mintern had become a proverbial thorn in their sides and had no intentions of letting up.

His investigation into the assassination of a fellow agent became mythical during his brief, tumultuous career. Dale knew there was no bringing back the murdered federal agent — his friend. His goal, unbeknownst to his superiors, was two-fold. Dale would find evidence of illegal activities, anything that might be used to file charges, something that would finally stick, and lock each of the ten suspects up in prison for the rest of their lives.

He would also search for his partner's leather bag, which contained a small fortune. Mintern knew what was in it. He had watched Douglas inventory it before someone murdered him. The bag had never been located, and one of the ten people at the Starlight Lounge that night either had it or knew where it was. Mintern would intimidate, discredit, or arrest them—*all* of them—for duty and pride's sake. He would find the treasure-filled bag as a personal achievement, a reward.

THE SNOW fell heavy on a late December afternoon. Mintern was returning to Detroit after visiting an Ohio congressman in Cleveland, his third visit to the crooked politician's residence in the past few weeks.

Dale wanted to be home for Christmas. No particular reason. There was no one waiting for him. No one to hug or snuggle. No children. No pets. It was a nostalgic holiday, and he thought back to when he was a small child, how his parents, whom he adored, would spoil him at Christmas. Dale was nostalgic that way. It brought back beautiful memories. He wanted to be home for that reason, and because he had been on the road for so long, he needed a break.

Gusting north winds blew thick, wet snow across Lake Erie's choppy, frigid waters and onto the narrow highway, making visibility more than problematic. Hungry and tired from the long journey and weary of the weather, he pulled into a small diner on Highway 2, east of Toledo, where he waited out the storm.

With the sun setting low on the western horizon, Dale

Mintern took the last sip of his coffee and settled the bill, leaving a healthy tip on the table. He buttoned up his heavy overcoat in the damp vestibule and shuffled his feet through wet snow to his vehicle. He had waited out the snow squall for hours with dozens of other exhausted travelers and was anxious to get back on the road.

Shots rang out as he reached for the handle on the driver's door. Shards of glass flew in his face. The noise was deafening, and the disorienting feeling of confusion and weakness consumed him. Heavy, wet snow cushioned his fall.

DALE MINTERN had been shot three times. He should have died. The surgeon told him as much when he awoke at ProMedica Hospital in Toledo, where he spent most of the next few weeks recovering. A gunshot to the hip was the least of his problems. The two bullets he took to the chest caused significant complications. They were the worst of his injuries. That's what the doctor told him, but he disagreed.

Dale had missed Christmas.

After nearly six weeks of recovering at home, he was on his way to the familiarity of the FBI offices in Detroit. Dale liked familiarity. But when he arrived at the building on Michigan Avenue, everything had changed, including the unrecognizable face that sat at the reception desk.

Short, somewhat round, and redheaded, the secretary greeted him with an awkward smile. "Agent Mintern," she said. "The deputy assistant director would like to see you in his office, sir."

"What's this about?" Dale asked.

"I'm not sure, sir. He asked me to let you know he wants to meet with you immediately, sir."

Dale made his way to the third floor of the Detroit FBI field offices. Reaching the top of the staircase, he turned left, proceeded to the corner office, and knocked. The assistant director pointed to the chair across from his desk. Dale sat, peering over the AD's shoulders, staring out the large window that overlooked the Detroit River in the foreground and Canada in the distance. The director spoke first and told Dale he was glad he hadn't died. Dale thanked him and told the director he was delighted to be back.

The AD winced. "A lot has happened since you've been recovering, Dale."

Uneasiness overcame Dale. "This doesn't feel like a welcome home meeting, sir."

"I'm just saying that a lot has happened in the past two months."

Dale leaned forward, still tight from prolonged inactivity. "You've always been straight with me, sir. What's your point?"

The assistant director got to the point, and Dale's stomach twisted. There had been ongoing investigations from the highest level of the bureau. "The highest level," the director repeated. "Allegations from very influential people. Mayors, congressmen, and powerful attorneys accuse you of harassment. And it gets worse. Claims have been made about you threatening witnesses. They said you were searching for the treasures never recovered from the night of the raid on the Starlight Lounge."

Dale sat back in his chair, wondering if he'd lost his will. Not the will to live, of course. But the will to fight. He'd been off the grid, out of the fight, so to speak, for a few months. And he was relaxed. Maybe too comfortable? Possibly. The painkilling drugs he had been taking for his injuries had affected him, but to what degree? He didn't seem to care. Dale stared out the window over the DA's shoulders, lost in contemplation.

"Are you hearing me, Dale?"

"Yes, sir. I'm listening."

"I don't think you are. This is serious, and I need you to pay attention to what I'm saying — what I'm about to say."

Dale nodded, his shoulders hunched.

"While you were recuperating, charges have been prepared, not filed, but they could be — if you challenge the bureau's decision. I'm sorry because there is no easy way to say this, but today will be your last day with the FBI."

Dale was reminded again that he had pissed off too many people. The wrong people. The ones with power and influence. The bureau, he was told, was still in its infancy and couldn't afford the negative publicity a trial might bring. It couldn't happen, so they struck a deal. He would resign immediately and receive an unprecedented two-year severance package.

Former FBI Special Agent Dale Mintern relinquished his badge and service weapon.

CHAPTER THIRTY FOUR

Present Day - Friday, November 5

Not hearing from Kathy for the rest of the afternoon wasn't concerning. She could handle herself, and besides, Kenny was with her. I looked forward to our conversation this evening and learning how their visit went with Billy Bartlett. Sure, I wished I had joined her and Kenny at the interrogation in Inkster, but I also knew it could be dangerous. She didn't want to put me, an inexperienced, part-time cop, in harm's way. I understood. Didn't like it, but I accepted her decision. What choice did I have? I would have a large glass of wine ready for her when she got home.

Across from my desk, high on the wall, a large clock — green and yellow, a gift from the local John Deere dealership — showed one hand up and the other down. It was six o'clock and time for me to leave the store in the capable hands of Jim Anderson, AKA George McFly, for the next three hours. I was whooped, ready to go home for a drink, and excited to see my wife.

I shut down my computer, shuffled a pile of papers into a neat stack, and picked up my cell phone to check for messages. Nothing from Kathy. I deleted a warning about my expired car warranty. I sent another weekly reminder to join AARP to the trash bin. The last message caused my body to stiffen. I leaned back in my chair, tucked my left fist under my right elbow, extended my arm, and reread the message.

I know you have the gold coin. I want it. I'll be in touch. Don't fuck this up. Do not contact the police.

Thinking it might be a prank, or someone texting a wrong number, I stared at my screen. It was an unknown number.

I sent a quick reply. *Who is this?*

Your worst nightmare.

Seriously, this isn't funny. Who is this?

This is not a joke. The gold coin was not in the restaurant safe. I know you have it, and I want it.

Holy shit! What was happening? I had trouble processing the information. Was this a joke? If so, it wasn't funny. *Not* funny. I squirmed in my chair and tried to wrap my head around what I was reading.

Are you there, asshole? The message prodded me.

Who are you? What do you want?

I tugged the hair on the back of my head and waited while my tormentor composed a follow-up message.

It doesn't matter who I am. I want the gold coin. You have 24 hours. No fakes. If I don't get it, a family member or friend will die. Maybe both. Maybe I'll kill you. I'll be in touch.

My hands shook as I pumped on the screen. *I don't know what you're talking about. I don't have any coins.*

It took a few minutes before the next message came through. I nervously tapped my fingers on the desk.

I know your wife's a cop. She has connections. Have her get the coin. She better be the only cop you get involved with. 24 hours. That's it.

I tried redialing the unknown number. No answer.

AFTER SEVERAL attempts to contact Kathy, my cell phone delivered a recognizable ding.

I read the text message. *In a meeting. I'll call you back.*

SUPERMAN. I texted back.

Direct and straightforward. Kathy would understand. Seconds later, my phone rang. I couldn't remember when I'd felt so relieved to hear my wife's voice. Simple breathing felt laborious at that moment.

Kathy was blunt. "What's going on?" I could tell she was on the move, walking, pacing. She'd probably skirted out of an important meeting to call me.

My chest felt heavy. "Are you okay, Kath?"

"I'm fine. Where are you? What's going on? Are *you* okay?"

Superman was our secret word for "I'm in trouble." Since we started dating, it had been ingrained in our subconsciousness and training. It was to be taken seriously. Nothing else mattered if either of us uttered the word 'Superman' out of context. Survival instincts kicked in. It became a priority.

"I'm fine, Kathy, but we have an issue." My heart rate was elevated, and my breathing pattern was irregular.

"Talk to me."

"Check your phone. We're being threatened. I just sent you a copy of the texts I received from an unknown number."

"I'm reading them now. When did you receive these?"

"Ten minutes ago, maybe fifteen—I don't know. My head is whirling. I've been trying to call you."

"Sorry, Rick. It's been a long day. I'm back in Lansing now. Kenny and I had a confrontation with a bad guy this afternoon."

Damned Billy Bartlett!

Kathy told me she and Kenny had discharged their weapons during an altercation in Inkster. There were protocols and specific departmental regulations they needed to follow.

"Shit. Okay. We can chat about it when you get home. Is Bartlett dead?"

"He is not. He sneaked out the back window of his apartment and is currently on the run."

"All right, listen, I need you to come home safely. Right now, though, I'm more than a little concerned. I need to know what I should do about the messages I received. He — I guess it's a he — wants the gold coin, the *real* gold coin. Said we had twenty-four hours. Also, the text messages said he knows you're a cop. He told me not to get the police involved. I'm worried about you."

She told me I did the right thing, calling her. I hoped she was right. Her voice was calming. It probably had to do with her training and experience. I was told to expect a call from Bill Evans. He would require access to my phone. Maybe he could find the source of the text messages. She sounded hopeful but not convincing. Part of the process, I presumed. My mind raced. My blood pressure elevated.

"So, should I just go home and wait to hear from you? When will you be back?"

"Yes," Kathy was quick with her reply. "Go home, and, I might suggest, no alcohol tonight. You need to stay sharp. I'll call you with my ETA when I'm on my way. Right now, I've got my hands full. You should call Bob and Dan and let them know what is happening. Please make sure they understand the seriousness of the matter and the importance of keeping a tight lid on it. Tell them I will assign security details to their houses for the next twenty-four hours. After that, we'll re-evaluate the threat levels."

"Yes, ma'am. I love you. Please be safe."

"I love you, too. Keep your phone with you at all times, and of course, let me know if you receive any more threatening messages."

After the call ended, I sent Kathy one more text. *BTW, where is the gold coin?*

I have it.

I CALLED Scruggs and told him everything I knew, which wasn't as much as I wished. There'd been a threat to me, my family, and my friends; I reminded him he was my closest.

"Be vigilant," I advised him, instructing him to call Jo immediately, telling them to stay home tonight. "Maybe take tomorrow off as well. Don't answer the door for anyone." I told him not to be alarmed with the MSP security detail posted outside his house. "They'll be discreet," I promised, although I didn't know the protocol. It felt comforting saying it.

Scruggs had just closed his shop and had pulled out of his parking lot when I called. Said he and Jo had dinner plans, somewhere fancy. After all, it *was* Jo, and it *was* Friday night. She was going to be pissed. Oh, well. She would be safe, and that was all that mattered to me.

I entered the town square. The traffic was congested as it usually was on the weekends. The long line to enter the Social Club reminded me to call Brewster. I grabbed my phone from the center console. An incoming call vibrated in my hands.

I answered nervously. "Hello. This is Rick."

It was Bill Evans. Said he was on his way to my house and wanted to know if I was home. My ten-minute ETA would be pretty accurate. I asked him how confident he was in finding the origins of the text messages. His pause told me all I needed to know.

"Honestly, Rick, the chances are slim. Finding those listening devices in your store made me look like a hero, but it was relatively simple. It's easy whenever there is a physical, tangible device. With cell phone technology, there are many more variables. With Internet scrambling and VPN networks, it's easy to hide the caller's identity. I'll do my best, but let's see what happens, okay?"

"Understood," I replied, not fully understanding.

Click.

My phone was not synced with the loaner vehicle, so I scrolled through my contact list and dialed Brewster. He answered on the first ring.

"I'm glad you answered Brewster. Where are you?"

"Heading to Dina's office," he said. "It's Friday. Date night. We're heading to the blues bar in Ann Arbor for music and dancing. You and Kathy should join us."

"I thought Dina didn't work on Fridays."

"She has an emergency patient. What's up? You sound winded."

"Listen, the reason I'm calling is important. You guys shouldn't go to Ann Arbor tonight."

My conversation with Brewster was shorter than it was with Scruggs. He had been a cop. He'd been in the business, for Christ's sake. I explained everything to him as best I could, the same way I'd explained it to Scruggs. He listened and asked questions. Told me having a protective detail stationed in front of his house was unacceptable. I told him tough shit.

"Have a date night at home," I suggested. "Roleplay. Do whatever makes you happy. Just don't go to Ann Arbor tonight. It's too risky. Stay home. Stay safe."

He had more questions than I had answers. As soon as I hung up the phone, I knew he would reach out to his contacts for more details. By the end of the next hour, he would probably know more than I did, and I was married to one of the lead investigators.

"I understand," he said.

His answer sounded vague. "What are you going to do, Brewster?"

"Just what you recommended, Rick. I'll pick Dina up from her office, take her home, cook a delicious meal, and break out the handcuffs."

"Perfect. Pick a good safe word. Send me photos."

He was still chuckling when I ended the call.

I PULLED into the driveway where Bill Evans waited. We shook hands and went inside. He pulled a thick, black portable computer from his leather bag and set it on the kitchen table. I scooted to the refrigerator and opened a couple cold beers. Passing one to Bill, I sat next to him and guzzled half a beer, remembering what Kathy had said to me. *Might I suggest no alcohol tonight?* Yep, I remembered correctly; it was a suggestion.

Bill copied the contents of my phone and returned it to me. He requested my security password, which I provided. "This might take some time," he said. "I'll take a copy of your information home and see what I can uncover."

I nodded. "Do whatever you can to find the source of those messages."

"I'll do my best." He swallowed the last few drops of his beer.

My phone rang as I escorted Bill to the front door. I glanced at the caller ID. It was Brewster.

Bill waved as he stepped off the front porch. I answered my phone with a chuckle. "Need my handcuffs, Brewster?"

He wasn't laughing. "Dina's been abducted!"

"What?"

"I'm at her office. Her car is still here. The door to her office is unlocked, and she's gone."

"Maybe she jus—"

"Stop!" Brewster said. "I checked the video security tapes. A man wearing a black mask grabbed Dina from the front of her office and dragged her to the parking lot. He struck her on the head and tossed her into the back of a black SUV."

I pulled the phone away from my ear. "Bill! Hold on, don't leave yet—sorry, Brewster—Bill Evans was just leaving my house, and I thought he could help. We're on our way."

"I'm searching for clues." Brewster sounded calm and more relaxed than I might have been in his position. "Give Kathy a call immediately," he said. "Let her know we need to act on this quickly. Understand? I don't want this place swarming with cops I don't know or don't trust."

CHAPTER THIRTY FIVE
Present Day - Friday, November 5

I FIDGETED WITH MY KEYS, ANXIOUSLY WAITING FOR KATHY TO answer. When she did, the words blurted from my mouth.

"Are you on your way home? How close are you?"

"Yes. Sorry, I should have texted you my ETA. I was following up on a bunch of phone calls."

"Meet me downtown at Plaque Attack Dental Clinic. I'm heading there now. Dina's been abducted."

"What the hell are you talking about?"

"That's all I know, Kath. Bill Evans was at our house when Brewster called. Said he had videos of Dina being smacked on the head, dragged to a black SUV, and stuffed into the back seat."

"I'm less than fifteen minutes out. I'm on the way."

I fired up my truck and followed Bill Evans. Flashing red and blue lights reflected off the trees.

My head was spinning. Who else should I call? Who else might be in danger? Was this guy—or guys—targeting me, Brewster, and our families, or was anyone else in danger? Neighbors? Friends? Mayor Ben? Is anyone else from our lunch crowd in jeopardy? What about Ward Watkins? Was he in trouble? The single beer wasn't providing the numbness I needed. "Shake it off." My dad's voice popped into my head. "Get your shit together."

Good advice.

Bill drove fast, and I rode his bumper. We passed the

Social Club on our right, where the crowd at the front door flowed down the sidewalk. A few blocks later, we turned left at the bronze statue of a Native American Chief. Screeching to a halt behind the dental clinic, I saw Brewster's Lincoln Navigator. It was still running. Bill and I hopped from our vehicles and rushed inside. We found Brewster in Dina's office.

"Fill me in." I sounded like a cop.

"I'm kicking myself in the ass, buddy. I never let Dina see emergency patients without being with her. There are too many weirdos out there looking for drugs and painkillers."

"Yeah, okay. We can rehash this guilt trip later. Right now, I need to know what *you* know. Kathy is on the way."

"Here's what I know." He placed his elbows on the desk and rubbed his forehead. "Dina answered her cell at about 5:30p.m. A man said he was in extreme pain. Said he had a swollen face and a foul taste in his mouth. A typical abscessed tooth, right? I was ready to drive her to the clinic, but she told me to get ready for our date night and pick her up later. Said we would head to the blues bar from her office."

"What time did you leave the house to meet her?"

"Just before you called me, at 6:22p.m. I checked my phone. I was on my way to pick her up."

"So, what did you find on the security footage?"

"At 6:10p.m., Dina was leaving her office. My guess is that the guy, the fake emergency patient, didn't show up for his six o'clock appointment. She was probably pissed. The video is hard to watch. Dina was locking the door, and a guy wearing a ski mask walloped her on the back of her head. At least six feet tall and strong, the guy dragged her to his vehicle. After tossing her into the back seat, his vehicle left the camera view. "

Bill Evans intervened. "Can I have your seat, Bob? I'd like to review the footage myself."

Brewster stood up and waved Bill into the ergonomic chair. We left him to his business and stepped outside, grabbing an empty table behind the candle company, next to Dina's office. Minutes later, Kathy pulled into the lot, ignoring the designated yellow lines, and shut off her vehicle, blocking the circling traffic.

She exited her vehicle and made her way to our table. A short, scrawny dude wearing a Harley Davidson t-shirt mumbled something like, "Hey lady, you can't park there." Kathy flashed her badge, snarled, and may have even let out a low growl. The skinny wannabe grabbed his underage-looking girlfriend's hand and kept moving, never looking back.

"Hey, Bob," she said.

Brewster stood from his chair and welcomed her embrace. "Thanks for coming so quickly. We need to find Dina. I'm worried."

"I understand," Kathy said, backing away from the hug but still holding his hands and staring into his eyes. "You've been through this before, Bob, when you were in my position. Let's chat and see what we can uncover. You've probably already spoken with Rick about what happened, but I need to hear it myself. Please sit."

Brewster replayed the scenario for Kathy, as he had done with me. She scribbled in her spiral notebook. Kenny and Steve pulled up behind Kathy's Explorer. Exiting their vehicles, they rushed to our table. I briefed the Erickson brothers on what I knew. Kathy continued speaking with Brewster. I listened in on their conversation. He found Dina's purse and phone on the passenger seat of her car. Strike one. We wouldn't be able to track her cell phone.

"Here's what I've learned today," Kathy said. "Maybe these small pieces of the puzzle can help us visualize the bigger picture."

Kathy said the two punks from the construction business, Lowell Thomas and Billy Bartlett, had been friends with someone matching the description of our suspect, Tyler Jackson, the fake fire marshal.

"I don't know how this ties together," Kathy said. "But there is a connection between these guys and the construction site." She turned to face Kenny. "Can you grab the information Jean Simmons prepared for us? Maybe we can find a connection between the construction workers and Tyler Jackson. He has to be involved in this."

"Got it," Kenny said.

"Grab your laptop as well," she yelled as he walked to his car.

Kenny was headed back to join us when another state-owned vehicle pulled into the parking lot. Two female crime scene investigators opened the doors and walked toward us.

KATHY INTRODUCED her CSI colleagues to the growing group at the outdoor table. She instructed the two agents—Debbie and Patti were their names—to work the scene inside and out. "See what you can find," she told them. "No clue is too small." They hustled next door to the Plaque Attack Dental Clinic.

Kenny slid the papers from the manila envelope, and

while we waited for his computer to fire up, Kathy provided us with a recap of recent activities. She retold the story about meeting with the owner of the construction company, Jean Simmons. Summarized the subsequent encounter, and the gun battle, at the Parker Ridge Apartment complex with Billy "Bully" Bartlett, an employee of the construction company and a close friend of the recently deceased Lowell Thomas, who'd been killed by the State Police in Hubbard Lake. She reminded us that Billy Bartlett was still on the loose.

Steve passed around a photo of Bartlett and his extensive rap sheet. "We have issued a BOLO for his arrest."

Kathy said, "Great. We need to find him. Also, we discovered Bartlett and the deceased Lowell Thomas had a friend who visited them at the construction site in Redford from time to time. We have positively identified this person as Tyler Jackson. He's our number one suspect and presumably involved with Dina Brewster's abduction. I can almost guarantee he's the person who sent the threatening texts to Rick."

"How do we find him?" I asked.

She pointed at the papers in front of Kenny. "Let's start with the DMJ Construction employee list. If we can find a connection between any of their twenty-six employees and Tyler Jackson, that would be a great start."

Brewster looked around. "What about his house at Hubbard Lake? Do you think Tyler Jackson would ever return?"

Kathy shook her head. "Highly unlikely. The house is under twenty-four-seven surveillance, and besides, the detectives in Alpena found nothing significant that would warrant his return."

Kenny worked the keyboard on his laptop. Everyone else leaned in and listened, hoping for a clue, praying for something that might be important, a tiny sliver of evidence we could use to find Dina. Kathy focused on the papers and began reading the names. She called them out as Kenny punched the keyboard. Employees' names were read aloud alphabetically as we waited for the Internet to catch up with our anticipation.

For the next twenty minutes, Kenny told us about each individual on DMJ Construction's payroll. Charles Akens, misdemeanor possession, fifteen years ago. Walter Allen, public intoxication, recent. William Baker, indecent exposure, public urination. Simon Conners, disorderly conduct. David Kettering, petty theft. Thomas Richardson, drunk driving, second offense. On and on it went until he finished with Frank Zimmerman for trespassing.

Kenny slapped his palms on the table. "Shit. Twenty-six employees, twenty-six at-bats, twenty-six strikeouts. Now what?"

It was nearing eight o'clock as the crowds thinned. I saw the manager of the candle shop place the closed sign on the entrance door. The two young CSI investigators, Debbie and Patti, walked towards us from the dental clinic.

Kathy shrugged. "Find anything?"

Patti shook her head. "Too much information to process immediately. We found no tangible evidence from the abduc— Oh, sorry, Mr. Brewster. The *disappearance*. There are dozens of fingerprints. Probably Doctor Brewster's patients and staff. It'll take a while to get through them all. Debbie and I will head back to the office and get started."

Kathy nodded. "Great. Please make it a priority."

"You know we will," she said.

Patti and Debbie pulled away.

My phone vibrated. I looked down at a new text.

I thought I told you no more cops! Get me that gold coin or the bitch dies.

I nudged Kathy and stealthily handed her my phone. She read the message that had just flashed across my screen. She bit her lower lip and returned the phone to me as Bill Evans emerged from Dina's dental clinic.

Bill rushed to our table. "I found something!"

CHAPTER THIRTY SIX

Detroit, Michigan - 1945
'Never Quit'

For the thousandth time in the past ten years, Dale woke up not knowing where he was. The feeling of disorientation and hopelessness seemed to be his entire existence for many years. It was something he'd learned to live with. Was this *really* living? Of course, it wasn't, and he knew it, but doing something about it didn't feel like an option.

It sure wasn't a comfortable living, not like he remembered and often dreamed about, but it was a lifestyle, a choice, his current position in life, and Dale came to terms with the fact that it would never be better, so he dealt with it. Somehow, today felt different, and not in a good way.

Squatting in a dark alley, surrounded by rodents and garbage, he stumbled to his feet and brushed a sticky substance from his trousers. Was the odor from the trash? He couldn't tell. He didn't care. Looking around, he found no one else in sight.

The morning sun peeked above the horizon from another country and danced across the black waters of the Detroit River. He could see the Ambassador Bridge and the fading lights of Canada in the distance, but somehow couldn't find a street sign. *Where am I? How the hell did I get here?* Repeatedly, the same questions for nearly a decade and never an answer, at least not an acceptable one, and even if he could change the outcome—could he? He reasoned, probably not.

He ran his fingers through his long, stringy hair. Dale Mintern bent over, threw up again, and wondered how life got so shitty. He wiped the slime from his beard and sat back down. The tears welled in his once bright blue eyes. Reminiscing as he often did, he thought about better days and happier times. He remembered being the good guy once. He didn't feel so good at the moment. Christ, he felt nothing for so long; Dale wondered if he was even human anymore. It was a terrible existence, living day to day, meal to meal, scuffle to scuffle.

He stood up, which had become more challenging by the day, and gazed toward the magnificent Ambassador Bridge. Something caught his eye. Something he hadn't seen before. A billboard. A Marine recruitment advertisement.

'Face the Future. Never quit. U.S. Marines'

For the first time in a very long time, Dale thought about John Douglas, his Marine buddy, his cop partner, his FBI colleague, his friend. Flashing memories, good recollections, and beautiful thoughts came to him less and less, but when they did, they were vivid—like it was a dream.

He closed his eyes and thought about his enlistment day in the Marines. He could still feel the warm salt water breeze blowing in from the Pacific Ocean. The smells he remembered from the streets of northern San Diego pulled his chapped lips into a slight grin. He recalled the faces of his fellow soldiers. He relived the sweat, the pain, and the commitment. A flashing smile from a dear friend, John Douglas, cleared his head—if only for the moment. *Boot camp*, he remembered. That's where they first met. He lost control again.

Dale Mintern, now a frail man, a shadow of his former prowess, fell back hard against something metal and cried. For a long time, he lay there and sobbed. Not knowing what to do or where to go, he forced himself to his feet and wandered aimlessly for an undetermined time in an unknown direction.

He was heading away from the Detroit River into the heart of the city. That's all he knew. Sometimes he considered taking a plunge in the river, but today, like most days, he didn't have the commitment—unlike his Marine days. He stumbled through the dark streets of Detroit for what felt like hours. It probably was. His internal clock was a combination of the rising sun and the noise from the growing traffic. A few horns sounded, whistles from the traffic cops pierced the air, and he knew the soup kitchen would open soon. His internal clock worked. His inner compass was broken.

Turning an unmarked corner, looking for something recognizable, he heard shouting. A voice echoed off tall buildings and blended confusingly with the growing noise on the busy streets of the Motor City. Dale was confused, expecting trouble, and ready, as he always was, for a confrontation. His head was on a swivel.

"Hey there. Are you alright?" Dale's body pivoted, and his mind raced. Voices in his head were becoming ubiquitous.

"I said, young man, are you alright?" The calls grew louder.

Turning right, he saw an elderly man waving his arms high. The stranger was standing on the cement steps of a church. A church he had walked past a hundred times and yet, couldn't remember the name or even the street.

Something is wrong with me.

Dale rubbed his palms. They felt sweaty. His knees buckled, and his head reeled. His heart rate quickened, creating a strange sort of dizziness.

What the hell is going on?

The man descended the cement steps, approached him, and smiled. "You look troubled, young man. Is there anything I can do to help you?"

St. Joseph's Catholic Church.

It was the last thing he remembered.

CHAPTER THIRTY SEVEN
Present Day - Friday, November 5

BREWSTER ROSE FROM THE TABLE, ARMS WIDE. HE HUSTLED toward Bill Evans. Everyone stood. And listened. Bill asked Brewster if he had used the SmartStuff security app at his house.

Brewster's arms were high. "Yeah, so?"

"I checked your security systems. You and your wife use tracking devices that turn on and off certain devices in your home and your businesses, right?"

"Get to the point, Bill."

"I got a ping on your wife's tracker. Follow me."

We gathered our belongings from the outdoor table at the candle shop and followed him next door to the Plaque Attack Dental Clinic.

Bill sat at Dina's desk and maneuvered the mouse around the desktop. The rest of us circled him, staring at the computer screen.

"Here—right here." Bill pointed.

Kathy's eyes darted around the screen. "What are we looking at?"

"It's the last known location of Dina."

Brewster moved forward, standing shoulder-to-shoulder with Kathy. "What do you mean, last known location?"

Bill pumped his finger at the monitor. "Pay attention. You and Dina have identity trackers set up on your

SmartStuff security system. Where is your tracker, Bob?"

Brewster fumbled with his pocket. "It's on my key chain."

"What's its function?"

"It turns certain things on and off at my house when I arrive or leave. It's creepy but convenient. I never have to unlock doors, turn lights on, or anything. It's like a secretary on a chain."

"Where does your wife keep her tracking device?"

"How the hell should I know?"

Bill gave us a geeky stare. "Well, wherever Dina keeps it, she still has it, and I got a hit. At 6:12 p.m., it left this office. It's currently at the intersection of West Chicago and Telegraph Road in Redford Township. It's been there for about forty-five minutes."

Kathy said, "I thought you said her key chain was still in her car, Bob?"

"It is. I saw it."

Kathy stared over Bill's shoulder. "Well, the tracker is obviously not connected to her key chain. Can you pinpoint the location, Bill?"

He scribbled on a legal pad. "Yep, here's the address. A place called the Rib Shack."

Kathy ripped a sheet from the yellow legal pad and walked away, holding her phone to her ear. I heard her directing Patti and Debbie, her CSI investigators, to change routes and meet her at the address in Redford.

I JUMPED into the passenger seat of Kathy's Explorer. Brewster rode with Kenny, and Steve followed, driving solo. Lights flashed as we traveled at a high rate of speed on I-94 towards Redford. Kathy contacted the Redford Police Dispatch. Her call was redirected to the cell phone of the lead officer on the scene. The conversation blared over the car speakers.

Lieutenant David Kozlowski with Redford PD answered the call. Kathy explained the situation. The Redford cop sounded confused. He said he was at the Rib Shack and was following up on a domestic dispute call. She clarified the urgency and filled him in on the abduction in Dunville.

"Really? All the witnesses here described it as a domestic."

"It's much more than that, Lieutenant. Can you preserve the scene until we arrive? And keep the witnesses onsite, please. We'd like to question them as well."

"I'll do my best," said Kozlowski. "Many have already left. We have contact information and statements from those we interviewed. I hope that helps."

"I appreciate that. Can you also find out if the restaurant has security footage of the parking lot?"

"I can tell you they do," he said. "I've reviewed the files. A black SUV, traveling northbound at high speed on Telegraph Road, lost control and jumped the curb. It bounced violently into the parking lot of the Rib Shack, barely missing a few pedestrians. The SUV ran into a light pole. The female passenger jumped from the vehicle and ran southbound into an empty lot where there was ongoing construction. Another one of those damned marijuana dispensaries. The male driver then chased the female, grabbing her by her jacket and ripping it from her body. We found the jacket on the ground in the empty lot. Then he dragged her back to the SUV."

"Was there anything in the pockets of the jacket?"

"The only items we recovered were a pack of gum and some dental floss."

"How did they leave?"

"Believe it or not, after he tossed the female into the back seat, he started the vehicle and drove away, northbound on Telegraph Road. There was significant damage to the front end. I'm surprised it was drivable. I've already put out a BOLO on the vehicle."

"Did you get the license plate?"

"Negative. The security cameras pointed west, away from the restaurant, facing the street. It only recorded the front of the vehicle. No plates were visible. When the driver rushed from the scene, he backed up, trampled the bushes near the neighboring construction, and drove over the curb."

Kathy's conversation blared over the speakers, and I hunched forward, listening intently. The Redford cop told her there were traffic cameras three miles north. Kathy said she needed to review the past two hours of video files from that intersection and told the Redford Lieutenant she would have her CSI detectives follow up.

She ended the call by asking the Redford PD to tape off the area, letting the Lieutenant know she would arrive in less than thirty minutes. It was already past 8:30. She called CSI agent Patti Trombly.

"Change of plans," Kathy said. "You and Debbie go directly to the Redford Police Department. Let me know if you find anything on the traffic cameras. I'll follow up with you later."

THE REDFORD PD did a great job securing the area and keeping the thrill-seekers outside the perimeter. The Rib

Shack parking lot and the neighboring gravel lot — the soon-to-be Head Shack, another marijuana dispensary — were cordoned off with yellow crime tape. A throng of spectators held their smartphone cameras high in the air, recording what they could from a distance. Bright lights from their cameras lit up the scene.

Kathy introduced herself to Lieutenant Kozlowski. The clock was ticking, and she needed to find Dina.

Steve entered the Rib Shack to interview witnesses who were still at the restaurant.

Dina's brown leather jacket, found in the empty construction parking lot, was searched again. No tracker was found. I saw Kenny and a few Redford cops set up a search grid and heard Kenny speaking with one of them.

"Our technology specialist with the State Police confirmed the female victim had a tracking device on her body when she entered this parking lot. According to him, it's still here. Let's find it."

Kathy and I hustled into the restaurant, where Steve interviewed witnesses. Daniel Herkimer, who proudly wore an "assistant manager" badge on his ill-fitting jacket, directed us to his office. He guided us to the monitor on the desk and repeatedly played the camera videos for Kathy, stopping here and there for a second look. Ten minutes later, she thanked him for his help.

"My team will want to review this video again, Daniel," she told him. "Please make a copy for them."

"Yes, ma'am." He addressed her with a sloppy salute.

I walked back outside and met with Brewster in the parking lot. He was questioning witnesses who had already met with Steve. Said he learned nothing new.

Kozlowski called out for Kathy as she exited the restaurant's front doors. He waved her over. "Special Agent Cooper, may I have a word with you, please?"

Brewster and I moved in their direction. The Lieutenant and Kathy waved us off. We shrugged in unison, walked south to the gravel parking lot of the future recreational pot dispensary, and looked for Kenny, staying within earshot of Kathy's conversation.

"What have you got, Lieutenant?" she asked.

"First, please call me David. It will keep our conversations shorter."

"Perfect," she replied. "I agree. Call me Kathy."

"Great, Kathy. We have a lead."

"I'm listening."

Our dispatcher had received a call from a concerned motorist. The troubled driver called 911 to report what he thought was a drunk driver. Said a black SUV with a damaged front end was driving recklessly at a high rate of speed and nearly sideswiped him. The suspicious SUV was eastbound on the Jeffries Freeway when the man called. Said it exited the freeway and turned northbound on Beech Daly Road.

Brewster and I took a few steps closer.

"How about the license plate?" Kathy asked.

"Nothing yet. My team is working on it. Hopefully, we'll have more information shortly."

Daniel Herkimer was taking photos on his cell phone under the front awning of the restaurant. Kathy waved him over. He hustled to meet her.

"Mr. Herkimer, is there a private area in your restaurant that my team might use for an hour?"

"Absolutely." He beamed. "You can use the employee

break room. I'll kick everyone out of there right now." He looked winded from the short sprint.

"Be polite, Mr. Herkimer. We'll be inside in five minutes."

"Yes, ma'am." He saluted her again and hurried towards the entrance.

Brewster and I followed Kenny as he headed in Kathy's direction. Kenny said he had found the tracking device.

"It must have fallen out of Dina's jacket pocket during the scuffle."

Kathy threw a thumb over her shoulder. "Kenny, can you grab that DMJ Construction folder from your car and meet us in the employee break room? We need to take another look at the employee list. Also, we never found out who previously owned DMJ Construction. We need to find out why they insisted that Jean Simmons keep Lowell Thomas and Billy Bartlett on her payroll."

"Will do."

Steve finished his final interview as we reentered the restaurant. We waved him over, and Daniel Herkimer escorted us down a brightly lit hallway. I side-stepped the single file of people to answer a call from Scruggs. Our conversation was short, probably because I was short with him. He wanted to know where I was and what we were doing—requesting our current location. He wanted in on the action; I was sure of it. I probably would have had the same questions if I were in his shoes. I kept the answers vague. Told him he was nearly an hour away, there was nothing he could do to help, we'd be on our way home shortly, and left him with a few other ambiguous reasons for him not to make the journey. Not that I didn't want him with us. Of course I did, but I had heard a few whispers from the Redford cops, probably wondering why an ex-cop and a reserve cop were involved in an official police investigation. Kathy no doubt regretted letting us join her, and the last thing I wanted was to bring another civilian into the mix. She didn't need one more person to answer for and keep safe.

Ending the conversation to satisfy his need for inclusion and, in the same breath mitigating his desire for travel, I advised Scruggs he might reach out to Bill Evans to see if he needed any help. Bill was still in town at the dental clinic.

"He might want your help," I told him.

"You're an asshole," he said.

Click.

Shortly after 9:00 p.m., we took our seats on wooden chairs in the break room. I tucked the phone into the breast pocket of my flannel shirt. Behind me was a clean kitchen counter area, a large refrigerator, and a microwave. A unisex restroom was on the right. The room was larger than I expected, with two means of egress. We'd entered through one, and the second led to the employee parking lot in the rear of the building.

Kenny set the manila folder on a pine table that matched the chairs. The table was large enough to seat twelve people comfortably. There were six of us: our Dunville team of five and Lieutenant David Kozlowski. We all sat at one end, closest to the employee parking lot.

The assistant manager entered the room with his hands full. The robust Daniel Herkimer set two overflowing baskets of ribs and chips on the table and asked what we wanted to drink. He placed a stack of paper plates and napkins in the center and headed back to the kitchen for beverages. Kathy gave him a nod of appreciation as he passed.

Kenny opened the folder, shuffled through the papers, and fired up his computer. Everyone else reached across the table for the BBQ ribs.

His face twisted as he found the information he had been looking for. "Elaine Jackson-Mintern," Kenny said. "She's listed as the previous owner of DMJ Construction."

"Huh." I cocked my head.

Steve turned to me. "What?"

"Mintern," I said. "Is that a coincidence or what?"

Kathy's eyes met mine for a long moment and then back to Kenny. "What's her husband's name?"

He shrugged. "It doesn't say."

"Do you have her current address?" Kathy stood and walked to Kenny, peering over his shoulder.

Kenny read from the screen. "Her residence is 15865 Bayberry Court, in Livonia, Michigan. I don't know if it's current or not. Let me check." He tapped on the keyboard.

Lieutenant Kozlowski excused himself from the table and walked to the far corner of the room to accept an incoming phone call.

The assistant manager and another helper entered the room carrying beverages. Kathy thanked Daniel and his helper, telling him they would square up later. Herkimer told her it was on the house and mentioned he had a cousin in Baltimore who was a police officer. He thanked us for our service and offered another awkward salute.

"Here you go," Kenny continued. "Elaine Jackson-Mintern. Caucasian, no criminal history, a few traffic citations, sixty-three years of age, brown eyes, five-foot-two inches tall, no children, married to a sixty-five-year-old

Caucasian male named Dale Mintern Junior."

"Fuck!" I screamed. A greasy chicken wing landed on my lap. I jumped from my chair.

Brewster slid back fast, avoiding the grease splatter.

David Kozlowski returned to the table, ignoring the commotion. "We got a hit on the license plate. The 2020 black Chevy Tahoe is registered to a business called D & E Properties."

Kathy asked. "Where is this business located?"

Kenny pounded on his keyboard.

I wiped barbecue sauce from my jeans.

"It's the same address!" Kenny exclaimed. "Bayberry Court. Livonia. The principal owners of D & E Properties are Dale Mintern Junior and Elaine Jackson-Mintern. They must have an office in their house."

Kathy addressed the Lieutenant. "David, we'll follow you. Can you have another car meet us there?"

"Absolutely. I'll call it in on the way."

"Do not have them approach the suspects' house until we arrive."

"Understood."

We ran out of the employee break room of the Rib Shack and hustled to our vehicles. Daniel Herkimer inquired about the urgency. Kathy told him we had a lead that needed to be acted on immediately. He frowned and asked if we were coming back.

"Probably not, but thank you for your hospitality and help."

Daniel Herkimer's face lit up. He had a great smile. Then, it got better.

Kathy turned toward him and gave him a proper salute.

CHAPTER THIRTY EIGHT
Present Day - Friday, November 5

KATHY CONTACTED A FAMILY FRIEND, WILLIAM CARLTON, A respectable judge from Michigan's First District in Monroe County, and petitioned for an expedited search warrant. She had eyewitness accounts, video surveillance from the Rib Shack parking lot, and confirmation of the suspect's license plate from the traffic cameras that the Redford Township Police had provided.

The judge said little, just listened. Even an untrained ear like mine could hear the sounds of silverware clinking and people chatting in the background. It was close to 10:00 p.m., and the cocktail hour was in full swing. I guessed he was at a bar, probably schmoozing with other political muckety-mucks. Judge Carlton asked for a few minutes to review and consider the information.

"I have your number, Agent Cooper."

Click.

"He'll approve it, right?" I asked.

"Oh, yeah."

She called Patti, letting her know we had left the scene on Telegraph Road. Priorities had changed since their last conversation. Kathy gave her the address in the neighboring city Livonia. Told her and Debbie to meet us there.

Red and blue lights flashed. No sirens. The Redford Lieutenant took the lead. I rode shotgun with Kathy. Brewster rode with Kenny, and Steve brought up the rear.

We traveled at high speeds eastbound on Schoolcraft Road, which merged into the Jeffries Freeway. Vehicles slowed and moved to their right as the flashing lights of our four-car convoy flew by them. At Farmington Road, we exited the freeway, turning right. The police caravan turned left onto Blue Skies Lane between Six-mile and Seven-mile Roads. GPS had our target's location less than six blocks away.

Kathy turned to me. "You and Brewster need to stay back. This is an official police matter."

"I'm an official police officer," I said.

"Not here," she said. "Not now!"

The Lieutenant called Kathy, letting her know he needed to inform Livonia PD of our intent—something about rival pissing matches. Kathy consented and clarified the State Police had the lead on the investigation. She didn't want any cowboys on her turf. Passing the Redford Police backup vehicle parked on the corner of Blue Skies Lane and Bayberry Court, our convoy turned right. The backup car pulled in behind us. Kathy checked her phone. She smiled and told me the judge had approved the warrant.

We were in an exclusive neighborhood, every yard beautifully landscaped. Flowering trees, brick pavers, rock gardens, water fountains, and dark green manicured lawns were abundant.

Their water bills might be more than my mortgage.

The convoy skidded to a stop outside the elegant entrance. The target house, a sizable colonial estate, was on the left near the beginning of a cul-de-sac. The paved circular driveway made parking easy. Flashing red and blue lights bounced off the manicured shade trees. Porch lights from curious neighbors added a contrasting white hue.

Kathy stepped out of the car and repeated her directions for Brewster and me to stay back.

The house faced east. Lieutenant Kozlowski and Kathy approached the lustrous paneled wood door and hopped up two steps onto the front porch. Two officers from the backup vehicle hollered they would cover the south side of the estate. They hustled left.

Kenny and Steve bolted in the opposite direction. Kenny stayed on the north side—the right—as Steve continued to the backyard, securing the estate's west.

"Open the door. We have a warrant!" Kozlowski shouted.

"Don't move! Get down on the ground!" Steve shouted from the rear of the property.

One of the Redford cops hustled to cover Steve as he detained a suspect in the backyard. The other officer never gave up his position on the east side of the house, keeping their eyes on the garage doors.

"Clear!" Steve shouted.

The front door opened. Elaine Jackson-Mintern appeared stunned as Kathy pushed her way inside the vestibule and secured her with handcuffs. Kozlowski brushed past them and advanced toward the kitchen.

Brewster and I slipped closer to the front door and stared into the spacious interior. We saw Kenny enter through a rear patio door near the kitchen. With his pistol in a registered firing position, he rushed inside and made eye contact with the lieutenant. Nodding his head to the left, Kozlowski bolted down the hallway. Kenny went right, heading for the garage.

Clearing the immaculate three-car man cave, he pressed

the opener. The garage lights lit up. As the first garage bay opened, I heard Kenny calling out to the Redford backup team, shouting his name and position. He probably didn't relish the thought of dying by friendly fire. The two cops entered and joined Kenny. In the right bay sat a vintage red and white Corvette convertible. In the middle bay was a bright red Ferrari Purosangue SUV. The left garage bay was empty.

"Damn. Nice cars." They hustled inside, glancing back with envious looks.

"I TOLD you! I wasn't running. I stepped out on the patio to smoke a cigar."

"Sit down," Steve pushed Dale Mintern Junior into a plush kitchen chair.

Kathy and Kozlowski had already escorted Dale's wife, Elaine, to another part of the large estate.

Steve shoved a finger in Dale's face and scowled. "I didn't see any cigars, and innocent people don't run when confronted by law enforcement. Do you know why we're here?"

"I'm telling you, I wasn't running. Where's my wife?"

Dina was missing, and they needed information fast.

Kenny leaned forward and growled, "We're investigating the abduction of a friend. We know you're involved. You better tell us what's going on. Where is she?"

Steve repeated the question more forcefully.

"Okay! Listen, I had nothing to do with this," Dale scooted his chair back. "This is about the gold, right? That's my guess — and if I'm right, that little prick and his buddies are out of control. They've messed themselves up on drugs and can't think clearly anymore. I can't control them. This isn't my fault!"

"What isn't your fault? Who are you talking about?"

Dale raised his palms, pumping them wildly. "My asshole nephew. My wife's brother's kid."

"What's his name?"

"Tyler."

"Tyler, what?"

"I just told you. He's my wife's brother's kid. Jackson. Tyler Jackson."

BREWSTER AND I had already sneaked our way inside, quietly, through the open front door. We stood motionless in the large vestibule. We heard the Erikson brothers question their suspect. Brewster's posture stiffened when he heard Dale mention Tyler Jackson's name. Anticipating his reaction, I stepped in front of him, grabbed him by his shirt, planted my feet, and held him against the shiny wallpaper, preventing forward movement.

"Don't do it," I told him, looking into his wild brown eyes. "Let them finish questioning him. You're only going to make things worse if you go in there."

Brewster slid backward along the wall and slapped my arms with a forceful downward motion of his right forearm, escaping my grip. I stayed close, shadowing him, maintaining a safe distance.

I saw Kathy exit a hallway to our left. She turned to Brewster and me with a glowering look. "I thought I told you two to stay outside!"

"It's all good," Brewster lied. "You were gone a while, and we thought you guys might be in trouble. It's all good," he repeated.

Kathy shook her head and threw her hands high in

frustration. She hustled toward the kitchen and pointed at the table. "What's going on?"

"His nephew..." Steve pumped a thick knuckle into Dale's chest. "His nephew is involved in Dina's kidnapping."

Kathy nudged Steve aside and bent down, placing her hands on her thighs. Her brown eyes fixed on the moist blue eyes of Dale Mintern Junior. "You'd better answer our questions quickly. Right now, you're an accessory to kidnapping. If anything else happens to her, I'll make sure you never see the outside of a prison wall again."

"I didn't do anything!" He rubbed his chest.

Patti and Debbie gave Brewster and me a quizzical stare as they passed us in the vestibule. Kathy hustled from her suspect and met them at the threshold between the living room and the kitchen.

"I need this house turned upside down," Kathy whispered. "I don't believe they're telling us everything they know. If you could find any physical evidence of their involvement, that would be helpful. I need leverage. Got it?"

They nodded and disappeared down a hallway. Kathy made her way back to the kitchen and assumed her authoritative position. With her hands on her knees, she stared into Dale's eyes. "You're going to be in jail for a long time," she growled. "Your wife told us about her nephew. Said you provided him with information about the gold coin." She shoved her finger in his face. "I'll have my arrest warrant shortly, Dale. You're about to be introduced to a lifestyle you've never imagined."

Dale slapped his thighs and barked, "Listen, my wife didn't tell you *shit!* You know why?" He leaned forward, spittle forming at the corner of his mouth. "Because she has no fucking clue what's going on! Elaine is an angel. She's the only one who stuck by me these past fifty-plus years!"

"That's not what she's telling us. So, if you think you ca—"

"Knock it off!" Dale shouted. "Stop your bullshit! My wife didn't tell you anything." Dale looked like he had a hard time breathing. His face tightened, and his head fell forward. He placed his palms in the air and inhaled a deep breath. After a moment, he composed himself and continued. "If this *is* about the gold coin, my wife and I had nothing to do with that—or anything that may have happened to your friend."

"You seem to know a lot about something you claim to know nothing about. You'd better tell us what you *do* know."

Dale Junior slid his chair back, away from Kathy, wiping tears from his eyes. "My childhood was filled with stories from my dad," he said as he wept. "It was always a quest for him. Finding the treasure, wealth beyond the imagination, he would say to me. It obsessed him."

Kathy stepped back, providing space for him to continue with his story. "So, your father was Dale Mintern? He was an FBI agent?"

Dale Junior nodded.

"How are these stories of your father related to the abduction of our friend?"

Dale wiped his eyes again. "I'm getting there. My dad would sit in his den for hours every night except Saturday, studying his notes. He followed hundreds of leads, determined to find the treasure." He rolled his eyes. "Treasure. Ha!"

Kathy asked, "What was different about Saturday?"

"Saturday was my favorite day of the week. Dad would

spend the entire day at this homeless shelter downtown. He ran the place. Most weeks, he would take me with him. I loved those days. They're my favorite memories. Then, Saturday evening, it was TV night. Just the three of us watching television. It was the only night of the week he allowed us to watch."

Brewster and I shuffled closer to the action.

"So, your father railed you with stories of a hidden treasure." She prompted him to continue. "Go on, and get to your point quickly."

"I want my wife with me," Dale demanded. "Get Elaine. I need to see that she's all right." His head hung low.

Steve volunteered and left the kitchen. Minutes later, he returned with Kozlowski and the female suspect, still in handcuffs.

"You can remove those from her." Kathy pointed at her wrists. "Have her take a seat at the end of the table."

Elaine rushed quickly to her husband. Dale did his best to reciprocate her affection. With her arms wrapped tightly around his chest, she sobbed. "What's going on, Dale?"

Kathy said, "Mrs. Mintern if I allow you to be present in this room, you need to stop talking and only speak when you're asked a question. Do you understand?"

She met her husband's eyes, then turned to Kathy and nodded.

"Great. Now, back to you, Dale. Quit stalling and finish your story. Where is your nephew, and where is our friend?"

"I screwed up." Dale sniffled loudly. It sounded like he was trying to suck a milkshake up his nose. He shuffled his feet, glanced at his wife, and continued.

"Dad's FBI partner had a leather briefcase that held all

the valuables from a gambling raid in Detroit. Before he could submit it into evidence, he was murdered. Shot in the back of the head. Anyway, like I said, our family had very little money. Dad knew if he could track down the gold coins and other valuables, he could afford a much better life for my mom and me. He knew the cash was already gone, probably gambled away. Before my dad passed, he showed me where he had kept his secret files and made me promise to continue the search if he died without finding the treasure. I was sixteen years old when he died. Massive heart attack."

Kathy said, "So, you've been obsessed with this *treasure* like your father was?"

"Maybe for a few years after he passed, sure. Once I graduated from high school and headed to college, I didn't give it another thought until I heard the news story about a gold coin being found in Dunville. That's when I got my dad's secret file from my safe. I hadn't even thought about it in decades."

"Where is this safe?"

"In the master bedroom."

Kathy tipped her head toward the Lieutenant. He returned the nod, helped Elaine from the kitchen chair, and escorted her down the hallway.

"Dale," Kathy said. "Listen to me. This is very important. I don't believe you're a murderer, but people *have* been murdered since you've been involved, so pay attention. I need to know the whereabouts of your nephew, Tyler Jackson."

"Find my SUV, and you'll probably find that prick. He stole it. I'll give you the license plate number. You can track him down that way."

"Was it a black Chevy Tahoe?"

"Yes ma'am."

"When did he steal it?"

"A few weeks ago."

"Did you report it stolen?"

Dale shook his head. "Tyler said he was borrowing it, but I *knew* I'd never see it again."

Kenny said, "I'm not sure you *want* your SUV back, Dale. Your nephew smashed it up pretty good this evening."

CHAPTER THIRTY NINE

Detroit, Michigan - 1945
'I Used To Be a Cop'

DALE MINTERN SAT UP STRAIGHT AND FAST, WHICH SURPRISED even him. Waking up warm and comfortable wasn't familiar. Not in recent memories, at least. Not for a long time, in fact. Hell, it didn't feel natural. Something was different. *What was happening?* He checked his surroundings and found no one standing over him. What the hell? There was nobody to fight with.

A red-headed priest entered the room with a broad smile. Dale let out a guttural sound that didn't sound human, drawing attention from the adjoining room.

"It's good to see you moving, young man. How are you feeling this morning?"

Dale surveyed the room. "Where am I? What's going on?"

The priest beamed. "Relax, relax. We were worried about you."

"Who are you? Where am I?"

The priest clapped his hands together. "You're safe, young man. That's the easiest way to begin our conversation. *You're safe.*"

"Am I dead?"

"No, son." The priest laughed. "You are not dead. In fact, thanks to the grace of God, our loving sisters, and the help of our parishioners, you are very much alive."

Dale's attempts to stand up failed him. He fell back into the cot.

Two nuns entered the room, each smiling at their miracle. "It's so good to see you awake," one sister, heavier set than the other, said with a smile.

Dale settled back against the wall. "How long have I been here?"

The other nun knelt at his bedside and grabbed his hand. "Son, you've been resting for almost five days."

"What happened?"

"Well," the heavyset sister replied. "Only *you* can tell us what happened. All we know is the good Lord delivered you to the steps of our church."

Dale scrunched his forehead. "I don't remember anything."

"And that's fine for now," the priest said. "Let's get your physical strength back first. Then we can work on your spiritual faculties."

The skinnier nun released Dale's hand and flashed a smile. "I'll fetch you some food and water. Don't go anywhere." She laughed and retreated from the small room. The chubby nun followed.

All alone with the tall, pie-faced priest, Dale said, "I feel sick, Father."

"I'll bet you do," the elderly priest nodded. "How you looked when we took you in, well, son, I'm not sure you would have made it through another day."

"I should be on my way." Dale's attempts to stand failed. He fell back, once again finding the wall behind him.

The priest gently placed his hands on Dale's shoulder, leaning forward. "You should lay back and get some rest, young man. Accept your fate and let us help you. Let God help you."

"Am I not free to go?"

"Of course, you are free to go anytime you'd like, but I'd like you to listen to what I say before you rush out of here. It won't take long. I'm usually pretty direct."

Dale nodded.

"Young man, we were going to contact the hospital when you passed out on our church steps, but law enforcement follows when we contact emergency services. We weren't sure if you had any other issues, you know, *besides* your demons."

Dale paused, lowering his eyes. "I used to be a cop."

"Is that so?"

He craned his neck. His voice was weak. "Yes. It's a long story, Father."

The priest took Dale's hand and knelt on the side of his cot. "Well, I hope you stay with us long enough to share. We have some terrific parishioners here, young man. Many of them volunteered their time and services to keep you alive. As long as you're here, you are part of our family. Should you leave us before the Lord feels you're ready and fall back into your wicked ways, just know that I can't ask them to sacrifice again."

"My name is Dale. Dale Mintern," he breathed out with a heavy sigh.

"It's a pleasure to meet you, Dale Mintern. I am Father Malloy."

Dale fell back into a comfortable position on the cot, pulled the wool blanket over his head, and closed his eyes.

CHAPTER FORTY
Present Day - Friday, November 5

STEVE REJOINED THE INTERROGATION. "WE NEED TO FIND YOUR nephew before he harms our friend's wife. Where is he?"

"I wish I knew." Dale wiped the snot from his upper lip. "Actually, I'm glad I don't know where Tyler is. After the botched robbery at that bar in Dunville, he threatened to kill me. Said I was an idiot. Said I should have known the coin in the safe was a fake. I didn't tell him to rob the place."

"Do you have a phone number for him?" Steve asked.

"Nope. Like I said earlier, my nephew is a drug-addicted piece of shit, a total loser." Dale looked around, thankful Elaine wasn't in the room to hear his outburst. "And he doesn't own a phone. He buys those cheap, untraceable ones from whatever convenience store he's close to, in whatever shitty neighborhood he's staying in."

Steve's face tensed. "So, you don't know where he's staying?"

"I'm sorry, I don't. Tyler's grandfather, Elaine's dad, left him a house in northern Michigan. It's somewhere near Alpena."

"Hubbard Lake."

"Yeah, that's it—Hubbard Lake. Maybe you can find him there?"

"We've already searched that property. Tyler wasn't there. One of his friends was there, though. He was shot and killed."

"He only has a couple of friends. Let's see, Bill and Lowell. Yeah, that's it, Billy and Lowell. I don't know their last names or where they live, but maybe the names will help. You've got to believe me. Whatever my nephew and his loser friends are involved with, I had no part in it."

"Well, your nephew has one less friend," Steve told him. "Lowell Thomas was the one who was shot and killed."

Kathy's face was inches from Dale's. "You already admitted being involved in the robbery at the Social Club in Dunville."

"I did no such thing! I told you I knew about the robbery at the bar because I saw it on the news. After I saw the television report, I *knew* who did it. Who else would it be? The night the news reporter aired her story about a gold coin being found in Dunville, I pulled Dad's secret files from my safe. Tyler was swiping another free meal from my wife at our house that night. I *may* have had a few too many glasses of wine and *may* have spouted off information that I shouldn't have, but that doesn't make me guilty. Listen, that news report made me feel young again. I felt like I was reliving my teenage years, looking over my dad's shoulders as he sat in his den, plotting his treasure map, putting together pieces of his evidence puzzle. I felt alive."

Kathy said, "Dale, if there is anything you can do to help us find your nephew, I will make sure the district attorney will do everything to go easy on you."

"There's nothing to go easy on," he shouted. "Spouting my mouth off to a deranged sociopath is a moral defect, not a crime. I feel guilty because I never should have spoken out loud with that asshole in my presence, but I never helped him and his friends plan anything."

Steve asked, "Do you know where we can find your nephew's friend, Billy Bartlett?"

"I'm sorry, I don't. Billy stopped by now and again when Tyler was in town, but I never asked him where he lived, and I didn't care. Mostly, when Tyler brought his friends over, I buried myself in the den and read a book. I like to read."

Lieutenant Kozlowski walked into the kitchen with Elaine Jackson-Mintern. He handed a thick folder to Kathy and assisted Elaine to a chair before retreating from the busy kitchen to answer an incoming phone call.

Dale pointed at the folder. "Those are the files from my dad. That's his life's mission. Solving the mystery of riches and wealth. It's the only tangible memory I have of him. Please, don't destroy them.

IT WAS nearly eleven o'clock when I stepped onto the flagstone patio near the front entrance to give Scruggs a call. Brewster followed. The bright flashing lights of the police vehicles had long since been muted. Neighbors had closed their curtains and blinds. The waning gibbous moon glowed in the clear skies and illuminated the mature trees in the exclusive neighborhood. A dog barked in the distance.

I called Scruggs. It went directly to voice mail.

He's probably pissed at me.

I meandered between two tall decorative types of grass, approached Brewster, and asked him how he was doing. By his expression, I already knew. Still, I had to ask. He said he had a good feeling about finding Dina. I believed his instincts.

I *needed* to believe.

He kept checking his phone. Waiting for a miracle call?

Maybe. He was edgy, and I wished there was more I could do. He waved me back inside, and we entered the vestibule together.

Our movement caught Dale Junior's attention. He stood from his seat slowly and faced us. "Whose wife was abducted?" The question seemed sincere.

Brewster raised his right hand.

Dale placed his hands together as if to pray. "Please know that I had nothing to do with that. I can explain if you can afford me a minute or two."

Brewster inhaled a deep, audible breath.

Nobody asked Dale to be seated. He stood tall and looked straight into Brewster's eyes.

"What's your name?" Dale asked.

"Brewster. Robert Brewster."

"Mr. Brewster, I feel terrible. If I'd had any knowledge of what these assholes, these unfortunate members of my family would do, I would have come forward sooner."

Brewster closed the gap. "Do you know where my wife is?"

Kathy quickly placed herself between Brewster and Dale. Holding her hands in front of her, palms facing forward, she spoke calmly. "Bob, I don't believe he was involved in Dina's disappearance. He may have been an unfortunate accomplice." She turned to Dale, raising an eyebrow.

Then, stepping closer to Brewster, she whispered, "He might even be a useful idiot, but this wasn't his plan. It wasn't his idea. He was not part of Dina's abduction."

Brewster stared at Dale for a long moment, his eyes narrowed, and his fists tightened. "If I find out you had anything to do with my wife's kidnapping, you'll be the sorriest person on this planet."

Dale nodded, sat down, and turned to Kathy. "So, is it true?"

"Is what true?"

"The treasure. What my father spent his life searching for. Did you find it? Did you find the treasure?"

Kozlowski rushed back into the kitchen. "We found the vehicle!"

The commotion level amped up in the kitchen. So did the adrenaline. Kozlowski said the black SUV was located back in Redford. Cops were already onsite, and the perimeter had been secured.

Kathy directed Steve to assist agents Patti and Debbie in escorting the Minterns to the Redford police station for written statements. She told Steve he could cut the couple loose afterward.

"After you provide your sworn statements," Kathy said, glaring at the traumatized couple, "I want you to come directly home. Do you understand?"

They nodded.

"You're not out of the woods yet, and if I need further information from you, you had better be home and answer your phones. Got it?"

Dale's eyes widened. "Did you find the treasure? I need to know!"

Nobody responded during their rush to the front door.

CHAPTER FORTY ONE

Detroit, Michigan - 1956
'In Times of Need'

IN THE LATE AFTERNOON SHADOWS OF THE ART DÉCO-STYLE skyscrapers, with the Detroit River in the background, sat the oldest active rescue mission in the city. Initially opened in 1908 to support his parishioners, a young priest of St. Joseph's Catholic Church thought the small building would outlast him and the needs of the disadvantaged people in his congregation. Twenty years later, the Great Depression proved him wrong, sadly.

In 1929, the land surrounding his small rescue mission on Larned Street, a few miles from the Ambassador Bridge and three short blocks from the construction of the new tunnel under the Detroit River, wasn't expensive—nor was it affordable. The depressed property values in Detroit matched the diminishing donations to the church. People hurt. They were broke. The youthful priest needed help and wasn't shy about asking for it.

Soliciting major Detroit-based businesses, the priest asked for help, and in typical form, many came through. Midwesterners stuck together and helped each other. It's what they did.

Donations from the largest corporation in Detroit were welcomed. Companies like Stroh Brewing, Vernor's, General Motors, Chrysler, and others donated generously to his efforts. Even Henry Ford, a devout Episcopalian who had recently moved his manufacturing facilities from Detroit to the neighboring city of Dearborn, was generous.

Adjacent land was purchased, contractors and parishioners contributed time and materials for the construction, and in the fall of 1930, the doors were open to serve the public.

Over a hundred donated cots were strategically placed in the large auditorium, providing a safe and warm place for the people to escape the weather and the seedy streets of a depressed Midwestern manufacturing city. Volunteers cooked and served two meals per day, seven days a week.

The young priest designed the beautifully handcrafted sign hanging above the front door.

'Serving God's people in times of need.'

DALE MINTERN pulled into the parking lot of the rescue mission on Larned Street and smiled. Every Saturday, without exception for the past ten years, this was his routine. The twenty-minute drive from his modest house in Allen Park gave him the time he needed to reflect. Reflect on his faith, his family, and, of course, the people in need.

He used to be one of those people.

The *Father Patrick Malloy Community Center* was where Dale's life changed ten years ago. Then, back in 1945, the rescue mission was smaller. Much smaller. The aging priest, the founder of this beautiful community center, had rescued Dale from the steps of St. Joseph's Church and saved his life. Now, over seven years since his passing, Dale was doing what he could to honor the priest's legacy.

Dozens of needy folk lined the front of the building on Larned Street, waiting to enter, eager to be out of the frigid

March weather and looking forward to a warm meal. The charity wasn't supposed to open for another half-hour, but Dale recognized the painful looks on their collective faces. He felt their suffering.

Dale shivered, gazed past the community center, and surveyed the large chunks of ice floating downstream in the Detroit River on a journey to Lake Erie and beyond. He vividly remembered many nights when he found no way to escape the brutally cold Michigan weather. Today he viewed it from a different perspective, a sober perspective, and it looked much different from what he remembered.

It was almost peaceful.

Shaking off the moment and possibly frostbite, he hustled to the main entrance and unlocked the doors. Kissing the fingertips of his right hand, he reached up, touched the handcrafted sign, and led the flock inside.

IT WAS Saturday night. Television night. With Dale in his favorite chair and his wife, Marge, on the sofa to his right, they smiled. Jackie Gleason, Art Carney, and Audrey Meadows made them laugh. They loved to laugh.

Dale helped many needy people today at the community center. Now, he was with his beautiful wife, relaxing, sipping Coca-Cola, and watching *The Honeymooners* on their new television. Elaine was days, if not hours, away from delivering their first baby. It felt like a perfect day.

Dale and Marge Mintern had prayed together every day since their wedding ten months ago. They prayed for their health and the well-being of others. They asked God for forgiveness. Lord knows Dale was asking a lot, but he also had much to be thankful for. Today, he was grateful that the good Lord had answered their prayers.

Ten years ago, he woke up feeling comfortable, believing he might have died. Father Malloy, the nuns, and wonderful parishioners had cared for him for many weeks. It had to be this way because he couldn't care for himself. He had lost track of time, feelings, and, most embarrassingly, bodily functions.

Eventually, Dale had recovered. He knew he was one of the lucky few. Food, water, and rest decontaminated his body. Prayers and tears cleansed his soul. Months later, he would still battle fits of demons. Physically, emotionally, and spiritually.

Father Malloy had warned him of the devil's persistence and told Dale to expect these evil visits from time to time, maybe even for the rest of his life. "Always expect a miracle," the elderly priest would say. "God works at His own pace."

Remembering those profound words from nearly a decade ago, Dale reached for Marge's hand and smiled. She beamed back, rubbing her belly.

Early the following day, Dale heard Marge say something to him he hadn't heard in all the time they had been together. "We're not going to church this morning, Dale," she announced. "It's time."

Dale Mintern Junior was born on March 22nd, 1956.

CHAPTER FORTY TWO
Present Day - Friday, November 5

THE CARAVAN OF COP CARS LEFT PERMANENT BLACK MARKS ON the circular driveway as they peeled out of the Minterns' upscale neighborhood. Turning south on Farmington Road, the lights flashed, and sirens howled en route to the location of Billy Bartlett's truck in Redford.

A few blocks from making a left turn on Five-mile Road, the Channel 6 Action News van passed us, heading north in the opposite direction. I glanced over my left shoulder to see the van make a U-turn.

Kathy scowled.

We followed Lieutenant Kozlowski and the backup patrol vehicle to the address in Redford. Kathy radioed a request to block Sumner Street, preventing the news hawks from interfering with the investigation. They wouldn't be far behind. We skidded to a stop on the dirt street in front of a two-story house that had seen better days. Redford cops and paramedics attended to a frightened couple on the large front porch.

A handful of cops stepped off the porch. Kozlowski introduced Kathy to his team and asked for a briefing. Brewster and I slid silently to the edge of the cop perimeter and listened.

"We've already performed a probable search on the house," one officer said. He turned and pointed to the front porch. "The occupants are Chuck and Vicky Waters—

husband and wife. They have no criminal history, and, frankly, they're terrified and confused. They were hit pretty hard, probably knocked unconscious. Paramedics are attending to their injuries. Our technicians are searching the room where their tenant was living."

Kathy glanced at the frightened couple. "What does the tenant have to do with this, Officer Dudek?"

"According to their statements," Officer Dudek pointed towards the destruction, "someone pulled that black Tahoe into their driveway, crashed into the fence, and blew the horn for a long time. The Waters' tenant, a white male named Billy Bartlett, ran down the stairs and pushed Mrs. Waters out of his way. She fell back, hit her head, and was bleeding pretty bad. When the husband stepped in to help, he was punched. The tenant rushed from the house and met the person who had been driving the Tahoe. They jumped into Bartlett's truck. A blue Ford Ranger."

Kathy winced. "We already have a BOLO for Billy Bartlett and his Ranger. Have you cleared the Tahoe?"

"We found nothing tangible. My team is currently dusting for fingerprints. I'm told the tenant moved in four days ago, on Monday. Chuck Waters said Bartlett's lease on his apartment had expired, and he needed a place to stay for a couple of weeks. Apparently, the Waters' rented a room on the upper level for extra income."

Kozlowski said, "We're patrolling the area for his dark blue Ford Ranger. It's an older model and shouldn't be hard to spot. The body's been lifted, and he has large off-road tires."

An unidentified Redford police officer interrupted. "Special Agent Cooper, your CSI team is at our station. They are reviewing the traffic cameras in the city, but you should know, there aren't as many as we'd like."

"Thank you." Kathy nodded and turned back to Officer Dudek. "So, what happened next? After Billy Bartlett left the house?"

"Neither of the injured residents saw anything. Their neighbor, however," he pointed to the small brick bungalow with the manicured lawn to his left," witnessed Billy Bartlett. She recognized his face. Bartlett hopped into the driver's seat of the blue truck. The other man, the driver of the damaged black Tahoe, shoved a woman into the passenger side and then jumped into the truck next to her. They peeled out quickly, driving west, towards Beech Daly Road. They couldn't tell us if the vehicle turned north or south."

"Special Agent Cooper? Ma'am?"

The cops on the postage-stamp-sized lawn turned in unison to assess the interruption. Kathy looked to her right and placed her hands on her hips.

"Dan, what the hell are you doing here?"

The officer gave Scruggs a quizzical stare. "He says you know him, ma'am. Said you were expecting him."

Kathy exhaled a long, irritated breath. She grabbed Scruggs by the elbow and motioned for Brewster and me to join her. We met near the aging, cracked sidewalk.

"Listen, Dan," she whispered loudly, glancing at each of us with the look of a displeased mother. "I don't know how you found us or who told you where we were, but I'm glad you're here."

"Really?" Scruggs beamed.

"Did you drive your pickup truck here, Dan?"

"I did."

"Where is it?"

"It's at the end of the street, right behind your vehicle. I had to park there because your cop buddies wouldn't let me through. I told them you were expecting me."

"Brilliant, Dan," Kathy said, in a way that didn't make Scruggs look brilliant. "Now, here's why I'm glad you're here. You, Rick, and Bob will walk to your truck, get inside, and go home, back to Dunville. Do you understand?"

"But I thought I would be able to—"

"Enough!" she shouted. Looking over her shoulder at the group of cops on the front lawn, she gave a slight nod. Kathy turned back with a scowl and addressed us in a low, guttural whisper. "Listen. I shouldn't have let Rick and Bob join me on this trip, but it's a decision I can live with. The situation has elevated from finding Dina's tracking device to locating and apprehending a couple of violent criminals. I cannot have you guys interfering with a police investigation. So, Dan, I'm glad you cared enough to track us down and offer your help, but the best way you can help is to give Rick and Bob a ride back to Dunville."

Lowering his head, Brewster punched me gently in the shoulder. "She's right, Rick. We *are* interfering with her investigation. We should leave and let the police handle this."

Kathy nodded at Brewster, bowing in such an understated manner as to not be noticed by anyone else. She appreciated his consideration and yet was skeptical of his motives. He'd backed off without a fight. It was not what he did.

We moseyed along the aging sidewalks to Scruggs's shiny silver F-150. I gave Brewster a side glance. He shrugged, ignored me, and kept walking.

After stopping briefly for Brewster to peek into an open window in Kathy's Ford Explorer, we jumped in Scruggs's truck. With me in the passenger seat and Brewster in the back, he fired up his F-150.

We drove west to Beech Daly Road and turned right. Brewster kept looking over his shoulder. A few blocks later, he asked Scruggs to pull over.

Scruggs pulled into a Dunkin' Delicious parking lot. "You need a coffee, Brewster?"

His body was still twisted, staring out the rear window. "Yep. I need a few minutes to sort things out."

Scruggs slipped into an empty space. "Whatever."

Brewster exited the vehicle and walked to the brightly lit donut franchise. I turned in my seat. "How the hell did you find us, Scruggs?"

He beamed. "I followed the secret clue you gave me. Are you impressed?"

"What clue? I didn't give you any coded message."

"Yeah, you sorta did. After we spoke, I hustled to the dental clinic and met with Bill Evans. He was just about finished when I arrived."

"So, Bill told you where we were?"

"Nope, he said it was a police matter. Wouldn't tell me shit. Told me that Dina had a tracker on her and that you were pursuing the device's last known position. I glanced at his notepad on the desk, memorizing several keywords he had written. Then I drove to the Rib Shack. I pulled into the parking lot, walked inside, and told the hostess I needed more information on what had transpired earlier. Shit, I was grasping at straws. I had no idea what I was asking for. I didn't even know what had happened earlier. She hustled away from the greeters' stand and returned with the manager. He started telli—"

"Assistant manager."

"What?"

"Daniel Herkimer. He's the assistant manager."

"Whatever, but yeah, that was his name. So, anyway, he told me the cops left in a hurry. Said he overheard talk of them heading for Livonia. He must have thought that I was a cop because he saluted me as I left the building. Then I drove north on Telegraph to the Jeffries Freeway and headed west towards Livonia. As I approached the exit for Beech Daly Road in Redford, I noticed a cop car and an EMS vehicle heading north on the overpass. I knew I was still a few miles away from Livonia, but something told me to follow them. It just felt right. Anyway, I made an exit for Beech Daly and followed them. Before they even turned on Sumner Street, I knew something big was happening. Red and blue lights lit up the sky. I pulled down the dirt road and immediately recognized Kathy's vehicle. She should get that huge dent fixed, by the way. And that, my friend, is how I ended up sitting with you in this donut shop parking lot. Are you impressed?"

"Actually, I have to admit it. I *am* impressed."

Brewster opened the door behind me and pulled himself in. He handed each of us a coffee and placed a box of donuts on the console between us. He spoke as my phone rang. I flashed the caller ID to him and Scruggs. Paulie was calling. Damn, the clock was just past midnight. I had planned to call him a half-hour ago. Huh? I wondered where I stored the mental note to call him.

I smiled, pressed the green icon to answer the call, and

then the speaker button. "Paulie, how's it going, brother? I'm here with Scruggs and Brewster. You're on speakerphone, rock star. How was the show in Chicago?"

"I need help, boss."

"What's up?"

"I'm in trouble."

"What's going on, Paulie?"

"I'm in jail, boss. I've been arrested."

CHAPTER FORTY THREE

Present Day - Saturday, November 6

I SHIFTED IN MY SEAT, UPSET WITH THE NEWS. DAN LEANED RIGHT, and Brewster tilted forward.

"Son of a bitch, buddy," I said. "What happened?"

"Drugs, boss. The cops said our tour was a front for a drug trafficking operation. I don't do drugs, boss!"

Brewster said, "Settle down, Paulie. Take a deep breath."

Paulie wheezed. "I'm scared, Brewster. This place is a hellhole. There are crazy people everywhere."

"I understand, buddy. Listen, we're going to get you out of there as soon as possible, but for now, you need to understand it won't happen quickly and most likely not tonight. Do you understand?"

"I guess."

"Where are you?"

"Cook County Jail."

Scruggs chuckled. "Have you seen the Blues Brothers?"

Paulie snorted and asked what he should do.

Brewster, having the law enforcement experience, provided him with seasoned advice. "Don't make friends. Don't make enemies. Avoid eye contact. Never whine, and certainly never shed a tear. No weakness. Hang tough. I'll arrange for an attorney and post your bail in the morning. Right now, we're in the middle of our own shit storm, but know this: we'll be thinking about you, got it?"

The call ended, and we fell back into our seats. Brewster

took a few moments to send a text. He explained to Scruggs and me what might happen next. Said Paulie would need an excellent criminal defense attorney and didn't want him represented by a Chicago public defender. Told us he had sent a message to Susan Winston, Mayor Ben's wife, to call him as soon as possible.

"She's the best criminal defense lawyer I know," he said. "I'll have her work on getting Paulie released on bail, which will hopefully be reasonable, but he's in some deep shit. He's going to need our support."

Scruggs and I nodded. There wasn't anything to say. Paulie's freedom was in jeopardy, but Dina's life was in danger, taking precedence.

My phone dinged with a text message.

I told you no cops, asshole! Now you went and fucked everything up. You have exactly two hours to get me the coin, or the chick dies.

An unsettled look telegraphed my emotions and caught the other two's attention. I read the text aloud and asked Brewster for advice.

"Respond to him. Tell him we need more time. It's midnight, and there's no one to contact. Stall him any way you can."

I did what Brewster recommended, even offering a few flawless diamonds as an incentive to prolong his deadline.

Fuck You. Two Hours.

I SENT a copy of the text message to Kathy. She responded almost immediately, and not with her most nurturing voice. I had the call on speaker.

"Where are you?" she asked.

Brewster gently slapped me on the back of the head, sort of.

"On our way home," I lied.

Kathy snarled, or I imagined she snarled through the phone. "I'm not playing games with Dina's life. Text him back and let him know we have the coin. Tell him it's in Lansing. Steve is on his way."

Brewster said, "Kathy, when Steve gets to your office, have him take a photo of the coin, front and back. It needs to be next to something with a current date, like a newspaper. Have him send that photo to Rick's phone, so he can use it to extend the deadline if needed. This Jackson guy might be crazy, but I don't believe he'd jeopardize losing the coin over a little more time. It could save Dina's life."

"Done."

Click.

BREWSTER TAPPED me on the shoulder. "She's on the move."

I tossed my hands in the air. "What are you talking about?"

"Kathy left the suspect's house. She's heading north on Beech Daly. Quick, everybody duck!"

"How the hell do you know that?"

"Shut the hell up. Get down!"

Brewster lay flat in the spacious back seat. I slid down and buried my head below the window. Scruggs smacked his head on the console, trying to conceal his tall frame from view.

Brewster, still staring at his phone, sat up. "All clear. She turned on a side street, one block north."

We watched her headlights from the Dunkin' Delicious parking lot as she traveled east on Student Street.

Scruggs looked in the rearview mirror. "How are you following her?"

"Most likely the same way you found us."

"A tracker?"

"Yep. Before we left the scene on Sumner Street, I tossed my tracker into the open passenger window of Kathy's car."

Kathy weaved through the diverse neighborhoods of south Redford. We trailed her at a safe distance. Brewster called Kenny for an update and put him on speaker phone. Assuming there would be no negative repercussions from sharing information with Brewster and believing he was far away from the active investigation, Kenny said he and Kathy had split up. She covered the south side of town while he focused on the north end.

"Right now," Kenny said, "I suspect everything and everybody. It's nearly one o'clock in the morning, and the neighborhoods are quiet. Anything out of the ordinary is what I am looking for. I've stopped at least a dozen times at houses where the lights were still on, peeking in garage windows, hoping to find that Ford Ranger. When an alert citizen startled me, I even had to pull my badge once."

"Appreciate the information, Kenny. Be sure to call me with any news."

"You got it, Brewster. Are you home?"

"Uh, well, not yet. We stopped for coffee and donuts."

"Oh, okay. Stay positive, buddy. We'll get your wife home safely."

My phone vibrated. A text message. I opened it. It was a clear photo of the 1933 gold coin. Steve had placed it on the front page of today's *Lansing Journal* newspaper.

Perfect.

I asked Scruggs to stop the vehicle. He pulled into the small parking lot of a local playground. With shaky hands, I forwarded the text photo and told the guy the coin was one hour away. The response took me by surprise.

I'm not dealing with you anymore, asshole. Your wife, the cop, will deliver the coin to me.

Where should I tell her to meet you? I responded.

Fuck you. Text me her phone number.

Shit. Kathy answered my call on the first ring and began the conversation. "Are you guys at the Social Club?"

I may have stuttered a bit. "Uh, no, we stopped for coffee and donuts."

Her cop voice was unmistakable. "Where did you stop?"

"Uh, at the donut shop." Another stutter.

Brewster slapped me upside the head again.

"You guys are up to something, and I don't like it. I had better not see you guys anywhere around Redford."

"You won't."

"I just received your text, Rick," Kathy said. "I have to go."

Brewster spread his arms wide, palms up, and leaned in. "What the hell is wrong with you?"

Scruggs laughed.

I glared at him. "You're not a good liar either."

CHAPTER FORTY FOUR

Present Day - Saturday, November 6

SPEEDING ALONG BEECH DALY ROAD, TRAVELING NORTH, KATHY'S Blue Goose Ford Explorer turned west onto Grand River Avenue. She called Steve Erikson. He told her he was on his way back. Thirty minutes away, maybe less. Kathy explained the change of plans, and he didn't like it.

"Tough shit," she told him. "Get here as quickly as you can. We'll figure this out when you arrive."

Kathy's caller ID didn't recognize the incoming number. It was a local area code. She answered. Maybe Tyler Jackson had a second phone.

"Special Agent Cooper?"

"Yes?"

"I don't know if you remember me. My name is Jean Simmons from DMJ Construction. We met a few days ago."

"Of course, Jean. What can I do for you?"

"You told me Lowell Thomas was dead."

"Excuse me?"

"You said I didn't have to worry about him anymore. You said he was shot and killed, up north, in Hubbard Lake."

"That's a true statement, Jean. I didn't lie to you. Lowell Thomas will never bother you again."

"Then why did his truck just pull into my construction site?"

"What?"

"My security alarm notified me of a trespasser. I checked

the video camera feed and saw Lowell Thomas's truck."

"Describe the vehicle, Jean."

"One word: redneck. It's a mini pickup truck with huge tires. Do you know what they say about guys needing big tires? Little dicks, that's what they say. I'm telling you, that prick is still alive."

"It's not him, Jean. It's *not* Lowell Thomas. Billy Bartlett has his truck. We've been searching for him all night."

"Should I call the cops?"

"I *am* a cop, Jean. Please, let me handle this. Don't contact anyone else. This is a hostage situation, and someone very close to me is in great danger. Keep this between us. Do you understand?"

Jean Simmons said she understood. Kathy asked Jean if there were additional cameras on her property. "No. I had one camera installed in the corner of my building. It lets me know if anyone is pulling into my driveway. That's it."

"Could you tell how many people were in the vehicle?"

"No. The video quality isn't great. Both vehicles were clear, but I couldn't see inside them."

"What do you mean, *both* vehicles?"

"The mini pickup truck was followed by a real pickup. It was bright red with huge tires. Another redneck, I suppose—with a tiny dick."

"Are they in *your* building, Jean? The yellow one? Is that where they would go?"

"There's no way they can get into my building. It's locked tighter than a nun's legs. They're probably in the storage warehouse near the back of the property. It's where they used to party."

"Are you talking about the two-story light blue building?"

"Yep, that's the one. Smells like weed."

"Jean, you just made my night. I will call you as soon as possible. Thank you so much."

KATHY PLACED a three-way call with the detectives. She shared the information from Jean Simmons, and they discussed their options. It was decided that the local police would not be informed. Too much was at stake—mainly Dina's life. They would need to act alone. Kenny asked if they should reach out to Brewster and inform him of their progress.

Kathy let out a heavy sigh. "Those knuckleheads are nearby."

"You think?"

"I'm not stupid."

"Shit," Kenny admitted. "I spoke with Brewster a while ago. He wanted to know how things were going."

"And you provided him with an update, I suppose?"

"Sorry, Kathy. I thought he was back in Dunville and wouldn't be able to interfere with our progress."

"If you were in Bob's position, would you have gone far from the action?"

"No way."

"Well, then. The three stooges are lurking nearby. The good news is they don't know exactly where we are, so we can forget about them for the time being. Let's put our heads together and decide how we're going to breach that building and rescue Dina. Kenny, find a convenient place for us to meet. I'm on my way. See you shortly."

Steve hightailed it east on I-96.

Kenny pulled into a twenty-four-hour restaurant one

mile west of the construction site and fired up his laptop. Searching Google Images of the DMJ Construction property, he studied it closely. Recon was critical. He found the only access was the gravel driveway, which was unacceptable. It appeared they would need to go in on foot.

Westbound on Grand River, Kathy pressed the accelerator hard. No lights. No siren. Adrenaline pumping at max capacity.

Hold on, Dina.

CHAPTER FORTY FIVE
Present Day - Saturday, November 6

On a dark, twisty, dirt road near Lola Valley Park in south Redford, Brewster sat up straight and slapped the back of my head. A gentle slap, but a slap nonetheless.

"Kathy's on the move. Let's go!"

He stared at the tracking app on his phone, leaning forward between the seats, providing guidance for Scruggs. I was in the passenger seat and kept my eyes open for anything suspicious—like a blue mini-pickup truck with oversized tires. There wasn't much happening on the streets at this early hour. The technology directed us north, then west. We drove slowly past the two 'blue goose' vehicles in the dimly lit parking lot on Grand River Avenue. We ducked our heads. Scruggs continued a few hundred yards farther and turned left, across the street, into an empty auto repair shop, which was dark, unlit, unassuming, and perfect for our reconnaissance.

Two blue Ford Explorers, one pristine and the other with a dent in the rear door, sat in George's Coney Island restaurant on Grand River Avenue. The soft white glow from a laptop reflected off the windows. Not much action, otherwise. Fifteen minutes had passed. Brewster continued to stare at his phone, his face twisted. He leaned forward. "What was the name of that construction company? The one that Dale Mintern, or his wife Elaine, owned?"

"DMJ Construction," I said.

Brewster rubbed the back of his head and pointed at his phone. "That has to be why they're here. DMJ Construction is about a mile east, just inside the Redford border. Let's head over there and check it out."

I shrugged. "What if they leave the parking lot?"

"We can still track them. Let's check out that construction place."

Scruggs pulled out of the parking lot and pressed the pedal hard. We headed east. Passing George's Coney Island on our left, a blue goose Dodge Charger drove past us in the opposite direction.

Scruggs turned his head right and mumbled, "Shit."

"Did Steve see us?" I asked.

"I hope not."

Brewster leaned forward and tapped me on the shoulder. At least he didn't smack me on the head. "Rick, didn't you and Kathy have a recent meeting at that construction place?"

I shifted in my seat, looking over my left shoulder. "Yep. We met with the construction site owner a couple of days ago. It's where Tyler Jackson's buddies, Lowell Thomas and Billy Bartlett, worked. That was the day she and Kenny shipped me back to Dunville. After that, they had that shootout at Bartlett's apartment in Inkster."

"So, it makes sense, right?" Scruggs interjected. "Bartlett *couldn't* return to his apartment in Inkster, so he rented a room from the Waters in Redford."

Brewster pointed through the windshield. "The construction site is on the right. Drive past it and turn right onto Cherokee Street. The map says a county park borders the back of the construction site. Make a right and another right."

Scruggs feathered the gas and brakes, pulling a hard right on Cherokee Street and then right again on Fargo. Gravel crunched under the tires as we passed the "Wayne County — Your Adventure Begins Here" sign. We drove another fifty yards on the gravel path, ignoring the 'Park closes at 10:00 p.m.' warning, and pulled into a large, dark parking area. With light cloud cover and no artificial lighting, another car, parked at the far end of the parking lot was barely noticeable.

I pointed. "Who else would be here this time of night?"

Presuming it was just a sexual rendezvous, Scruggs parked a distance away. There were no lights on in the other car. It wasn't bouncing up and down, and the windows weren't fogged. He winked at me and got out of the truck to take a stroll. Brewster and I also got out. We stayed put and watched Scruggs shuffle over to the vehicle and peek in the window.

I hollered, "What do you see?"

Brewster shushed me.

Scruggs replied in a loud whisper. "It's a Ferrari."

I whispered back with a sideways glance at Brewster, "Anyone inside?"

"Negative."

"Huh." I checked the surrounding area. The woods seemed quiet.

Scruggs shuffled back to the truck and dropped the tailgate. "I'm chilly."

Pulling out a sweatshirt from a duffel bag, he put it on under his jacket and tossed a black hooded sweatshirt to Brewster.

"Thanks," Brewster said. "Got anything for Rick?"

Scruggs nodded, pointing to the golf bag in the bed of the truck, and then to me. "There's a vest and a sweater in there. It's going to be too big for you, though."

I put the large sweater on under my jacket and zipped it up.

Brewster said, "Okay, guys, I have no idea if anything is going on at this place or not. If there is, we need to be prepared. Pull out your phones."

We did.

"Go to your display settings and turn on the dark theme. Make sure the brightness level is all the way down, and for Christ's sake, make sure your phones are silenced."

"Got it."

"Done."

Brewster placed his phone in his jacket pocket and surveyed the blue building. "It looks to be about two hundred feet long. I don't see any vehicles outside."

Scruggs pointed. "That large bay door in the middle of the building has tire tracks in the gravel. They probably parked inside."

"I don't know what's in the front of the building," Brewster said. "I'll take a stroll around the near side and check it out. Rick, you're the squirrelly one. See that radio tower antenna at the far end?"

I nodded, knowing what he would say next.

"I want you to climb that tower and work your way into the second floor or onto the roof."

"Great," I mumbled and shuffled my feet in the loose gravel.

Brewster told me to suck it up. Said it wasn't that high, don't look down, I would be alright, and a few other words of encouragement designed to reduce my fear of heights. They didn't work. Would I climb the tower? Of course. Would my knees still shake? Of course.

Turning to Scruggs, Brewster pointed at the blue building. "Stay in the woods across from those bay doors. Out of sight," he said. "If they went in that way, they'll come out that way. Be alert."

Scruggs pumped an enthusiastic thumbs-up.

Brewster press checked his Glock and asked if we were carrying.

I nodded.

Scruggs winced.

I told Scruggs it was probably better he wasn't armed because he couldn't shoot straight anyway. He shook his head but didn't offer a smart-ass rebuttal. He knew I was right.

We shared fist bumps, and I pointed toward the building.

"Let's go."

We traversed the tree line, trudging through the deep, wet leaves. On our left was the county park and the woods. On our right was the long, narrow blue building. My heart rate spiked from the adrenaline rush. I slapped Scruggs on his back at the halfway point across from the bay doors. He slipped into the woods. I continued to the far end of the building, constantly scanning my surroundings, looking for movement—or trouble.

At the triangular antenna tower, I glanced back at Scruggs. He was already out of sight, camouflaged in the tree line. With a hand on the rusty tower, I peeked around the corner. High above me, mounted to the side of the building, was a mercury vapor light. Thankfully, it was not turned on or not working. Either way, it was dark. Which I appreciated. Nothing else caught my attention.

Clutching the rusty metal with weak knees, I began my ascent. The triangular tower was wobbly but seemed solidly anchored to the building. The large second-floor window closest to the antenna tower was too far for me to reach. At least ten feet away.

I continued climbing to the top, carefully stepping onto the shingled roof. My shaky legs were pleased to be standing on a shallow pitch.

Shuffling slowly and as quietly as possible, I inched my way along the ridge of the roofline. I looked around to gain my bearings from thirty feet in the air, trying not to look down. Brewster was nowhere in sight. He must have moved forward to the front of the building. To my right, I spotted Scruggs and froze.

Oh, no. Fuck.

I crouched lower, now balancing on all fours. All of my joints shaking. Adrenaline pumping. Ringing in my ears grew louder. I had to remind myself to breathe.

Scruggs was on his knees in the gravel parking lot, just outside the tree line. His hands were tied behind his back, and his head was bent forward, chin touching his chest.

He looked like a trapped animal. His ponytail had come undone. Disheveled shoulder-length hair covered his face. A large shadow stood behind him with a gun pointed at his head.

This is not good.

SITTING WITH Kenny in Kathy's Ford Explorer, Steve asked, "So, what's the plan?"

Kathy shrugged. "I'm winging it. I'll text the scumbag and let him know I have the coin. Let's see what happens."

"Not much of a plan."

"Do you have any better ideas?"

He shrugged.

Kathy baited the hook and sent a text.

I have the coin. Where are we meeting?

"How long do you think it will take for him to answer?" Steve asked.

"Not long, I'm betting."

Where are you? Came the quick reply.

"I told you," she said and then replied.

15 minutes away.

15 minutes away from where?

Redford

Send me a picture of you holding the coin

Kathy reached for her phone. Kenny stopped her. "Let me and Steve get out of your car. Any reflection of our faces could kill this deal. Also, make sure nothing gives away your position when you take the photo. Use the portrait mode on your camera. It will blur the background."

The Erikson brothers stepped out of the vehicle. Kathy snapped a selfie, gave a thumbs-up, and they hopped back in. Kathy sent the text, waiting for the reply.

You're cute.

Focus on the prize.

Your friend here is a nice prize.

Kathy took a long minute to reply. Almost afraid to ask.

Send me a photo of my friend.

Her phone dinged.

The photo wasn't pretty. Dina looked like she hadn't slept in days. The bruises and dried blood on her face mixed with tears. Kathy grimaced, showing the photo to Steve and Kenny.

The perp texted back.

Ten minutes. I'll text you with a meeting place. You better be alone.

You better have my friend.

"Grab your phones and download the SmartStuff app," Kathy said, providing Steve and Kenny with her personal login credentials.

Reaching in her purse, she removed the tracking device and stuffed it into her panties. "If Tyler Jackson pulls a fast one on us and we get separated, this is how you can find me."

They nodded.

"Steve, I want you positioned across the street from the construction company. When Tyler Jackson leaves, follow him and confirm that Dina is in his truck. Kenny, I want you to trail me — at a safe distance, of course — knowing that the tracking app will locate my position if you lose sight of me. Got it?"

Kenny stared at his phone, his head cocked. "This stupid security app is asking me if I want to pair a new tracking badge. What does that mean?"

"Probably a glitch."

Kenny's face twisted. "It's telling me there's another tracker in the vicinity and asking me to push the sync button to pair the device. What should I do?"

Kathy pounded her fist on the dashboard. "Son of a bitch. Look around. On the floor."

Steve picked up a small, white rectangular device from under the passenger seat.

Kathy checked the security app on her phone. "It's *not*

Rick's tracker," she said. "His is still in Dunville. He always leaves his keys in his truck. I'll bet Brewster planted a tracker in my car."

CHAPTER FORTY SIX

Present Day - Saturday, November 6

BREWSTER LOOKED AT HIS CELL PHONE SCREEN AND WINCED. He answered.

"Where the hell are you?" Kathy growled.

"What?"

"Don't stall!" Kathy shouted. "Where are you?"

"Well, we're sort of on a mission."

"Are the other two stooges with you?"

"Yes, ma'am."

"Are you in Redford?"

"The gig is up?"

"Where the hell *are* you?"

Brewster whispered. "Listen, I don't know if we're on to anything, but we just hiked through a county park that borders the DMJ Construction site. I'm on the east end of a warehouse. I don't see any vehicles, but lights are on inside."

"Pay attention," Kathy scolded him. "There are *so* many things you *don't* know. You could be in danger."

"Talk to me."

"First, you are indeed in the right spot. I received a call from the construction company owner this evening. She confirmed that Billy Bartlett is on her property. Hold on. I'm putting you on speakerphone. Are you still there?"

"Yes."

"I have Steve and Kenny on speaker. Like I was saying, I spoke with the construction company owner. She confirmed that Billy Bartlett drove a Ford Ranger onto her property. Tyler Jackson and Dina were in the truck with him. A second pickup truck followed them with two more individuals. I have no idea who these people are, but I can assure you, they are not friendlies. Do you understand?"

"Copy that."

"I'm waiting to hear from Tyler Jackson about the location of the transfer. He's demanding the gold coin for Dina. Said he would get back to me in ten minutes with a meeting location. Just so you know, Steve will be positioned across the street from you, and Kenny will track me electronically. Are you guys at the blue building near the back of the construction site?"

"Yes. Scruggs is covering the rear of the building, and Rick should be on the roof looking for a way to breach the second floor."

Kathy shouted, "What the hell do you guys think you're doing?"

Brewster peeked around the metal dumpster and whispered loudly, "We were just checking this place out, Kathy. Trust me, we had no idea they would be here."

"Is there anything else you're *not* telling me, Bob?"

"Well, there may be more people involved. We spotted an expensive Ferrari in the park behind the construction site. There was no one inside the vehicle."

"What model is it, Brewster?" Kenny asked.

"How the fuck should I know? It's a bright red Ferrari. How many of those are you going to see in Redford?"

Kenny huffed. "It's probably Dale Mintern's car. He had a red Ferrari in his garage."

Brewster scanned the area. "Do you think he's double-crossing us? Helping his nephew with the kidnapping?"

Kathy shrugged. "If he is, he's the best actor *I've* ever seen."

Bang!

The gunshot startled Brewster. He hit the ground hard.

Bang!

The second blast brought his awareness to a higher level. He scrambled behind a commercial dumpster, diving headfirst into the gravel.

"Shit! Shots fired!" Brewster barked into his phone. "Two shots. From inside the building."

Kathy's phone dinged.

Brewster's phone vibrated.

Kathy stared at her phone.

So now you know where I am. Bring me the gold coin. Come alone, or both of your friends will die.

Brewster read his text.

They've got Scruggs.

In a crouched position, gun at the ready, Brewster searched the surrounding area. High on alert.

"Who got shot?" Kathy asked.

Brewster peered around the commercial dumpster, staring into the shadows of the construction equipment. "Don't know." He checked his perimeter. "I'm thirty yards from the east end of the building behind a large green dumpster. There's nobody outside. Their vehicles must be inside the building. There's a large garage door at the rear of the building. It's where Scruggs was positioned. Hold on." He checked his phone. "It's Rick."

He connected the calls. "Are you there, Rick?"

—

"I'M INSIDE," I said in a low voice.

Brewster whispered, "I've got the whole team connected. They can hear you. Talk to us. What's going on?"

I sucked in a heavy breath. My heart leaped from my chest. "The whole main floor is wide open. There are two pickup trucks parked in the center of the building, and there is shit everywhere: crates, boxes, truck engines, and a workbench below a large crane, and—"

Brewster's voice tightened. "Settle down. How many people, Rick? Describe the scene."

"Dina and Scruggs are secured. Dina is tied to a chair, and Scruggs is sitting on the floor, duct-taped to a pole. That Dale Mintern guy has been shot. Looks like he's lost a lot of blood, but he's twitching. The other guy who was shot looks like the photo I saw of Billy Bartlett. He is definitely dead. The back of his head is missing."

"Take a deep breath, Rick," Kathy said. "I need you to stay focused. Do you understand?"

"Sorry about this, Kath."

"Don't worry about that right now. We need you to paint a clear picture of what's happening and where everyone is positioned. Understand?"

"Yes, ma'am."

"How did you get into the building?"

"The roof access door near the HVAC unit was unlocked. The ladder brought me down to a maintenance closet."

"Where are you now?"

"Some type of office. The back of the building has an upper level. A hallway extends the entire length of the narrow second floor, with staircases on either side. Between the stairwells are about a dozen rooms. Four or five of them have large windows that overlook the main floor. I'm in one of *those* offices, closer to the east side of the building. The rest of the building is wide open, with tall ceilings."

"How many people can you see on the first floor?"

I slid up the wall and peeked over the windowsill. "One, two, three, four…seven. There are seven people. Dina and Scruggs, the two guys who were shot, two hillbilly looking mongrels, and that fire marshal guy, the one who looks like Mark Harmon."

"What type of weapons?" Kathy asked.

"It looks like the fire marshal is holding a pistol. The two hillbillies are strapping AR-15s."

"Okay, listen up. Steve and Kenny are already on their way to the county park. They will enter the building through the roof access door. Understood?"

"Yes, ma'am."

"Are you armed?"

"Yes, ma'am."

"Don't shoot them. Got it?"

"Yes, ma'am."

"Let's keep this line open. If anyone leaves that building, let us know immediately. Brewster, see if there is any vantage point for cover. If there is— hold on."

KATHY LOOKED at her phone.

Where are you?

Traffic. Five minutes.

You're stalling, bitch! If anyone but you shows up in this parking lot, both of your friends are dead – on the spot – no second chance.

Kathy composed a long text.

I want my friends alive. You walk them to my car, and I'll hand over the coin. Pull anything stupid, and I hit the panic button in my car. You'll be swarmed with cops in minutes. I want the hostages. I don't give a shit about this coin.

She let out a long exhale and said, "Okay, I'm back. We have five minutes. Here's the deal: Brewster, I need you to find a vantage point for a clean shot near the front door. Tyler Jackson will walk Dina and Dan out of the building in exchange for the coin. Steve and Kenny will take a staircase on either side of the building to the lower level and take down the hillbillies. Rick, you stay where you are. Do you understand?"

I WATCHED through the large glass window as the scene unfolded below me. "There's a problem with your plan, Kathy."

"What is it?" She huffed.

"Right now, the fire marshal dude is untying Dina, but one of the goons just smacked Scruggs upside his head. They're leaving him there, duct-taped to the pole. I think he's out cold."

"Shit. Good to know. They're probably planning on keeping Dan hostage until they confirm the gold coin, or they'll keep him captive for their getaway. Are there any heavy objects in your room?"

"Yeah, it's an office. There's a desk and a couple of large chairs. Why?"

BREWSTER DASHED to a construction vehicle parked near the front door. "Kathy, when you enter the lot, there is a white Bobcat tractor thirty yards from the front door, not quite in front, but close. I'm positioned behind that tractor. Stop your vehicle near me. Close enough for a clean shot."

"Okay, great, Bob. So, Rick, listen closely. I'll park just past Bob's position, about thirty yards from the front entrance. Use your best judgment, and when you think Tyler Jackson and Dina are about twenty yards outside the building, I want you to find the heaviest thing you can handle and throw it through the office window. Got it?"

"Distraction?"

"Yep."

"SHIT!" I shrieked, covering my mouth quickly.

"What?"

"Steve and Kenny are standing behind me! They scared the hell out of me."

"Perfect. Fill them in. It's go time."

KATHY'S EXPLORER crunched the thick gravel as she idled into the parking lot. She probably wondered if Jean Simmons was watching on her video feed, snacking on potato chips and sucking a beer as the scene unfolded.

She drove slowly to her left, toward the blue building. A line of neatly parked construction vehicles was on her right. Focusing on Brewster's hiding place, she veered off-center slightly, pulling beside him as he huddled behind the tractor, attempting to make his nearly six-foot frame invisible.

STEVE AND Kenny shoulder-pressed Colt M4 carbines and turned to me with a focused nod. They darted down the hallway in separate directions. I peered through the dirty window, watching the hectic scene below unfold. Scruggs looked like he was coming to. Dale Mintern twitched.

One of the hillbilly goons walked Tyler Jackson and Dina to the front door, covering them from behind. The other hillbilly stood close to Scruggs, nervously tapping his foot.

The door opened. Tyler Jackson and Dina stepped out, leaving the goon with wild eyes in the door frame. Tyler held Dina tight with his left arm, pulling her close. His right hand held a large pistol. It was pressed firmly against her temple.

Twenty yards. Kathy told me twenty yards. At the pace he was shoving Dina, I figured each step to be about a one Mississippi, so I counted. One Mississippi, two Mississippi, three Mississippi, and so on, until I reached the magical number. Then, on the count of twenty, like an Olympic athlete competing for the gold medal, I swung a heavy leather chair with steel legs with all of my strength.

Smash!

The impact shattered the large window. Shards of glass flew in every direction. I fell backward, smacking my head on the side of the desk. Then I heard gunshots, lots of gunshots. How many? Who the hell knew? I wasn't counting. I jumped to my feet and looked out the broken window.

Two bodies lay motionless on the cement floor. One near the front door and the second near Scruggs. I watched Steve and Kenny rush the two hillbillies, kicking their weapons aside.

Protocol, I guess. They won't need them anymore.

Scruggs screamed in agony.

Oh, no! I thought my buddy might have been shot. Leaning over the broken window frame, I stared down at him.

He threw his head back to scream again and smacked it on the metal pole where he was still duct-taped. "Ow!"

"Scruggs, are you alright?" I shouted.

"What the fuck is wrong with you?" His agonizing scream filled the building.

"I saved your life!" I shouted back and noticed his right leg was bent in an unnatural position.

Steve and Kenny hustled to Scruggs and removed the oversized, heavy chair covering his lower torso.

He screamed again.

WHILE STEVE and Kenny executed their duties flawlessly inside the building, Tyler Jackson stood twenty yards outside the front door, in the gravel construction lot. His body stiffened from the sound of gunshots that emanated from the building behind him. He lost the tight grip he had on Dina.

She took advantage of the distraction and smashed down hard on the arch of Tyler Jackson's right foot. Then Dina dropped to the ground.

Brewster spun from the side of the Bobcat tractor and leveled his Glock.

Aim small, miss small.

The gun hammered against his palm. Two shots found their mark. The first shot—center mass—sent Tyler Jackson reeling backward with a look of bewilderment. The second shot, a millisecond later, sent a pink misty cloud airborne.

He no longer looked like the handsome Mark Harmon.

HUGS AND kisses were plentiful, tears shed, and pats on the back were generous. State Police officers secured the crime scene with bright yellow tape. Small yellow cones were placed near the spent cartridges, preserving the evidence for the CSI investigators. Photos were taken from every angle.

Statements were recorded. Paramedics treated the wounded and confirmed the deceased. The coroner's van was escorted through the busy construction site.

Dina kissed Brewster one more time before she became the guest of the Redford paramedics. She would be transported to St. Mary's Hospital, a few miles away.

Dale Mintern Junior didn't look good. I overheard a paramedic whisper 'critical condition' as he was placed on a gurney and slid into a waiting ambulance.

An IV combination of antibiotics, sedatives, and painkillers dripped into Scruggs's right arm. Before they slid him into the ambulance, he called my name. I hustled closer to him. His hair looked wild. He reached for my right arm with a goofy grin and slurred, "I love you, man!"

The medicine must have kicked in quickly.

The coroner zipped up four black bags. Tyler Jackson, Billy Bartlett, and two hillbillies were taken away. They would not be missed.

After what seemed like hours, and probably was, the parking lot emptied. Steve and Kenny walked toward the back of the property, heading for their vehicles in the county park. Brewster walked alongside, hoping the security code Scruggs had given him for his shiny silver F-150 was accurate. After all, Dan was stoned out of his mind. It's not what he did.

I clutched Kathy's hands and gazed into her eyes. "I'm really sorry, babe."

After a long, tight hug, she planted a passionate kiss on my lips. "There's nothing to be sorry about. You did well tonight."

"I love you, Kath."

"I love you, too. And you can show me how much you love me when we get home."

"Deal."

I jumped into the passenger seat of the Blue Goose Explorer. Kathy weaved around the remaining vehicles and headed for the exit. At the far corner of the ugly yellow building, she turned down the gravel path. At Grand River Avenue, I looked to my right. The Channel 6 Action News van had parked on the scraggly lawn. The good-looking reporter with purple hair shoved a microphone in the face of Lieutenant David Kozlowski. Our eyes met. He looked perturbed.

I threw my head back and laughed.

Kathy gave me a quizzical glance. "What's so funny?"

"Nothing, Kath. Life is good."

EPILOGUE

I TOOK A SEAT IN A PLASTIC CHAIR THAT MUST HAVE BEEN engineered to be uncomfortable. The monitor above the ticket counter confirmed the Amtrak train had been delayed, which wasn't surprising. I spent my time people watching and guessing what everyone did for a living. It was a hobby, and I had no idea how accurate I was with my instincts, but it kept my mind occupied. During the thirty-minute exercise, I identified dozens of sales reps, twice as many college students, two professors—they were easy—tweed jackets, plenty of moms, and a woman who looked like a nurse. She could have been the CEO of a major company. Who knew? Still, my averages were pretty good, I thought.

I took another peek above the ticket counter and noticed Paulie's train would arrive any minute. I gave up my seat to a cosmetologist and hustled to the arrival gate. Along the trot, I ran my fingers through my shaggy hair, tucked in a favorite flannel shirt, and combed my two-week-old beard with my fingers. I was excited to see my buddy.

Quack. Quack. Paulie's jeans looked less than crisp. His signature aloha shirt, a blue floral pattern, seemed to hang on his weakened frame. Loosening the grip on his suitcase, it hit the floor with a thud. He gave me a huge hug.

I reciprocated the act of love and then stepped back with a sour expression. "You stink, dude."

"Sorry, boss."

I grabbed his roller bag and strolled down the long

walkway. He waddled beside me. During the hour ride home to Dunville, he regaled me with stories of playing at Buddy's Blues Club: the crowds, the engineers, the sound, the mix, the lights, his performance, the women, and the adrenaline. "Damn, boss." He beamed. "I've never been so pumped."

That seemed to take his mind off the sad stuff, at least for now. The short stint he did in Cook County Jail? Hell, that could wait. He would share those stories with me when he was ready.

After listening to Paulie's ramblings, it was my turn to speak, and I was direct. "I'd like to get the band back together."

He sat up straight and tugged on his wrinkled shirt. "Really, boss?"

I smiled. "On one condition."

"What's that, boss?"

Our eyes met. "You can never call me *boss* again."

"It's a deal, boss— *Shit!* You got it, Rick!"

I laughed. "So, I've been thinking about this for a while. I've already spoken to the drummer of the Group Therapy Band. He's not dissatisfied with his bandmates. In fact, he likes the guys, and they've been together for many years. However, he told me he wouldn't object to experimenting with another band."

Paulie nodded in deep thought. His eyes sparkled with anticipation. When I dropped him off at his place, his spirits had elevated. He bounced up the driveway, turning for a final wave. I pulled away from his home and dialed Susan Winston as I headed for Main Street.

Mayor Ben answered the phone. "Hey, Rick. I understand you've had some exciting adventures." He laughed.

"It's been an interesting week."

"My week was interesting as well. Of course, you knew I was re-elected, right?"

"I have not been *that* far out of touch, Ben. Congratulations on your re-election, Mr. Mayor."

"I couldn't have done it without your support. I really appreciate it."

"You're the right person to run this village, and if you weren't, I wouldn't have supported you."

He chuckled and thanked me again for my support. Then I told Ben I needed to meet with him about this year's upcoming Holiday Festival. I told him I had a few ideas that he would find interesting and beneficial.

Ben chuckled. "What's this going to cost me?"

I didn't chuckle. "It'll cost you your next re-election bid if we *don't* meet."

"We could grab breakfast tomorrow."

"No can do, Ben. I'm meeting a guy at my hardware store first thing in the morning. He's going to repair my leaky roof. Let's meet tomorrow at Brewster's Social Club. The restaurant, not the bar. I'll buy lunch. Meet me at noon. You won't be disappointed."

"See you then, Rick. Do you need to speak with Susan?"

"Please."

I let Susan Winston know I'd picked up Paulie from the train station and thanked her for her efforts in getting Paulie released from Cook County Jail. She told me it wasn't as difficult as she'd imagined, and her bill would reflect it. Said Paulie was a good guy, and she liked him, but he had got caught up in some shit that was way over his head. Susan told me the lead guitarist in the band, a trouble maker named

Ron Snelling had worked a deal with his buddy, a drug runner named Salvador Hernandez. Together, they conspired with a few other people across the Midwest to use the concert tour to distribute large quantities of methamphetamine to dangerous gangs. I asked if Paulie was out of the woods, and she confirmed he would need to travel to Chicago at least once more and appear in front of a Cook County Judge. Susan assured me it was just a formality. The case against Snelling and Hernandez was rock solid. They would go away for a very long time.

"Paulie is as innocent as a newborn baby," she said.

"Did you learn that phrase in law school?" I chuckled.

"Don't push your luck, Rick. I haven't sent you my final bill yet."

"Just kidding, and thanks again for everything you did for Paulie and me. I won't forget it. We need to get together soon for dinner."

"I'd like that. It's been a while since Ben and I have hung out with you and Kathy. I can't wait to hear the details of your adventures this past weekend. I've heard third-hand accounts, and if the *real* story is anything close to what I've been told, you and your wife are pretty badass."

"It's what we do." I chuckled.

She snickered. "You're so humble."

"Don't I know it?" We both laughed out loud.

I hung up with Susan and called Kathy. "Hey, babe. I dropped Paulie off at his house. I'm heading home."

"I'm just leaving St. Joe's Hospital."

"How is Dale Mintern Junior doing? Did you show him the coin?"

She let out a soft breath. "Dale Junior is doing better. The bullet missed his major arteries. He's expected to make a full recovery."

"Are *you* all right?"

"After I gave Dale the coin, he clutched it in his hands for a long time and wept." She spoke in a soft tone. "It was quite touching. I don't think I've ever seen a more genuine smile."

"Did you scold him for trying to help us?"

"Absolutely not. Dale was enjoying the memories of his father and his childhood; besides, he just got shot by his own nephew! He didn't need any negative vibes from me." She laughed. "By the way, did you speak with Ben?"

"He's meeting me for lunch tomorrow at the Social Club."

"Do you think he'll have any problems with our plans?"

I chuckled. "Not at all. Ben is a smart politician."

"Well, you guys better start rehearsing."

"Yep. I'll call the guys next. By the way, did Gary find a buyer for the diamonds?"

"He did. Said we wouldn't believe what we got for them."

"Great. Are you on your way home?"

Kathy let out a long breath. "Soon. I'm taking a quick detour to River Rouge."

"That's not exactly on your way home, you know."

"I understand, but I'm going to stop by for a quick visit with Danny Gonyea."

"Does he know what you discovered? Are you going to tell him?"

"Tell him what?" Kathy sighed. "That his father murdered a piece of shit gangster named Sam Durocher over eighty years ago?"

"Yeah, well, I guess I was just curious."

"I promised to return his father's gun to him personally, and that's what I plan on doing. Am I telling him his father killed someone with this gun? No, I'm not. What good would it do? I'll tell him the evidence was inconclusive and leave it at that. I'll return the gun, thank him for his time, his service to this great country, and thank him for helping us with our case. That's it."

"You're a good human being, Kathy."

"That's the best compliment I could ask for."

KATHY AND I arrived at the County Fairgrounds shortly after 5:00 p.m. The traffic was heavy and blocked country roads for miles. I pulled my brand new burgundy F-150 limited edition pickup truck into the gravel drive and waved over a county sheriff. I flashed my backstage pass and bypassed the long line of vehicles.

"Break a leg," the cop shouted as I drove over the grassy field to the large building at the back of the property.

Scruggs, Paulie, and I had played many gigs in the past, but this would be the largest. Unlike past performances—bars, weddings, private parties, and corporate events—this was as close as we would ever get to being rock stars.

The temperature this evening was well above average. Clear skies and warm weather brought people in from surrounding counties by the thousands. Food trucks and souvenir vendors lined the fairgrounds. The atmosphere was electric, the night perfect.

I parked in the performers' parking lot next to the large building. A team of volunteers offered to grab my instruments and take them to the green room. I declined.

After losing a classic Fender guitar at a gig many years ago, I had become more vigilant. "Please take my amp," I said. "I'll take care of the instruments." I lifted the two guitars and a pouch of harmonicas from the back seat and headed backstage.

Kathy hugged me tight and set off to mingle with the growing crowd.

Hundreds of people gathered around the front of the elevated stage inside the enormous building, positioning for the best view of the concert well before the opening act. Thousands more mingled in the carnival-like atmosphere outside, where the unseasonably warm weather elevated their spirits.

We weren't scheduled to be on stage until 9:00 p.m., but other ceremonial events took place before our performance. I met up with Paulie, Scruggs, and our drummer, Jerry. We shared laughs in the green room, sucked down a few water bottles, and soaked up the energy. A few people lined up to sign the heavy cast on Scruggs' right leg. His ponytail swung proudly as he soaked up the adulation.

At 7:00 p.m., Mayor Ben Winston spoke into the microphone and introduced the spokesperson for the *Dunville Dispatch*, Sarah Owens. The crowd clapped loudly as I accepted my "best hardware store of the year" award. I held the plaque high and stepped closer to her for photos. Professional makeup hid Sarah's lingering bruises.

From the elevated stage, I spotted Kathy standing in a large gathering of friends. Around her neck, in a beautiful setting designed by Joan King, dangled a sparkling two carat round diamond. I blew her a kiss.

I waved to Gary and Joan. Then, I saluted Ron

Grimwade. He and his wife, Laura, had driven north from Atlanta for the show and would spend a few days at our house.

Dina Brewster caught my eye and waved both hands high in the air. When she did, the reflection from the stage lights sparkled off a similar diamond necklace. Recently having my chipped tooth repaired and my teeth polished, I returned the wave and flashed a pearly white smile. Dina looked good. You could hardly tell she had been beaten half to death a few weeks ago.

Scruggs's wife, Jo, approached a gathering of dozens of people mingling near the beer tent. She scanned the crowd, made her decision, and moved in for the kill. Like a lion stalking a gazelle, Jo separated the weakest from the herd and set off to make a new friend.

HIGH RANSOM, the opening act, finished their short set and joined us in the green room. They were initially billed as tonight's main act, but my meeting with Mayor Ben and a significant anonymous donation to the Dunville athletic department influenced the lineup. We shared high fives with the band and congratulated them on their performance.

Due to the quality and the provenance of the diamonds we found inside Brewster's Social Club, Gary King was able to auction them for a much higher price than we expected. In a group decision, two diamonds were made into necklaces for Kathy and Dina. Kathy took the lead in our adventures, and Dina nearly got killed, for Christ's sake.

After our six-figure charitable donation, the remainder of the windfall was divided evenly between the rest of our rag-tag group.

—

JERRY TWIRLED his drum sticks between his fingers, a limbering exercise we'd grown accustomed to over the past few weeks of rehearsal. Scruggs and Paulie stood in the corner of the room and warmed their vocal cords, harmonizing with each other on a classic Beatles tune.

My emerald green Paul Reed Smith custom guitar was slung over my shoulder. I ran through several fingering exercises and checked the tuning.

The door to the green room opened inward. Mayor Ben poked his head inside, giving us the thumbs-up sign.

"It's time, gentlemen. Break a leg."

I rocked on my feet. Jerry tapped his sticks on the wall. Paulie rolled his head from side to side, and Scruggs hobbled over.

We shared a group hug. "Let's do this!" I beamed.

Brewster's voice boomed from the microphone on the elevated stage. "Are you ready to rock 'n' roll?"

The overflowing crowd screamed back. Arms waved high in the air, and cell phones flashed. The hooting, hollering, and whistling was deafening. I shook off the goosebumps.

Brewster riled up the large crowd, pumping his hands in the air. "I said...are you ready to rock 'n' roll?"

The yelling and whistling grew louder. Adrenaline coursed through my veins. I made eye contact with the rest of the guys as Brewster waved us forward.

"Ladies and gentlemen, please welcome to the stage...Paulie and the Misfits!"

THE END

Thanks for reading. If you liked this book, let me know with a review on Amazon. Your positive comments will help others discover **The Mintern Report.**

ACKNOWLEDGMENTS

As I reflect on the time spent writing *The Mintern Report*, I think about the many good friends and family members who helped along the way. Those who listened to my ideas, those who helped me shape the book, and those who endured the early versions of the manuscript with honesty and encouragement. Without all of you, this story would still be stuck in my head.

Thanks to Nevin Spreerbrecker, the talented Michigan artist who designed the cover. Your artwork captured the spirit of the book beautifully.

The coaching, critique, and direction I received from author Benjamin X. Wretlind helped to polish my book in ways that weren't possible on my own. I couldn't have had a better editor. Thanks, Ben.

Special thanks to my son Ken Coppens, my sister Patti Trombly and my good friend Bob Brewster for reading and critiquing the many early drafts. Your candid thoughts, comments, and feedback on character development and plot direction mean more to me than you know. You're the best.

Finally, I'd like to thank my wife, Kathy. Writing this book took much longer than I had expected. She not only tolerated my obsession, but she encouraged it. Her creativity, ideas, suggestions, and influences are sprinkled throughout the book. Without her patience, love, and support, this book would not have been possible.

ABOUT THE AUTHOR

R.D. Coppens is a retired sales rep who lives in a rural town in southeastern Michigan with his wife, Kathy, a former educator. They have five wonderful children and four beautiful grandchildren.

Made in the USA
Columbia, SC
22 August 2023